No. 1 Bestseller

"FASCINATING"
—The New York Times Book Review

"FIRST-CLASS"
—Clifton Fadiman

"BEST"
—Saturday Review

"REAL THRILLS"
—Harper's

"COMPELLING"
—Minneapolis Tribune

"SPINE-TINGLING"

THE SALZBURG CONNECTION

HELEN MacINNES

FAWCETT CREST • NEW YORK

THE SALZBURG CONNECTION

THIS BOOK CONTAINS THE COMPLETE TEXT OF
THE ORIGINAL HARDCOVER EDITION.

Published by Fawcett Crest Books, a unit of CBS Publications,
the Consumer Publishing Division of CBS Inc., by arrangement with Harcourt Brace Jovanovich, Inc.

ISBN: 0-449-24053-3

Printed in the United States of America

29 28 27 26 25 24 23 22 21

To Gilbert, always.

THE
SALZBURG
CONNECTION

1

THE LAKE WAS COLD, BLACK, EVIL, NO MORE THAN FIVE hundred yards in length, scarcely two hundred in breadth, a crooked stretch of glassy calm shadowed by the mountainsides that slipped steeply into its dark waters and went plunging down. There were no roads, no marked paths around it; only a few tracks, narrow ribbons, wound crazily along its high sides, sometimes climbing up and around the rough crags, sometimes dropping to the sparse clumps of fir at its water line. The eastern tip of the lake was closed off by a ridge of precipices. The one approach was by its western end. Here, the land eased away into gentler folds, forming a stretch of fine alpine grass strewn with pitted boulders and groups of more firs. This was where the trail, branching up from the rough road that linked villages and farms on the lower hills, ended in a bang and a whimper: a view of forbidding grandeur and a rough wooden table with two benches where the summer visitor could eat his hard-boiled eggs and caraway-sprinkled ham sandwiches.

But now it was the beginning of October, and the tourists had gone from this part of Austria. Each July and August, they came pouring through the Salzkammergut, the region of innumerable lakes that stretched eastward from Salzburg toward the towering mountains of Styria. Some were beginning to penetrate this remote section of the Styrian Salzkammergut although the other lakes offered more in ready-made pleasure: boats for hire, swimming pools and picture-pretty inns, petunias in window boxes, waitresses in dirndls, folk music and dancing and general Gemütlichkeit. A few visitors lingered into September. And a few is just too many, thought Richard Bryant as he came over the last rise in the trail and saw the dim outline of the picnic table near the edge of the water. September might have been safe enough; it certainly would have been warmer, made things easier for me. Still, I wanted no risk of even a single tourist camping out with some mad notion to see the sunrise. This is one dawn which I would like to have very much to myself.

So far, there had been nobody following. He had driven through the little village of Unterwald, his lights out, his engine running gently, and had left it as deep in its predawn sleep as when he had entered it. Just beyond the last dark house he met the trail, at an almost right-angled turn, that climbed eastward to the lake. There, he had to put on power to get him up the steep grade past the inn—Waldesruh it was called appropriately, even if it was misspelled: its final *e* had been lost somewhere in the eighteenth century and never found its way back. And once past Waldesruh's sloping meadow, he could switch on his parking lights to keep him from sideswiping the dense trees that now edged the narrow way. He had only hoped that the sound of his engine would be smothered enough by the forest of larch and beech through which he was traveling. Half a mile from the lake, he had parked the Volkswagen in a gap between the trees that the foresters had made to get the timber down to Bad Aussee's lumber mills, drawing the small car under the drooping branches of some tall firs. He had swung his bulging rucksack onto his back and set out on foot. The rest of the trail was safer without a car.

Bryant halted before he reached the meadow, studied it carefully as he regained his breath, eased the heavy load on his back. Yes, he decided as he looked at the deserted picnic table and the dark loneliness of the lake, he had chosen the right time of year—perhaps a little earlier than he had first planned, but safe enough. No tourists. No woodcutters either, once daylight came. For the last month, they had stripped the bark off the trees they had felled in the early summer and left to dry out, but now the last chained load must have been trucked down to the valley; he had seen no signs of prepared timber lying on the forest floor. That was one worry canceled. Even the logs that were only good for fuel had been already chopped into regular lengths and stacked neatly under roofs of bark; they'd be picked up later, once the piles of wood around the village houses began to thin out. So, no foresters. The climbers also were gone—they were of the summer variety, hoping for good weather; they would do better in this Styrian area to plan their climbing for autumn. The hunting season had started, but two days ago

10

there had been an unexpected break in the crisp sunshine—a break for me too, Bryant thought. Wise hunters would wait another day, until the mists and drizzle lifted from those mountainsides. As for any fisherman, the lake itself eliminated that problem; it was too deep, too dark, had too many mysterious currents. (Trout preferred the other Styrian lakes that were fed by waterfalls and overflowed into small shallow streams with clear pebbled bottoms. But here the outlets were the same as the water's source: underground streams, hidden springs, a constant filling and emptying by invisible forces.) And skiers would find no packed snow until December at least. Yes, Bryant decided again, he had chosen the right time of year. And he had chosen the right time of day, too. Dawn was only a hint, night faded slowly, and the sun had some distance to travel, once it rose, before its light overreached the high precipices at the eastern point of the lake. By that time, two hours at most, his job must be finished.

He knew the lie of this land well enough. He had been here in May, again in July, had taken photographs (his trade nowadays: camera studies of alpine scenes which filled large expensive calendars for Christmas giving), and had examined them over and over again, memorized the blowups. Even so, as sure as he was of the terrain, he had decided against the middle of night and had chosen approaching dawn to make his move. Darkness might hide him from any keen eyes scanning the bare mountainsides edging the north side of the lake, but it could deceive his eyes, too: one false step, a slip, a stumble, and a loose stone would split the silence, perhaps start a small slide of splintered rocks. There was always the danger of that on a steep slope, naked of bushes or trees, such as the one he would have to cross for a short distance before the track would take him down to the water's edge. So he had decided on the gray hour leading into dawn, when shapes were indistinct, patches of trees seemed dark blots, and only the sharp line of jagged peaks was etched clearly against a softening sky. He could move quickly, surely; reach his objective, do the job, and be back at his Volkswagen just as daybreak was complete.

He shouldered the rucksack once more, set out at the same quick pace, but he left the trail before he reached the open meadow, keeping to the edge of the forest that was now thinning out as it tried to climb the lower slopes of the

11

mountainside, onto the narrow track that wandered eastward for a short distance before it divided and drooped one thin arm down toward the lake, vaguely pointing—so it had seemed from his photographs—to the one patch of green on that naked shoreline. And that was his target: the steep bank where boulders were held together by the roots of contorted trees, straining to keep the whole mass from slipping into the deep waters. To the casual observer, the mountain's plunge into the dark lake seemed endless. In fact, there was an outcrop of rock forming a ledge not more than twelve feet below the surface. It was a clever hiding place the Nazis had chosen.

He allowed himself another brief pause at the last group of trees before he stepped onto the track which would lead him over that desert of stone. A very tilted desert, at a good fifty-degree angle. He was too hot, much too hot for the task that lay before him. He laid aside the camera and tripod he carried, slid the heavy rucksack carefully from his back, peeled off his thick wool gloves, pulled off his green loden jacket and bundled it inconspicuously under the low branch of a fir. His motions were quick and neat. He was of medium height, sparely built, but strong enough, certainly wiry. His brown hair was grizzled, his complexion ruddy, with high color in his cheeks where their fine veins had been broken by wind and sun and snow. He could pass for an Austrian—his Salzburg accent was now indistinguishable from the genuine article. Sometimes, he wasn't sure what he had become. An expatriate Englishman? He disliked that adjective. But he had never returned to England since he had quit his work with British Intelligence in Vienna in 1946. And here he was back on the job, of his own free will, unasked, unpaid, risking everything. A damn fool? Hardly. This was a job he should have done twenty years ago; and it still needed doing.

Besides, he thought as he stood under the cover of the trees while his eyes scanned the bleak mountainside ahead of him, you know more about that lake down there and what it hides than any of the bright boys in London or Washington. And if you tried to approach them now, giving them your information, letting them do the work and face the dangers, they might very well ask you why the devil you hadn't reported all this in 1946? And that would be hard to explain to men who had never been in Vienna when it was filled with ruins, both of buildings and of people. You could tell them

12

you had been tired of the whole bloody war; it had turned sour—for it kept going on in hidden ways. Now, an ally had become the enemy and the peace was splintering around you. You were tired of informants and their pieces of half-truths and rumors and improbable facts, dredged up to gain money and papers and escape. You were tired of frightened men's hoarse whispers over sleazy café tables set up in ill-lit, ill-heated cellars where the sickly sweet smell of death lingered behind their walls. There was one you did listen to; you strung him along, made him sweat a little because he must have been a Nazi, and a member of the SS at that, if his tale were true. (How else could he have talked about this little lake, given it the right name—Finstersee—although few people outside of this Styrian Salzkammergut region had even heard of it; how else could he have known what was buried there?) And when you had heard all of this fantastic story, you had the pleasure of telling him there would be no *quid pro quo*: you were a civilian now; he was two days too late in coming to you. As for his story, you did nothing about it. And he scarcely had time to take it to the Americans or the Russians or the French. He was found with his neck broken beside a pile of rubble, not far from the café where he had talked so much in the hope of passage money to Argentina.

Time to move, Bryant decided. Nothing had stirred on the dark mountainside or down at the lake, and the peaks on the opposite shore were developing a nice swirl of mist. He hoped it would spread. He picked up the tripod and camera, wondering if he could afford to discard them with the jacket. But no, he thought; if any stray hunter met him, he would need a self-explanatory excuse. Photographers were known to work at strange hours in odd places—it wasn't the first time he had risen before dawn to capture a sunrise. So camera and tripod went with him, his passport to innocence. He swung the cumbersome rucksack onto his back, stepped onto the open mountainside, walking carefully but confidently. He noted that his heavy gray sweater and gray trousers blended perfectly with the jutting crags around him. He smiled briefly. That wasn't any lucky accident; it was a necessary precaution.

It might seem ridiculous to expect that the Nazis—after all these years—were still posting guards around here, or that they had possibly installed a man in a nearby village like Unterwald to patrol Finstersee. And yet he had only to

13

remember Lake Toplitz, some three miles to the south, and nothing seemed ridiculous about the patience and determination of a handful of totally committed men. Even as their army was surrendering in north Italy, with Berlin in flames and Hitler dead, a last stand in the Bavarian and Austrian Alps now impossible, they were planning for the future. Top-secret Intelligence files—the hard core of power for any resurgent force—were sealed in watertight chests and lowered into Lake Toplitz. The news of that had come out only years later when Toplitz proved there must be something worth guarding in its deep waters. Two British agents—but they could just as easily have been American or Russian or French —had been left to bleed to death on the crags above Toplitz, their bellies slit wide open.

He averted his eyes from the crags through which the track was leading him, thinking that there was at least one difference between Toplitz and Finstersee: the Intelligence agencies of the big powers hadn't yet learned about this little lake; and the Nazis, for that reason, might not be expecting trouble. His chances were fair to good, especially with the mists spreading on the opposite shore. It was going to be a fine morning of clouds and drizzle. He increased his pace on the last few yards of downslope, leaving the track which had decided to start climbing again, and almost slid into the clump of twisted trees at the water's edge. He sat down thankfully among the rough boulders. Phase one was over.

Not too bad an effort, he conceded as he glanced at his watch. After all, he was reaching forty-six, and that was twenty-two more years than he had carried in 1944 when he had parachuted into the Tyrol and organized his Austrian agents among its mountains. It was surprising, though, how the old tricks came back. Reassuring, too. He chose the flattest part of rough ground for laying out his equipment, braced his feet against the roots of a tree so that he would not slide into the lake before he was ready, and began unpacking the rucksack. Phase two would not take so long: checking and donning of gear. He had practiced constantly in this last week, making sure of the routine, recalling everything he had learned last summer when he had bought his equipment and tested it, over and over again, in the same depths of water he would have to face here. The hidden ledge did exist, some twelve feet under the surface. He had made sure of that, too, last summer, with the help of Johann.

Johann would be in a sour mood when he learned he had been left out of the action, but one man was less conspicuous than two, and why risk two lives when one was more than enough? With that, Bryant pushed his brother-in-law out of his mind—not quite admitting he didn't trust Johann's judgment once the chest had been recovered—and concentrated on unpacking and checking.

He laid out the suit—a dry suit it was called, made of thin sheet rubber in contrast to the newer wet suit type of foam-neoprene that fitted the body like a second skin. But the dry suit, hood attached, came in one piece instead of five; it had been simpler to pack, lighter to carry, and with the front opening he had chosen, it was fairly easy to put on and quick to take off. And for his purposes, it was speed at the end of this job that was absolutely imperative—if necessary, once he was out of the water, he could rip the suit off. It should be warm enough over the long wool underwear he was wearing specially: he did not intend to stay more than thirty minutes in that cold lake, the maximum safety time for forty-degree temperature. The summer months must have taken some of the bite out of Finstersee, but he had had to plan for what might be possible, not for what he hoped would be probable.

Next, he drew out the contraption known by the ungainly name of single-hose regulator, one end fitted with a mouthpiece, the other to be screwed into the small valve of his scuba tank. Now the tank itself, a junior model chosen for easy handling but with sufficient compressed air for fully thirty minutes at the depths he would have to work in, was pulled gently from the rucksack. He had decided on this small size of scuba tank ("kid stuff" his instructor in Zürich last summer had called it) because it was considerably lighter to carry and less bulky inside the rucksack. He didn't need the regular scuba: he wasn't a sportsman going into deep waters; he was sticking on that ledge, twelve feet below. And he had better, he told himself grimly.

He unpacked a weighted belt which would let him drop down from the surface. Dark blue sneakers, something to give his feet a grip on the ledge and yet not cause added difficulties when the time came to rise to the surface. Mitts of foam-neoprene, tight but easily pulled on if he first wet his hands. A knife, one blade serrated. A strong wire cutter. (Both of these would be strapped to his leg.) A thirty-foot stretch of quarter-inch nylon cord, braided to prevent fouling, and a clamp to fasten one end of the cord that he would coil around the tree nearest the water; a second clamp, with quick release, to fasten the other end around his waist. A piece of rubber tire to protect the tree's bark from any friction. An underwater light. A waterproof watch with illuminated numerals. A slab of chocolate and a flask of brandy to be left beside his camera and tripod, all covered by his clothes which he was now stripping off. He secured the neat pile with a heavy stone. Methodically, he began donning his gear.

He was ready. He pulled sharply on the rope coiled on its cushion of rubber around the base of the tree, testing the clamp. It would hold. The other end of the rope was already firm around his waist, the remaining loops neatly gathered in the crook of his left arm. He glanced at his watch strapped over the mitt on his right hand, making sure that nothing interfered with the wrist seal of his suit. He checked the light hooked securely to his belt, adjusted the mask which would let him see sideways as well as above and below, and started regular breathing. Then, gripping the rope in his left hand, with a twist around the wrist for extra security, playing it slowly out, keeping it taut with his right hand, he took a step backward into the lake. Its bank went straight down. As the water reached his shoulders, he remembered to check his descent and raise his right arm above his head so that his left hand could open the wrist seal briefly and let the air in his suit be pushed out. Then he gripped the rope with both hands again, removing the strain from his left wrist, and sank slowly down into a black-green world.

It was worse than he had imagined. Cold shock, as his face went under, and blind slow motion; a feeling of being trapped in darkness. With an effort, he forced down the split-second panic that attacked him, and kept his breathing regular. His feet touched something solid under slimy mud. He could stand on it, he could turn slowly, carefully. His right hand could free its rigid grip on the rope for a moment and fumble for the flashlight at his belt. He switched on its powerful beam. By stooping, and that was the way he would have to move, he could direct the light in front of his feet. Yes, he had found the ledge.

It was about two feet wide at this point. How long? The beam showed a short stretch of ten feet, no more, before the ledge vanished. Nothing on that section. He turned slowly, remembering not to dislodge any silt by a quick or careless movement—muddied waters could take hours to settle again, and his job would be made impossible even before it had properly begun—and looked along the other stretch of ledge. It was just about the same length; the trees above him had marked almost the middle of this outcrop of rock. And near its end he saw a heavy mass, blacker than the waters around it.

It's too big, he thought at first; I'll never raise that weight by myself. And then, as he came closer, leaning forward— slowly does it, small sure steps, keep a grip on the rope and the breathing regular—he decided it wasn't a chest at all, but a lump of stone that had fallen down the mountainside and ended here with a thud. It was only when he was close to it and could stoop over with his flashlight full on it that he saw it was really a huge lump of mud and mosslike growths. He unsheathed his knife and went to work on the deposit of twenty-one years, cutting and scraping gently, always mindful of the danger of disturbed silt, until he struck something hard. It glinted under the light. His depression vanished. It was a chest made of some bright metal that did not rust. Not iron, thank God. If it was aluminium, it would be all the more easily raised. (After all, the Nazis who had lowered it here wouldn't want any difficulties in salvage. They planned ahead, those boys.) His one problem now was to get it free of the mud, and then ease it along to the spot where he had descended.

He began scraping cautiously at the encrustation until he found that, if he got his hands against the box and pushed up against the caked deposit, it peeled off like a matted carpet and floated away in broken chunks. There were long fraying fragments of hemp on the side handles of the chest, all that was left of the cords that had lowered it. He pulled them off quickly. Too quickly. There were shreds of thin wire imbedded in the cord, and their broken edges ripped the palms of his gloves. Lucky his suit hadn't been torn by one of those thin jags of wire—that would have been real trouble. He worked more carefully, using wire cutters, and at last released the chest completely. Now to secure it, his way.

He released the clamp at his waist and started twisting the free rope around the chest and through its handles. Under water, its weight was no problem, and once he had it freed from the mud it had settled into, the task was only a matter of care and quiet movements. He used all the rope he could spare, and then clamped it to hold. The hardest job, because it was most worrying, was to find the place where he had descended. But by tugging on the rope overhead every few steps back along the ledge, lifting the chest with him as he moved so that it lay always beside his feet when he paused, he found the spot where the rope no longer strained at an angle between his hand and the tree, but fell straight as a plumb line.

Quickly, he released the buckle of his weighted belt, the flashlight hooked to it, and let them drop away. The wire cutter, which he had been too late to use when his mitts had been torn, went too. He started to float. Keep a firm grip on the rope, he warned himself, and don't hold your breath; move slowly; *don't hold your breath!* He rose to the surface, half swimming, half pulling upward on the rope, and hauled himself onto land. He staggered toward the cover of the tree. He tore off the mask, wrenched free from the rest of his equipment. The fresh air twisted his lungs. Twenty-seven, he noted with difficulty, twenty-seven minutes all told. The box ... Better rest before he salvaged the box.

He did more than rest. He collapsed, face down, his cheek against the tree's root. When he became conscious again, he had lost a valuable twenty minutes. Daylight was spreading from over the eastern ridge.

He rolled slowly over on his back, and lay there, unable to rise, his body heavy with fatigue. He was chilled to the bone. He shivered violently, remembering the last few minutes under water when the cold started to penetrate his body; colder, colder, the embrace of death. He sat up with an effort. Everything seemed out of control. He wanted to fall back again, let himself drift into deep, deep sleep. He rubbed the back of his neck, gently; that was where the headache began that encircled his brow. The box could wait. He had made sure it was lying safely on the ledge, well wrapped in tight coils of rope. First, he must drag himself to his clothes, get some brandy down his throat, get this suit off, get his flannel shirt and sweater and thick trousers onto his body. Something warm, for Christ's sake, something warm and light. His body felt as if it were encased in a ton weight.

It took him another half hour to accomplish these simple things. And then, suddenly, he began to feel more in com-

18

mand. His chin, which had been exposed under water, felt frozen. And his hands were stiff. The palms had been scored by the rope when his grasp had slipped. Now that he could see the sun and breathe the fresh air, he would admit the worst moment down in that pit of darkness—the moment when he had rid himself of the weighted belt and the flashlight, sensing them go over the edge and sink into the depths; and he was left with only his grip on a quarter-inch thickness of rope to keep him from drifting out over that abyss too.

He had drunk all the brandy—its only effect was to bring him up to normal—and eaten some of the slab of chocolate to give him energy. He was far behind schedule now. He ought to have been back at the Volkswagen by this time, heading down into the valley where the highway would take him back home to Salzburg for breakfast. But as he worried, he worked. He removed the knife from its sheath and bundled the rest of his gear around the tank, empty now and heavier, and added the stone that had anchored his clothes. That should be weight enough. He would tie the package firmly with the rope once his use for it was over, and drop it all into the lake. Four feet out from the bank wouldn't cause too much of a splash, he hoped; the bundle should sink as far as his belt had traveled.

He was ready to haul up the chest. He had bandaged his hands with a shredded handkerchief, and was preparing to dampen his wool gloves to give them some grip (the torn mitts were now bundled with the suit), when the sun came out from behind a cloud and shone right along this side of the lake. He took cover among the trees and boulders, staring through the branches at the opposite shore thick in fog with the mountainsides above it shrouded in low-lying clouds. And they were stationary. So I'll have to wait, he thought gloomily, I may have to wait until dusk this evening. Where was that prevailing wind, damn it, that brought mists and rain from the huge mass of storm-breeding mountains far to the south? But at the moment, Finstersee looked like a stretch of dark-green glass. It was almost too still. That could mean bad weather. Perhaps, he thought, hope surging again, I may not have to wait in this trap until evening. For trap it was, with this side of the lake washed in early-morning light.

He sat there for almost an hour, kneading his body to keep the circulation moving, rubbing his legs, watching the lake. And at last the wind was rising, sweeping clouds from the

19

south, packing heavy mists down over the treetops. The sky was shrouded, the sun obliterated, and all the bare slopes of crag behind him were swathed in gray. Visibility was scarcely ten feet. I'll manage it yet, he thought, and moved quickly.

He unfastened the rope but left its coil around the tree, safely padded with the tire, and pulled on its end until he had taken up the slack on the ledge below and he could feel the chest resist. Now let's say you are bringing in a thirty-pound salmon, he told himself. He stood a little to one side of the tree, again made sure the piece of rubber was in place, and began to haul. His hands hurt like hell, but the less attention he paid to them the sooner the chest would be raised. With four short pauses, letting the tree take the brunt of the dangling weight, he made it. The chest broke the surface, tilting dangerously. Rapidly, he cinched the rope around the tree. He reached for the box with both hands and lifted it safely onto solid ground. It had become much heavier to handle. He carried it into the small encampment of boulders and trees, placed it beside his rucksack. He kept staring at it. It was heavier but smaller. It seemed to have shrunk. Then he remembered that the glass face on his mask, by underwater refraction, had magnified everything.

He was smiling as he carefully peeled the piece of tire from the tree, slashed the rope to free the chest, added all those bits and pieces to his weighted gear, keeping one length of cord to tie the package securely. He carried the bundle to the water's edge. It sank reassuringly. He threw the knife after it. He eased the chest into the rucksack, a tight fit made more difficult by a padlock. The flap couldn't be fastened over its top but at least he could carry the weight on his back, leaving his hands free for camera and tripod. His hands ... The woolen gloves were in shreds over the palms, but he kept them on. The cold air was shrewd and damp. Better wet gloves than nothing. They'd offer some protection when he came to the job of hiding the chest.

He must hurry. Every second counted more than ever now. He moved out from the small group of boulders and trees, with a last glance around to make sure that he had left nothing behind. He was so pressed for time—this shore of the lake was blanketed in mist, but the wind from the south had blown too strongly and the high edges of the peaks opposite him were beginning to be cleared of cloud—that he didn't use the track that had brought him here, but struck

20

along the lower slope of mountainside, following the shore line as his guide through the white fog toward the picnic ground. It was one of those times when the feeling of urgency drove every pain out of his body and made the impossible seem simple. Tomorrow he would ask himself, How in hell did you manage that? Today he was too intent on reaching the edge of the meadow even to doubt he could make it. And he reached it. The mist at the western end of the lake was so thick that he couldn't see the picnic table or the trees that had covered his climb up onto the mountainside almost four hours ago. His timing had been shot to pieces but at least he had some luck now, just when he needed it most, with the weather. He almost walked past the three ungainly boulders that lay some twelve feet from the water's edge.

They were piled together roughly, as if some giant hand had thrown them from the mountain, aiming for the lake, and missed. Bryant found the gap at ground level between two of them where one had tilted against the other, and eased the rucksack off his shoulders. Gently, he pulled back the dry grasses and the thorny branches of a wild rosebush that were part of the circle of growth that surrounded the boulders. (In summer, this spot had been a mass of color.) He laid his tripod on top of the stalks and stems to keep them down for the brief moment he needed, and used a knee to hold the branches aside. He lifted the chest, rucksack and all, and pushed them sideways into the gap as far as he could stretch. He was careful to leave the straps pointing toward him. When the time came to remove the chest, he would need them for haulage. There was no way of reaching down into the gap from the top of the boulders, for they met together in a tipsy embrace. And they were the height of a man, well grounded in the soil, as if they had taken root there. It would need a bulldozer or dynamite to force them apart. When he lifted his tripod and helped the grasses and dried twigs to stand upright again, the gap was screened. The rosebush bobbed back into place, leaving a few hard thorns piercing his trouser leg, and covered everything.

He backed away, his eyes looking with satisfaction at the naturally disguised gap. It didn't exist. As the mist blocked it from his view, he made for the dim shadow of the nearest tree and reached the forest that had led him early this morning onto the mountainside. Here, visibility was better—the massed firs seemed to be balancing the clouds on top of

21

their heads. His quick pace slackened to a slow march; he could now let himself admit he was just about at the end of his strength. But he was careful enough to avoid the direct uphill route to the tree where he had hidden his jacket. Instead, he circled widely to the north to approach it downhill. He'd know it at once, with its low sloping branches and the track starting eastward only a few feet away.

He took off his sodden gloves, shredded and torn, and dropped them into the first piece of underbrush he passed. It was better to do that and tell Anna he had lost them than let her see the damage and start imagining the kind of dangers he had been through. He would be home for breakfast, after all, a late ten o'clock breakfast. An eleven o'clock breakfast, he emended, noticing the time on his watch. It was now twenty minutes to nine. He would tell Anna just enough to keep her from asking questions—last night, he had only disclosed what was absolutely necessary for her to know in case something went wrong. Even that had terrified her. He remembered the sudden whiteness of her face, the thin drawn look of her cheeks, the droop to her lips, the blank stare as if she could see no future at all. She didn't weep, she didn't exclaim. But the touch of her hands had been ice-cold with fear. As cold as he felt now in spite of the shelter of the forest. He would be glad to button that jacket right up to his chin. And there was the tree he was looking for, with its thick low-slung branches.

And there, also, were two men.

2

AUGUST GRELL HAD BEEN WAKENED BY A SOUND. HIS MIND, half-thick with sleep, couldn't place it. A car traveling up the hill to Finstersee? But in that case he ought to have heard it traveling through the village. His small inn stood on a rising meadow just above Unterwald, its back close against the woods that covered the lower slopes of the mountain. He pushed aside the bulky eiderdown and left the warmth of his bed. He crossed over the scrubbed-wood floor to the window. If there was a car taking the hill trail, he could see no lights. There was only the thick blackness of the forest, a thinner blackness of the sky. Dawn was slow in coming at this time of year. There wasn't a light in the village, so they had heard nothing. A bunch of peasants, he thought as he climbed back into the high bed. You could rely on them to pay no attention except to their own lives. Twenty years of being the owner of the Gasthof Waldesruh had convinced him of that.

He hadn't even got his head back on the pillow when the telephone rang. He moved quickly, slipping his feet into wool-lined slippers, pulling his old coat over his nightshirt as he crashed through his bedroom into the front hall where the telephone stood on the reception desk. Perhaps it had been the telephone that had wakened him and not the sound of a car. In any case, Anton was up at the lookout on Finstersee; if any car drove up to the lake, he'd hear and see it.

Without switching on the light, Grell fumbled for the receiver and found it. A man's voice asked, "How's the weather up there?"

Grell said guardedly, "There has been some mist and heavy cloud." The man could be a hunter, making sure that the mountains were clear enough for a day's shooting before he drove up all the way from the valley.

"You might listen to the weather reports."

"I'll do that." Grell smiled as the line went dead. That had been no ordinary hunter. He closed the inside shutters before he switched on the light and looked at the clock on the wall, which never had missed a minute in the twenty years he had lived here. It told him the time was 4:36 exactly. The "weather report" would be transmitted one hour later than the telephone call. He would be ready for it.

But first, even before he started heating some coffee or getting dressed, he had better make contact with Anton and learn whether anything had been heard or seen at the lake. The lookout was actually a cave with a narrow entrance at the foot of a high cliff on the south shore of Finstersee, which a detail of German sappers had transformed into a weatherproof, dripproof room with a gallery leading through the rugged stone to a much larger room commanding the southern hillsides right down to the valley. They had even installed a field telephone between this blockhouse and Waldesruh, which had been taken over as company headquarters by the German occupying forces. It had been part of a vast plan for hundreds of strong points to make a last stand feasible. But all the frantic labor in March and April of 1945

23

had come to nothing. The secrecy of it had been useful, though: the peasants had been trucked down to the valley, only a few men with useful skills kept here to work as they were told, no explanations given; they had never guessed the full extent of these fortifications. And if the gallery and larger room had never been filled with ammunition or gun emplacements, the small room facing Finstersee had justified its existence. The heavy door closing the narrow entrance to the original cave was completely hidden by the tops of the trees that grew right up to the cliff face; some branches even brushed the door's natural timber. An apparent fissure in the rock, well to the side of the door, had been carefully fashioned to give the room enough air and—just as important— to allow a telescope to keep its sharp eye on the opposite side of the lake. Anton wasn't always stationed up there, of course. But there had been an alert last week, and Anton had spent the last four nights and days in his eyrie.

August Grell re-entered his bedroom, closed the shutters before he turned on the light near his desk, unlocked its top, and rolled it up. Now he reached in to pull out the pigeonholes; they came away in one piece, a screen to block the gap that lay behind. Carefully, he placed this unit against the wall, keeping the pigeonholes upright so that they held their pieces of writing paper and envelopes and bills intact. The desk was old-fashioned and deep; the disclosed gap easily held his communication equipment. It was a strange mixture: the latest in short-wave radio transmitters with tape attached for high-speed receiving and sending (Russian model); a schedule for transmission—kilocycles changed according to the month as well as to the day of the week (an adaptation of the Russian methods that had worked very well in America); the usual one-time cipher pads, with their lists of the false numbers that had been inserted into the code for the sake of security, each small tissue-thin page easily destroyed after it had guided the decoding; a small decoding machine (American), seemingly accurate but which he often double-checked with his own methods; a two-way radio, the size of his palm, with which he could make contact with Anton (British invention, Japanese manufacture), but which he rarely used—open communications without being coded would be extremely dangerous if the Austrians really started having suspicions about this district; and the old but infallible field telephone (German), which always gave him pleasure to

24

use. It was a good piece of workmanship, and would last another twenty years if necessary.

He lifted it gently out of its hiding place, and rang Anton, less than two kilometers away. They talked in quick German, accurate and literate, dropping the slow dialect of the South Tyrol from which they were supposed to have come.

Anton sounded brisk enough even if he hadn't had much sleep; the cold was penetrating, but he wasn't grumbling. He was too excited by August's call—a sign that something might be brewing. "Then that alert last week really meant business?"

"I'll know soon," August told him guardedly. "What's the outlook up there?"

"Nothing ten minutes ago."

"Look again."

There was a long pause. "The light is poor as yet, but I can see nothing moving either at the lake, or on the slopes, or at the picnic ground. Nothing."

"Keep watching."

"Yes, sir."

"And the weather?"

"The lake is clear so far, but some streaks of mist are beginning to drop down on this side. Might be bad."

"Even so, keep watching." Bad weather could come quickly in these mountains, but it could clear just as unexpectedly. "And don't call me *for any reason* after five-thirty."

"Not if I see—?"

"It will have to wait. I'll call you the first moment I can. Got that?" The message from control came first. And it could be delayed; that had happened before. He would be given a stand-by signal, and stand by was what he had to do.

"Understood," Anton said, not debating the point.

Anton was a good lad, August Grell thought as he replaced the telephone, then the disguising front of pigeon-holes, before he rolled down the lid of the desk and locked it. He was a cautious man; extra trouble was no bother at all if it ensured success, and it usually did. He shaved and washed in ice-cold water from the ewer in his room, dressed in heavy clothing, locked his old gray coat safely in the wardrobe—the marks on its shoulders and collar, where he had cut off his insignia, barely showed after all these years; and although it was now faded and tight, it was a comforting reminder of the best years of his life. SS Oberstandartenführer, equal and more to a lieutenant colonel in the army. Not bad for a man thirty-two years old. Only three years older than Anton was now. And what was Anton? A corporal in the East German army. Well, that was hardly fair, even if it was comic. Anton had "defected" to West Germany, picked up a new identity in Stuttgart which got him into Switzerland, received a new set of papers in Lucerne which took him to Milan, set off from there for the Dolomites, and then, with all the documents needed to establish him as the "son" of August Grell, he had made the usual surreptitious trip from the old South Tyrol over the mountains into Austria as a "refugee" from Italian domination. The politics and power struggles of Europe had been a great help to Anton and the young men like him in disguising the purpose of their various journeys. They were all good lads, if the stories Grell heard were true, and he had heard plenty of quiet stories. He wasn't completely isolated up in Unterwald. In the summer, along with the usual mixture of climbers and hikers, he had his special visitors. When skiing started in late December, he had more. This grapevine was important: not just reports and rumors, but something to keep hope alive and morale high.

What was Anton's real name? Grell had often wondered, just as Anton must have wondered about his name. It made no matter. The important thing was that they got on better than Grell had expected when Anton arrived here five years ago to replace Grell's "brother." He missed Anton's help in getting a good hot breakfast ready on the kitchen table. (In between seasons, there were few visitors; the two men managed by themselves, with a local woman—who was reliable in the sense that she was too stupid about politics and too much in need of extra money—to cook a solid dinner and scrub the floors.) He had to settle for a slab of cheese on a hunk of bread and some heated-up coffee, which he carried through to his cold bedroom. He locked its stout door, got both his radio transmitter and his schedule for transmission out of their hiding place along with his decoding equipment, had time to put another call through to Anton (mist thickening steadily all along this south side of the lake; visibility probably zero in five minutes; nothing seen on the mountainside opposite), switched on a small electric heater near his legs, drank the coffee as he checked the schedule for the exact wave length according to the day (this was Monday) and month (October).

The first signal came through exactly on time. The message was brief. He knew before he decoded it that either the alert was over or there was more to come. And that was what the message told him: *Stand by for second weather report. Utmost importance.* "Second weather report" meant another hour of waiting. There must have been additional information to add to the message, and it was being evaluated or checked. He destroyed the top flimsy of the cipher pad, so small it was less in size than a book of matches. The next little page was ready for the next transmission, when a new series of false numerals, scattered through the body of the message, would have to be eliminated before he could start transcribing the columns of digits into letters and words.

Utmost importance. Then something was stirring. He called Anton, and got no answer. He called again in five minutes. No answer. Worry now smothering his anger, he waited five more minutes. This time, Anton answered. Grell was so relieved that he forgot to lash out with a few well-chosen curses.

Anton was cheerful if somewhat breathless. "I took a quick scramble down to the lake."

"You're a damned fool—"

"But I'm blind up here. The mist is draped over me like a white curtain."

"How is the lake?"

"Clear of mist so far, but the light is still poor."

"So you had a perfect view of nothing." Grell's voice was heavy with sarcasm.

"I took binoculars with me. There *was* nothing." (Richard Bryant, at that moment checking over his gear, would have been delighted.)

"Don't leave your post again! I had to call you three times. And don't contact me around six-thirty. I want no interruption then."

"There has been a delay?"

"Yes."

"That might mean something." Anton was excited.

And I hope it doesn't, thought Grell. He would prefer no trouble around Finstersee. He didn't want Austrian Security to be attracted to his domain. If there was trouble, it would

27

have to be handled with caution and skill and maximum concealment. "It might," he agreed with little enthusiasm. "Stay at your post!"

"Yes, sir."

There were no more delays on the six-thirty transmission from control. The message was lengthy and explicit. Control seemed to be giving Grell as much information as possible, as if they did not want him acting blindly should the emergency develop. Yet they were as careful and cautious as his strong sense of security could wish. They had even used code names for places and days of the week, so that he had two jobs to do: first, decode the message; second, further decode the names in the text. Then, with all the information fixed in his mind, he burned the evidence, replaced his equipment, locked desk and bedroom door. He took the coffee cup through to the kitchen, made sure the lights were off, picked up his loden cape from where it had been drying near the stove, before he left the inn by its back entrance and stepped into the wood.

The mist lay heavily over the top of the trees, and the open spaces were filled with it. He cut across the trail, saw nothing but thick white cloud where the picnic ground should have been, and made his way through the trees on the southern side of the lake toward Anton's lookout. As he plodded up through the forest at the steady pace of an expert climber, he reviewed in his mind the information he had decoded. (Some aspects of it puzzled him in spite of its clarity. He would think about them later.)

The message he had received could be divided into seven parts.

One: A report, *mentioning Finstersee,* had been intercepted last Wednesday when it was being transmitted to Warsaw by an Intelligence agent stationed in Zürich. It dealt with the documents that had been sunk in certain Austrian and Bohemian lakes. The Zürich agent stated he had excellent reason to believe that Finstersee should be added to the list of Austrian lakes.

Two: Another report from Zürich to Warsaw had been intercepted yesterday (Sunday). It had been transmitted by the same agent, who now had reason to believe that he would have definite information on Finstersee by this coming Friday.

Three: At 4:45 A.M. this morning, a third message from Zürich to Warsaw had been intercepted. It was a communication of high urgency. The Zürich agent was convinced that the Finstersee operation had been advanced by several days and *might even now be under way.* He demanded the immediate dispatch of two suitably trained operatives to Salzburg, there to await his arrival. Extreme measures might be necessary.

Four: The Zürich agent had been seized, as of 6:00 A.M. this morning, and was now being held. Examination in progress. Further information was expected about his employer in Warsaw, the importance—if any—of Salzburg itself, and the threat to Finstersee.

Five: Reinforcements were being sent at once to the Gasthof Waldesruh. Two men would arrive late this afternoon or early this evening. Others would follow, if required. Usual identifications.

Six: In the interest of speed, any urgent news or questions from Waldesruh should be directed to Zürich. Telephone to be used only in most extreme emergency; call must be thoroughly disguised and brief. Otherwise, usual radio contact with regular code must be used.

Seven: Definite orders to handle this situation with care. There must be no repeat of the events at Lake Toplitz. Austrian Security must in no way be alerted.

Not by me, thought Grell, I'll make sure of that. But why the general reference to Warsaw? The Zürich agent couldn't be in the pay of the Poles, or why was "further information expected," even needed? And that eliminated the Russians, too, for they knew everything Polish Intelligence planned or accomplished; the Poles had become merely another arm of the KGB. Or were the Americans being ultradevious? Or the British, or the French? Germany, either East or West? He might as well add every nation to the list; there wasn't one of them that wouldn't take wild chances to discover the secret of Finstersee. We are fighting the whole damned world, he thought, not without pride, as he reached the lookout. He signaled, and Anton opened the narrow door.

Anton was wrapped in army blankets, his sleeping bag neatly folded on the low wooden platform covered with dried fir that stood in the warmest corner of the room. Food supplies were on a high shelf. Two small kerosene stoves were producing some heat. He had fixed a lamp to give him some light, and had shaded it so that its glow wouldn't be seen from the outside. He had books and magazines, a set of chessmen, a couple of decks of cards. Anton knew how to get along.

Grell nodded approvingly and went over to the telescope. The mists were clearing on the peak above him—that much he had been able to notice on his way up here—but they were heavy over the lake and the mountainside opposite. The telescope might be blind for another hour, even two. He changed his plans. "We'll have to go down," he told Anton. "It's the only way we'll have a chance of seeing them."

"Expecting visitors?" Anton was busy putting out the stoves, folding his blankets, adding his cape to his heavy gray suit. He lifted his hunting knife and rifle, held them up for confirmation. Grell nodded, drawing back his own cape to show he was equally armed.

"Any idea of what we'll meet?" Anton asked as he blew out the lamp and Grell opened the door.

"None."

"What *do* we know then?"

"That we have broken someone's code and we have got him for questioning. Come on! There's no time to waste." It was now half past eight.

It took them only ten minutes by the direct route to come down to the picnic ground. They crossed it at a run, relying on the mist to conceal them. Swiftly they climbed through the forest, following the path to its eastern boundary where the mountain track began. Anton set off across the open slope to see if anyone was actually down by that important cluster of boulders and trees by the water's edge. Grell waited, regained his breath, kept an eye on the forest trail they had just climbed in case any unwelcome visitors, delayed by the bad weather, were now making their way up. Not everyone had Anton's ability to lope along a cloud-streaked mountain track. He had the confidence and the instincts of a chamois; and he knew every meter of ground.

Grell edged into the cover of a thickly branched tree. Everything seemed peaceful. Yet, the agent who had been caught in Zürich had sent that message to Warsaw: the

30

Finstersee operation might even now be under way. If so, thought Grell, they'll be using two men. Three would increase the difficulty of concealment, although it had taken three to lower the chest into the lake—himself and a couple of lieutenants, while a squad of five had guarded the picnic ground. He never stood here without remembering that night. And its almost failure.

They had lowered the chest, expecting it to sink to the depth of fifty meters at that part of the shore line. (Finstersee was estimated to be a hundred and twelve meters, just about the same as Toplitz, at its central depths.) Barely four meters down, the chest had come to rest on something solid. And could not be eased off. It was firm on some underwater ledge. And just at that moment, as they prepared to haul the chest up and try some place else, a light had been flashed across the lake from the picnic ground, warning them to move out. He had one of the lieutenants cut the chest free, well below water line so that no strands would be seen floating under the surface, and they had left with two large coils of unused rope and a pneumonia case. The other lieutenant had died, too, but much later; he was suspected of trying to buy his way out of Vienna with his story of that night. For twenty-one years it seemed as if the traitor had been eliminated before he had a chance to talk or be believed. But now? It began to look as if the execution had been too late. Someone must have listened, someone must have believed. And waited . . .

Anton was coming back. Grell stepped out of cover to show himself, looked down as his foot brushed something in the underbrush. He pulled aside a low branch and picked up a green loden jacket. It had a Salzburg label, but no name.

"Nothing at all," Anton reported, keeping his voice low. "I searched among the boulders and trees. No sign that anyone has been there."

"Someone has been here." Grell held out the jacket, folded it again, and replaced it. "He must be somewhere out on that mountain."

"Only one man?"

Grell could agree with Anton's disbelief. But nothing made sense at this moment. Any man who was foolish enough to scout around a hillside in a soaking mist without his jacket was hardly the kind of agent that Warsaw would hire. (And why Warsaw? Why hadn't the message gone to Moscow

31

direct? Nothing made sense.) Irritably, he stared at the track leading eastward along the mountain now beginning to clear of mist. "He must be somewhere out there," he insisted in a hushed but angry voice.

"Yes," agreed Anton very softly. He had his sharp blue eyes on the trees above them, some distance to the west. "But he is coming from the wrong direction. I think I know him. Yes. He's that Englishman who is married to Johann Kronsteiner's sister. He's a photographer in Salzburg."

"Kronsteiner the ski instructor who keeps a shop down at Bad Aussee?"

"Also a guide in the summer season. He's all right. We checked him out when he brought that bunch of students to stay overnight at the inn last July. Remember?"

Grell remembered. Johann Kronsteiner was one of those amiable dolts, handsome and charming, who climbed and skied their lives away. "He has a girl in Unterwald, hasn't he?"

"He has a girl in every village between here and Salzburg."

"Has his brother-in-law noticed us yet?"

"Yes. He is walking down to meet us."

"He is, is he?" Grell turned around slowly to face the oncoming man.

Richard Bryant had seen the two men just as the younger one had noticed him. He had no time to step behind some cover. And perhaps it was better that he hadn't made the try. These men had the instincts of hunters. Both were facing him now, and he could recognize them: August Grell and his son Anton, from Unterwald, where they kept the small inn that stood on the meadow above the village. They both wore loden capes that ended just where their gray knee breeches met their heavy woolen stockings, heavy boots tight-laced over their ankles, and a look of definite speculation.

Bryant reached them, greeted them nonchalantly, and then looked around him vaguely. "I left my jacket somewhere here," he explained, and noted the quick glance the two men exchanged. They hadn't expected that admission. Had they thought he would pretend he had just arrived at the lake and hadn't hidden any jacket? They don't catch me as easily as that, he thought, as he found the jacket. It seemed to be folded as he had left it, and in the same place. "I had an idea of getting a photograph with the early sun on the lake, but the clouds closed over just as I reached here. Then I had a brighter idea. The hill to the north of the wood seemed clear, so I went up there for a shot of sun struggling through mist. Very effective, you know, if you can have long enough exposure."

"You got quite another kind of exposure," Anton said, looking at Bryant's sweater fuzzed with fine beads of rain. Grell was smiling, very much at ease, but his glance rested on Bryant's hands.

"Got trapped on the hillside, couldn't even see this wood. I fell, nearly lost my camera. So I sat down and waited for the clouds to lift. That's what all good mountaineers do, isn't it?"

Anton nodded. "Did you hurt your hands badly?"

"Just a scrape." Bryant looked down at the rags of handkerchief wound around them and laughed. "This gave me something to pass the time. Pretty messy bandaging, though." He laid down his camera and tripod, peeled off his sodden sweater, slipped his arms quickly into the warmth of his jacket, buttoned it gratefully. He still needed a sweater, but a dry one. He repressed a shiver, and privately cursed the bandages he had left on his hands (he had thought he might need them for handling the steering wheel on his way home) while he talked casually. "My name is Bryant. I stopped off at your inn, last July, when I was taking some pictures around here." Anton remembered now, yes indeed he remembered; Herr Bryant had sat out in front of the inn and drunk a tankard of beer. The older Grell kept his silence and that same benevolent grin on his face. "I think I'll head for my car and start back to Salzburg. It has been a long time since breakfast." He saw the same quick glance pass between them when he mentioned his car. His frankness puzzled them, perhaps. And they were puzzling him a little. Everything seemed normal, as if they were only a couple of hunters out after marmot and had been cheated by the weather, too. He could see the shape of their rifles under their lodens. What else were they hiding there? Knives? That would be less noisy than firing, but of course the butt of a rifle could be just as silent. And just as lethal.

He began walking down toward the picnic ground. They came with him. Anton was saying it wasn't much of a day for anything, and he wouldn't mind a lift in Bryant's car as far as the inn. August Grell spoke his first words. "We might all have breakfast there. You'd feel the better for it. And you

33

can dry your pullover at the stove. You'll need it on your way home."

"Thank you," Bryant said. "That sounds a fine idea. Only —" What else could he do except play along with them? They were huskier than he was. August was a solid mass of a man, red-faced, brimming over with good health. Anton, perhaps thirty years old at most, was six feet and strong-muscled. The safest thing was to keep on being the harmless photographer, who certainly wouldn't refuse a hot breakfast at the Gasthof Waldesruh.

"Only what?" asked Grell.

"I'm late as it is. My wife will start worrying."

"You can telephone her from the inn." There was no arguing allowed by that tone of voice.

The three of them passed quite close to the spot where Bryant had hidden the chest. Whatever happens, he thought, it has been a good morning's work. "You know," he told them as they reached the trail that ran downhill to Unterwald, "I shouldn't be surprised if this mist has cleared in a couple of hours. I might get my photographs yet. It would save me coming back tomorrow or the next day."

"What's so urgent about the photographs?" Anton asked.

And that gave him a chance to talk about the book he was planning on the lakes in this part of Austria. He had photographed sixteen of them so far, at various times of year, at various times of day, to show—as he could explain at length and with real enthusiasm—their various characters, their amazing changes of mood. August Grell was interested; Anton seemed impressed. Bryant, in spite of his exhaustion, felt his spirits pick up. Yes, a good morning's work, he thought, as Grell and he drove the short distance to the inn. (Anton had decided there was too little room for his long legs and had taken a short cut down through the wood.) Bryant wondered a little when Grell told him to park the car at the back of Waldesruh, but otherwise there seemed no attempt at secrecy. Grell hadn't blinked an eye when a couple of villagers walked past, but gave them "Grüss Gott" and a wave of his hand.

Anton was already there. He had added wood to the big earth-colored stove and set a pot of coffee on one of the openings of its black iron top. Now, he was whistling as he moved cheerfully around the large kitchen. It seemed as if the two men used only one corner of it when they were by

34

themselves. It was a practical place. Cooking utensils crowding the niches above the stove, pots and pans hanging from a beam, a smell of cheese and apples and freshly ground coffee, scrubbed-wood floor and tables, blue-patterned tiles around the oven and sink. And the remains of one man's breakfast. Bryant's glance flicked quickly away from the single cup and saucer and plate. One man. Where had the other been? "I think I'll call my wife," he said easily, and waited for an abrupt refusal, a reversal in manner.

"This way," Grell said with a polite gesture toward the dining room. He led Bryant through the ice-cold room with its chairs up-ended on bare wooden tables and its rows of mounted heads, antlered and glassy-eyed, staring down from the walls. "We have only one telephone, but this is a very simple inn. And we do not charge much, no more than fifty schillings a day for everything."

"Very reasonable." Fifty schillings meant about fourteen in English currency, two dollars flat in American. "I must remember that."

"Over there," Grell said, pointing proudly at the desk in the entrance hall. Tactfully, he headed for his bedroom and left Bryant alone.

Bryant looked at the telephone and then at the front door just a few paces away. It was barred. Probably locked, too. Even so, if his car had been out there, he would have been tempted to try that door. He fought down the impulse to try it anyway. Once he was outside, someone in the village would see him. The Grells could hardly stop him leaving then. But it would be a mistake on his part; he would only confirm any suspicions they had, and he would be watched and followed and menaced for the remaining days he was given to live. *If* they were Nazi agents, that was. He wasn't sure about them any more than they were sure of him. He picked up the receiver, knowing that if August Grell was an agent he must have devised a way to monitor any conversation on this telephone.

At last he heard Anna's low voice, uncertain, hesitant. "I'm fine," he told her quickly, trying to keep her from asking any questions that might give him away. "Sorry I'm late. I'm in Unterwald. I was delayed by the mist and got properly soaked, but I'm drying off at the inn—the Gasthof Waldesruh—and Herr Grell and his son have invited me to breakfast. I'll be home around midday. By one o'clock at the latest." There, he thought, I've named them. They won't risk anything happening to me here. "Stop worrying," he told her, suddenly cheerful.

"Dick—"

"Yes?"

"Perhaps you ought to telephone Eric Yates right away. He called you early this morning. He seemed really upset when I told him—"

Bryant cut in, even if he wanted to know what she had told Yates. (He hoped to God she had kept Yates guessing; he was pushing far too hard.) "How early?"

"Just—just after you left. He said it was something about the book. I couldn't quite understand."

"Where is he staying in Salzburg? Did he leave a number?"

"It was a long-distance call from his home."

"Zürich?" Bryant was incredulous.

"Yes. And such a strange time to call! He sounded so sharp, almost angry. Do you think he won't publish your book? Was that the reason he—"

"He'll publish the book all right. I have a contract *and* an advance."

"I was worrying in case we would have to give that back," she confessed. "But that was the least of my worries. Oh, Dick—I'm so glad you're safe."

"This isn't the first time I've been caught in a mist," he told her quickly, before she could add anything more. "See you soon, darling," he ended abruptly, and cut her off. He counted out some money to cover the cost of the call, and left it beside the telephone. As for a call to Zürich—Eric Yates could wait. Is he checking on me? Bryant wondered. Yates was becoming too damned curious. Last week he wanted to know when the completed set of photographs would be ready. He had mentioned Finstersee in particular, yet in a careful way. Too careful for Bryant's taste; he had replied vaguely that he would be up at Finstersee by the end of this week, possibly next Friday. But that hadn't been enough for Yates, seemingly. He had made this phone call shortly after one o'clock this morning just to test if Bryant was still in Salzburg. Was that it? He can trust me, Bryant thought irritably as he moved into the dining room.

We were together in the war and did the same kind of work, too. Yates has contacts with British Intelligence, may

36

even be working for them. He knows perfectly well that anything I find in Finstersee is going to be handed over to our side. What does he want—everything spelled out? I had to give him a hint, back in June, just to make sure he could act as a go-between when the time came for that. I need his help. He is the quick route to the right people in London. But any more of this pressure and I'll start thinking about my old friends in Washington. I have at least two there who will remember me from the old days.

But that was just momentary annoyance, he told himself as he returned the cold stare of the beheaded deer on the wall. There was a personal stake—call it vanity—in showing London what he could do.

"I see you admire our collection," Anton was saying at the kitchen door.

"Impressive. How many did you bag?"

"Some," Anton admitted modestly. He was a handsome fellow, with clear blue eyes and brownish hair and healthy skin. "My father shot most of them. Including the chamois." He pointed to the head mounted over the door. "Do you do much hunting?" Something caught his eye in the hall behind Bryant, and he took Bryant's arm and drew him firmly but politely into the kitchen. "Do you?" he asked again.

Bryant didn't glance back at the hall. He had heard the telephone click as August Grell had lifted the receiver. "No. It's on the expensive side, isn't it?"

"Depends what you kill. Breakfast is ready. Shall we start?"

That was a neat turn-aside from costs, thought Bryant. The fee for killing a chamois could come as high as four thousand Austrian schillings. It seemed that August Grell didn't do too badly, considering he owned a simple little inn that charged fifty schillings a day in high season. He swallowed the hot coffee and hoped it would pull him together; all he wanted to do was lie down in front of that warm stove and sleep. He couldn't eat much, after all. He was completely exhausted physically; and mentally he seemed to be dissolving in worry. He could scarcely listen to Anton's constant chatter. He was thinking of August Grell and what kept him so long on the telephone. Or why he had even needed to use the telephone at all. Something is wrong, Bryant's instincts kept telling him, something is wrong.

"Look," he told Anton, rising to his feet, reaching for his

sweater, "I really must go. It's well after ten. Time I was on my way to Salzburg."

"It only takes an hour and a half," Anton protested. He looked almost alarmed, nervous.

More like two hours in my condition, thought Bryant. Last night he had taken fully three, dawdling his way carefully through the night. "Sorry I can't say good-bye to your father. Give him my thanks, won't you? Perhaps I'll bring my wife up here for some skiing in December. You do open then for skiers?"

"Yes, of course! We have no ski lift here, of course, no special slopes. But there is good ski-running. That is the best sport anyway. Here—let me show you on this map." Anton had followed Bryant as he talked, and was now rummaging in a dresser drawer near the back entrance. "You can ski for thirty kilometers across—"

"I'd be satisfied with three," Bryant said. "You overestimate me, Anton." He unlocked the back door, began to pull its heavy weight inward.

"Wait!" said Anton softly. "I think I hear my—"

Bryant half turned his head to see where the blow was coming, ready to dodge. He was a split second too slow. The side of Anton's right hand, hard as steel, cracked the back of his neck. He keeled straight over like a tree under a woodsman's axe. His hand fell away from the door, his face hit the floor, and he lay quite still.

3

AUGUST GRELL CAME OUT OF HIS ROOM TO FIND ANTON, A nervous look on his face that pinched his lips and tightened his eyes, waiting in the hall. Grell froze, then burst into anger. "He has left? Hell take you, you let him leave!"

Anton listened in silence to a string of curses, but his eyes were widening and his lips beginning to ease before he asked too innocently, "Didn't you want him to leave?"

Grell looked more closely at the spreading smile. He ran through the dining room, burst into the kitchen, halted abruptly. He stared back at Anton, then he went over to kneel beside Bryant. Yes, his suspicion was right. The man was dead. "You were too quick," he told Anton grimly.

"I aimed for the side of his neck, but he jerked his head around and the blow caught him right at the back of—"

"So I see." Grell rose to his feet, picking up Bryant's sodden sweater.

"There was no choice. He was leaving. He had the door open." Anton felt the side of his hand. It was numb. He shrugged his shoulders. "Why did you bring him here anyway?"

"Because I wanted him for questioning. I wanted no body found near Finstersee. I wanted no repeat of Lake Toplitz."

"It had its uses," Anton suggested. "It scared them all."

"And made everything twice as difficult for us." Grell glanced at his watch. "All right, all right," he said irritably. "You take his jacket, wear it. Get him loaded into the front seat of the car and cover him with your cape."

"The back seat would be better—gives me more room."

"You won't have time to move him out of the back seat into the front, and that's where you'll need him when you leave the car. Whiten your hair a bit—use some flour. Not too much! Where's his hat? Didn't he wear a—"

"Here's something," Anton said as he searched in a deep pocket. "A beret! Imagine wearing a beret with a loden jacket," he added contemptuously. "Who was he working for?"

"It would be nice if we could ask him, wouldn't it?"

"Oh," said Anton, and shrugged his shoulders again. "Don't think we would have got much out of him."

"He has a wife," Grell said simply.

Yes, that always made a good threat, Anton thought. But why blame me for what I had to do? After all, Bryant would be alive and tied securely to a chair, ready for questioning, if old Grell hadn't been caught up in all the precautions he took for security's sake. He was secretive about the methods he used for an emergency call, but he wouldn't have locked himself up in his bedroom if he wasn't decoding the double talk that had come over the telephone in thick, rich Saxon dialect. "Didn't *you* find out anything?" Anton asked, challenging as much as he dared, his eyes innocent.

"If he hadn't died today, he would have been killed tomorrow." Grell hesitated, then added, "Two men were being sent from Warsaw to Salzburg. They intended to get the chest from him, and then silence him completely."

"But he hasn't got it. I searched the trunk of his car in case he had carried it that far before he doubled back through the woods to get his jacket."

Grell studied Anton with amusement. But his tone was gentler now. "And what about his equipment? You think that all a man has to do is take off his shirt and dive into Finstersee? There is more to it than that." He relented completely. "You're right. I don't think he could have found the chest."

"This jacket is too small. I can't button it." Anton laughed at his wrists popping far out below the cuffs.

"You aren't going to be seen closely by anyone. You'll drive quickly through the village, climb the hill at high speed—give every appearance of a good driver who takes chances. You are someone going home in a hurry."

"His wife—how much does she know, I wonder?" That's what we should be worrying about, thought Anton. A faked accident to Bryant would be easy; but loose ends might be more difficult to deal with.

Grell was reflective. The woman must have known something. Why else would she have sounded so upset? As if she knew that Finstersee was a dangerous spot, yet dared not mention it. But she had spoken about Yates's call from Zürich quite freely. Grell allowed himself one small deduction. "She does not know everything, or else she would never have mentioned a man called Yates."

So that's what all his telephoning was about, thought Anton; he was checking on the name of Yates. "And who is he?"

"A man who has been sending messages to Warsaw from Zürich."

"The man we caught?"

"Come on, come on," Grell said brusquely. "Time to get Bryant moved out of here."

Anton took his cue. "How far do I drive?"

"Well outside of the village—beyond the old church on the high meadow. There's a sharp curve at that point. You go around it, and just where the road—"

"I see what you want." But, thought Anton, not that old cliché! Every time I hear of a car going over a cliff and ending in flames, I wonder who pushed it. He repressed a weary sigh, said diplomatically, "I'll start a skid and stop the car near the edge. I'll put his jacket around his shoulders, leave him slumped over the wheel, smash the window, take my loden, and get out of sight. And don't worry, I'll keep my gloves on all the time."

Grell was frowning as he pulled and tugged at the sweater to fit it over the body. "It may not be enough. The skid, I mean."

"Well, I'll turn the car over on its side—it's small enough."

Grell shook his head. "Better push the car right over the edge of the road." That should be easy. It was a third-class road, with soft shoulders and no railing, narrow and rarely used except on market days. And Monday wasn't a market day.

He's in love with his cliché, thought Anton, and restrained his amusement. The trouble with the old was that they had their set patterns. He rather enjoyed the idea of a skid around the corner, just to remind him that he had been an expert driver once. A secondhand motorcycle was the most that Grell thought appropriate for him in this job.

"Understood?"

"Yes, sir."

"And remember—get quickly through the village."

Anton nodded. He pulled the crumpled beret into an angle to cover the right side of his head, which would be seen from the more populated side of the street. Three hundred and forty people lived in Unterwald, but most of the houses were scattered down over the fields, some barely in sight, as if each and every one of them wanted its own view of the valley below. At this time of day, the children would be in school, the women would be hanging their washing under the broad eaves on ropes strung across their third-floor balconies, the men would be sawing timber for a winter of wood carving. Some would see the car, certainly, but they wouldn't see too closely. Unterwald would be no problem. "You know," Anton said as he got ready to hoist Bryant over his shoulders, "I quite liked him. I was beginning to believe his story until I heard you start telephoning. What gave him away?"

"He trusted too much in a friend."

Anton's quick blue eyes studied the other man's impassive face, as if trying to read the riddle. Old Security-Conscious wouldn't tell him, not until this emergency was over and done with. So he risked a probe. "The man whose code we broke? The one who is in our custody right now?"

Grell began to smile. "That isn't a bad guess," he conceded.

"Name of Yates?"

Grell laughed. He liked to see bright intelligence in the young. We'll need all we can get of it, he thought. "You are doing well." He pulled the door wide, walked out between the two neat piles of logs that stretched along the entire back of the house almost to the balcony overhead, and opened the door of the car. Bryant had left the keys in the ignition, ready for a quick departure. He really had thought of everything, that little amateur. I'd better go up to Finstersee right away, decided Grell, and make a careful check of that patch of boulders and trees down at the shore line before I send in my report. Rope burns on a tree, slime from the lake where the chest had been dragged over stones would tell me the real story. Then I'd know whether he managed to get the chest, or whether he was just on a scouting expedition.

Grell looked casually to either side of him. No one in sight. He nodded to Anton, waiting at the threshold. Anton was shaking his head, the expression on his face openly well-I-never. "What is it?" Grell asked quickly.

"So friend Yates alerted Warsaw to get Bryant?" Anton asked as he passed Grell.

"Yes. Now hurry—don't overplay our luck!"

"Nice people," Anton commented as he lowered the man he had murdered into the car and swung off his loden cape to cover the body. "I'll circle back around the hills. See you in a couple of hours."

Luck, Grell had said. More than luck, thought Anton; we must have some good ears and eyes stationed around Europe. I have been told that often enough, but it's reassuring to find it is true. We may be few as yet, but that's the way every real power group started. Not in huge masses—that's something to be used later. Not even with popular approval— only the democracies think in terms of the majority, and they are no model for us. They waste themselves in talk talk talk and self-indulgence. We have better brains than most of them and a sense of realism they never possessed. One thing East Germany showed me and that was the fat-cat weakness of the West. The Communists have more to teach us; we can learn something from them. They have the right idea about power and how to get it and how to keep it. Look at Russia today: eleven million Communists, that's all, controlling more than two hundred million non-Communists. China is the same: nineteen million Communists as the élite group over seven hundred million people. Popular approval? That's a laugh. Just give us all newspapers and radio stations and TV channels, and we'll give the people all the five-year plans they want; and we'll see. . . . Crazy, are we? It can be done. Because it has been done. And we'll do it better. Better than any Russians or Chinese. And we'll be clever this time. The way the old Germany handled the Jewish problem was worse than a crime, it was a blunder. We'll handle the Jews the way Russia does—a few for a showcase, the rest nothing-men. Yes, we'll succeed where the old Germany failed; we'll use all its greatness and repeat none of its mistakes. And it *was* a great country. Our enemies could destroy our homes and our nation, but we still have our brains and our courage and our perseverance. We don't give up, we don't compromise. And we have a cause. Universal peace through world domination. Why should we let the Communists have that plum?

He took the hill road out of Unterwald at a good strong speed. It was empty of any traffic, and the next mountain village was at least fifteen minutes away. A nice lonely stretch. His speed increased. There was always an exhilaration in twisting and turning along the shoulders of the hills. In the distance, he could briefly glimpse the black onion-shaped cap on the white bell tower of the little church standing boldly on its high meadow; then it would be blocked from view by another wooded slope. In and out, twist and turn, soaring above the placid valley that lay far below to his left. The mists had lifted, leaving only dampness to bind the earth road more securely. His one complaint was the weight of Bryant's bent-up body, which kept falling against his legs with each swerve and curve. Now he was almost at the church itself, rounding the turn with a screech of brakes.

And then the skid started, much more of a skid than he had intended. A real skid. Startled, he swung the steering wheel to his right—no, that was wrong—he must turn into the direction of the skid. He remembered, too, to take his foot off the brake and press lightly on the accelerator. He had veered right across the narrow road, the rear tires already digging into its soft shoulder. He felt it yield. He swore, reaching for the door handle, but his legs were jammed by Bryant's sudden weight, and there was no time, no time at all—

The car slipped over the treacherous edge of the road and plunged downward, twisting and turning, twisting and turning.

4

THE TELEPHONE RANG, PULLING ANNA BRYANT TO HER FEET. She pushed back her disordered hair, tried to wipe the dried tear marks from her tight cheeks, and stood holding the edge of the table. She was afraid to answer. Could it be Dick? It had to be, it had to be. She left the warm kitchen and ran through the narrow corridor, past the darkroom and the storeroom, into the little front shop. She caught the receiver on the seventh ring. "Yes?" she was asking, afraid to say "Dick?" But it was his voice.

She leaned against the counter where the cameras were displayed, staring at the wall with samples of his pictures scattered over it. It was daylight out in the narrow little street, people were up and around. And his voice was telling her that he was fine, that he was drying off at the inn, he'd be home around midday, he'd be home, he'd be home. . . . "See you soon, darling," his cheerful voice said, and he had hung up before she could ask if everything was all right.

It must be all right, she thought. He must have found the chest and hidden it. Or else he wouldn't have sounded so confident. Perhaps it had been easier than she had thought, after all. Except for that mist. She drew a long breath. The truth was that she had scarcely hoped to see him alive again. Last night, as she had listened to him over their late supper, watching him eat, unable to swallow a bite from her own plate, she had felt only horror and fear and the cold anguish of her world smashed to pieces again. But he had been right: he could do the job; and he had done it. She paused before one of the pictures on the wall, touching it lightly with her hand. It was a study of Finstersee, taken from the picnic ground in early July, showing the meadow scattered with flowers and, behind it, the deep green forest and, behind that, the mountainside of gray barren rock. But it was on the three tilted boulders at the edge of the meadow, garlanded at their base by wild roses and lupins and long-stemmed daisies, that her eyes rested.

As she returned to the kitchen through the long stretch of the old house, she heard her brother's footsteps clumping around in the spare bedroom overhead. One thing about Johann as a guest—he gave good warning that he was about to come downstairs. She moved to the kitchen door that led out into the stone hallway and unlocked it so that Johann could enter, for the dark vaulted hall was both the main entry from the street for all the people who lived in the apartments above and the only means to start climbing to the various landings. It was a complicated business living in the Old Town of Salzburg, but the Bryants had thought themselves lucky to find a flat over the shop and, like everyone else who lived in this section, had grown accustomed to coping with seventeenth-century surroundings. Walls bulged and floors sagged, but everything was kept repaired and painted and people talked of character and charm. Inconvenience was never mentioned except by those who moved away to the more antiseptic suburbs—that was Dick's phrase for the modern houses spreading out over the hills that surrounded Salzburg.

Anna, looking around at the disorder of her kitchen, was almost disloyal to Dick. Somehow, the parlor furniture from upstairs had infiltrated down here piece by piece—there had never been much of it but it certainly made the large room seem small. Originally, it hadn't been a kitchen either. But Dick had decided that it was easier to cook here, when they were working late in the darkroom, and to eat here too. Now—just what would you call this room? she wondered. She smiled, knowing Dick's reply: the warmest and most comfortable in the whole house. I had better start clearing things, she thought, and stood wondering where she'd start, and then heard through the half-opened door the quick clatter of Johann's heavy shoes as he came running down the stone staircase outside.

"Careful!" she called in alarm. The stairs were worn, deceptive, dark. She heard him slip and fall. He was cursing everything in sight as he burst into the kitchen. He calmed down when he saw her. "Bloody hell," he ended, rubbing his

45

backside. "Last week I climbed over the Dachstein, got caught in snow flurries, hiked back to Bad Aussee in pouring rain, took neither a fall nor a cold. All I have to do is come to Salzburg for three days and I start sneezing and splitting my—" He became aware of the kitchen's state, of his sister's appearance. Dirty dishes were uncleared from the table, the sink was littered with pots and pans, the lamps were on and the curtains tightly drawn although it was broad daylight out in the streets. Anna's hair seemed to be falling in pieces around her thin, pale face. She was wearing the same sweater and skirt he had last seen when she had brought him broth and her special brew of herb tea yesterday evening. And in spite of the comfortable warmth of the kitchen, she was huddled in an old coat of her husband's which usually hung on the back-door peg. "Have you been down here all night? What's—"

"Nothing is wrong," she told him, decidedly, cheerfully. "Except with you. You shouldn't be up and dressed. Another day in bed would do no harm."

"I'm all right." His voice was thick with his cold, his eyes looked more gray than blue, but the flush of fever had gone. "One day in bed is enough for me." He switched off the light, pulled back the curtains, and stared out at a honeycomb of other people's houses around their tight little courtyard.

"You should stay indoors—"

"We'll see, we'll see," he said irritably. He was hungry, but the kitchen was a mess and his appetite was beginning to leave him. Anna never had been much of a housekeeper, but this morning she had surpassed herself. "Anna, you look awful. Will you go upstairs and make yourself decent, and we'll get this mess straightened up so that a man can enjoy his breakfast?"

"Yes," she said, latching the coat back on its peg as she left. She climbed the stairs quickly. I'll get him fed before I give him the news about Dick's absence, she was thinking. Dick had said she could tell Johann everything. Everything, that was, except the hiding place of the chest. Or about its contents. No one was to know that. Not at this time. And I was only told about it in case things went wrong, in case Dick never got back. She had been given full instructions what to do if that happened. But she wouldn't have to do anything. Dick would be home to take charge as he always did.

She washed away the sticky streaks of tears, combed her fair hair into its soft wave, added lipstick to her pale lips for some courage. Johann was going to be angry. He was going to be more than angry. She went downstairs slowly.

He had solved the problem of the dirty dishes by shoving them inside the small sink beside the pots and throwing a drying towel over the heap to get them out of sight. He had ground fresh coffee and was putting the kettle to boil. "That's more like it," he told her as he gave her a quick glance. "You're short of food—there are three eggs and not much bread."

"I only want coffee." She had made a big supper for Dick last night.

"But what about Dick's breakfast? He'll need something when he wakes up."

"I'll get some more food before then." She began breaking the eggs into a bowl.

"He takes it easy, doesn't he?"

"In between assignments. The book is all ready now. The photographs are waiting to go to Zürich. He may take them there this week."

"Why not mail them?"

"Oh, Dick wants to see the publisher himself about some details. Well—he is not exactly the publisher. He's the man who runs the Zürich office of the American publishing house. It's a New York firm—" She stopped whisking the eggs, glanced across the kitchen. Johann did not seem impressed. "It's a very important firm," she told him severely.

"I know, I know."

"It was a very generous advance: a check for three hundred American dollars."

I could live for three months on that, thought Johann. "Any chance your Zürich friend would like a book on mountain climbing?" He watched the answering smile on his sister's face. No, she wasn't unhappy. So there hadn't been a quarrel between her and Dick. Yet why had she sat up all night? Breakfast first, he thought, and then I'll find out. He sat down at the table to wait in silence. Anna's cooking was better than her housekeeping provided no one disturbed her concentration. It was on the simple side, of course; Dick's taste in food was simple. But what chance had she ever had of being taught how to run a house or bake Linzertorte? Aged fourteen she had been when the Russian shelling of

Vienna had stopped and the horde of soldiers poured in from the east. There hadn't been a woman or girl in that part of the city—yes, some had been younger than Anna, some five times her age—who hadn't nightmare memories of that day of liberation. No one spoke of it any more; it was something dead and buried like the corpses under the burned ruins of the Cathedral. No one spoke of it; all was silence, all seemed forgotten. Seemed ... How often did the memory steal unexpectedly into a man's mind and make him want to seize the whole bloody world by its filthy throat and break its hypocritical neck?

"Johann! *Please* eat it while it's hot."

She had set before him his favorite omelette, fluffy and soft, slightly sweetened, filled with heated apricot preserves, powdered on top with fine sugar. He turned his head aside and blew his nose violently. "Has Dick any spare handkerchiefs? This cold is all in my head now, blast it."

"I'll get them. And his slippers."

"They won't fit."

"They are better than shoes that are damp," she told him severely. "You men!"

Yes, he thought, you men. ... He had almost finished the small omelette before she came running downstairs. There had been no other sounds from the bedroom overhead except her quick light footsteps. He frowned, pouring himself a mixture of hot milk and coffee, and then, as she placed the handkerchiefs at his elbow and the slippers beside his feet, he asked quite simply, "Where is Dick?"

"Your shoes are really sodden," she told him, and poured her own cup of coffee. She didn't sit down, though. "That must have been quite a shower you were caught in. Where were you anyway?"

"On the Mönchsberg."

"With a very pretty girl who is probably dying of pleurisy right now. Oh, really, Johann, couldn't you just have taken her to a café or the movies?"

"We were at a café and we were at the movies, and then we walked along the heights to see the view."

"At midnight?"

"There was a full moon until the rain came. And stop worrying about Elisabetha. She had my cape. How do you think I got soaked?"

"Elisabetha. No, I don't need to worry about that one."

48

"Anna," he asked quietly, "where is Dick? Sit down. No; across the table from me. Have some more coffee. Where is Dick?"

"He went up to Finstersee."

Johann stared at her, put his cup down slowly.

"But it's all right, Johann. It's all right. He is at Unter-wald right now. That was Dick telephoning me."

"From where?" he asked quickly. There weren't so many telephones in Unterwald.

"From the Gasthof Waldesruh. He was going to have breakfast with Herr Grell and his son Anton."

"I thought you told me all the photographs were ready."

"They are."

"Then he didn't go up to Finstersee to take some more shots? He went up to Finstersee to—" He couldn't finish. Anger choked him. Then he thought, That's impossible; Dick must only have been taking another look around. He calmed down. "What did he tell you?"

"Everything."

"And what is everything?" His anger was rising again. Dick wouldn't have told Anna anything unless he was actually taking action about that damned chest. "Did he really believe that a box was lying on the ledge?"

"He thought he would see, at least."

"But it was only an informant's story—years ago—and he didn't even believe it then. I know. We laughed about it together when he told me, and that was a long time ago."

"There is a ledge at that part of the lake."

"I know! I'm the idiot who found it for him!"

"He told me that, too," she said gently. Johann had taken a party of amateur climbers up around Finstersee last summer and brought them back close to the shore, just at the point where Dick thought the chest might be hidden. And Johann had started telling the girls in the party that the lake was so deep, so filled with strange currents, that no one would swim there. Anna could imagine the scene well enough: time out for rest, the girls teasing Johann about his wild statements. She could see his handsome tanned face smiling as he weighted the end of his climbing rope and threw it out into the lake to let it keep on sinking, sinking. And as the girls turned away impressed, he had dropped the rope into the lake in front of his feet. And the weight had touched ground just about four meters down by his calcula-

49

tion. "He told me he asked you to find some way to see if the ledge existed, and you did. And you know, Johann, I don't think you would have bothered if that informant's story hadn't been haunting you too."

"Well, after what happened at Toplitz—" He didn't end the sentence. She knew about Lake Toplitz, that he could see by her face. But he was willing to bet that she hadn't been told about the two bodies there, or how they had died. "When did he leave? Come on, Anna. Tell me it all."

So she told him. Everything except the hiding place, and about the chest's contents. That was a promise she had to keep.

"He might have taken me along," Johann said bitterly when she had finished. "He needed another man." If Finstersee contained anything at all, the Nazis would be watching.

"You had a cold. You can't go diving with a cold. Dick said that could make you pass out and—"

"He rushed this job. I was laid up, and he seized the chance to ditch me. Doesn't he trust me?"

"Of course he does. It's just that—just that—" She was in trouble, so she stopped.

"It's just that he wants that chest to go to the bloody British or the damned Americans." His anger was returning.

"He says the only important thing is that the Nazis never find it again," she flashed back at him. "And you like the British and Americans, so why swear at them? Besides, he is English, isn't he? He found it, so it goes to them. Isn't that fair?"

"No! It was in an Austrian lake. It's ours by right."

"But we are neutral. We'd do nothing with it. We'd lock it up safely and then forget about it. But the Nazis won't forget. Nor the Communists. Dick says they'll infiltrate our—"

"That's his excuse." Johann paused. The contents of the chest must be valuable, then. "Did he tell you what was in it?"

"He didn't want to talk about that." Which was true.

"You really don't know?"

With difficulty, she kept her eyes from flinching. "He said I did not need to know that," she said, feeling her throat go dry. But that was true, too. Dick refused at first. And then, when I insisted, he told me. Not so much because I insisted but because he realized he had to—in case something went

50

wrong. But it didn't, and now I can forget all about the chest. If only Johann doesn't keep asking, asking, asking.

But Johann was off on his own train of thought. "Then *he* knows!" Johann said swiftly. He thumped his fist on the table, spilling his coffee, rose to his feet. "I'm going to phone."

"Whom?"

He halted. Felix Zauner was the man to deal with this problem: he had been with the Austrian State Tourist Department for a number of years, and then—after the Toplitz incident—he had gone into business for himself. He had opened a sports-equipment shop in Salzburg, a very small business which allowed him plenty of free time for his particular hobby of skiing. He had a few branch shops, too, although that wasn't known except by the men whom he had staked. Johann was one of them. Felix was the silent partner, with his name not even mentioned, far less over the door. He was equally casual about money matters or a share in the profits. All he needed were a few men he could trust who knew the mountains, and who wanted no Nazis or any other foreigners complicating Austria's revival. His friendship with Johann was quite open; he liked Bryant and had a kind of gallant affection for Anna. But what had stopped Johann short on his way to the telephone was Felix's words when they had last discussed the possibility of Nazi secrets hidden in lakes other than Toplitz. "Let them rot there," Felix had said. "That's what they deserve. Unless, of course, there's definite evidence that the Nazis are raising them to use again. Then we'll move. And if anyone else is idiot enough to think he could find these documents—these old Hitler boys will get him before he even reaches the spot, and another good man will be dead. Tell your brother-in-law to stop being curious. He isn't serious by any chance, is he?" And Johann had said no, he didn't think Dick was anything more than curious.

Anna was watching him and wondering and guessing all the wrong reasons for his indecision. "But we don't know anyone here to whom we could report all this about Finstersee. And why report Dick? You wouldn't do that. He isn't hurting Austria. Please wait until he gets back and talk it over with him."

"Why didn't he tell me about the diving gear? What kind was it anyway?" And I told Felix he was only curious.

51

"Don't shout!" she pleaded. "I don't know what kind. It is something he used for underwater pictures this summer."

"Where did he buy it?" Not in Salzburg, certainly. Word would have drifted around. And there had been no talk of Bryant dabbling in underwater pictures, either.

"I think in Zürich."

He's a closemouthed bastard, thought Johann. He stifled some stronger language, thinking of what he was going to say to Felix, and came back to the table to get another handkerchief. He blew his nose again, and that seemed to clear his brain for a moment. "Anna! He can't have found the chest! Don't you see? He never would be having breakfast at the inn with anything as valuable as that chest lying in his car. Now would he?"

She was silent. I won't have to tell Johann any lies after all, she was thinking, and relief spread over her face. "No," she said, at last.

Johann's resentment faded. She's as glad as I am, he thought, that Dick failed. Felix was right: some things were better left to rot. "Just as well he didn't find anything. He'd be in danger, and so would you. It isn't only the Nazis we have to worry about. Did you know that a couple of Russian tourists in Bad Aussee were politely escorted to the frontier? They weren't what their passports said they were. And then there was that Frenchman pretending to be an Italian schoolteacher on vacation. He was wandering around Lake Toplitz trying to find out whether we had salvaged more documents there. He left along with the Russians."

"Have we salvaged *all* those documents? Dick thought not."

"And what gave him that idea?"

She half dried her hands and went over to a drawer in the little writing desk where Dick had filed that newspaper clipping of last week. Someday, she thought, we'll have a real kitchen and a real living room, both separate, both neat. "Here," she said, giving it to Johann as she returned to the sink. She glanced at the clock. "Oh, dear! I ought to have done the shopping first. The soup should be on by now."

Johann watched her with amusement; you could depend on Anna to plan things the wrong way round. And yet, in the darkroom, her work was excellent. Even Dick, who fussed and fumed about texture and light and shade and flawless prints, admitted she was good. Now she had decided to let the dishes drip and fetch her coat and shopping basket from the crowded closet near the door. By the time she was ready to go, he had read the clipping. It was date-lined Vienna, and only a few days old.

Since the first diving operations in Lake Toplitz during the summer of 1959, when various chests that had been sunk there by the Nazis in 1945 were recovered, there has been considerable speculation in informed circles concerning the contents of these discoveries. It was officially announced, at the time, that among the items recovered from the lake was a cache of counterfeit English five-pound bank notes amounting to more than 25,000,000 Austrian schillings in value, as well as plans for U-boat rockets. (The details were given in the August 11th publication of the German magazine "Der Stern" of 1959.) But until today silence has been officially maintained about subsequent discoveries, leading certain interested people to believe that documents might still be hidden in Lake Toplitz. Such ill-founded beliefs can now be laid to rest. According to a reliable source, the documents have been identified as German records and receipts of the period 1936–39, including a list of Balkan agents working for the German Reich at that time. A government spokesman stated today that all diving operations ceased some years ago when it was officially decided that our Styrian lakes had given up the last of their secrets. Such operations were highly expensive to maintain and, without further results, a waste of time and money.

"What got into Dick? It's obvious we did fish up the documents, too." And they were scarcely worth the trouble, thought Johann. Now that hoard of counterfeit bank notes and the submarine rockets had been something; but a list of Balkan agents, who probably never survived the war anyway ... He laughed.

"Is it?"

"Of course it's obvious! It says here—"

"It doesn't say anything of the kind. 'A reliable source,' it says, and that's all. What reliable source?"

"But the government spokesman—"

"Is stating the truth, and just read again what he says. It simply means we stopped diving."

"But it says here—" Johann insisted.

"It doesn't." Anna was impatient. "It is simply trying to give that impression. It's trying to convince people like your

53

Russian tourists and Frenchman that they are wasting their time. Which means there must be *some* interest starting up in the lakes again, enough to worry our government and make them want to discourage prowlers. It's—it's hidden diplomacy. That's what Dick says."

"That's what Dick says," he mimicked, and then laughed.

"Yes," she said, blue eyes large with indignation.

"But he doesn't think they are going to be discouraged?"

"Some of them won't be. They know that the Nazis sunk several chests, and these held more important things than the names of Balkan agents."

"So that's what triggered him off!" Johann lit a cigarette and poured the last of the coffee. "He's a crazy idiot," he added, shaking his head.

"Yes," she flashed back at him, "only a crazy idiot would have given shelter to a fifteen-year-old refugee with a three-months-old baby in her arms." The door closed behind her, leaving him staring at nothing.

The coffee was cold, but he drank it. The cigarette tasted like floor sweepings. It was the first time Anna, in all these years, had even mentioned Vienna to him. Dick had kept his silence, too, except for one brief explanation of why he had brought her to Salzburg. "I took her away from everything that reminded her of what Vienna had suffered." And it was Dick who had arranged for the adoption of the child. That was part of the therapy. "It was Anna's only chance. And mine. Rape distorts a girl's mind, leaves revulsion and fear in place of trust. For months, even when she would share my room willingly, wouldn't leave, wouldn't go out into the street unless I was with her—she wasn't afraid of me somehow, only afraid of being abandoned again—she would flinch if I ever touched her hair, tremble against her own will when I put a hand on her cheek." So, thought Johann bitterly, it was a stranger who found my sister wandering in the ruined streets—the family friends she had hoped to find either dead or scattered, new addresses unknown. I wasn't any help to her then, when she needed most help. I wasn't even there.

But what good would a sixteen-year-old kid have been anyway? He hadn't described himself as that, of course, back in those days. He was a veteran, a courier for the underground that the Americans and British had formed in the mountains both south and north of the Italian border; he was a man, a grown man by his reckoning, a very big man

54

indeed. Hadn't he, a city boy born and bred, made his way to the mountains when he was only fourteen? The Germans weren't going to make a stiff-backed Nazi out of him as they had done with Josef, his older brother—killed in Poland, which was one way of settling Josef's savage political arguments with their father. (Come to think of it, it was his father who had turned Josef into a Nazi before the Germans even arrived.) And his father wasn't going to convert him into being a fellow-Communist—Marxist was his way of describing himself; Father had always liked the intellectual touch—and sharing the martyrdom of a Nazi concentration camp. Yet the old man was tough. He had survived.

Yes, he had survived to come home after that great night of liberation and find what his comrades had done to his wife and daughter. He solved that problem even more quickly than he used to solve all the problems of the world: he hanged himself from an exposed and blackened beam in the ruins of his house. As for Mother . . .

Johann drew a deep long breath. Yes, that was all his mother had needed to push her out of this world. She retreated; first mentally, then physically. The day after she died, Anna made her way out of the Russian zone. A fifteen-year-old girl with a three-months-old baby in her hands. On foot. With only the clothes they wore. He had tried to imagine that journey, and couldn't. Wouldn't. That was more honest. The past was past. . . . He was thinking too much about it, today. Perhaps because Anna had been thinking about it. Had she sat all through last night remembering?

He rose abruptly, went through to the shop. Here everything was neat and businesslike. He admired the display of cameras, the expensive gadgets that tourists liked to drape around their necks, and the photographs on the wall that were Dick's real interest. Mountains, glaciers, forests and meadowlands, lakes (yes, Finstersee was there among them) and alpine villages with their half-timbered houses, wooden walls rising from white plaster, balconies set into alcoves under deep eaves. There was a picture of Unterwald, too, with the Gasthof Waldesruh standing peacefully against its background of trees. Suddenly, Johann frowned. He hesitated. Then, obeying his instinct, he moved quickly to the telephone. He hoped Felix Zauner wouldn't still be reading a newspaper over his cup of midmorning coffee at Tomaselli's. But Felix was in his office above the Getreidegasse.

"And where are you sneezing from?" Felix wanted to know.

"I'm in Salzburg, staying with Anna and Dick. Look, Felix—what do you know about the Grells, August and Anton Grell? They keep the inn at Unterwald."

"Pleasant enough. Efficient. The old boy is pretty conservative, though. I couldn't interest him at all in turning his place into a real ski lodge. I have an idea for a ski lift up from the valley, but so far he says it would only ruin Unterwald." Felix laughed. "It's the first time I've ever heard a little more prosperity spread among the villagers being called their ruin."

Johann wiped his nose, repressed another sneeze. The shop was cold.

"Why do you ask?"

"I don't know," Johann said slowly. He hadn't any real reason, only a small worry that had started out as a simple question. He frowned again at the picture of the Gasthof Waldesruh. "It's just that Dick went up to Finstersee early this morning—"

"Oh?" Felix's quiet voice was now serious.

"And he telephoned Anna from the inn. He was having breakfast there."

"Why not?"

"The inn is closed at the moment. At least, it looked very closed when I was up visiting Unterwald two weeks ago."

"I didn't think you noticed anything when you were with Trudi." Felix might be making a mild joke about Johann's girl-in-every-village, but his next words went right to the heart of Johann's question. "So they invited him in for a hot cup of coffee. Why does that puzzle you?"

"He doesn't know them except by sight. They aren't friends of his. I was wondering if they were—well, perhaps a little curious about his photographing the lake." Now that he had said it, it sounded damned silly.

"I'm a little curious about everything," Felix said with a laugh, "including that cup of coffee. It's more than I was offered when I visited Unterwald. When do you expect Dick home?"

"He's on his way now." Johann turned his head quickly as the shop door opened, but it was Anna coming back with her shopping basket piled high. "He will be here around one o'clock. Anna is just about to start making liver dumplings for the soup." She laughed as she passed him, hurrying toward the kitchen, already slipping one arm out of her coat.

"I'll bring around my camera after lunch and hear what Dick advises. It's letting in too much light. I may have to get a new one. See you all then. My love to Anna. And I think you should stay in bed."

Johann went back to the kitchen and warmed his hands at the stove. "That was Felix."

"What did he want?" Anna asked absent-mindedly.

"He needs a new camera."

"Well that's nice for us." In the summer months the shop did a brisk business, for everyone who visited this part of Austria came to Salzburg and everyone visiting Salzburg liked to wander through the narrow streets of this old part of the town. That was one of the reasons Dick had chosen to live here rather than on the outskirts, which would have been cheaper as well as given them a garden and a view of the mountains. If Dick's book did well, if it led to other books of the same kind, perhaps they could afford both a shop on the central Neugasse and a house on a distant hill. Something like Johann's, only nearer to Salzburg. "What's wrong, Johann?" He was too quiet.

"I had better shave." He left without looking at her. He was beginning to regret his call to Zauner. Perhaps he had been too quick. Felix might well be more curious about Dick Bryant than about the Grells. And yet, he thought, there really is no harm that can come to Dick. Not now. If Dick had actually found anything in Finstersee, had refused to hand it over to the proper authorities, there could have been big trouble. Thank God I won't have to feel guilty for that, thought Johann. Being neutral could be a very unpleasant business.

5

IT WAS HALF PAST ONE, AND FOR THE LAST TEN MINUTES ANNA had been trying not to look at the clock. Johann was moving around the kitchen in one of his restless attacks. Another day of living in this enclosed space, he thought, and I'd start pushing the walls out. How could people live in towns or cities? The more he remembered his own place, not much bigger than this but standing free and alone on the hill road outside of Bad Aussee, the greater became his impulse to gather his few things together, find his jeep in its usual parking place, take the highway home.

The shop door opened.

It could be Dick, although he usually came in the back way; it was nearer the square where he left his car, for in this part of the Old Town no automobiles were allowed. Anna was on her feet and running toward the shop before Johann could even turn around. He followed quickly.

It was a stranger who had entered the shop, a man with intelligent brown eyes, dark hair, pleasantly rugged features, and a brisk but polite manner. He was fairly young—about thirty-five or less, Johann decided—and fairly tall, but not quite Johann's six feet. He was in good condition, Johann noted too, someone who wasn't spreading into his thirties. He was an optimist about weather; he wore no coat, no hat, just a tweed jacket and dark-gray flannels. He carried a neat camera bag strapped over one shoulder and two yellow boxes of film were in one hand. That explained his visit.

He addressed Anna. "Guten Tag, gnädige Frau. Ich möchte—" He paused, searching for the next phrase.

"I speak English," Anna said. "I am sorry. The shop is closed for lunch. Until half past two."

He looked at the door behind him which was very much open. "Then I'm out of luck." He had a very disarming smile.

"I forgot to lock it," she confessed, softening visibly. She liked his attempt to speak German; that was politeness, at least. Too many foreigners would not even take the trouble. From his voice, he was American. He would be in a hurry; they always were. "At the moment, we are very busy. If you want your film developed and printed quickly, you should try Lieleg. That is on the right bank, the other side of the river. They are reliable—"

"But only after half past two?"

She was almost amused. Any other day she would have laughed. She glanced at the clock.

"Actually," he said in his easy way, slipping the boxes of film into his camera bag as if he were glad to get rid of them, "I came here hoping to speak to Mr. Bryant. My name is Mathison, William Mathison. Are you Mrs. Bryant?" She nodded. He looked over her head toward the hall door. "Mr. Bryant?"

"No," said Johann, and studied the American more carefully.

"This is my brother, Johann Kronsteiner. My husband is not here at the moment. May I take a message?"

A sad and lovely face, thought Mathison, both old and young. But under the gentle mask of politeness, there was some deep anxiety that was pulling her attention away from this room. This had been the wrong time to come here in every way, he decided; his luck was out. But then, it had been out for the last four days, ever since he had arrived in Zürich from New York. He said, "I'm staying overnight at the Salzburger Hof. Perhaps your husband would telephone me there when he returns, and we could arrange to meet?" He produced a card from his wallet. She looked down at it with a frown. It was her brother who took charge then, padding forward in soft slippers that were too small for him.

"William Mathison," Johann read from the card, "Attorney at Law." He exchanged a look with his sister, and went on reading the names in the bottom left-hand corner of the small piece of pasteboard. "Strong, Muller, Nicolson and Hodge. 61 Wall Street, New York 5, N.Y.—and who are they?"

"My law firm. They represent Newhart and Morris."

"Dick's publishers," Anna prompted Johann. "Did they send you here?" she asked Mathison. "But why?"

"Well," he said, keeping his voice as easy as possible to calm her new anxiety, "for the last four years, I've been retained—" Hell, he thought as he noticed the baffled faces, let's cut out the jargon. "Whenever Newhart and Morris have a problem, they call on me. And I try to help."

"And what's the problem here?" Johann demanded.

"It's simple enough, possibly just a—"

"It's simple enough, so you came all the way here from New York?" Johann's voice sounded belligerent.

Mathison turned to the woman. "It's only a matter of a letter which I think your husband wrote to Newhart and Morris two weeks ago." He took a folded sheet of paper out of his wallet and handed it over. "This is your husband's signature?"

"Of course. Was it wrong of him to write his publishers? He *did* wait to hear from New York," she told Mathison reprovingly. "He thought that someone over there should be in touch with him now that his book was ready to be published."

Mathison stared at her blankly for a split second. "Then he received the check he mentioned in his letter? And signed a contract?"

"But of course!" The touch of reprimand faded from her voice and face. "Didn't you know?"

Mathison shook his head. He gestured to the letter in her hand. He said gently, "That's the first we heard of Richard Bryant. Now please don't start worrying. We'll clear this up quite easily." Like hell we will, he thought, but he spoke reassuringly. "It's just some kind of bungle in the Zürich office. Or perhaps in New York," he added to soften a hard look from Johann Kronsteiner. "Something has been misfiled, or gone missing in the mail. That happens now and again."

"Didn't you see the samples of my husband's work? He took them to Zürich—in June—when he went to see Mr. Yates."

Johann cut in. "Perhaps Newhart and Morris know nothing about Mr. Yates either."

Mathison restrained himself and said patiently, "Eric Yates has been their representative in Zürich for the last six years. He usually does send samples of the work of any European author he is recommending to Newhart and Morris, but in Mr. Bryant's case there has obviously been some oversight." And what samples were they, what kind of work?

Johann was angry. It was obvious he thought that the stranger's "problem" was something invented by a bunch of Wall Street lawyers to let some New York publishers escape from their contract. "You can't get the check back anyway. It has been cashed."

"I never suggested that Mr. Bryant should return the check," Mathison said acidly. He noted the relief on both their faces, and pressed on with the first small advantage that had come his way. "All we want to know is the date of the check, the amount, anything you can remember about it. That would help track it down. So would you tell your husband all that? He has possibly kept some record—" Mathison, talking easily again, preparing to leave, walked over to the wall where the pictures were displayed in order to get a closer view of them. "I've been admiring these," he said. "Some beauties here. Did your husband take them?" They

60

weren't signed, but the studies of various lakes were named in a rough pencil scrawl in Bryant's writing on the gray mat that framed each one. "What camera did he use?"

"A Hasselblad." Her voice sounded strained.

He turned to look at her, pausing in his slow progress down the line of camera studies.

She was trying to appear normal, slightly amused. "Your check helped pay for it."

"Money well spent," he said, and went on with his inspection.

"I'm so glad you like these samples. They will be part of the book. It's a study of Austrian lakes," she said quickly.

He swung around again and caught the glance passing between Johann and his sister. What on earth have I wandered into? Mathison wondered. Don't these two innocents know that Newhart and Morris are publishers of books dealing mainly with science? Books filled with words and authority? And if they used any photographs or illustrations, these were more likely to deal with the trajectory of rockets, or geological slices of contorted rocks, or the interior of a bathysphere, or the exterior of the moon? But art books? No, that wasn't in any Newhart and Morris catalogue. And what was worrying these two at this moment—his interest in the pictures? Yet these were the samples Bryant had offered Yates. He turned back to the photographs. "I would pay good money for a copy of this kind of book myself," he said tactfully. "It should sell very well, I'd imagine. Your husband really knows texture. Take this, for example." He studied the quality of a mass of soft-petaled flowers growing around three giants of heavily grained rock set in a sea of grass against a background of forest and crag climbing to a gently clouded sky. This picture wasn't named. "Oh, I see," he went on, discovering the explanation for himself, "this is a detail of the end of this lake." He pointed to a photograph a short distance away, and went over to it. Finstersee, it was called. "A grim name. How do you translate it? The dark lake, or lake of darkness?" He glanced around at Mrs. Bryant for her answer, but she was standing quite rigid, hands clasped tensely. Her brother's eyes had narrowed. My tact isn't doing so well today, Mathison thought. So he left the photographs with only a passing look at the last one, Lake Toplitz.

"Doesn't that one interest you?" Johann wanted to know.

Mathison studied the Austrian's face. He was a handsome

type, strictly open-air, lean and powerful, a man of quick reactions. Perhaps his trade or profession needed that kind of reflex, but the challenge in his eyes at this moment was puzzling, disconcerting. "I thought I had wasted enough of your time. Sorry if I've been a nuisance. Well—I'll be going."

"Without seeing my brother-in-law's records? We were talking about them, I believe." The sarcasm was heavy and didn't altogether suit Johann.

Mathison's surprise deepened. So that's the reason for his truculence, he thought: this character thinks I used the check as an excuse to get in here and study these photographs. Then his explanation seemed so wild that Mathison pushed it to the side of his mind. He said quietly, "We were. Is it possible to see them now? I thought Mr. Bryant might have them locked in his safe."

"We don't need to lock things up in Salzburg," Johann said curtly. He looked at his sister. She had stopped staring at Finstersee, thank God, but now her eyes were fixed on the clock over the shop door. Damn this American who had talked of time.

"It's almost two," Anna was saying. "Oh, Johann—it's almost two."

"Get Dick's files, that's a good girl. Go on, Anna. Get them." It was better to start searching for them instead of watching a clock and thinking of Dick. Better, too, to call the American's bluff and show him the record of the check and get rid of him.

"It would save me coming back here again and troubling your husband," Mathison said, and that at least seemed to make good sense, for she nodded and hurried toward the back of the house. The kitchen possibly lay there; the appetizing smell of soup was growing stronger by the minute.

The silence in the shop was complete. Mathison was careful to keep away from the photographs of the lakes and looked out the window at the narrow street. It was barely twelve feet wide—about the breadth of his living room back in New York—and edged by just the suspicion of a sidewalk. Two men were walking there. Slowly. They were dressed definitely for Salzburg, in capes and dark-green felt hats each with a chamois brush sprouting at the rear of its squashed crown. He might have paid them no more attention, transferring his interest to a couple who had the right idea about life—a boy and a girl, holding hands, laughing at something preposterous—if one of them had been able to resist staring at the shop door. It was then he remembered seeing them before, at the end of the short street, as he had walked slowly up here from the Altmarkt searching for Bryant's address.

Suddenly, the silence was broken. Anna Bryant's clear voice, carrying through the tunnel of a hallway, was welcoming someone and then explaining to him about the stranger from America.

"Bryant?" Mathison asked quickly, turning away from the window.

Johann shook his head. "Just a friend of the family," was all he said, but even that was an admission he was relaxing. He greeted the man with evident relief. "Felix, come in. Glad you got here."

Mathison thought it wiser not to look too hard at the man whose family privileges included the use of the kitchen door, so he contented himself with a polite nod as Anna Bryant murmured a quiet introduction to Herr Zauner, and then turned away to open the large Manila envelope she had brought him. There wasn't much in it, but the contents were neatly arranged and across its flap was written, in Bryant's handwriting, *Yates*. He took out the documents, placing them for all to see on top of a counter, and began going through them. "Businesslike," he said approvingly to Anna Bryant, who stood beside him.

"Yes, my husband is a very careful man," she said with pride.

So careful, indeed, that—among the copies of the letters he had sent to Yates and of the one letter to Newhart and Morris—there was a photograph of a check for three hundred dollars. A wide and happy grin spread over Mathison's face. "This is all we need," he told her. "Do you mind if I photograph it, Mrs. Bryant? That's the simplest way to put it into our own records." He took out a neat camera only two inches long, switched on the lamp on the counter after exchanging its bulb for the high-intensity one that he carried in his bag along with an adapter for foreign sockets, laid the check under the bright beam.

"You come prepared," Johann said, leaving Zauner in his corner. He looked curiously at the check. "It's made out in

63

New York! The First Maritime Bank of New York." He studied the signature. "Emil Burch. Who's that?"

Mathison didn't answer. He was busy photographing the copies of Bryant's letters to Yates. And there was no use in alarming Mrs. Bryant, for the flat truth was that Newhart and Morris did not bank with the First Maritime. Neither did they have anyone called Burch who was allowed to sign their checks. And although Johann, breathing down the back of his neck, or the family friend standing silently against a wall might not believe it, the last thing that Mathison had come here to do was to add to Anna Bryant's trouble. "Just one thing: the contract. It isn't in this file." He switched off the light, and closed his camera, placing it carefully in his carrying bag.

"No. Mr. Yates has it. He promised last Wednesday—or was it Saturday?—when he phoned. He promised it would be here soon." Her thoughts wavered. "He is always telephoning," she said, trying to sound amused. She made an effort to complete her answer. "We—that is, my husband—signed two copies of the contract. In August, no—in July; yes, July."

Mathison helped her. He was beginning to see the pattern. "And after signing, Mr. Bryant sent the two copies back to Yates, who was going to send them to New York for the publisher's signature. One copy would stay in New York, the other was going to be returned to Yates to send to you. Was that it?"

She nodded.

"And the check was sent to you through Yates?"

"In August, the beginning of August." She was definite about that.

Johann cut in brusquely. "Isn't that the usual way? I mean about this Yates fellow sending on the contract?"

"It's the usual way," Mathison said reassuringly, his eyes on Anna Bryant's white face. But nothing else about this whole case was in the least usual. There hadn't been one mention of Bryant's name, far less a contract, in the files of Yates's office in Zürich. He began putting the copies of the letters and the photographed check back into their envelope. Not one real letter from Yates, he observed again; just two notes which must have accompanied the check and the contracts, and these were friendly and brief, making no specific mention of any business. One said: *Here it is! Glad it came through so quickly. Good luck with the Hasselblad. I hope it*

won't be long before you can get to Zürich again. Yours . . .
And the other: *We kept these as straightforward and simple
as possible. Just return them to me with two samples of your
fine sloping scrawl and I'll attend to the usual routine. It may
take time, but I've had the go-ahead signal from the Great
White Father in New York, so all is well. Yours . . .* A very
skillful job, Mathison thought. His lips tightened. "I'll
straighten all this out in Zürich," he said. He pocketed the
letter which he had brought with him, and re-exchanged the
light bulbs. Well, that's about all, he thought. "I can't thank
you enough, Mrs. Bryant. You've been more than helpful.
I'm sorry I had to—"

"You know," said Felix Zauner, leaving his quiet corner, "I
should have thought that everything might have been
straightened out by this time if you had gone to Zürich first."
His voice and manner were nonchalant, his eyes watchful.

"I did." Mathison let that have its effect while he studied
Zauner openly for the first time. To the facts he had already
noted—medium height, solid construction, neat tweeds—he
could add reddish hair thinning and receding, a high forehead, an aquiline nose, prominent cheek bones, gray eyes
with fine lines at their corners, lightly tanned skin. Zauner
was waiting, his head cocked slightly to one side, eyebrows
raised just enough, lips almost pursed. Mathison took the hint
and went on. "Unfortunately, Yates was just leaving as I
arrived. He is visiting a couple of scientists in Germany
whose articles caught his attention—he thinks he can get a
book out of each of them. I'll see him when he gets back on
Wednesday."

"You had no time at all to bring up Bryant's name?"

"No time at all." It was better to look inefficient than to
blurt out the unpleasant truth: Yates had laughed off Richard
Bryant—merely an old acquaintance who was always con-
cocting some wild scheme, bit of a joker, didn't do to take
him seriously.

"But I don't understand," Anna Bryant said slowly. "Mr.
Yates is in Zürich. He called us from there."

"When?"

"Last Wednesday, then Saturday. And then—very early
this morning."

"From Zürich? You are sure?"

"I took the call. He left a message for my husband to
65

telephone him in Zürich." Her voice trailed as she glanced up at the clock.

"Have you got that num—" Mathison, watching her face, cut off his question. "I'm sorry I—" he began awkwardly, and then finished quickly with "Good-bye. And thank you, Mrs. Bryant." He offered his hand, and she took it, trying to answer his smile. Her fingers were ice-cold.

"Sure you haven't forgotten anything?" Johann called after him.

I had better not, thought Mathison as he stepped onto the narrow sidewalk and joined the brisk stream of foot traffic. This was a town of walkers; they knew how to step out, had little time for dawdling. That was how he came to notice the two men again. They were still in the Neugasse, now at its lower end, preparing to stroll up its short curve once more. Mathison pretended to ignore them, but he was quite aware of their scrutiny as he passed them. Why should they be interested in me? he wondered. Is Bryant's shop so closely under observation that anyone who spends any time there is immediately worth noting? And what makes Bryant so important as all this? Or perhaps I'm crazy, perhaps they are two men closing a business deal, taking the air, waiting for a friend, discussing a family problem. He stopped to light a cigarette, look at a window displaying wood carvings and chessmen, choose the moment to glance back up the Neugasse. They hadn't left it; they had turned at the top of the street to resume their patrol.

Mathison went on his way, following the gentle slope of this maze of sixteenth-century houses and lanes down to the riverbank, where he would start dodging cars and buses again. From there, he couldn't miss his hotel. He kept thinking about the Neugasse. It was none of his business, he had to remind himself sharply. His first job, right now, was to telephone New York.

"What did you make of him?" Johann asked Felix Zauner as they watched the door close behind the American. "And why did you keep him here, Anna?"

"Keep?"

"Answering all those damned questions."

"Someone had to." It wasn't the American who puzzled her; it was Eric Yates. A vague fear, undefined and all the more frightening because of that, began to stir at the back of her mind. "I'll get you something to eat," she said in a low voice.

"That's more like it. I'm starving. Look, Felix, do you think he was an American agent? You should have seen the way Finstersee drew him. Like a magnet. He—" Johann noticed Anna had stopped abruptly at the doorway to the hall and was looking back at him with wide eyes. "He could be one," he ended lamely. I made a mistake there, he thought; she knows I must have told Felix about Finstersee.

"Quite possibly," Felix said. "The rumors about Finstersee might well attract dubious types." He watched Anna's face.

"What rumors?" She kept the fear out of her eyes. "He was only trying to help us. I know. I felt it."

"Anna and her instincts," Johann said jokingly. "She liked him, so she trusted him."

What rumors? she kept asking herself. There could be no rumors unless Eric Yates had spread them. Or Johann, if he had talked too much to Felix. Or Felix himself?

"My dear Anna," he was saying, "never trust anyone unless you *know* he is on your side."

"Sometimes not even then," she said bitterly. She walked slowly into the long hallway, looking down at the Manila envelope in her hands.

"And who was that Parthian shot aimed at?" Felix asked, keeping his voice amused for Anna's benefit.

"Me," Johann said glumly. "You weren't supposed to know about Finstersee. Felix, why don't you tell Anna who you really—"

"How's your cold?" Felix asked quickly. Anna was within earshot.

"I haven't had time to think about it in the last hour. Perhaps that's part of the cure."

Anna had reached the kitchen. Felix moved swiftly over to the door that separated the shop from the hallway and was usually forgotten, so that it stayed open most of the time. He closed it gently. "I'm leaving for Unterwald," he said very quietly. "Are you feeling fit enough to go there, too? You'll have to look after Anna, first—get her settled with a neighbor or take her over to my house. She can't be left alone here. You see—I have bad news." He paused. But Johann had got his message. "Yes," Felix added gently, "Bryant is dead."

"How? Where?"

"His car skidded off the hill road near St. George's

Church. I got word from the Bad Aussee police just before two o'clock. After you telephoned me this morning, I called them to keep an eye open for his Volkswagen and let me know when it passed through Bad Aussee. But he took the other road."

"Was he alive when they found him? Could he talk?"

"No. His neck was broken. He had been thrown out of the car as it fell down the slope—the door had opened, been wrenched off its hinges as the car turned over and over; it was lying not far from his body. It's the only thing left of the car."

"It burned?"

"At the bottom of a gully where it landed eventually. They haven't been able to get near it so far."

Johann was scarcely listening. "I don't believe it, I don't believe it! A skid? Dick was too careful a driver. And he knew that road, he knew—" Shock gave way to pain. "Anna— how am I to tell Anna?"

Felix Zauner had no answer for that. Each man had to find his own way to tell his bad news. "While you're with Anna, I'll use your phone. Did the American mention where he was staying?"

The practical voice was like a bucket of water doused over Johann. He stared at Felix. Half-angrily he said, "The Salzburger Hof. And he left a card. Somewhere." He gestured contemptuously at the counter. "Business as usual?" he asked bitterly, turned on his heel and left.

At least, thought Zauner as he moved quickly to the counter and found Mathison's card, Johann is under control again. Small help he would be to Anna if he started going to pieces right now. Besides, urgency waits for no man. He picked up the telephone and got through to his office. "Dietrich," he said crisply, "I'm just about to leave. Any further reports from Unterwald? God, they are slow! Here is something else for you to worry about. I want all information on a William Mathison, American, possibly staying at the Salzburger Hof. If he isn't, check all the other hotels in town. Give him complete surveillance when you trace him. Yes, complete! And find out from Vienna if they've got information about him. Also, if they would reach New York and verify his firm there, I'd be grateful. Here's its name: Strong, Muller, Nicolson and Hodge. They are said to be lawyers. He is also employed by a publishing firm called Newhart and

Morris. Got all that?" He waited while Dietrich repeated the names. Careful man, Dietrich; sometimes almost too careful, he thought wryly. "One more thing: when you are talking to Vienna, ask them what they know about Eric Yates, a British subject possibly, now living in Zürich. ... That should hold you until I get back. Tomorrow or the next day, depends on what I find in Unterwald. Unless, of course, you uncover anything that would bring me back here in a hurry. You know where to call me." So the pebbles were cast and the millpond would ripple. How little, how much?

He frowned at the picture of Finstersee as he passed it, his steps slowing to a halt. Whose agent had Bryant been? Not one of ours, he decided, or else I'd have been told to contact him when the first rumor about Finstersee began filtering through Intelligence circles last week. Strange how such a rumor could start in the undercover world. It could develop from a hint, one phrase, that some quick-witted listener picked out of seemingly innocuous conversation; it could be a word, one name, in an intercepted message. All it needed was the knowledge to understand what the hint or word or name might mean, and you had the beginning of a rumor that no intelligence-gathering agency could afford to leave unchecked. If Bryant had somehow been the source of that current rumor about Finstersee, his death would arouse real interest in it. Unless, of course, his death was an accident. In that case, even the quick wits of Western Intelligence might be inclined to drop Finstersee into their wait-and-see files. Once there, most rumors gradually suffocated from a lack of clear information. Yes, Bryant's death had to be an accident.

As Zauner entered the narrow hall, his pace slowed again. Bryant an agent? Right here in Salzburg for all these years? No, he decided, Bryant might in some way have stumbled upon some information, but that's about all. He was too cantankerous, too quixotic to take orders from anyone. Not once, in all these years, did he have contact with any known Intelligence agents who had floated in and out of Salzburg. He might have been a sleeper, of course, but surely he would have been activated at the time of the Lake Toplitz incidents. He could have been very useful there if he had been a trained agent. His war experience? Negligible for what an agent had to face today. And once peace broke out, the British had ditched him quickly enough. No, if Bryant had any information about Finstersee, the most he would do with it was to sell it to the highest bidder. And who would that be?

"Felix—" Johann called worriedly, "come in, listen to this! She isn't going anywhere. She is staying here. That's what she keeps saying." He threw up his hands in despair and rose from the table where he had been sitting opposite Anna. "You persuade her," he said, and went over to stand at the window.

Zauner looked at Anna in complete disbelief. Her face was set in a blank white mask, letting neither tear nor cry escape. Her arms were folded tightly around her, her eyes staring into space. "Anna—" he began, wondering if she could even hear him.

"I'm not leaving. I stay here."

"That is not wise. Believe me. Please—"

"I am staying." Her voice was low but decided.

Zauner moved over to Johann. "Get her out of here. And call a doctor. He will give her a sedative and she'll sleep through the night. I'll have to leave now." He glanced at his watch and swore. "You'll make sure she doesn't stay here by herself?"

Johann nodded.

Zauner hesitated, went back to Anna. "I am so sorry. So terribly sorry. Anna—"

"Please leave me alone."

Zauner retreated. "You'll have to persuade her," he told Johann almost angrily as he opened the back door. "Do a better job with that than you did with breaking the news of Dick's accident."

"I didn't even have to break the news—she seemed to know the minute she saw me." But the door had closed before the sentence ended.

"Accident," Anna repeated. She shook her head slowly.

"We don't know yet—not until we get up to Unterwald. I'll find the truth for you, Anna. I promise that."

"And promise me—" She bit her lip, tried to remember what he had to promise. At last she said, "Those things I told you this morning—Johann, you must tell no one about them. No one."

He came over to her, pulled her chair around gently so that he could look closely into her eyes. "Why not, Anna?"

"Dick said no one. I promised him for both of us."

There was no choice. "I give you my word. I won't fail

you." He kissed her cheek. "But why did he want no one to—"

"For safety," she said quickly. For the safety of a box of papers. She began to weep as her hands went up to cover her face.

For her safety, thought Johann. Yes, Dick had been right. Anyone who knew as much as Anna could be in serious danger if the word got around. He could take care of himself; but Anna? "I'm going to call Frieda Dietrich. She and her husband will look after you until I get back here. You'll go with them?" He didn't wait for her answer, but hurried away from her tears toward the telephone.

6

WITH SOME CALCULATION OF TIME ZONES AND ADVICE FROM the hotel porter on placing transatlantic calls, Mathison reached James Newhart by half past ten in the morning, New York time. Or rather, he was stopped by the usual defense perimeter of cool-voiced secretary. "Now, Linda," he told her, "don't give me that sales-conference routine. Nothing really starts until eleven o'clock at those Monday meetings, and this call is costing him schillings by the second. I'm in Salzburg." That sent her off at a run, and Mathison had barely time to arrange an armchair and disentangle the long extension cord of the telephone, so that he could sit in front of a picture window with a real view, before Newhart's voice boomed in his ear.

"Easy with that baritone, Jimmy."

"It's those damned bulldozers outside." Newhart dropped his voice to normal. "Can you still hear me?"

"Loud and clear."

"Why Salzburg?"

"I drew too many blanks in Zürich."

"I called Yates to expect you. Wasn't he co-operative?"

"He was just dashing off to Germany. You may get two new authors."

Newhart's voice lost its edge. "What about his files? Or his secretary?"

"Nothing and nothing. So I decided to try this end of the puzzle. I think it's solved, more or less, but it isn't pleasant.

71

The Bryants seem to have been thoroughly taken."

"What?"

"I'll write out a full report for you, and I'll add some things I wouldn't want to discuss over the telephone, but here's the gist now. Bryant has kept a small file of his dealings with Yates. He also has a photograph of the check he received, through Yates, supposedly from Newhart and Morris. Three hundred dollars' advance, drawn from—"

"Advance for what?" Newhart broke in.

"A book of photographs of Austrian lakes—"

"Bill, you're kidding!"

"I wish I were. They are very good photographs, too, so good they really are worth publishing. That's the sad thing about it all."

"Bryant has three hundred dollars of our money." Then a new worry came into Newhart's voice. "What kind of contract did he have?"

"His copy hasn't been returned to him yet. And I don't know whose three hundred dollars he has. The check was supposed to come from you, but it was signed by Emil Burch. The bank was First Maritime of New York. Forty-third Street branch."

There was a long pause, complete silence. Then Newhart said slowly, "Just a minute and I'll jot that down. Emil Burch?"

"B as in boy, *u* as in uncle, *r* as in robin, *ch* as in church. But you'll have a copy of the check and the other documents as soon as I can get my film developed and printed. Yes, I did some photographing myself."

"Then Bryant was co-operative." Newhart sounded relieved.

"He wasn't there. Mrs. Bryant was very helpful."

"Did you tell her the whole thing must have been a misunderstanding?"

"No. And you wouldn't have, either, if you had seen the tension she was under."

"They've got to be told sometime."

"That's not my job." At least, I hope to God it isn't, Mathison thought. "And anyway, shouldn't we have a talk with Yates first of all? What do you want me to do? Get back to Zürich and meet him when he returns on Wednesday morning? But I'd really prefer you to send someone from the firm, and I'll stand at his elbow and be ready with legal

72

advice. You'll have to do something about Yates, won't you? I can't do that, you know."

"There couldn't be some mistake?"

"When you see my report along with the evidence, I don't think you'll have any doubts."

"But Yates has always been completely reliable, a very good man—"

"I know, I know."

"Didn't he have anything to say to you?"

"We had only time for a few words. He thought we were taking Bryant too seriously. He says the man is just a psychopathic liar who wouldn't risk facing any real trouble."

"Yates thinks he could handle him alone?"

"So I gathered. And I admit I was inclined to believe him. But in fact he hasn't handled Bryant as yet. Has he? So I came to Salzburg. And I saw the check. It does exist. Just who is Emil Burch?"

"We are taking action on that right now. Linda is getting the manager of First Maritime on the other wire for me. So we had better sign off."

"Do I stay here and see Bryant himself when he gets back? Or do I return to Zürich and start throwing my weight around there?"

"I think Zürich—no, perhaps you should see Bryant himself." There was a pause. "I'll have to call you later about that, Bill. I have a conference waiting, and I can't cut that. Actually, I've nothing but conferences today, one after the other. Look—I'll call you much later; make it the end of the day. Around seven?"

"Your time?"

"That's right. It will be around midnight your way. Okay with you?"

"Well, I'll have to give up that champagne supper with the polka girls over at Ossi's Feinschmecker Restaurant, but I'll be here." Newhart actually had a laugh coaxed out of him, which, for a Monday morning like this one, was no small triumph. "My hotel is the Salzburger Hof. And not a bulldozer in sight. Good-bye, Jimmy."

"And thanks, Bill. I mean that."

Mathison set down the telephone by his feet, lit a cigarette, and sat studying the view of the Old Town opposite him. Had he been too quick to judge Yates? Was Richard Bryant quite so much the injured party? Could he have arranged for Mr.

Emil Burch to send him that check, faked something that looked like a contract, concocted Yates's brief notes?

Well, let's see. . . . Bryant had written a letter to Newhart and Morris two weeks ago. Three days later, it was on James Newhart's desk. He had tried to straighten the matter out right away, by a telephone call to Eric Yates in Zürich. The call had been taken by Yates's secretary, Greta Freytag—he was away on one of his business trips. She hadn't known much about Richard Bryant except that he had visited the Zürich office last summer. She was not sure about any contract; however, she would search Mr. Bryant's file and call back. But when she did, she could only report that she couldn't find any file at all. She would search further, she promised, and suggested that Mr. Yates would be able to answer all Newhart's questions when he returned at the end of the week.

But Yates had explained nothing, actually. He had been astonished and politely regretful. Bryant was a very light acquaintance of many years ago, so light indeed that Yates had only remembered him with difficulty when he had dropped in for a social call at the Zürich office last summer. There had been no business talk between them whatsoever, just a general kind of conversation about publishing. Perhaps Bryant had assumed too much, or had jumped to wrong conclusions—he might be a psychopathic personality with delusions of authorship; there were plenty around who'd take one word of friendly interest as a definite promise to publish. In any case, Yates would telephone Bryant right away and tell him he had better drop his wild story about a contract. A couple of well-chosen phrases would sober him up.

"I wonder," Mathison had said when Newhart called him with the full story.

"You don't think Richard Bryant will be so easily scared off?"

"I don't imagine he would have written to you unless he had something plausible to back up his statements. His letter is very specific, you know. He considers you his publisher, bound by contract and an advance."

"Any use telephoning him ourselves?"

"Not at this stage. He would only repeat what he stated in his letter. We'd have to see his evidence. What did Yates report back to you, by the way?"

"A complete foul-up. Not Yates's fault," Newhart added

74

quickly. "He's a very competent and capable fellow. You know what he landed for us on that last business trip? A manuscript from a couple of physicists working in the field of elementary particles."

"But he landed nothing for us in Salzburg?"

"He phoned several times, and only got a polite brush-off from Mrs. Bryant. Her husband always seemed to be out. However, Yates is persevering—"

"Let's call Yates now. I'll be at your elbow. And I have some specific questions to ask *him*." Mathison listed them carefully. But they were never answered over the telephone. It was Miss Freytag who took that call. Yates had come down with grippe and was at home nursing a temperature. And when Mathison questioned her about a file on Richard Bryant, she froze completely. There never had been any file, she insisted now. She had been mistaken.

"I don't like it," Newhart was forced to admit. "It looks as if there has been some kind of office bungle and they are trying to cover up. Why the hell can't people just admit they made some small mistake, lost a couple of letters or something?"

"What letters?" Mathison asked. Poor old Jimmy was flapping around, trying to find some simple explanation to some simple problem. But nothing was as easy as that, especially with a possible lawsuit looming over the horizon.

"You're right," Newhart admitted slowly. "We know nothing. We'd have to talk with Miss Freytag face to face. We'd have to get Yates to take this really seriously—he thinks my worries are exaggerated, that he can handle Bryant with a couple of sentences. And we'd have to find what possible basis there could be for the story this Bryant fellow has cooked up. Is that what you are thinking?" And as Mathison nodded, Newhart said gloomily, "A lawsuit could be more trouble and expense than a trip to Zürich. That's where to begin, obviously. It could all be settled in a couple of days. Bill, you handle this. When can you leave?"

And that was why Mathison had been sent chasing over to Zürich. Last year, it had been to Amsterdam, to settle a threatened suit for a supposedly broken contract, a three-day visit that had stretched into two weeks before the author turned out to be an unemployed draftsman with more time spent on money-making schemes than on his own drawing board. Jimmy Newhart was developing quite a sixth sense for picking out a trickster. And Bryant was his present choice for that kind of character. Yet, thought Mathison, it wasn't any feeling of guilt about any cooked-up scheme against a New York publisher that had created the scene in Bryant's shop today. The moment of real tension did not arise when I was looking at his file on Yates. Or even photographing his records. It arose when I looked at the photographs on the wall, and it didn't involve just Mrs. Bryant, whose nerves were on edge long before I arrived. (Remember the way she came running through from the back of the shop as I stepped in the front door and then stopped as she saw me—a stranger about whom she knew nothing—and the excitement and welcome on her face drained away into disappointment?) Her brother became as tense as she was, more so if you add up the obvious facts about him: a husky man, the kind whose job must keep him in the open air much of the time, an extrovert with a carefree look and impudent humor once he stopped being suspicious—not the type to panic easily. And what was wrong about paying so much interest to a first-rate camera study of the lake with the dark name— what was it called? . . . Finstersee.

He rose, coiling up the extension cord roughly as he carried the telephone back to the bedside table. Time to get out and take some photographs of his own before the light faded. It was a fine afternoon now, with clear blue sky and strong sun, but the high wooded ridge that jutted up behind the Old Town was already shadowing the tight-packed roofs that stretched along the bottom of its cliff. Soon the rest of the tall stone houses, made miniature by the medieval spires, renaissance towers, baroque domes that soared above churches and palaces, would be covered by that soft-gray blanket of premature dusk. He found his camera bag, took out his Rolleiflex. And at that moment there was a scraping of a key in the lock of his door. Possibly a maid with towels, he thought. But it was a man who entered, quickly and silently. He was dressed in dark-gray overalls and held a telephone in his hand. He stopped abruptly as he saw Mathison.

"What do you want?" Mathison asked in German. His two years' army service in Berlin had left him with an authoritative bark when he needed it.

"I am sorry to disturb you," the man said, hesitating, mustering some composure. "I did not know the gentleman had returned to his room."

You're half an hour late, thought Mathison. He didn't reply. The onus of proving the innocence of his presence, as his heavily legal friends would say, was certainly not his to bear. He simply stared at the telephone the man was now keeping close to his side, as if it were part of his trouser leg.

"Your telephone is out of order, sir."

"It seemed all right to me."

"I have orders to change it." The man was thin, young, undersized, and sweating slightly at the temples.

Poor guy, thought Mathison, you are doing your job, but I've a strange suspicion it seems necessary only to you. "Shall I test my phone?" he asked blandly. "Or could it possibly be a mistake? Are you sure you have the right room? This is 405."

The man seized the excuse with a slightly embarrassed grin. "Then it is a mistake." He made the pretense of checking in a small notebook. "I'm looking for 305. I'm on the wrong floor." And with many apologies, the nervous man left as quickly as he had entered.

Mathison looked down at the small Minox lying in his camera bag. It looked lonely, he decided. Especially with all those telephones needing to be exchanged. After all, the film it contained was all the proof he had of Bryant's file on Yates. So he thought for a minute and then removed the valuable roll of film, wrapped it carefully in a sheet of soft tissue from the bathroom, dropped it into the breast pocket of his shirt, disliked the small bulge it made and decided it was too close to warm skin anyway, found a thin Italian matchbox in his raincoat pocket, flushed the delicate little sticks of wax matches down the toilet, and inserted the covered film neatly into their place. The flap-over lid closed and no more. It was secure.

He looked around the large bedroom for a hiding place, something so obvious that no one would think it of any importance. Beside the ashtray? No, it had better be somewhere he could touch it and reassure himself it was safe. He slipped the box into the deep pocket of his tweed jacket, added a half-smoked pack of cigarettes. Not original, he told himself, but you'll know what is happening to it. Then he filled the Minox with a new roll of film, snapped a few quick pictures of Salzburg through glass before he dropped the miniature camera back into the bag and replaced it on a wardrobe shelf.

77

All that trouble possibly for nothing, but at least—as he had photographed the town through the window—he had determined where he was heading with his Rolleiflex. Right up there, crowning its own massive hill to the left of the wooded ridge, was the Hohensalzburg, the enormous castle old in story. It was girded with walls and battlements, plenty of space for strolling and climbing around its towers, plenty of light, too, for it overlooked everything from its eyrie. That's for me, he thought, and grabbed his coat.

Outside his hotel, there was a short stretch of busy street before he reached the long low bridge to take him over the strong flow of the river. He didn't notice the man then. But halfway across the bridge, when he almost collided with two women carrying a load of packages and turned to apologize, he saw the stranger who stopped abruptly, not far behind him, to light a cigarette. Mathison paid little attention, thought nothing about it until ten minutes later, when he was striking quite a rapid course through the Old Town's mixture of narrow streets and broad squares. (His long search this morning for Neugasse 9 had given him basic training in some necessary geography. Distances here were actually short; they only seemed complicated because so much was grouped in so little space.) He had cut around the Cathedral, walked briskly past the white marble fountain which had been built for watering horses two centuries ago, became aware he was about to take a wrong exit from the square, veered quickly to reach the right one, and saw the man again. Same raincoat, same height and breadth, same fair hair, same man. It might have been coincidence, of course; Salzburg was the kind of place where you could keep remeeting people. Only, thought Mathison, it was odd that this one was always the same distance behind him. The man wasn't lighting a cigarette this time; he was completely absorbed in the beauties of the marble horse pond.

Mathison increased his pace and in a few minutes reached the cobbled street that backed right up against the steep rise of the castle's hill. Here he could take the funicular for a quick ride up to the castle itself. And he was in luck; the cars were now finishing a descent, and he wouldn't have long to wait until they were hauled uphill again. He bought his ticket and stood in the waiting room with a half a dozen varied characters. No sign yet of the man in the raincoat. Then everyone filed out of the waiting room to find places in the nearest car, and Mathison could only wonder if the man was now arriving and buying a ticket. The idea amused him, although he felt annoyance too. Who the hell would want to have me followed? he wondered; and then he decided the whole thing was ridiculous and his imagination had been running wild.

But the man was doing more than buying a ticket. He was using the few minutes before the scheduled departure uphill to put in a hasty call over the attendant's telephone. "I picked him up in the hotel lobby, but I think he has seen me," he told Dietrich at the other end of the wire. "He is bound to notice me on the funicular. He's on his way to the castle. So get someone up there as fast as possible to take over. I'll keep near him to mark him out. In case that's difficult, here's the description of what he is now wearing: fawn tweed jacket, two vents in the back, well-cut; narrow dark-gray trousers; light-blue shirt, blue tie; brown shoes; raincoat at present over his arm; camera. And he's—sorry!" The man jammed the phone back in place and made a dash outside to the funicular.

It was a quick, steep-angled haul through boulders and small trees, tunneling through the lower wall and the first huge bastion. Once on foot, Mathison began his climb of exploration around ramparts, across inner courtyards, up staircases to the tops of other walls. He was so astounded by the inventive genius of the medieval mind—this place was a complex of fortresses guarding the Archbishop's palace on the crest—that he stopped paying attention to the man who plodded behind him. One idea he did borrow from the man: he put on his Burberry to keep the sharp breeze from freezing him. He took his last photograph from a railed platform that twentieth-century Salzburgers had built to keep tourists from falling over the side of a bastion, and then stood with the wind whipping at his coat as he looked southward over the plain far below to the mountains with their jagged peaks.

"Is it safe up there?" a girl's voice called. He turned to see her hesitating on the wooden steps (again, courtesy of the twentieth century) that led to his vantage point.

"Safe but cold," he warned her, holding out his hand to steady her as she reached him. "The view is worth a chill, though. Magnificent."

She studied his face. "An American?" she asked, breaking into English.

"You always can tell, can you?" And I thought my accent wasn't so bad, he thought ruefully.

She was looking around her. "I never dare come up here alone," she admitted, trying to clear her wind-blown hair away from her eyes. She hadn't much success. Her hair was dark brown with golden lights in the rays of the late-afternoon sun, long tendrils escaping from her fingers as she reached to take hold of a railing. "Heights scare me a little. But it is a wonderful view."

"When you can see it," he said with a grin. "Perhaps I ought to hold on to you while you keep two hands on that hair." He gripped her arm lightly while she smoothed her hair back from her temples. But its length and thickness defeated her.

"I give up," she said. "Would you help edge me off this platform? This is the point where I mustn't look at my feet or I freeze."

They retreated down the solidly built steps and stood in the calm of a sheltering wall. She found a comb in her pocket and combed the tangles out of her hair until it fell smoothly to her shoulders. Now he could see her eyes, wide-set and large, dark gray in color. "That's better," he told her approvingly. She smiled, pale pink lips curving softly, widely. There was a touch of pale pink, too, over the broad cheekbones, but whether that was due to the wind or skillful application with a light sure hand, he couldn't tell. Eyebrows and lashes were enchanting even if the sure hand had been at work again. A short nose and a rounded chin completed a pretty picture. He felt a touch of annoyance with himself, and some sadness too; ten years ago, when he had been twenty-five, he would have just accepted the sum total rather than take a bloody inventory. And then he became amused as he felt somehow that she was taking her own inventory. It couldn't have been altogether adverse, for she wasn't saying good-bye, walking on, leaving him to follow at a polite distance. Instead, she was beginning a conversation as she slipped the comb back into the pocket of her coat. It was one of those expensive tweed jobs, fuzzy and soft yet somehow cut with slender shoulders, and its hemline was the shortest he had seen since he had left New York. Her legs, fortunately, were excellent. He liked the white mesh stockings, too, and the flat-heeled shiny black shoes with their silver buckles.

She was saying, "I have been wandering around here making my good-byes. What about you? Is it hello or farewell?"

"Both."

They had begun walking slowly down a cobbled path. "You mean," she said in horror, stopping abruptly, so that her heel almost skidded on a worn stone and he had to catch her elbow to let her regain balance, "you mean this is your first and last visit?" She looked down at his hand on her arm. "And thank you. You really are very quick, aren't you?"

"And tenacious," he said with a grin, keeping hold of her arm. "I'll just make sure you get along this road without twisting an ankle. Are you positive this is the right direction, by the way?"

"For what?"

"For a drink at that restaurant. There is one somewhere around here."

"Near the cable railway," she told him. She gave him that same warm and charming smile. "And I think a drink would be perfect. We'll give a toast to a quick return to Salzburg. You do intend to come back, don't you?"

"I hope so. You sound as if you were a native."

"I'm from Chicago. I came here last spring. But now—" She sighed quite openly. "Oh well, money does run out. And my father refuses to send any more except for the fare home. Tomorrow I leave for Zürich to visit my grandmother for two or three weeks. Father's orders." She laughed then.

"Zürich? I may be there myself for a week or so."

"But how fantastic!" she said delightedly, and halted abruptly again, almost slipping, letting her weight rest on his arm for a moment.

"And how dutiful of you," he said with amusement. "Do you always obey your father?"

"It's economic necessity," she reminded him severely.

"What about a job? If you like Salzburg so much—"

"Oh, I made some extra money in the summer months. Translator, sort of a guide for special parties, that kind of thing. But the season is over now and jobs are scarce for foreigners. So it's Zürich for me. At least that gives me two more weeks abroad. Any excuse is a good excuse for travel, don't you think? But what about you? Are you on holiday or business?"

"Business." And he remembered the man whose business it had been to follow him. He glanced back, but the path was

81

empty. So were the fortifications. The man had vanished. "The light's fading," he said. "We'd better hurry."

She was somehow amused. "We'll be all right. Look!" She pointed to the courtyard lined with houses that lay ahead of them. There was a large tree with children playing around it, and lighted windows, and the sound of women's voices as they worked indoors. "And that's the main entrance gate around the corner at the other end."

So people lived up here, he thought. He kept an eye open for the man who had followed him so persistently. He could see only half a dozen men, who looked like guides or caretakers or artisans. She was watching him curiously, as if she had noticed his interest in the people. He said lightly, "I suppose these are the fellows who build all those wooden catwalks and railings? Now *there's* one who is obviously a tester." He pointed to a massive figure who was carrying an outsize tankard of beer across the sloping cobblestones. "His job is to jump three times daily on each wooden step so the tourists won't break their necks."

"He's an artist," she said with a faint giggle. "Some of them live up here, too, you know. There's an international school of fine arts—I took some classes here last spring."

"You are full of surprises."

"Hi, Jan!" she called to the artist, and waved.

"Hallo!" he called back in German. "Don't forget the dance next week!"

"He's Polish," she explained as she walked on.

"Refugee or devoted party member?"

"Refugee." She disengaged her arm from his.

"If you want to explain to him that you are leaving Salzburg, I'll wait at the gate."

"I hate good-byes," she said curtly. "Besides, artists never notice anyway whether you come to their parties or not. As long as there's a crowd, they're happy."

Now what did I say to annoy her? he wondered. Or perhaps she would like to be at that party more than she will admit. "Well, what about that toast to Salzburg and a quick return?" he tried.

"Let's have it in town." Her voice was back to normal. She glanced at her watch. "Yes, that's the best idea. It always seems so spooky up here when it gets dark."

Or she might see more of her artist friends, he thought. And as she said, she hates good-byes. "Anything suits me.

Don't you think we had better start having names? I'm Bill—Bill Mathison."

She studied him. "Yes, that suits you. And I—I'm Elissa."

"That suits you completely." Soft, pretty and romantic, and different. "Elissa what?"

"Lang. Elissa Lang. It's really Eliza-Evaline, shortened by me aged nine."

"Your first revolt against the family?"

"And my most successful one. Nothing since has been half so permanent."

"You haven't done too badly," he said teasingly. "The last one brought you six months in Salzburg." He made a guess at her age and thought of something around the early twenties, although in some ways she seemed older than that—it was difficult nowadays to pin a precise number of years on most women. "So what now? Back to college?"

"I've finished with all that," she said indignantly. "It's another world."

"No more picket lines, demonstrations, or LSD parties?"

"You know what? I don't believe you take me seriously."

"I wouldn't mind trying," he said softly. Then he retreated instinctively, and covered that slip in his emotions by looking at the view. They had come out of the gateway of the castle onto one of its lower terraces. Dusk was deepening rapidly. The lights in the town at their feet were a handful of diamonds scattered on a dark velvet cushion. On the black curve of river, the reflected gleam from the bridges was rippled by the strong currents. Almost reaching eye level were the peaks of the other hills that rose on either side of the riverbank. And far beyond all that—the mountains, ringing the town around.

She studied his face. He is different from what I expected, she thought as she changed her mood to suit his. "Let's walk down instead of taking the funicular," she suggested. "It's always fun to see the domes and towers coming up to meet you." Why, she thought again in surprise, this man may even be what he says he is. I won't have to cover my interest in him with pretty prattle about their Excellencies the Prince-Archbishops who held court for centuries in the heart of that fortress while their judges held court above the torture chambers, or about their mistresses, or about all the little footnotes to history which usually make an hour pass easily and safely. I might even relax and enjoy myself. He's attrac-

83

tive, definitely; a twentieth-century romantic. "And this is an evening for walking, isn't it?" she added gently. She slipped her arm through his, and they started down the steep road.

"It will have to be a very quick drink," she said regretfully as they entered a bar-restaurant that lay, tucked into a spare space between two Grimm's fairy-tale houses, on the narrow street near the base of the castle's cliffs. She stole a glance at her watch and frowned a little.

"You can't have dinner with me?" Mathison asked, guessing what was coming, masking his disappointment, looking around for a quiet corner. The place was so small that he hadn't much choice. Fortunately, the half-dozen customers were grouped before the bar, and the lighting was so artfully dim that they only appeared as a cluster of silhouettes in a haze of cigarette smoke. He pulled off his raincoat and hooked it on a wall. He selected the table farthest from people.

"I'm so sorry, Bill." She stretched out a hand to touch his as he sat down beside her on a narrow bench against the roughly plastered wall. "It's my last night in Salzburg. I already promised— Oh, if only I had known we were going to meet—" She paused abruptly. Her voice brightened. "I have an idea. I'll telephone while you order the drinks. Better stick to Scotch or beer. Avoid the Martinis. The man behind the bar is Italian and he is devoted to vermouth."

He watched her walk to the telephone near the door. She had her coat around her shoulders, and he had the odd idea that she was perhaps leaving him, that she was going to slip out of his life as quickly as she had stepped into it. But she came back to their table as the drinks were arriving. She was walking slowly, and, as she reached him, he saw that the small frown had returned to her brow. It cleared as she became aware he was watching her. She sat down, pushing back the coat from her shoulders, and let him help ease it off. But she looked dejected. "It can't be as bad as all that," he said with amusement. "Didn't your idea work out?"

She shook her head. "I've got to keep my appointment tonight—just can't even be late for it. Sorry."

"We'll have dinner in Zürich."

"Where are you staying?"

"I may have to move. A bankers' conference is going to take up most of the rooms next week. But what's your address?"

"My grandmother lives out of town and refuses to have a telephone. But I'll be in Zürich often enough. I have a friend there who will put me up at her apartment if I stay overnight."

"Then give me her number."

She hesitated. "I wonder. You see—" She was trying to soften her excuse. Then she shrugged her pretty shoulders, looked down at her bare arms. "I don't like bothering my friend *too* much. There is nothing so annoying as a phone that keeps ringing not for you but for someone else. She—well, she—"

"I promise I won't pester her. I'll only call once and leave a message that I'm in town. She wouldn't object to that, would she?" He had his address book and pencil ready. She gave him a number, slowly, as if she were trying to remember it, or perhaps because she had something else on her mind. "That saves a lot of trouble," he told her reassuringly. "Of course I could have given you the Newhart and Morris office number, but there's a dragon called Miss Freytag who guards the entrance to Yates's office—that's the head man around there—and she is allergic to social calls. Business is business is business."

She was sitting very still. Suddenly, she laughed and said, "No, I don't think I want to leave any messages with a dragon. She'd breathe flames all over them." She looked down at her hands. "When do you expect to reach Zürich? And how long will you stay?"

"I'm not sure in either case. I'll know more about it later tonight."

"You are so mysterious." She sounded as if that idea delighted her. Her eyes turned briefly to look at the door as two people entered.

"There's nothing very mysterious about a phone call from New York."

"From your friend the publisher? You know, you never did tell me why he sent you here." She adjusted the watch bracelet on her wrist, studied her hands. It was exactly six o'clock.

"Just a simple matter of checking on a contract for a book." The door of the restaurant opened again, and this time a man entered. As he took off his dark-gray coat, he looked around the room. Seemingly he decided against a table and went to the bar instead.

"It must be wonderful," she said, now completely relaxed, half dreaming, "to have a job like yours. I mean, a real career with travel as part of it."

"That only happens now and again. I'm mostly in New York."

"You never think of going back to Denver? Why didn't you settle there after law school? You sounded as if you liked open-air life."

He laughed, thinking that she had learned quite a lot of little things about him on that walk down from the castle. But although he had long got over Nora and a broken marriage—these things hit you hard when you were serving overseas—he wasn't the type to talk about something that had once almost broken him too. When a man had been spread-eagled on that kind of wheel, he became very wary of any repeat performance. There had been Joan and Mary, Clarissa and Peggy and—yes, there had been plenty of them, perhaps too many. A man got into a routine of independence just as easily as the routine of suburban commuter.

"But don't you? Bill—what do you really like?"

"That's quite a question—" he began, and stopped short in surprise. She had looked at her watch, openly this time, and was rising as she pulled her coat back over her shoulders. He rose to his feet, looked around for the waitress to pay his bill.

"No, please don't come. Finish your drink, Bill."

"Nonsense! I'll walk you home."

"But I'm not going there. My friends are waiting for me just around the corner, at the Marionette Theater. We are driving out to Schloss Fuschl for dinner."

"Very gemütlich," he said. And the message was very clear: a car meant a fixed number of people; if he took her to meet her friends it would only look as if he were trying to crash their party. He helped her put on her coat properly. "Sorry I kept you."

"I'm not." She was smiling up at him as he took her hand. "I never knew that walk down from the castle could take so much time. I usually do it in twelve minutes." Impulsively, she kissed him on his cheek. "And I do want an answer to my question. I'll hear it in Zürich," she said very softly. Then she was walking to the door, her heels clicking lightly on the tiled floor.

Mathison sat down at the table. It was small and lonely. He finished his drink, paid, and reached for his coat. The evening ahead of him seemed small and lonely, too. Damn it all, he told himself angrily, you were a perfectly happy man wandering around by yourself this morning, or exploring the castle this afternoon before you met any Elissa. You are still you, and Salzburg is still Salzburg, and that's that.

He was at the door when he remembered his camera lying on the bench where they had sat. He turned to retrace his steps and almost collided with a man who was unhooking his dark-gray coat from a wall peg. Well, he didn't stay long, thought Mathison; did his girl stand him up?

He left the little room with its warm smoke-spiraling air, the encrusted candles guttering low on red tablecloths, the crowded pack of baying voices at the bar, and stepped out into a street that was now dark with early-autumn night, and cold. He was thinking of Elissa's last question. Bill—*what do you really like?* A man could answer that differently every five years of his life, and yet be giving the truth. He turned down the short run of narrow street to reach the square with the marble horsepond. He was so deep in his own thoughts that he never noticed the man in the dark-gray coat who walked a discreet distance behind him.

7

AT SIX O'CLOCK, JOHANN KRONSTEINER DROVE BACK TO UNTER-wald from the scene of Bryant's death. The village was quieter now than when he had first arrived over an hour ago. The groups of people had faded away into the warmth of their lighted kitchens, talking in subdued voices about the accident that had taken place only a few miles from their own home. The where of the accident seemed to shock them as much as the how of it. It was this constant murmur of "accident" that had made Johann drive to St. George's Church even if the light was fading rapidly and he would have to scramble down to the burned-out car with a flashlight in one hand. One of the policemen from the Gendarmerie at Bad Aussee had accompanied him; two were staying to talk with August Grell when he returned to the inn—he had gone hunting up around Finstersee, it was said, and hadn't yet heard about the burned car—and the fourth policeman had left with the ambulance and Richard Bryant's body. Now, as he swung himself out of his jeep, Johann saw that Felix Zauner was standing at Postmistress Kogel's door (it was one of the few houses where there was a telephone, Johann remembered, and if he hadn't been plunged into gloom he would have been amused at Felix's artful position), and there was Trudi, too, waiting anxiously, keeping Felix company. He called his thanks to the Gendarme and went over to the lighted door. Trudi took his hand. He stood close beside her, but he said nothing at all.

"Did you get down to the ravine?" Felix asked.

Johann nodded. The car had cooled off enough to let him examine it.

"Then you saw the body behind the steering wheel?"

The charred corpse had been transfixed by the wheel's column; there had been no possible escape for him. No possible identification either.

Trudi Seidl said in her soft voice, "Who could it have been? There's no one missing from Unterwald. Besides, we saw the car drive through the village. There was only one man in it then." She was a dark-haired, dark-eyed girl with glowing cheeks and an easy laugh, but tonight there was no smile on her full red lips and she watched Johann anxiously. "The police say it could have been a hiker—there was a Frenchman here on a walking tour. He stayed with my aunt last night; the inn was closed, old Grell said. He left before eight this morning. Do you think it was him?"

"Did it take him two and a half hours to hike to St. George's?"

Felix said, "He could have visited the church to see the wood carvings, or strained an ankle, or anything. We won't know he isn't the man until we find him at one or the other of the hill villages."

"He could have cut down to the valley, taken a bus or a train from there, and be in Munich by this time." Johann looked hard at Felix. And *you* should have said that, he thought.

Trudi's worry increased. She found the logical solution. "Come and have supper with us, Johann."

Johann looked at a lighted ground-floor window of the

88

Gasthof Waldesruh, perched on its meadow above the village. "I'll go to the inn first. August Grell is back, I see."

"The Gendarmen are talking with him now. He only got back half an hour ago."

"And young Anton? Where is he?"

"But didn't you know?" asked Trudi. "He's on holiday. He left last week."

Johann looked at Felix again, standing there so silently with one foot on Frau Kogel's threshold. "Did you find out if anyone saw him leave?"

"We heard his motorcycle," Trudi said quickly. "You know how it roars. It woke everyone up in the village last Thursday morning. Johann, what's wrong with you?"

"Johann has a theory and he doesn't want it spoiled," Felix Zauner said wearily. He cocked his head as the telephone rang. "Excuse me." He hurried indoors.

"He's been doing that for the last hour, either sending calls to Salzburg or getting them," Trudi said. "He's a funny kind of man. I never know what he's thinking."

"He's just worrying about his business back in Salzburg. Never thinks anyone can do anything right except himself."

"It was some day he chose to come up and try again to talk old Grell into his ski-lodge idea. Doesn't he take a refusal?"

So that is Felix's story for being at Unterwald, Johann thought. But why isn't he at Waldesruh, right now, watching Grell's face as the two Gendarmen talk with him? Felix has his own methods, that's for sure, but they certainly aren't mine. He bit his lip and frowned, then blew his nose. "Damn this cold, it's almost better but I can't think straight." All he kept feeling was that he and Felix were being drawn apart, and he couldn't understand any of it. Felix, the bright one, didn't seem to be aware of it, while he, who never pretended to be one of the clever ones, was seeing a long friendship—well, not end exactly, but certainly change. I've never criticized Felix before, he thought, and the idea disturbed him.

"Come and eat with us," Trudi pleaded.

"Later. But I'll give you a lift to your house."

"I'll keep some food for you." She drew her heavy cardigan tighter around her throat. "Are you sure you are warmly enough dressed? I don't like the sound of your cold."

"You should have heard it yesterday." He helped her into the jeep. They drove the short distance in silence. "I'll leave the car here," he told her, driving it over the grass to the side of the house. "I may be very late."

"I'll wait."

She always did. He kissed her, hugging her close. Then abruptly he picked up his loden cape from the jeep and started back to the main street of the village.

It was sparsely lit, especially now that the curtains were drawn over the windows. But there was a smell of wood smoke in the sharp air, a reminder of warm stoves and supper tables and families safely gathered together. What was it that Dick used to say about the villagers? Easy live and quiet die . . . For a moment, he envied them and thought of Trudi. But what chance had he of marrying her now, of marrying anyone? He'd have a sister to look after for the rest of her life. She wouldn't have enough money to live on: Dick was the earner; she only helped him complete the photographs he had taken. She couldn't afford to pay the rent on Neugasse 9. And after she sold all the equipment, and squared any debts, what would she have left? That's a hell of a thought to have on the day your brother-in-law died, he told himself angrily. But it was there to nag him, and he couldn't forget it. Money was something he used to laugh at; he made it, he spent it, and he didn't want too much of it, for it did strange things to a man. Tied him down to possessions, turned him into something different, and not always for the best. Money might breed plenty of evil, but the lack of it could be the root of misery. His depression increased.

Felix Zauner was waiting for him at the corner of Frau Kogel's house.

"Everything under control in Salzburg?" Johann couldn't resist asking, but Felix didn't respond to his needling. He merely nodded, deep in his own thoughts. "Coming?" Johann was already three steps on the way to the Gasthof Waldesruh.

Felix caught his arm and pulled him back into the shadows of the Kogel eaves. "Must you, Johann?"

"I've a good excuse: I'm the brother-in-law."

"But why go up there? If he is what you think he is, Grell could become suspicious of you. He might think Bryant told you more about Finstersee than he actually did." Felix pulled his green velours hat farther down over his high brow; the lines at the corners of his eyes deepening as he looked at Johann narrowly. "It isn't possible that Bryant did tell you more? You aren't keeping anything back, are you, Johann?"

"I told you all I knew. And I'm telling you now that Dick's death is no accident. Do you really believe he would let any stranger drive that car? He didn't even let me touch it."

"You also saw the palms of Dick's hands. He might have been glad to let someone else drive. What caused those marks, I wonder?" The quiet voice was casual, the gray eyes sharp.

"I don't know. I'm going to ask old Grell if Dick explained them to him."

"Be careful what you say to Grell," Felix warned again. "Don't even hint you think it wasn't an accident."

Johann stared at Felix. Then he nodded. "I might be next on Grell's list?" he asked, trying to joke it off. But he felt too close to the truth to get much humor into his voice. "You *know* there is something wrong about the whole thing. For instance, why was Dick only wearing his sweater? The villagers saw him, or someone, driving in his green jacket."

"He was too warm, he removed it."

"You find an answer for everything."

"Johann, if there are any Nazis around here, we're going to get them. It may take a little time, but we're going to find them and rout them out."

"And send them with a smack on their knuckles back across the border? Why don't you get them on a murder charge? Then you'd have them—permanently."

Felix Zauner's patience slipped. "Because, you idiot, a murder trial would bring out the reason why Bryant was killed. We want no more interest in Finstersee."

"And if the Nazis pull up that box from Finstersee?"

"How can they, if we've scattered them? It will be a long time before any try to come back to Unterwald. Once we gut out the nest, they won't have a place to operate from. They'll keep trying, of course, but we'll keep watching. And they will know that. I told you in Salzburg, and I tell you now—"

"Are you coming?" Johann moved off slowly.

"We had better not go in together. When I do join you—"

"I'll scarcely know you."

"And take care! He has a couple of possible friends up there with him."

Johann halted. "Who?"

"Two strangers who came here this evening. They're putting up at the inn for a few days of shooting. Trudi's aunt has been making beds and cooking all afternoon." Felix grinned.

"And that's my excuse. The inn is open. I'll have dinner there. Maybe even stay the night."

"By God," Johann looked at Felix with frank admiration, "I believe you would." He turned on his heel and crossed the street, following the line of houses until he reached the trail that branched up toward Finstersee. He climbed it for a few minutes until he reached the Waldesruh meadow with its short path to the inn's front door. From his vantage point, he looked down on the village. He couldn't see Felix, but Felix would be watching him, timing his entry. Did Zauner really enjoy this kind of life? he wondered. He rapped hard on the oak door and then opened it.

The big ceramic stove in the dining room had been lit, but Frau Hitz had to wear a shawl around her shoulders while she set a table. She was in one of her cross moods. She was tired. She had been at work since Herr Grell had sent word this noon that he wanted the whole place aired and cleaned and heated, not his room, of course—she was rarely allowed inside it, and never alone—but there was plenty to do without that and a full dinner to cook besides. "They're in there," she said as a return for Johann's greeting. "Drinking." And she nodded her head, sparse-covered with thin white hair pulled back in a knot from her white face, toward the kitchen. It was the most she would allow herself in disrespect for a man's world where women scrubbed the floors and men trailed over them in dirty boots. She looked at Johann's shoes, earth-caked, and went on with her work.

They were laughing in the kitchen, and warm, with their coats off and their legs stretched out. Johann loosened the collar of his cape. "I'm Kronsteiner," he said. "Can I see you for a minute, Herr Grell?" He nodded to Karl and Max, the policemen from Bad Aussee, whom he knew well. He merely glanced at the two well-dressed, well-fed strangers who sat apart. The laughter died into silence.

August Grell, red-faced and beaming, had been refilling the beer mugs. "Come in. Sit down. Will you have some beer?" Then he halted, his expression changing to one of sympathy. "You are Herr Bryant's brother-in-law? Herr Kronsteiner, forgive me. I didn't recognize you in your winter clothes. I can't tell you how sorry I am. A dreadful thing, dreadful."

"You were the last to see my brother-in-law, I believe." My voice is too tight, Johann thought, I'll have to ease up. He was conscious of the strangers' eyes studying him. He said to Max, who was the senior of the two men from Bad Aussee, "I suppose you've already asked most of the questions—"

"We have, Johann. There's nothing that is any help. Herr Grell met your brother-in-law up at the picnic ground, and invited him back here for breakfast."

"And nothing stronger than coffee was drunk, I assure you," Grell said.

"Was he ill?"

"No. He was cold and slightly damp. He had been caught in the mist. And he had scarred his hands on some rocks. Apart from that, he was well. A bit anxious about his wife. He telephoned her."

"I know. I was staying with them in Salzburg for a couple of days. Well—" He just didn't seem to be able to get an opening. "That's all that can be said, I suppose. Where's Anton?"

Grell's placid face did not move a muscle. "He's in Bozen."

"Back in the South of Tyrol?" Johann asked, startled. "Isn't that dangerous for him? After all, he left it without permission of the Italians."

"He has Austrian papers now. He'll be all right." Grell seemed amused. "He is hoping to bring his girl when he returns. At least, he is trying to persuade her to come north. They will be here next week if he has any luck. Did you have some message for him?"

"No. I just thought he must be here. In that telephone call—"

Grell was watching him politely. "Yes?"

"My sister thought her husband said he was having breakfast with the Grells."

Grell looked bewildered. "She must have got it wrong. *With* the Grells? Are you sure she didn't say *at* the Grells? There's quite a difference in one small word." He turned to his guests. "It's too bad that Anton won't be here to guide you around tomorrow. But perhaps we could persuade Herr Kronsteiner to take his place. He knows these mountains well. You like hunting, don't you, Herr Kronsteiner?" He faced Johann with a genial smile, his blue eyes widely innocent.

"There will be funeral arrangements," Johann said in a low voice.

Grell's smile faded. "Forgive me. I am so sorry. And please convey my deepest sympathy to Frau Bryant."

From the hall beyond the dining room there was Felix Zauner's voice calling, "Where is everybody? Grell?" Then his brisk footsteps echoed over the wooden floors and stopped at the kitchen door. Under his arm he had some heavy sheets of paper in a loose roll. "Glad to see the inn is open," he said, with a polite nod for everyone. He looked at the large stove where pots were drawn to the side of the heat, keeping warm, smelling deliciously. "Makes business more pleasurable when a good meal precedes it." He held up the roll of paper. "I had these diagrams and maps drawn to scale. They'll prove we don't intend to ruin Unterwald," he told Grell. "When are you serving dinner? Soon, I hope. This autumn air makes me—" He caught sight of Johann, and his voice changed. "I was sorry to hear about the accident, Kronsteiner. Very sorry."

Max placed his beer mug carefully on the table and rose. Karl did the same. "Yes," said Max as his parting word, "it was a bad thing, a very bad thing. But there was one mercy, Johann. Your brother-in-law died quickly, painlessly."

"Yes," said Karl, "not like that other fellow in the car. It's a wonder they didn't hear his screams in the village." He beamed around on them all, joined Max in his thanks for the beer, and lumbered out the back door after him.

Johann watched the grin on Grell's broad red face, forced and now fixed, as if Grell had summoned it and could not dismiss it. The two strangers sat unmoving. "Good night," Johann said, and followed the two policemen into the yard. As he closed the door, he could still see that rigid parting of Grell's lips.

Felix Zauner was saying quickly as he moved back into the dining room, "I'll get rid of my coat. Frau Hitz, would you be so kind as to show me where I might wash my hands?"

Grell listened to Zauner's retreating footsteps. He said, "Don't worry about him. He's just a sharp businessman. When he leaves, we can talk."

His guests had risen to their feet, but one of them had his eyes on the back door as if he were watching Johann Kronsteiner. "That brother-in-law is the one I'm worried about," he said in a hushed voice.

"What about Bryant's wife?" the other asked.

"We'll have to talk over that problem," Grell said.

"There have been two men watching her house all day."

"Ours?"

"No. We think they were the men that Yates asked for. But who gave them Bryant's address? Yates certainly couldn't reach them today." There was a thin smile on the normally pleasant mouth.

"Then there is someone in Salzburg who serves as a contact for Yates," Grell said thoughtfully. "Someone who was alerted by Yates before we picked him up this morning."

"That's possible. We were only monitoring his Warsaw sendings. If he made a telephone call to Salzburg—well, that was something we couldn't intercept. We find that he has at least two addresses in Zürich as well as his legal one. A very able fellow."

"Who was he working for? The Soviets?"

"I don't think so." The thin smile appeared again. "It was a Soviet agent who tipped us off about Yates."

"Was Yates working for the Americans then?"

"No. Definitely not. He has done enough harm to them to—"

Grell held up a warning hand as his ears caught the first sounds of distant footsteps, passing through the hall. The tight group of men separated to a more normal distance, raised their voices from a low murmur to a natural tone. "Yes," Grell was saying as he began leading the way into the dining room, "the chamois have disappeared. They seem to have all gone to the south of Styria. However, you never know your luck. Frau Hitz! Are you ready to serve dinner?"

Johann had halted at the corner of the inn to light a cigarette. Drawing ahead of him, the motorcycle and sidecar bumped over the rough cart track with a last friendly wave from Karl. Then it turned right for the road down to the Gendarmerie at Bad Aussee, its coughing and sputtering giving way to a steady growl. It was a clear night, almost cloud free, with the first stars glittering. The gibbous moon hung low in the sky; it would take another couple of hours before it was high enough to spread its light full on the mountainsides. The time couldn't be better: the village was silent; Grell and his friends would soon be at dinner; Felix was safely occupied. And I, thought Johann, am having supper with Trudi. He threw away his cigarette and took the road to Finstersee.

He made it in a quick fifteen minutes. Walking was as easy

as breathing to him, and the night held no problems once he had cleared the lights of Grell's kitchen out of his eyes. The liar, he thought bitterly, liar and liar and liar. So Dick was having breakfast at the Grells', was he? Anna didn't make mistakes like that, and she had been quite definite: Dick was having breakfast with August and Anton Grell. Those were her words. Perhaps, he decided, it was lucky for me that I didn't tell them that. They didn't like me much.

He halted at the edge of the picnic ground, studying the moon. Its light was even weaker here, cut off as it was by the mountain peaks that rose high above the lake. The first thing to do was to reach the small clump of trees and boulders on its north shore and try to find out if Dick had really been there. With the careful use of the flashlight that now weighed down the pocket of his cape, he might find some traces, some tracks. (He had enough experience in finding lost climbers who had strayed in the mists and been trapped in blind corners.) And if he found any sign that Dick had been crazy enough to visit that spot just above the ledge in the lake? Then that would have been enough for his death warrant. I'll know it really was murder, Johann thought. And if Felix won't take action, then by God I will.

He crossed the meadow, intending to cut up through the wood toward the track along the mountain's lower slope. His eyes, scanning the shadows around him, rested on the black shape of the picnic table. So this was where Grell had met Dick, was it? Another lie, possibly. He halted his steady pace, wondering what actually had happened, feeling the impossibility of ever reaching the truth through the maze of lies that Grell would invent. But at least there would be one piece of testimony from Anna about who was actually at the inn this morning. Anna didn't lie, Anna—

Incongruously, his mind jumped from Anna to the burned-out car. Yet logically, too. Anna said Dick took his diving gear with him. But the gaping mouth of the car's trunk had held only four blackened remains: the hub and twisted rim of what had been a spare tire, a jack, a wrench. Nothing else. In the back seat of the car, there was a crumpled small box that had once been the metal frame of a camera. Much of any diving gear would burn into ashes, but what about the weights in a belt, or a buckle, or clamps? What about a knife, a flashlight, or any metal parts in the scuba tank? The knife at least couldn't have burned to nothing.

Had Dick thrown his gear away? Not likely on the kind of money he made. Not likely with a job still to be done. Still to be done?

Johann walked slowly over to the picnic table, put his foot up on a bench, rested one elbow on his knee as he stared across the short stretch of lake toward the hidden ledge. He was remembering now the marks on Dick's palms. Rope marks. He had seen that kind of scar often enough; it happened to him if he slipped on a rock face and dangled briefly over a sheer drop, or when he was easing out a rope for a partner's descent and lost his grip for even one second. "God in heaven," he said softly.

His thoughts raced. Dick had done the job, had thrown the diving equipment away. And Anna had told a lie. She said Dick had found nothing. . . . Wait a minute, wait a minute, he reminded himself. You said Dick never would have been having breakfast at the inn with that chest lying in his car. *You* said that. And you asked, "Would he?" And her answer was "No." . . . The chest had never been hidden in the car. Dick had hidden it someplace else. Where?

Not on that bleak, bare mountainside. Not in the wood that led there: it was too vulnerable with hunters around; it was too close to the trail, too obvious. Dick was a cautious man. He would choose a hiding place that could be easily reached without attracting suspicion when the time came to retrieve it. Or rather, a hiding place that his friends the British could find without too much trouble. A place that Anna could identify for them, if things went wrong. Anna . . .

Suddenly he remembered this morning in the shop, remembered the way she had frozen beside him when that American had stopped at the detailed picture of Finstersee. He had frozen, too, because of his growing suspicions about the American. But was that Anna's reason? Or was the American looking at the hiding place? As I am doing now? he wondered in disbelief. He stared at the three boulders, silvered gray in the spreading moonlight.

Impossible, he kept telling himself. I've passed that picture in the shop a dozen times, thought nothing of it, it's a—what did the American call it?—a study in texture to show what a damned artistic photographer Dick could be. And to display it right there in the shop? Madness, complete madness. Except, he reminded himself, *you* passed it and thought nothing about it. And you wouldn't be giving it a second thought right now if you hadn't been standing close to Anna in the shop this morning, or if you had found one trace of diving gear in a ruined car.

He broke the spell of his thoughts, started across the soft grass. As he came closer to the boulders, he could see the black line of shadow where two met. Nothing could be hidden there. It was only a narrow cleft, a miniature crevasse. His excitement ebbed, and he was left with the hollow feeling of the man who has deluded himself.

He was turning away when he noticed the withered flowers and the rosebush. Their shadow wasn't as heavy as all that. He knelt, pulling them roughly aside, and found the cleft had spread as it reached the ground. He took out his flashlight and aimed its beam into the black hole. He saw the straps of a rucksack, and pulled. He had to lay aside the flashlight and pull with both hands. Pull heavily, pull slowly. The rucksack crushed the flower stalks, caught in the brambles. He tore it free. It was the chest, all right.

He knelt there for a long minute, not even touching the chest. And then he moved quickly. He hoisted the rucksack on his back, covering it with his cape. He pocketed the flashlight, pushed the dried stalks of grass and flowers back into place with his foot, and made for the nearest group of trees. From there, he reached the sparse edge of forest and slipped into its depths. There was no need to worry about cover now, only about direction, and his sense of that was built into him. Before he neared the back of the inn, he began a wide circle to avoid the village, making a long detour around the farthest stretch of fields. By the time he reached Trudi's house, he could feel sure that no one had seen him.

His jeep was standing in the deep shadows of the western side of the Seidl house. He hesitated. His first impulse was to drop the rucksack into the back seat and take off. But he was exhausted, although he'd recover quickly enough with some food and warmth; and he was hungry. His last meal had been breakfast. And Trudi would be waiting.

The heavy door was unlatched. He pushed it open carefully—it was old like the house itself and groaned easily. He stepped over the raised stone threshold that kept the kitchen free of any floor drafts, closed the door slowly, and paused. Trudi had left one small lamp, well trimmed, on the big table that stood in the center of the scrubbed wooden floor. There was food there, too, and the wood ashes in the old-fashioned fireplace glowed warmly. It was more friendly than any stove, he had to admit, although he had often been amused by the way Trudi's father had insisted on keeping that open fireplace, wide and black and smoke-stained, just because his grandfather and great-grandfather and their great-grandfathers had used it. Yes, it was an old house, all right, one of the oldest in the village. The wonder was it held together and kept the winter wind out—better than his own new house down at Bad Aussee. Gently he lowered the rucksack onto the floor at the bottom of the stairs that led up to Trudi's room. Her mother slept in a room at the back of the kitchen (once it had been part of the barn when Trudi's father farmed here); he could hear her steady breathing through the wall. He eased off his shoes as he unfastened his cape, and left them beside the rucksack. He moved silently toward the table and its covered plates. This was Trudi's way of saying, "Here's something to eat, and if you are too tired to see me, don't bother. I waited long enough, and I'm fast asleep anyway." She never meant it, of course. It was just to remind him that if he was an independent type, so was she. Or at least tried to be. But not very successfully, he thought with a happy grin.

He ate everything she had left for him. There had been enough for two men, and he needed it all. He sat for a while, his back comfortably near the warm hearth, and almost fell asleep. He roused himself. At least he had decided what to do with the rucksack. He had even answered the question why he had not left it in its hiding place. It was only safe there as long as Dick had been alive. His death meant that someone like Grell had been suspicious of him; and Grell wasn't the man to let suspicions wither away without a search. If I could find the hiding place, Johann reasoned, so could Grell. So could that American, the lawyer fellow, who studied the photographs so intently. Yes, once anyone guessed the chest was no longer sunk in the lake, the hunt would be on.

He rose, blew out the lamp, and moved quietly to the staircase. He lifted the rucksack and began his cautious climb, avoiding the third and ninth steps that creaked badly. He was careful with the upper landing, too. Inside Trudi's door, he could relax and move without such exaggerated caution. It always amused him, but it was part of the gamble and added to the fun of the chase. She had left her curtains undrawn so that the moonlight would keep him from falling over the heavy furniture. He laid the rucksack beside a low chest that stored all her carefully embroidered linens collecting for the day she would marry. He looked at the rucksack and then back at the sleeping girl, dark hair loose on the soft pillow. Marriage was something he could now afford. The thought nearly drove him out the door and back down the staircase.

Then she turned in her sleep, sighing a little, stretching her body under the white mound of eiderdown. He stripped off his clothes, dropping them on the floor. He bent over her, half wakening her with small light kisses. He bit her ear lobe gently. "Anyone at home?" he asked softly as he pulled the eiderdown aside.

Trudi awakened him at four o'clock as she always did. "Time to go," she whispered. She was already out of bed, wrapped in the heavy dressing gown he had given her last Christmas. The curtains had been tightly drawn and a candle lit.

"Too early," he grumbled, but she was shaking out his clothes, handing them to him one by one. He dressed slowly, longing for another hour of soft warm sleep. But Trudi was right. Time to leave before the village was stirring. Then he saw the rucksack and became wide awake. "Look, Trudi— I've got to go to Salzburg. I won't have time to stop off at my place. Would you keep this for me until I get back?" He nodded to the rucksack.

"Of course." She looked at it curiously. "What is it?"

"Just some equipment. It belonged to Dick. It was thrown clear of the car." He looked around the room, frowning. "We don't want your mother to find it and start asking questions about how it got here. Does she come up here much?"

"No, her leg hurts her badly. The stairs—"

"Even so, we'd better be careful. We don't want people to start talking."

She agreed with that. She watched him as he tried to draw the chest out of the rucksack, and then stared in horror as he took out his knife and slashed the canvas sides. "What a waste—" she began. "Oh, it's filthy!" She stared at the metal box with distaste.

"Get an old towel, will you? It will soon clean off."

"It needs a good scrub," she told him, but together they

began to get most of the dried green slime removed. "It must be valuable; look at the way he had it padlocked."

"I hope it's very valuable. For Anna's sake. She'll need every penny she can get for it. Look, love—once the funeral is over, I'll bring Anna out to my place, and she can get this box then. We'll keep it a secret between us. Right?"

"Won't the police want to—"

"It isn't their business. It's Anna's. Now where will we put it?"

"Under the bed."

The suggestion was so simple, so typical, that he almost smiled. "In here," he said, and lifted the lid of her linen chest.

"No!"

"Trudi," he said gently, catching her around the waist with his free arm, "do you know that's the very first 'No' you've ever given me? And just when I need your help most. Please, Trudi. We'll wrap it in a sheet. It can lie underneath. It won't dirty or crush anything. Come on, love." He kissed her neck, her chin, her lips. She still strained away from him. "All right. I'll just have to take Dick's equipment to my place and try to hide it safely there." He let go of her completely.

"Is it as valuable as that?" she asked slowly. "But surely no one would want to steal it."

"Wouldn't they? Do you know how much one of Dick's cameras cost him? Fifteen thousand schillings, and that was at a discount too."

She looked at him, completely shocked.

"So that box means money. Money for Anna. I won't have to worry about her future. I can think of my own. I can think of getting married, settling down." He hesitated, branched off to the main problem. "Oh, well—I must take the box down to my own house, try to find a—"

Trudi said briskly, "You are so careless about your place, Johann. Nothing is properly locked, the door key is where everyone can find it, and people keep wandering in and out to see you. No, no, that wouldn't do. Not if this box is so valuable."

"It is."

She began lifting embroidered mats and bolster cases and eiderdown covers and stacks of towels onto her bed.

The green-stained metal box was hidden. The linen was replaced after some rearrangement by Trudi to allow for the

101

addition to her hope chest. "Meine eigene Aussteuer," she said softly, sadly, as she closed its lid.

Johann caught her up in a massive hug. "It could be part of your trousseau," he said in his relief. "Once Anna is settled—" He could have bitten his tongue, but the promise was half out, and Trudi had seized it.

Her arms went around his shoulders. "Oh, Johann!" She kissed him over and over again. "We'll get married. Anna will have her box and we can get married!"

"Trudi, Trudi, we're late. Your mother will soon—"

She released him with a laugh. "That doesn't matter now."

"Oh yes, it does. We'll keep things just as they are. Meanwhile. Our secret. Right?" He picked up the rucksack. That must leave with him. Trudi would wash it and try to mend it. Better not have it lying around here.

"Our secret," she promised him. Her eyes were bright, her face glowing with happiness.

He gave her a last kiss. "You really are my best girl," he said softly.

Johann dropped the rucksack, covered by his folded cape, onto the front seat of the jeep and released its brake. He began pushing it away from the wall of the Seidl house. It was an easy and quiet exit, for the ground sloped downward to the road.

"Very efficient," Felix Zauner's low voice said at his elbow. "Need some help?" He was bundled up warmly, but he looked peaked and cold. "This would have to be the morning you overslept by twenty minutes."

"I tell you too much," Johann said, recovering himself as they both pushed. Quickly, the jeep swung onto the dark road that ran downhill to Bad Aussee. "Do you want a lift?"

"No. I am going back to my bed at Frau Hitz's place. She put me up for the night. Grell had only two rooms prepared at the inn."

"I thought you sounded a bit sharp-set."

"You sound on edge yourself. Anything wrong?"

Johann stared at Zauner through the cold bleak shadows. "I think I just asked her to marry me."

Zauner whistled softly. "And what is Elisabetha going to say about that?"

Johann shrugged. Elisabetha was not the kind of girl who

married. "I'm just a change from her Salzburg friends, that's all."

For a moment, Zauner said nothing. Johann had more sense than he had realized. Elisabetha, for all her charm and good looks, was a girl who brought misery. He clapped Johann's shoulder. "You will be better off with Trudi Seidl."

Johann said nothing.

"You love her, don't you?"

"I guess I do." There was a touch of amazement in Johann's voice.

Zauner was amused. "I don't see you as a married man."

"Neither do I."

Zauner's grin widened. "Let's get out of the cold," he said and climbed into the jeep, pushing the cape aside to make room. "Take me down as far as the first tree. I've got some news for you." He waited until Johann started up the engine, and once it was running smoothly enough he began talking. "It's about Anna. She didn't stay with the Dietrichs. They thought she was safely asleep, and she slipped out when Frieda and the children were having supper. She went home. She phoned them from there—at least, the American phoned them. He waited until Frieda came around to spend the night with Anna. So she's all right. But—" Felix Zauner's lips closed tightly, and he said no more.

"The American was with her?" Johann stopped the jeep. They were almost at the tree anyway. "That lawyer fellow?"

"Mathison."

"What in hell is going on?"

"That's what I'd like to know. What are your plans?"

"I was going to wash and change and then drive into Salzburg."

"Do that. As far as we know, they met accidentally. But—" Again there was that silence.

"*Is* he a lawyer?"

"We are finding that out. You know—" Zauner was choosing his words carefully—"there seems to be a lot of interest in Unterwald. That Frenchman, for instance, who stayed last night with Frau Hitz. She tells me he asked a lot of questions about visitors to the village. And three days ago, she gave a midday meal to two inquisitive foreigners who were also on a walking tour. She thought they were either Czech or Polish. They asked about visitors, too."

"Well, they weren't asking about Finstersee." But in spite of his cockiness, Johann was worried.

"They will do more than ask about the lake if they hear of a violent death—"

"Murder," Johann said determinedly.

"What motive was there?"

Johann had the impulse to say, "Plenty. You are sitting against Dick's rucksack right now—yes, it's under my cape. I found it where he had hidden it." But he clamped his lips shut. There was a brief silence. He gave Felix one last chance. "You don't want to name it murder, is that it? You want it to be an accident."

"We'll get Grell and his friends—if they are connected with it."

So this is where we part, Johann thought. He said angrily, "But not as murderers."

"You're a vindictive son of a bitch," Felix said lightly, and opened the jeep door. "I'll be staying up here for a day or so. I may yet persuade Grell to keep his inn open as a ski lodge. I didn't learn much tonight. They are a careful trio; they talk a lot and say nothing. But I had one small triumph. I rather think I have established peaceful relations with Frau Hitz. She should be a most valuable ally." He got out of the car, looked around him. The stars were almost gone; the moon was a pale ghost. "The most god-forsaken hour in the whole day."

"How do I get in touch with you? At the Postmistress's—"

"Better not call me direct. Phone my Salzburg office and let them reach me. Give my love to Anna."

"How long was she with the American?"

"I understand they met around half past six. They walked for almost an hour. And then he accompanied her home. But why don't you get to Salzburg and ask her yourself?"

Johann shifted from neutral into first and started with a roar down the hill.

Now that was unnecessary, thought Felix Zauner. He began walking up toward the silent village.

Around half past six, Johann was thinking. Just what had Mathison in mind? Some answers to a problem called Finstersee? Well, whatever the American had guessed or found out, it would do him little good. Not now. Let them all search Finstersee.

8

AT HALF PAST SIX, BILL MATHISON HAD HAD NOTHING AT ALL on his mind except the problem of dinner. It was too early to find a restaurant for that, and he seemed to have little luck in discovering another bar in this part of Salzburg where he might have a drink and put in an hour. In fact, this section of the town seemed devoted to large squares and fountains looking as lonely as himself at this hour. But perhaps his mood was colored by his disappointment over Elissa. It had all seemed to be going so damned well; and then the pleasant prospect had blown up in his face. A strange mixture, Elissa Lang: helpless, dependent, softly appealing; then capable, brisk, most definitely her own mistress. It could have been a really interesting evening. Well, there was always Zürich to continue what Schloss Fuschl had ended.

He had passed the massive front of the Cathedral and was headed for the arcades. Abruptly, he stopped and glanced back. Anna Bryant? Surely not. It was a woman, alone, standing in front of the giant doors, looking up at a church spire across the square, blindly staring, seeing nothing. Was she ill? He hesitated. It was Anna Bryant all right; fair hair silvered under the square's lights, cheekbones and jaw line as white and sculptured as the marble statues of the Cathedral behind her. She paid no attention to those who walked by. Waiting for someone? he wondered. He almost walked on, but the hopelessness in her face held him there. He stayed, watching, for a long minute. Then he went forward.

"Mrs. Bryant," he said quietly, and then had to repeat it.

She looked at him as if he were standing at a far distance.

"Can I help you?"

She came to life, but did not speak.

"I'm Bill Mathison." She must be ill; she shouldn't be wandering around these quiet dark streets by herself. She should be indoors instead of standing here, huddling into her coat, freezing to death. "Let me take you home," he said in German. He touched her arm. She came with him, unresisting.

Her pace was slow, unsteady. "First, please walk with me. A little." And that was all she said for the next fifteen minutes or so. He kept silent, too, letting her choose their direction. She wasn't ill, he had now decided; she was arguing something inside her own mind. Something highly emotional, painful. Perhaps there had been a quarrel, he guessed, when her husband returned; and she had left the house to walk the streets and fight out the rest of the quarrel by herself. I'll see her safely home, thought Mathison, and then retreat. This isn't my affair. Didn't I have enough of this kind of heartbreak of my own ten years ago?

"Thank you," she said at last, drawing her arm away from his, increasing her pace to normal. "I needed help, and you gave me it. Strange to walk through a town I love, among people I know, and yet feel so lost. Strange, too—" She broke off, remembering. That was the way she had first seen Dick. He had stopped, watched her, and his first words had been almost the same, too: *May I help you?* . . . That was so long ago. Twenty years . . . "Have you ever been in Vienna, Mr. Mathison?"

"No."

"Yates was there."

And what has Yates got to do with this aimless walk through Salzburg? Mathison looked at her worriedly. "Don't you think we should start getting you home?" They had reached the riverbank by this time, and the Neugasse was well behind them.

"That's where I'm going. That's where I shall stay. Not with friends. Johann was wrong about that, but I let him take me to their house because he must find out what happened. I *have* to know. Don't you see?" She looked at him pleadingly. "And I have to find out about Yates. I must know if I can really trust him. Or else everything has been quite useless, it has all been for nothing."

He looked at her with growing bewilderment. "Look," he began awkwardly, "I'm afraid I don't know what—"

"You do know Yates. What kind of man is he?"

"I've met him three—no, four times. Once in New York, twice on previous visits to Zürich, and then last week very briefly. He's a friendly type, free and easy—"

"Be honest with me. Please. I have to know."

"If you are worried about that contract, Mrs. Bryant—"

"It isn't the contract," she said sharply, angrily. "It's much

106

more, much more than that. Dick said—" She almost broke down. She looked away, stared at the river alongside them. "He said that if things went wrong, I was to go to Yates. Yates would finish what he had begun." She shook her head helplessly, kept looking away. "I don't know, any more. For the last few hours I have been trying to think, trying to put all the little pieces together. And I can't find an answer. No one in Salzburg can help me. Johann can't help me. You are the only person who could—perhaps—I thought—" She didn't finish.

They had been walking along the continuous stretch of quays that edged the river's bank, separated from the traffic in the street by a line of trees. Mathison halted, took her arm, turned around to retrace their steps. The moon had risen; the stars were out. "I'm taking you home," he said quietly. His guess had been wrong about any quarrel there, so wrong that he resisted making any more. "It's time you had something to eat. That's what everyone else is doing." There were few people out of doors now. Then his eyes narrowed as he caught sight of a man, strolling some distance behind them, who had quickly veered toward the nearest tree. *Am I being followed again?* Mathison wondered. *Why the hell should I be followed anyway?*

She was saying, "Dick trusted him. He is with British Intelligence. But now—"

"British Intelligence?" His thoughts swung away from the man who was now crossing the well-lighted street to reach its busier side of shops and restaurants. Clearly seen for that moment, he was the same man who had nearly collided with Mathison in the bar as he had turned to get his camera. Same man, same gray coat. "Eric Yates?"

"You didn't know?"

"How could I?" He almost laughed, but her face was too tense. "Men who work in Intelligence don't usually go around talking about it."

"He didn't. But Dick knew. He worked with Yates in Vienna. Long ago. At the end of the war."

An Intelligence agent as Newhart and Morris's European representative? That would send Jimmy Newhart's blood pressure soaring. "That was very long ago. Yates could have come out, couldn't he?"

"Dick said he was the kind of man who couldn't live without intrigue. It was his natural career. And it was he who came to see Dick in Salzburg last spring. Dick asked him what he was doing now. He said he was with the old firm. He said that quite definitely. Then I left the room and I don't know what else he said. But afterward, Dick seemed quite sure. That's why he went to see Yates in Zürich—" She bit her lip.

"Whatever made you imagine that I knew about Yates?"

"I—I thought there might be some—some way you could find out—whether he really is what he says he is. Your friends in Washington might have—oh, well, they might know about him." Her blue eyes, honest, perfectly serious, looked at him frankly.

"But I've no connection with Washington."

"None?" She didn't believe him.

He shook his head.

"Johann said—" She stopped, struggled with her disappointment. "Even Felix thought so."

"Thought I was some kind of American agent?"

"Yes," she said faintly.

"Now what could give them that idea?" he asked slowly, trying to puzzle it out. He was back in the shop again, talking about Yates and a contract. And looking at photographs. "Do they know Yates is a British agent?"

"No."

"They are just suspicious of anyone who came asking about your husband today?" Or who looked at photographs so intently? She hadn't answered. He tried again. "What made *you* believe I might be an agent?" he asked gently.

"You seemed so interested in—in the same kind of thing as Eric Yates." Her footsteps quickened. "We are nearly home. I'll have to go in by the kitchen door; that's the way Johann and I left. The front door is bolted. And please, Mr. Mathison, please forget all I've said. I've been so stupid."

Not stupid, he thought. Distracted and pressed to death with worries. Where was her husband, anyway? If she had him to talk to, she could have poured all her misgivings about Yates into his ear. Then suddenly he realized that she had done nothing but talk of her husband in the past tense. He said, he did, he trusted, he knew. *If things went wrong, Yates would finish what he had begun.* "Will your brother be at home now?" Mathison asked. He hadn't the courage to ask about her husband.

"No."

"There will be no one?"

"I want to be by myself."

"What about the friends you were supposed to stay with?"

"They think I am asleep. They gave me pills, but I didn't swallow them. I waited until dusk. Then I ran away. I had to walk, I had to get out of that strange room. I had to go home." She touched his arm, lightly, briefly. "Don't be so anxious. I am all right now. The time for weeping is over. I have been calm, haven't I?"

But a very strange calm, he thought, and his alarm increased. "I wish I could have helped you about Yates and—"

"Forget all that. Please. Don't talk about him to anyone. It could be dangerous for you."

"I can't quite forget all about it, Mrs. Bryant. After all, Newhart and Morris would want to know. In fact, they *ought* to know."

She thought over that. "I suppose so," she said slowly. "Yet—"

"They won't want any publicity, I assure you. They'll keep very quiet about this matter. But they must deal with Yates, don't you see? He can't go on doing their business with his right hand while his left is reaching out somewhere else." And reaching exactly where? Newhart would certainly need some pretty close accounting rendered to him. Then thinking of Newhart's strong reactions, Mathison unexpectedly remembered the time he had served on a presidential advisory committee dealing with the conflicts between scientific publications and classified information. That had been four years ago, but James Newhart must still know some classified people in Washington. "Perhaps I can help you after all. I have a friend who may have contacts in Washington who might know what questions to ask in London. That's where you really have to go to find out about Yates, isn't it?" He didn't altogether believe his own words; he was just handing out hope, that was all. She needed it.

But she didn't seize on his words, as if she were beginning to realize how impossible it would be to discover anything in Yates's world of silence. If, Mathison emended that, Yates was actually an agent. All these charges might be part of her grief: a search for someone who could be blamed and hated, labeled responsible. She frowned. Slowly she said, "I don't really trust him. And yet, to whom else can I go? I must find out what he really is. I must."

"Why don't you trust him?"

"There never was any contract for the book. Was there?"

She had a point there. "I don't know," he admitted frankly. "But I'll find out. That I can promise you."

She seemed to have lost interest. Or perhaps she only wanted to get home now. They were at the beginning of the Neugasse. Its shops were closed; lights were dim behind shuttered and curtained windows of the rooms overhead. There were few people walking through this little street at this hour. Not even the two men were to be seen, the men who had worn such complete (and new) Salzburg costumes and had patrolled so dutifully. They've been called off, he thought. They've gone, and no replacements either. "Thank you," she was saying, "you've come far enough, Mr. Mathison."

"Bill is shorter."

She tried to smile. "So is Anna. Good-bye."

"Not yet. How do we reach your back door? I'm seeing you safely inside. Come on now."

She led him along the Neugasse, passing the closed and darkened shop with its handsome display of camera equipment, stopped immediately beyond it at a large wooden door. It was the entrance to several apartments, he noted, glimpsing a neat list of names posted at one side: a lawyer, a dentist, a doctor of letters, and three families without titles or degrees, including *Richard Bryant*. He swung open the heavy door and stood hesitating on the threshold. They were entering some kind of hall, possibly oblong—for the street lighting only spread a few feet over the flagstone floor—and certainly cold and dark.

"Oh, someone has turned off the light," Anna said. "Just a moment." She took a step into the deeper shadows in search of the switch. The darkness seemed to give her courage. She faced him. In a tight low voice, she said, "They killed him. It was no accident. The Nazis killed him."

"Nazis?"

"Yes. As surely as they killed those two men at Lake Toplitz."

Good God, he thought, she isn't rational at all. She probably never has been. She's— He felt her grasp tight on his arm. "Now," he said as calmly as he could, trying to disengage her hand gone rigid as if it were trying to make him believe, "we'll get you inside your apartment." And I'll call a

110

doctor, he thought. "Where's that light switch?" Her hand went limp, left his arm. He heard the flick of the switch, but the hall remained dark. He groped for the switch, tried it, too. The hall stayed dark.

"Its fuse must have blown," she said. Her voice was now as normal as her words. "Don't worry. I can find my way upstairs even in the darkness."

He had found a matchbox, almost opened it, then remembered it was the one that held his Minox film, jammed it safely back into his pocket, began searching for the spare box he carried with him. "Please don't worry. The stairs are just beyond our kitchen door—that's the back entrance to our shop, actually. We have the apartment above—" Her voice broke off. We? She moved quickly toward the staircase that led to emptiness, her hand guiding her along the plastered wall.

The match flared and died. Mathison took two strides into the hall as he struck another. There was a loud crash as he knocked against some heavy object and sent it clattering over on its side. He held the match high, rubbing his knee with the other hand, cursing under his breath, and saw a collection of five large garbage cans standing neatly together with a sixth rolling backward and forward on the stone floor. Thank God Salzburg was a clean place; the cans' lids were all firmly chained down to defeat rats and roaches, and nothing had spilled. "No harm done," he said cheerfully. Except for a bruised knee and a burned finger where the match had burned too low. He dropped it, set the garbage can back in place.

"Sh!" Anna whispered. He struck another match and saw her pointing to the kitchen door. "Someone's inside! The light's on!"

Mathison reached her quickly. And as the match flickered out with his burst of speed, he could see a narrow line of light edging the bottom of the door. "Your brother must have come back." Thank heaven for that, he thought.

"Johann is in Unterwald." She found the key in her pocket at last, but she was now fumbling with the lock in her anxiety to get inside. He took her hand away, turned the key in the lock, pushed the door open. There was a receding clatter of heels, the sound of someone in flight.

"Stay here!" he told her as he entered the kitchen. He headed at full speed for a long hallway that must lead to the

111

shop itself. It was from there that he could now hear the lightly running footsteps. He heard, too, a sharp crash, then the scrape of a bolt being pulled aside, the opening and closing of the front door. He had to slow his pace as he went through the dark shop, avoided a stool that had been knocked over to block his way, pulled the street door open, spilled onto the narrow sidewalk. Nothing in sight. But he thought he heard the same running footsteps, and he set out after them. He turned the corner, only to see a pair of legs and the swing of a coat disappearing into another street. It was a woman, all right. He increased his speed, but by the time he had reached it she had vanished.

He slowed his run to a walk, if only because there were other people in sight now. This street was broader, busier. And filled with doors; doors and entrances and small court-yards and narrow throughways to other streets. The woman had vanished.

Quickly, he retraced his steps. At the corner of the Neugasse, he saw the man in the gray coat trying to look part of a shadowed doorway. Mathison went up to him. "Did you see her?" he demanded. The man looked at him nervously, tried to walk off. Mathison caught a gray lapel. "You could have seen her. Did you?" The man struck out wildly, wrenched free. As a sprinter, he was almost as good as the woman.

Mathison didn't even try to chase him. Too many doors, alleys, winding streets. Any stranger was handicapped from the start. But the man must have seen the woman, no doubt about that. And why had he looked so startled, so amazed, even before Mathison had spoken to him? Had he recognized her? . . . That was a double failure, Mathison thought angrily: I should have kept a grip on that lapel, even if I had torn it off.

He found Anna Bryant waiting in the shop. She had set back the stool in its place by the counter, turned on the light. She was standing in front of the wall that had held the display of Austrian lakes, staring at it in disbelief. He stared, too. The photographs had gone. All of them.

He said nothing, closed the front door, securely bolted it, followed Anna into the narrow hallway. She stopped at the entrance to a small interior room that had been partitioned off from the kitchen. It was a photographer's darkroom, he noticed, as she turned on its light, a neat businesslike place with sink and water faucets and worktable and trays. A drying cord was suspended over them. On another wall there was shelving, with rows of large filing boxes. They were clearly labeled *Duplicate Prints.* She went to one of them, examined the folders inside. Then she turned to a metal box on another shelf and looked through its envelopes. "The negatives have gone, too," she said quietly. "Both the duplicate set of the lake photographs and their negatives." She passed him quickly at the doorway and entered the kitchen.

It was in complete disorder. At first he thought the thief had rummaged wildly, and then he noticed the unwashed dishes, the littered table with its unfinished meal, the pots on a small electric stove filled with food now cold. It would have been a marvel if any prowler had found anything here at all.

Anna was standing in front of a small desk, more orderly than any other piece of furniture in this kitchen-living room except that one drawer was open. The thief must have been at work there when the fallen garbage can had sounded its warning. A cool customer, though, to wait until Anna's key was in the lock and make sure it wasn't a false alarm, some visitor for an upstairs apartment.

"Anything missing?"

She nodded. "The envelope marked *Yates;* the one you saw today. Everything that could connect Yates with Dick is gone."

"Or perhaps it is the other way around."

She closed her eyes, put her hands to her mouth.

"Come on," he said, taking her arm and leading her over to a comfortable armchair beside the big ceramic stove, six feet high, free-standing in a corner near the window.

"But who could have wanted to know all about—" She had been talking half to herself. She didn't finish her spoken thoughts but looked up at him, puzzled, fearful. She shivered, folded her arms tightly around her.

"Who would they be?" He had disbelieved her before, had thought she was irrational, ill. Now he knew she had been telling him the truth as she saw it; she might even have told him some real facts. "Nazis?" he ventured, if only to show her he was now willing to believe her. He still had the feeling he had stepped back twenty-odd years into another world. "How do I get this going?" He eyed the stove mistrustfully, risked opening its curved door just enough to see what lay inside. Glowing embers, dying slowly. There was enough life.

113

He looked around for the fuel this huge monster of decorated tiles, handsome enough in its baroque bulges, must gobble up. He could see no logs.

"Not the Nazis. Not this time." She spoke in a strangely flat, hard voice. "They do not need to find out any more about my husband. They have already taken action. Their way."

He found a coal scuttle on the other side of the stove. "No wood?" he asked, looking down at the heap of soot-black bricks under a heavy glove.

"We aren't allowed to use logs. Briquettes. They are safer."

He dropped only two on the embers so as not to smother them, left the door slightly open for increased draft, and hoped that would start warming the room again. She had shivered twice. People were always cold after shock. "Here," he said, taking a heavy jacket from its peg on the door, "put this around your shoulders."

The jacket seemed to comfort her. She said slowly, "That was a woman who came here. Wasn't it?"

He nodded. "A young woman. She moved fast. She knew her way around those streets." He looked at the cluttered kitchen and then at the opened drawer. "She knew her way around here too. She knew just what she wanted."

Anna looked at him blankly. "And now there's nothing—nothing to show."

"I took some photographs. Remember? I'll send you copies of the letters—" He stopped. His words were no comfort. It was the loss of the lake photographs that really appalled her. "I'm sorry, really sorry. It would have been a remarkable book." But again his words meant little to her.

"I promised him I'd never go near the lake. I was only to show—" She bit her lip cruelly. "All for nothing, it was all for nothing." She began to weep, silently.

He moved over to the desk, found a small directory, brought the book over to her. "Anna—please. What's the name of your friend? The one you were staying with. She will be worried about you. *Please,* Anna."

"Dietrich. Frieda and Werner Dietrich." She stared at him, suspicion rising. "But I won't leave here. I won't!" She quieted her voice. "I should never have left," she said dully.

He found the number, and then had to search for the telephone—it was in the shop. He listened to Frieda's worried exclamations for half a minute, eventually persuaded her to come around here and spend the night. He would wait until she arrived. He replaced the directory and, as he did so, he stooped to pick up a small scrap of paper that must have fluttered out of the book as he opened it. It was a telephone number, hastily written. It wasn't Bryant's writing, though.

Anna was watching him. She was in control again. The tears had stopped. "That is Yates's number—the one Dick was to telephone when he got back here."

He frowned at the number. Only one thing was clear: it wasn't the number of the Zürich office; it wasn't Yates's home number either. "May I copy this down? And I'll note your telephone number, too." He remembered that all Newhart and Morris addresses had gone with the stolen file, so he wrote them out for her as a kind of reassurance. "I'll be in touch with you," he promised. "Don't worry. We won't forget you. This isn't the end of this matter."

She stared across the room at the gaping drawer. "Perhaps Yates is responsible for that, too. He wants to take all the credit. He will give Dick none of it. None. He knows where to search. Now he has the photograph, the one that wasn't sent to him—it wasn't to be published. It was just a—" She broke off. "It won't matter now. He has everything." She rose. "I think I'll go upstairs. I'm very tired." She looked at the small lines of flame running around the edges of the briquettes on their bed of glowing embers. "Thank you," she said. "I'll need a warm stove in the morning." She added some more fuel, closed the door of the stove, adjusted a ventilator.

She is far from hysterical, he thought, as he noted her movements and the practical voice. If what she has been saying seems wild, then it is only because I know so damned little about anything. "I'll see you into the apartment upstairs, lock you in, and give Mrs. Dietrich the key."

The apartment seemed safe enough. No intruders here. And she was so exhausted, both emotionally and physically, that she might not even notice its emptiness. There would be bad days ahead for her, he thought, as he returned downstairs through the dark hall.

He had to wait almost ten minutes before Frieda Dietrich appeared. She was, he noted with relief, a placid blonde with a capable air and a kindly face. "I'll soon get this place straightened up," she told him, and he could believe her.

"Anna was never much of a housekeeper. Poor Anna! A terrible thing, terrible!"

"What happened actually?"

"His car went off a hill road near Unterwald."

"Unterwald?"

"It's up in the mountains southeast of here. Just beyond Bad Aussee. That's where Johann Kronsteiner has his ski shop. He's Anna's brother. Lucky she has him around. There's no one else. Of course, there's a niece in America, but she was adopted in Vienna by an American and his wife. An army officer in the American occupation forces. That was years ago, soon after the war. The niece was only a baby then, won't even remember her. You know what it's like with adoptions: people don't want the family to keep in touch. It's understandable, I suppose. Too bad that Anna never had any children of her own. Never could understand it. She's young, too. Only thirty-five. He was much older; she depended on him for everything. It's a terrible thing. Terrible."

Yes, Mathison agreed, it was a terrible thing. He backed away. "Well, now that you are here to take charge, I'll start thinking of dinner. Good night, Frau Dietrich. I hope everything will be all right." He looked around for his camera. He had dropped it somewhere in his chase through the house. "Here it is," he said, picking it up from the floor. "Good night. And lock this door after me, will you?"

"We don't lock our doors—"

"Do it to please me," he said with a grin. He left quickly, seeing all the amiable questions that were rising in her curious face. Let Anna deal with them, he thought. I'm just the innocent passer-by.

He headed back for the hotel. The evening was shot to pieces. He would have dinner in his room and work at his brief for Newhart, getting everything down as quickly as possible while his memory of the details was fresh. He would have it ready by the time Newhart telephoned at midnight. As he turned the corner into the busy street, he looked at the doors of the shops and houses, wondering again which one the woman had used to vanish behind. She was young, all right. A girl. And the stockings on her slender legs had been light in color, very light. Flat-heeled shoes. No one could have run like that in high heels. And swinging tweed coat, a neutral color from the distance ... That reminded him to look over his shoulder for a man in a gray raincoat, but he

116

could see no signs of anyone following him. That was one thing about losing your temper and losing it hard: it could discourage the other fellow.

In the hotel lobby there was a large decorative map of Salzburg and the surrounding country that brightened up one wall for the benefit of the tourists. Mathison studied it as he waited for the elevator. *Southeast of here, just beyond Bad Aussee* ... Yes, almost directly east of Bad Aussee was Unterwald, so unimportant that it had been given only the smallest printing. It was near a lake, a little blue oblong among the greens and browns and etched grays of the mountains. There was spider type, delicate, almost unreadable, stretching up the side of the narrow lake. He resisted the impulse to tip his head to read it more easily, just as he had kept his finger from tracing the road from Bad Aussee. With difficulty, he read the name sideways. Finstersee. Yes, definitely Finstersee. He turned away from the map, looking now at the selections of dirndls and lederhosen inside the display cases, showing—he hoped—more interest in them than he had done in the map. At last he could step into the elevator and reach his room.

The first thing he did was to take his camera case from the wardrobe and open the Minox. The decoy roll of film was gone. Ridiculous, he had told himself this afternoon, when he had inserted it; all that trouble possibly for nothing. Yes, that was what he had thought then. But now?

He fished in his jacket pocket, brought out the matchbox. He was shaking his head as he replaced the box in his trouser pocket—keep close my pet, keep close—took off his jacket, loosened his tie. He went over to the head of his bed and picked up the telephone. A double Scotch; sandwiches; a typewriter, with carbon paper; three separate orders, with a repeat added to the Scotch to see him through the evening. No real dinner or wine tonight, he decided regretfully: he couldn't afford to feel expansive and pleasantly lethargic on the job that he faced. And it was going to be quite something, to boil down events and words and facts into a straight brisk summary. Nothing longer than three pages for the completed brief, including the footnotes. Jimmy Newhart liked his reading crisp and clear.

He flopped onto the comfortable bed to wait for the drinks, lit a cigarette, stared at the ceiling. Now let's begin at the beginning, he thought. First, you noticed two men as you

117

entered the shop early this afternoon—hey, what happened to them? Shut up and concentrate! You entered the shop and met Anna Bryant. . . .

He felt like a man who was walking across a stream of whirls and eddies, managing not too badly, and then, all at once, had stepped into the steep drop of a deep pool and was up to his chin in rushing water.

He pushed away the typewriter at a quarter to twelve, studied the pages of his preliminary notes, and tore them into small pieces once he made sure he had left nothing out of the final concentrated report. There were two copies: one to carry with him, the other to mail at the airport as he left Salzburg tomorrow. He was taking no chances.

He read the report once more (with its appendage dealing with his own experiences that had made him take Mrs. Bryant's information seriously). The gist of it made clear that there were two separate problems for Newhart and Morris. First, there was a dubious contract and a peculiar check signed by some Emil Burch. Secondly, there was Bryant's death near Finstersee. And because Yates seemed so deeply involved in both problems, Newhart and Morris had been placed in a difficult if not doubtful situation. In one case, they stood to lose some money even if Mrs. Bryant didn't sue; there was a question of good faith involved here, or rather, the canceling of their employee's bad faith. In the other, it seemed as if their chief representative in Europe might be a British agent using their name as cover for his activities.

And that, thought Mathison as he burned the discarded scraps of paper one by one in the large ashtray, that is the joker in the pack. It had taken Newhart years to build up his firm (Morris had retired handsomely a couple of years ago), and now he might see its reputation and good will dissipated within a few weeks. If the newspapers started playing around with Yates's name— He didn't finish the thought. Even sly gossip, whispered rumors could be as dangerous as headlines. The Swiss, for example: how long would they let the Zürich office stay open if they thought it had been a center of espionage activities? There was only one consolation in the whole bloody mess. The British, presumably, weren't working against American national interests. At least, they were supposed to be on the same side of the fence. But he wouldn't describe the placing of one of their agents inside a perfectly innocuous American firm as exactly a friendly gesture.

It was time to get prepared for Newhart's call. He rose to bring the telephone over to the armchair near the window. The view was as spectacular at night as it had been by day, and at last he would have time to enjoy it while he stretched his back in a comfortable seat and propped his feet up. The architects and stonemasons who had built this town would have been astounded to see what effects electricity could bring to their work. The careful floodlighting had added another dimension. Maybe we can't build like them, he thought, as he remembered the tall glass boxes and slabs of metal cheese springing up over modern cities, but we do know how to use light. That wouldn't inspire any future poets, though; there would be few twentieth-century remains worth eulogizing once the barbarians destroyed the power plants.

He was halted abruptly by the telephone cord. It jerked him to a standstill at the foot of the bed. At first he thought it was tangled and couldn't make its full stretch to the armchair. But it was straight and taut. He sat down on the edge of the bed and broke into laughter. They really had been after his telephone, right from the start. They? He sobered up and looked at the neat black instrument in his hand. Latest model with microphone in place? He would need a screw driver to investigate. Perhaps a nail file might substitute. Before he could try, the telephone rang. Careful what you say, he told himself. But how was he to keep Jimmy Newhart in check? Jimmy not only raised his voice when he made a call, he got the most wordage out of every minute he paid for.

Mathison need not have worried. Newhart's call was his shortest on record. "Look, Bill, will you get back here right away? Yes, right away. When can I expect you? ... Sure, I know you'll have to juggle flights and connections. Try to get here by tomorrow night. Call me from Kennedy Airport, and I'll let you know where and when to meet. ... Cut out Zürich meanwhile. Just get here." There was a deep sigh. "Boy, you've given me one hell of a day." And on that note of gloom, the booming voice cut off.

So Zürich was canceled.

Meanwhile—whatever that meant. And there were two

119

good suits and six of his best shirts waiting for him in his hotel room there.

He searched for Elissa Lang's address in the Salzburg directory, but it wasn't listed. It was just possible, though, that the farewell party was still lingering over its last drinks or frugging its feet off. So he called the porter downstairs, who was a knowledgeable character, and enlisted his help in tracking down Schloss Fuschl. It was on a nearby lake, the porter told him. A little late, perhaps, to telephone but he knew the night porter there. Would Herr Mathison like him to handle the call?

It came through in a few minutes. No, he was assured most earnestly, there had been no party of six people from Salzburg tonight. No party of any size whatsoever. Not tonight. Definitely.

He put the telephone back on its table and went over to the armchair. He looked at the castle across the river, towering over everything. This afternoon, he had been followed all the way up there. Then suddenly no one was following him. And later he was followed again.

Meaning? Nonsense, he told himself angrily. The first man could have kept well out of sight once he saw Elissa speak to me. There were enough walls and battlements rising around that castle to let fifty men keep watch on two people who were completely absorbed in each other. And it didn't have to be a lie about Schloss Fuschl. Her friends could have changed their minds and taken her someplace else.

He called the hall porter once more and began discussing flights out of Salzburg tomorrow morning. That brought him back to his own world, and he stopped thinking of people whom he might never see again anyway. In that mood, he stubbed out his last cigarette angrily and went to bed.

But there was one postscript to be added to his day in Salzburg. It occurred early next morning, when he had arrived at the airport and joined a small group of people at the reservation desk. Ahead of him were two men. They had dropped the fancy dress and now wore stiff-looking business suits, but they were the same two who had maintained a dogged vigil yesterday afternoon outside Bryant's place on the Neugasse. They were trying, in a mixture of very exact German (for the benefit of the Austrian clerk) and a strange language that was difficult for Mathison to identify (used in quick discussion between themselves), to extend return tickets from Prague into the longer trip to Warsaw. That should be done at Vienna when they changed planes, the clerk kept repeating. But they were worried about connections and time, and so they argued for a useless two minutes. As they walked off in sullen annoyance, each carrying one small suitcase, the clerk had the last word. He shook his head sadly and said to his next customer, "They think they know everything, these Czechs."

9

WITH THE HELP OF THE FIVE HOURS' TIME LAG BETWEEN Central Europe and Eastern daylight-saving America, Bill Mathison arrived at the Newhart and Morris offices just as the staff was pouring out of the elevators to catch the evening trains and buses home. But on the eighteenth floor, where Jimmy Newhart had his suite, his secretary was waiting in the outside office. The three typewriters near its door were shrouded in gray plastic covers, their desks empty of papers, nothing in sight.

"Hello, Linda. I've never seen this place so quiet. It looks like the morgue. Are you working late?"

"I'm the hat-check girl tonight. I also keep cleaning women at bay." She took his coat and camera, picked up the hat he had thrown on a chair, and with her foot pushed his bag more closely against the wall where he had dropped it. She was in one of her brisk moods. He had never seen her quite so serious either.

"Had a bad day?"

She turned her eyes helplessly to the ceiling.

So he didn't waste any time on even one joke, but headed straight for Newhart's office. It was empty. He kept on going, to reach the inner room. Newhart was standing at its wide window, looking down at the street below him. "A fine mess," Newhart said, turning away from the giant excavation in the block opposite. "And that goes for Zürich, too." He was a short man, with a mass of prematurely white hair, a pugnacious face usually softened by an easy smile, and an excellent taste in clothes. His manner was capable but quiet, with occasional bursts of machine-gun energy. Tonight, he seemed strangely subdued. To begin with, at least. "Good to see you, Bill. Glad you got here so promptly. We're having a couple of visitors. Thought I'd brief you before they came. Well, how are you, how are you?" He shook Mathison's hand with a good hard grip, offered him the most comfortable leather armchair, and poured him a stiff Scotch. "I expect you need this," he said, but that was all the time he seemingly had for talk about the difficult journey.

"Here's my report," Mathison said, pulling it from the safety of an inside pocket. "And here's this." He produced the matchbox.

"Fine, fine." Newhart took them and laid them on his desk.

Mathison had to laugh at himself. He had imagined himself coming into Newhart's room, sitting back in a slight state of euphoria as he watched Jimmy open the envelope and start reading eagerly. Instead, he was watching Newhart pull a folded sheet of newspaper out of his drawer, smooth it neatly as he began talking across his desk. "As soon as you finished your call yesterday morning, I spoke with the manager of the Maritime's Forty-third Street branch. The minute I asked about someone called Emil Burch who had an account with him, I could almost see him freeze. He gave me a very polite but completely stave-off answer. Said he would call me back with available information if any. But within half an hour I had two quiet and efficient types from the FBI sitting in front of me." He nodded with approval as he noticed that Mathison had stopped lounging and was bolt upright in his armchair. "Yes, that's exactly how I felt."

"They are interested in Emil Burch?"

"They've been searching for him for the last six weeks. So have Swiss Security."

"The Swiss? What have they to do with Burch?"

"Burch also banks in Zürich."

"And just what is our government's interest?"

Newhart glanced at his watch. "I'll let them tell you about that. Yesterday, they were polite but cryptic. This morning, they paid a second call and were more informative. Enough, anyway, to scare the daylights out of me. Thank heaven they seemed friendly, though. I wouldn't like to face them if I had a bad conscience."

"And they are coming back tonight?" Mathison didn't hide his amazement.

"To talk with you. The name of Emil Burch triggered them off."

"And who is he actually?" That was something Mathison had been wondering about for the last twenty-eight hours, ever since he stood in Bryant's shop and stared down at a check.

Newhart's voice dropped instinctively. "It seems he acts as a paymaster for undercover activities against the United States."

Mathison's amazement changed to incredulity. "They're putting you on, Jimmy."

"You just wait and see about that. In the meantime, have a look at this article—it was published about two weeks ago." He consulted the date heading a page torn from the New York *Times*. "Yes, Sunday, September 18." He handed it over.

Mathison recognized it. He had read the article with astonishment and a touch of vague disquiet—just the kind of combination that helped fix any news item in his memory. He looked again at the headline. URANIUM LOSSES SPUR DRIVE FOR TIGHTER U.S. CONTROL OF FISSIONABLE MATERIALS. "I can almost quote you the first paragraph," he told Newhart. "The Atomic Energy Commission discovered that one of its industrial contractors had lost 'more than 100 kilograms of highly enriched uranium—enough to fabricate six atomic bombs.' Yes, I remember it. I also remember hoping pretty gloomily that someone, for Christ's sake, was doing something about it somewhere."

"Someone is," Newhart reassured him. "I know that we can expect a small loss of one or even two per cent in most manufacturing processes using enriched uranium. But this stuff was U-235—highly enriched—absolutely essential for nuclear weapons. That's the shocker. It seems we have been hitting a new high in carelessness. We are just too damned casual about such things—it isn't as if U-235 grew on trees or could be smelted like iron." And Newhart was off, into one of his newest interests. (He was publishing a book next spring called *The Nuclear Balance of Power*.)

Mathison lit a cigarette, listened intently as he smoked it slowly. The plants needed to produce highly enriched uranium were enormously intricate, occupied vast space, demanded fabulous investments. And, at first, success could not always be guaranteed. The process was exceedingly difficult; for instance, one part of it consisted of four thousand filtering stages. So it could be possible that any country racing to produce nuclear weapons might search for a short cut by procuring U-235 illegally.

"We just don't have enough safeguards at present against unlawful diversion of highly enriched uranium," Newhart ended his account, "and that's the reason why there have had to be investigations in the last few months. *Any* losses, even if caused only by bloody stupidity, need careful checking."

Mathison stubbed out his cigarette thoughtfully. "But what has all that got to do with Emil Burch?"

"Apparently—" Newhart began, and stopped as a buzzer sounded at his elbow. "They're here." He consulted his watch again. "And right on the button." He rose and went to meet the two men who had entered the room.

One was about forty, of middle height, and thin. His face was pale, and tired, as if he hadn't had much sleep recently. He was introduced as Frank O'Donnell. The other was John Lamberti, closer to thirty, fairly tall, broad-shouldered, a healthy specimen with dark good looks. They were both neatly and quietly dressed, with manners to match. They gave Mathison a polite but definite look as they shook hands, refused a drink, and seated themselves where they could see his face.

O'Donnell wasted no time. "I understand you made a copy of the Burch check that was sent to Salzburg, Mr. Mathison."

"I photographed a photograph, to be exact."

"More than once?" O'Donnell sounded hopeful, but he looked prepared for disappointment.

"Four times to make sure," Mathison answered with a grin.

"You have those photographs with you?"

"In that matchbox." Mathison pointed to the desk.

Newhart laughed. "Bill, you slay me. You do enter into the spirit of things."

"I'm glad I did. My hotel room was searched and my Minox emptied of a substitute roll of film I had left in it."

Newhart said, as O'Donnell's eyebrows lifted, "You never told me that when you telephoned."

"It happened later. A lot of things happened later. You'll have to read my report after all, Jimmy." Mathison watched

Newhart's face with some amusement as he picked up the envelope.

O'Donnell spoke quickly. "Apart from the check, is there anything else about Emil Burch in your report?"

"No."

"Would you mind if we got your film developed right away?"

"He's the boss," Mathison said, nodding to Newhart. "It's his lawsuit."

"You're not serious, Bill." Newhart was aghast, forgetting his worries about unlawful diversion of fissionable material and returning to the more everyday problems of settlements and costs.

"Let's say we are lucky that Mrs. Bryant isn't the kind of woman who sues."

"Mr. Newhart," O'Donnell asked patiently, "may we develop those films? The process will take only fifteen minutes or less, even to enlarge them. We'll have prints made tomorrow, but I'd like to have the film developed immediately."

"Couldn't be developed by better experts," Newhart said.

Mathison nodded his agreement, only worrying now that he might have used too much light (or too little) or moved when he was taking the pictures. If they didn't come out well, he'd have no one to blame except himself.

Lamberti was already over at the desk, lifting the matchbox, opening it carefully. He relaxed when he saw the tissue wrapped around the film. "Did you get that clear sample of Eric Yates's signature, Mr. Newhart?"

Newhart produced a letter from his drawer, and, along with the matchbox, it went into Lamberti's pocket. "I'll phone you the minute we get them scanned," he told O'Donnell, and headed for the door.

"Mr. Lamberti," Mathison called after him, "would it be possible to have an extra batch of all the prints? Bryant's file on Yates was stolen yesterday evening. I promised Mrs. Bryant I'd send copies of the photographs to her as a replacement." Lamberti looked interested, but he nodded and left without asking any questions. O'Donnell's eyebrows had gone up a further fraction of an inch.

"Stolen?" Newhart asked. "What the hell has been happening, Bill?"

"Read the report," Mathison said inexorably. "It took me almost four hours slaving over a typewriter last night, ruined

125

my dinner, spoiled my sleep. You don't want me to go all through that again, do you?"

Newhart drew out the three double-spaced pages from their envelope.

"Nothing there about Burch or missing U-235," Mathison told O'Donnell, who was allowing some amusement to show in his quiet gray eyes. "Just how important is this Emil Burch? Where does he tie in?"

O'Donnell looked as if he wished those questions hadn't arisen. He glanced toward the report—Newhart was now reading it with obvious concern—and seemed to measure a reasonable *quid pro quo*. "Anything we discuss here, you understand," he said to Mathison, "is completely confidential."

"Of course. So is that report, by the way. There may be nothing about Burch in it, but there's a good deal about Yates."

"That sounds interesting," O'Donnell said politely. If he was eager to read the report, he was managing to disguise it fairly well.

"There must be some close connection between Burch and Yates—"

"We don't know that yet. First we'll have to study the Burch signature on the check that Yates sent to Bryant. And then we have to compare it with Yates's own signature."

"Didn't you have Burch's signature for his First Maritime account to compare with one of Yates's letters in the Newhart and Morris files?"

O'Donnell nodded. "Burch's writing is upright and very exact. Yates's signature slopes forward and ends in a scrawl. We compared them yesterday and could find no link between them."

"What difference do you expect in the check I photographed?"

"We never expect. We just hope. A faked signature sometimes varies. It depends on whether the writer is using the correct pen for his forgery, or whether he is rushed, or paying less attention."

"You don't sound too optimistic."

"I'm not pessimistic either. A faked signature is a tricky business. Even Burch—or Yates—could make a split second's mistake."

All very interesting, thought Mathison, but it's getting me

nowhere. He tried again. "I'd really like to hear anything you can tell me about Burch. After all, I do represent Newhart and Morris. Anything detrimental concerning Yates is going to involve them in a great deal of unpleasantness. Now let's stop being a couple of lawyers," he said and won an answering smile. "I did hear in Salzburg that Yates is a British agent. Is Burch employed by the British, too?"

That really jolted O'Donnell. "A British agent?" He looked quickly at Newhart, who was in the middle of the report and seemed in no mood to rush his reading of it. "That's something new," he admitted wryly. "Emil Burch is certainly engaged in espionage, but I don't think he is in the employ of the British." He studied Mathison quite openly for a few seconds. "I suppose you are going back to Zürich?"

"That's possible."

"It might be very useful if you did."

To whom? wondered Mathison. "It might also be dangerous if I didn't know something about Burch." What exact business, for instance, did Yates have with Richard Bryant in Salzburg? Anything to do with Yates's possible connection with Burch's activities in the United States? "And I'm not talking just about myself. I could endanger your investigations if I am not properly briefed. You agree?"

Again there was a hint of friendly amusement in O'Donnell's eyes. "You press hard, Mr. Mathison."

"We may not have much time to waste."

O'Donnell obviously agreed with that. "All right," he said. He considered briefly. Then his voice became crisp, matter-of-fact, to suit his words. "We have been investigating a problem dealing with the security of the United States. As often happens in that kind of general probe, we came upon something unexpected. A man, quite above suspicion, was seemingly nervous about the repeated visits our agents paid to the plant where he held a sensitive post. Either he assumed they must know more about him than they actually did or his conscience started to bother him. Anyway, he approached us. Eventually, he made a full statement, admitted he had been recruited quite recently to supply information about the date of certain deliveries at his plant. He had only agreed to supply it, because it appeared harmless enough. And he needed the money. His first payment, however, had alarmed him; it seemed more than his information justified. He hadn't yet spent the money, and he turned it over to us. One thousand dollars in fifty new bills. We tracked their serial numbers to the bank that had received them—the First Maritime at Forty-third. A teller remembered one client who always requested used twenty-dollar bills. "New bills stick together," he said. But three weeks ago, old twenties were scarce, so he had to take a thousand dollars in new bills. He was annoyed. The check was drawn on the account of an Emil Burch.

"It could be a case of industrial espionage," Mathison tried.

"The methods used were too intricate for that." O'Donnell hesitated. He was thinking of the information that had been attached to the inside of a magazine and passed at the busy counter of a New York drugstore to a contact known only as "Tony." The payment, in turn, had been left at a "drop"—in this case, the space under a loose rock near a certain bridge in the park of the informant's home town. (All the man had to do that evening, when the park was fairly deserted, was to walk his dog.) "Tony" had arranged both assignations, using cryptic phone calls and excessive care in establishing contact. (He hadn't turned up for the first drugstore rendezvous; probably stayed in the background to watch the informant's behavior. That night, he had telephoned, arranging the same place and time for a meeting one week later.) He had set another meeting after the first was at last completed safely, but by that time the informant had confessed and two special agents were also there as interested observers. "Tony" was now being watched, all his contacts noted. It would take time before his network was fully discovered, but "Tony" himself had been traced. (That would have distressed him considerably. When he had left the Communist party eight years ago under orders to go underground, he had made the usual moves: all open contacts ended; records destroyed; a change of address from the West Coast to the Eastern seaboard, with a new name and new occupation. Two years ago, he had gone even deeper underground—and away from his old comrades completely—in a shift farther to the left. Again there was a change of name, address, place of occupation. He had concealed his moves well enough; to most people nowadays he seemed more bourgeois than his new set of unsuspecting bourgeois friends.)

O'Donnell shook his head over the deviousness of the

128

political animal's mind. "I think," he said quietly, "we can rule out any case of industrial espionage."

But Mathison hadn't finished the problem of Burch. "He had a bank account in Zürich, too. Right? Which is his main place of business?"

"Zürich. How did you know he banked there?"

Mathison nodded in the direction of Newhart, who was now rereading the last page.

O'Donnell was almost amused. "You have one of those retentive memories, have you?" I'd do well to remember that, he told himself.

"I can be equally good at forgetting," Mathison said pointedly. "So what about Burch? How does he make his money?"

"He is a dealer in fine books, manuscripts, ancient maps. He has his main office in Zürich, and opened up a branch office in New York two years ago. That was when he set up his New York account with the First Maritime."

"It must be an incorporated business." That made the opening of any foreigner's account in an American bank a fairly simple process. "All he needed was a recommendation from his Swiss bank that he was solvent and a good risk."

"He is certainly that. Money keeps coming steadily from Switzerland, enough to cover even the large withdrawals here. No complaints from New York at all."

"Couldn't Swiss Security give you any help?"

"They did what they could. All they could tell us was that Emil Burch's account in his Zürich bank is also in excellent condition. It gets its money steadily, too—from a numbered account."

"Ouch!" Swiss numbered accounts never had any information divulged about them. A matter of Swiss law. "So you'll never know who owns that numbered account or what is behind it."

"All we do know is that Burch's Zürich bank account is being used as a channel to other accounts abroad."

"It seems to me that Swiss Security might become interested in Mr. Burch himself."

"Give them time. He is an elusive man. Travels a great deal, leaves the running of his Zürich business to its manager."

"Searching for fine books, manuscripts?"

"And ancient maps."

This time, they both shook their heads. Mathison had

several more questions, but there wasn't any use in asking them. He had been given more than a fair share of answers as it was. He looked at the tired, haggard face sitting opposite him. There was one big question remaining, though. He risked it. "Why are you so sure that Burch isn't a British agent?"

"Because the British don't need what Burch is looking for."

"Meaning highly enriched uranium?"

"Now who brought that up?" O'Donnell asked blandly.

The British had their own supply of U-235, thought Mathison. So had the Russians, although they weren't telling anything to anyone. The French were now producing the necessary minimum after at least one disastrously expensive mistake. Mathison sat very still. He glanced over at Newhart. *. . . any country racing to produce nuclear weapons might search for a short cut . . . illegally . . . unlawful diversion . . .* "You worry me," he said softly.

Newhart looked up, gathering the three sheets of paper together. *"You* worry me," he said grimly, as he handed the report to O'Donnell.

O'Donnell was a quick reader. He seemed only to glance down the first page. On the second, he went back over the last paragraph, the one that dealt in detail with the constant surveillance of Mathison after his first visit to Bryant's shop. The third page—with emphasis on Finstersee and the parallel of Lake Toplitz given by Anna Bryant in talking of her husband's death near Unterwald—tightened his lips. "I'd like to study this. Have you another copy?"

"It was mailed from the Salzburg airport this morning. By the way, you can add a postscript about that. The two men who watched Bryant's house had come from Prague, but they were leaving for Warsaw. They were speaking Czech."

O'Donnell took a pen out of his pocket and actually noted the postscript in the margin. "All this goes farther than we are allowed to reach, but someone should certainly look into it. This Nazi angle, for instance—we can't afford to neglect that." He folded the report and replaced it slowly in its envelope. His brow was furrowed, his eyes thoughtful. "May I take this with me? I'll have it back in your hands by tomorrow night."

Newhart nodded.

"How many copies do you intend to make?" Mathison asked quickly.

O'Donnell looked surprised and then amused, but he answered frankly. "Two, if you have no objections. One for our classified files; one to pass along to the Agency. Europe is their business."

"The fewer copies the better."

"I agree." O'Donnell was frowning. "You know, Mr. Mathison—there are certain aspects of that surveillance in Salzburg which puzzle me a little. You were followed up to the castle; and then nothing? Not until you got down into the town again?"

"That's right. I thought about it, too. The only reason I could find was—well, I probably was under surveillance all the time, but I wasn't paying so much attention to it when I was up at the castle." He met O'Donnell's quick look with a smile. "I was with a girl."

"Oh . . . An old friend?"

"No. I met her up there. We wandered around together, went for a drink."

"I'm sorry I'm so stupid," O'Donnell apologized in his quiet, earnest way, "but I don't quite have the picture. She was a stranger?"

"Yes," Mathison said curtly. Then, if only to show it had been a pleasantly innocent meeting with a charming girl, he explained Elissa Lang. "Originally, Eliza-something-or-other. But she hasn't used that in years," he ended.

"From Chicago, you said?" O'Donnell asked mildly. "Forgive me if I ask one last question: are you meeting her in Zürich? I believe you mentioned something about her going there to visit her grandmother."

"Well, there was a tentative arrangement. But I doubt if I'll have time now to think of anything except Yates and his blasted files."

"Yes," Newhart broke in. "I've been wondering if he has used our name for any other bogus contract to establish confidence. That was what he was doing with Bryant, wasn't it? Play the poor sucker along and get a first claim on his information?"

O'Donnell nodded, but his thoughts were elsewhere. "Do you mind?" he asked Mathison as he took out his pen and jotted down Elissa or Eliza-something Lang on the flap of the

131

envelope. "Sorry to have bothered you about this. But it is necessary for us to get as complete a picture as possible."

That was a delicate reminder that without a mention of the brief episode with Elissa, Mathison's report could be considered incomplete. Either, thought Mathison with rising annoyance, I turn in a full record of my day in Salzburg or I shouldn't have submitted any report at all. Which was true enough, he admitted slowly. "I didn't think it was important," he said gruffly.

"It possibly isn't." O'Donnell pocketed his pen, ending that subject. "I must congratulate you on your report. It is really very expert."

"You're the professional, I'm the amateur; that's the difference in our approach," Mathison said, recovering some of his good temper. Elissa wasn't important, he felt sure of that. The professional had only given himself another footnote to check. This one would be a waste of time and taxpayers' money, but that was O'Donnell's headache. If he wanted to clutter up his records—

The telephone rang. O'Donnell was on his feet, picking up the receiver before it began its second ring. He listened without interruptions. At the end of the call, he said, "That's fine, John. How long will it take you to get prints made? Enlarged as far as possible . . . Yes, the whole film, a complete job. I'll pick them up. I have to take a late flight to Washington. See you." He replaced the receiver slowly, his mind now several thousand miles away.

"Well?" asked Newhart impatiently.

"It is possible that Yates and Burch are the same man."

"Yates *is* Burch?" Newhart's face drained of color.

"We need definite identification from the experts. But what the photograph shows is extremely interesting. Burch's signature on his check to Richard Bryant is less exactly written, more fluid. Three letters show a close resemblance to the same three letters in Eric Yates' own signature. That may not sound like much, but to the expert in handwriting it can mean a great deal."

"He must have been hurried," Newhart said, "or under some tension."

"Or contemptuous?" Mathison asked. "He was signing a check for a man he had duped."

O'Donnell looked at him, then nodded. "Good-bye," he told both of them, and shook hands warmly. "Thank you for

132

your help. It has saved weeks of searching." Weeks? he thought. It might have taken months to uncover Yates. Perhaps never, if "Burch" decided to cut his losses and fake his own death; those boys were supersensitive to the smell of danger. All Yates would have to do then was keep quiet, sit tight, play the innocent publisher. The Swiss wouldn't even have known that further search was necessary. He said to Mathison, "The Swiss may very well get in touch with you when you are in Zürich. You'd have no objections?"

"Would I be allowed to have any?" Mathison asked in wry amusement. But he could see O'Donnell's point. Now that he knew about Burch, his searches through the Zürich office files might produce something he had passed over last week. Or even Yates's elderly secretary, so tight-mouthed when it came to questions about her employer—for Yates had the power of hiring and firing his office staff—might unbend considerably once Yates was dismissed from his job.

"Switzerland is the host country," O'Donnell reminded him with an unexpected grin. That was something he was obviously never allowed to forget. "You'll hear from us," he promised Newhart, and closed the door quietly.

"I hope so," Newhart said, "but how much will we hear?" He had recovered his normal color, but he was obviously brooding about Yates. He sat down heavily at his desk. "You know what, Bill? I think I'll spend tomorrow in Washington, too. I just want to make sure that—"

"I'd leave it to that guy. There's no good in getting our wires all crossed. Besides, the fewer people who know about Yates, the less chance there is of broken security."

"My friends in Washington know when to keep their lips buttoned."

"Sure. But even discreet enquiries can start some speculation. You don't want publicity any more than the FBI does. Let them handle Washington."

"Well, I'd like you to get back to Zürich right away."

"Hey—give me a night's sleep at least! And a day to sharpen my wits. At the moment, all I can see is a long hot shower and a comfortable bed."

"What about dinner? We could talk—"

"I had dinner several hours ago." And he wanted no more discussions until he had got some thinking done. There was too much at stake here, and not just for the firm of Newhart and Morris, to be blown off in a fine cloud of talk.

"Bill—how much do you trust Anna Bryant? Oh, I could see from your report that you found her sympathetic. But trust is another matter. After all, it's only her word. And she was in a highly emotional state—must have been."

"Are you talking about the contract?"

"No. It's her statement about those god-damned Nazis." Newhart had served in the European theater in World War II, all the way from Normandy to Berlin. "You were only a kid at school, but I saw the liberation of one concentration camp, and I tell you—" He checked himself. "Okay, okay, I'll tell you another time. Better go and catch up on your sleep. I'll call you tomorrow. And Bill—thanks. I mean that."

Mathison left the small room, its photographs of family and friends beaming from every wall, crossed over the yards and yards of soft gray carpet in the outer office with its hunting prints and mahogany and copper lamps, entered Linda's preserve with its equally soft carpet (Audubon prints here, in dark-green frames), and found her knitting a thick-stitched sweater. She seemed to have worked some of her gloom away, for she looked up with her usual bright smile. But this time, it was he who was preoccupied. Tactfully, she said nothing.

"Oh, I nearly forgot," he said, almost at the door, putting down his bag and searching in his pocket. He brought out the letter that Bryant had sent to Newhart two weeks ago, the letter that had been the start of everything. He stood looking at it, remembering Anna Bryant's face as she had identified that letter.

"I'll take it to Mr. Newhart at once," Linda told him, and folded up her knitting. "Good night, Mr. Mathison."

"Good night," he said, still several thousand miles away.

One small letter, he was thinking as he went into the long corridor, one polite but businesslike letter packing a charge of dynamite. Finstersee ... What was so important about Finstersee that a man would risk his life?

10

WEDNESDAY WAS A DAY OF WAITING, AND MOST OF THURSDAY. Bill Mathison had to use considerable restraint not to telephone Jimmy Newhart with questions about O'Donnell: what have you heard, what's going on, what has he run into in Washington—deaf ears, bland smiles, gentle reassurances? Newhart's patience was certainly under similar strain. The idea of Yates, back in Zürich from his German trip, quietly at work in his office—in Newhart and Morris's office—was enough to boil Jimmy's temper into an explosion as high as Krakatoa.

Mathison made a protocol call to his own office down on Wall Street and had an amiable chat with Muller, one of the senior partners (Newhart and Morris business unfinished; this quick visit back to New York merely a matter of consultation). But apart from a couple of brisk walks in the crisp autumn air, and a lonely dinner at his usual steak house on Third Avenue (no good making a date with Peggy or Nan and having to break it), he spent the rest of his time in his own apartment. He had often wished for a couple of days to himself in the middle of the week; now, he had got them and he couldn't enjoy them.

His small apartment was comfortable—it faced south, so that the sun streamed in—and the white walls of the living room were covered with teak bookshelves in a broken-rhythm pattern at its sitting end. What was more, the shelves weren't cluttered with bibelots and cute bottles but actually contained books, some rather battered, for he had been gathering them together ever since he was in college, yet these old friends weren't saying much to him at the moment. He stacked pile after pile of records onto the stereo: Bach, Ravel, Haydn, Prokofiev, Mozart, Sibelius, Vivaldi, Shostakovich, Verdi, Fischer-Dieskau singing Schumann, Callas trying *Norma* (not her best effort; he'd have to find another recording), Schönberg, Bach again, and Bach. At least they kept him good company while his mind circled around the closely packed events in Salzburg. He had the odd, unpleasant feeling of being poised above his own life. Everything had come to a stop, and he was waiting. It was like the day after his final exams, or his induction into the army, or his interview for a job with Strong, Muller, Nicolson and Hodge. Just waiting, wondering, wishing, wanting, all wrapped up in a package of not-knowing.

The hell of it was, as he told himself several times on Thursday morning, he sensed something was going on in Washington. He even conjured up momentarily a small bare

135

ugly room with three serious men quite oblivious to their surroundings or the war in Vietnam or the threatened bust-up of NATO, so engrossed were they in—guess what?—three pages of William Mathison's typing. (That at least gave him a loud laugh, although that sounded damn silly, too, in the lonely apartment.)

By two o'clock on Thursday, he had finished his gourmet luncheon of slightly burned omelette, overmelted Brie, chilled Sancerre (at least that was a success) and left the cluttered mini-kitchen for Mrs. Pyokari to clean in her morning visit. He got his feet up on his favorite black-leather sofa, opened the book he was reading—a new novel about a British Intelligence network working in Berlin where the hero was his own best enemy, everyone was tired and old and cynical, all so meaningless, mess without end Amen Amen. The telephone rang. And it was Newhart.

Jimmy wasted no time. "Yates is missing."

"Yates?"

"Just had a call from that secretary of his. Miss—"

"Freytag. What did she have to say?"

"He didn't get back to Zürich on Tuesday night, didn't appear at the office yesterday morning or today. His housekeeper says he hasn't been home since a brief visit on Saturday."

When he was supposed to be in Germany, thought Mathison. It gave him a strange feeling to realize that when he had been working late in the empty Zürich office on Saturday, Eric Yates had been prowling through the town. "What else did you learn?"

"What else? Bill, it took me ten minutes to get all that out of Miss Freytag. The woman's practically hysterical. Scared stiff."

Old self-contained precise Miss Freytag? "I'd better leave for Zürich and take charge of his desk and papers. And when he gets back, I suppose I question him about the contract as a sort of lead-in to a telephone call with you? Or do you want to come over yourself?"

"That would emphasize everything, don't you think? We'll play it down. You talk with him, then keep him beside you while you call me. Right?"

"Anything in particular that you want me to say to him?"

"Use your own judgment. You're in charge, Bill. Just get this business cleaned up." Newhart dropped his voice to a normal tone. "Our quiet friend of the other evening is worried in case Yates has left for a long vacation."

So Frank O'Donnell was on the job. That was good news at least. "A permanent one, perhaps?"

"Could be. That Saturday-night visit to his house was to collect his passport."

Mathison restrained himself from asking which one; Newhart was in no mood for jokes at the moment. "How did our quiet friend find that out?"

"Swiss Security has been busy."

"I'm glad to hear someone has. What about our quiet friend himself?"

"He has just left on a long trip. Sent you his best. By the way, about that trouble you've been having with your stereo, the two men I recommended will be over to fix it this afternoon. Sorry I took so long to get hold of them, but they're quick. They won't delay you."

"I hope they know their business," Mathison said, recovering from his surprise. "I have a couple of imperative questions."

"They're fully qualified. Don't worry about that. Now two more things: I'm sending Mrs. Conway to Zürich—she's head of our translation department and a bit of a linguist. She lost her husband some years ago, by the way. She's a capable girl. She can manage the office there until I find a replacement for Yates. That's going to take some doing, I tell you."

Better luck next time, thought Mathison, and again restrained himself.

Newhart went on, "She knows something about the situation. I told her about that funny business with Bryant's contract. If you have to expand on that, you'll find you can trust her. She's extremely discreet."

That, thought Mathison gloomily, means she is past her first youth and has given up hope. "It might be simpler if you would send a man."

"Arnold is in Houston, Bernstein's wife is in the hospital, Johnstone is seeing an author through labor pains—complete revision of galley proofs or we'll have a turkey on our hands—and Paradine is on jury duty. Besides, none of them knows both French and German. Like to be a publisher?"

"Hardly worth the wall-to-wall carpeting. Hey—I nearly forgot. Did you get the prints of the photographs I took?"

"You'll have them this afternoon. I think—perhaps—you might even deliver them personally in Salzburg."

"Isn't that stretching the expense account?" Mathison asked with some amusement.

"Yes, but it may be cheaper in the long run. At least, that's what I am beginning to think. What's your opinion?"

"Yates was in your employ and empowered to act for you. You've always stood by any commitments he made. The fact that you never imagined he would make this kind of commitment is not much of a defense in a law court."

"Then it is possibly wise that you see Mrs. Bryant, explain personally."

"I think that's the least we could do. She is as much an injured party as you are. If she were less honest, you could have some kind of lawsuit faked up against you."

"Better get some signed clearance from Mrs. Bryant, don't you think?"

"That's necessary. And I'd suggest a token payment on that kind of quitclaim. What about the equivalent of the original advance—three hundred dollars?"

"So you think a copy of the contract might turn up?"

"Always possible. Pity it's such a small amount." She would need every penny she could get, Mathison thought.

"You advise giving her more?" Newhart asked worriedly.

"No. That would look as if we were cajoling her into signing. Which we are not. By the way, if you had been publishing a book such as Bryant's, what kind of advance would you have expected to pay?"

"Well, for a first book by an unknown author—five hundred would be considered generous. Some publishers would pay no more than four hundred, actually. Why do you ask?"

"Just curiosity, I guess." Yates really was cheap, Mathison thought. Even a couple of hundred dollars more would have meant a good deal to the Bryants. "It's really a hell of a thing," he said irritably.

"And none of our doing." Newhart was now indignant as well as angry about that. "Anyway, you clear it up. Get this business finished so I can start thinking about publishing once more. I have enough problems of my own."

"I'll handle this one. As quickly as possible."

"Do what you see fit. And good luck, Bill."

Mathison booked his overnight flight back to Zürich. He

ought to be there, even allowing for fog and drizzle, by early morning. Their time. Back to that again, he told himself, as he started repacking his bag.

In the kitchen, the house telephone sounded a raucous warning. Two repairmen about the aerial, the porter announced from the basement. They came up by the service elevator, both in gray work trousers, checked flannel shirts that had been through a hard day's crumpling, short zippered jackets soiled and sloppy. "This Mathison?" one of them asked, broad shoulders atilt with the large heavy box he carried in one hand.

You ought to know, thought Mathison as he nodded to John Lamberti. "In there," he said equally brusquely, pointing across the small hall. He looked at the other man, who had coiled yards of lead-in line over his arm. He was about Mathison's own height which meant, on good mornings after a deep sleep, five foot eleven. He was fair-haired; wore it long, shaggy at the neck, wild over the ears and forehead as if he had just come out of a wind tunnel. He was possibly near Mathison's age, too. Certainly no more than thirty-five. Features were even, a kind of handsome nothing face that made little impression, perhaps because it was kept so empty of expression. But once inside the living room, the blank look was wiped off, and the light-blue eyes were coolly appraising. Mathison appraised right back.

Lamberti dumped his heavy load on the rug and said, "Well, now that you've met each other, let's get to work. His name is Chuck, by the way."

"Charles Nield," the other said. He had a pleasant voice. He took out a cigarette and wandered over to look more closely at a Callot etching on the wall. He has a quick eye, thought Mathison; that is the only original I own, all four square inches of it. "Go ahead, Jack, I'll wait my turn," Nield called over his shoulder.

"We won't take long," Lamberti assured Mathison. "We know you are flying out this evening."

"Not the same firm?" Mathison was watching Nield with some speculation. "I thought you might be the Lamberti Bros."

Nield laughed. "Perhaps we ought to merge. We made quite a good double turn coming up in that elevator, I thought."

Lamberti glanced at his watch and concentrated on an

139

answer for Mathison. "Today's pretty exceptional. We thought we'd save time and a lot of security headaches if Nield came along with me. I can vouch for him. Sometimes it may be hard to believe, but he really is on our side."

Nield had wandered to the other end of the room, where he was selecting a record. It was the Rossini Sonatas for Strings. He turned it low. "D'you mind? After all, we are supposed to be testing the machine, aren't we?" Then he sat down in the most comfortable chair and studied the scrap of New York skyline that could still be glimpsed through the windows between the new high-rising apartments to the south.

"I didn't know you co-operated," Mathison told Lamberti and turned away from watching Nield. Cool, thought Mathison, very cool.

"In this case, we had to. Just as we've had to co-operate with the Swiss, and Nield's people are now talking with the British. It's an involved problem."

"Like Yates himself."

Lamberti nodded and plunged into business. "There are two things that Frank O'Donnell wanted me to tell you. Don't use that telephone number—the one that Mrs. Anna Bryant gave you."

"Yates's number? The one her husband was to call the minute he got back to Salzburg?"

"Right. The Zürich police have traced it. They want to keep the wire clear for any of Yates's friends to use. No good making the Swiss think you might be one of them; that just adds to their work, and they've got plenty."

"What did they find at that address? Any confirmation that Yates is Burch?"

"They found that, all right. So far, they haven't discovered exactly who are his bosses. That's what they are working on now." Lamberti studied the rug. "That's about all I can say on that score. But O'Donnell may see you in Zürich. He is there for a quick conference with Gustav Keller, his opposite number in Swiss Security. The second thing I have to tell you, actually, is Keller's description. This is to help you recognize him easily if he does get in touch with you. Keller is O'Donnell's height, but heavier in build. Gray hair, cut short. Dark mustache. Round face, high color, gray eyes. Small neat feet. Got the picture?"

Mathison nodded.

"So that's that. Two things: avoid using the telephone number—forget it altogether, in fact; and remember Gustav Keller."

Mathison nodded again.

"And here are the copies you wanted of your photographs." Lamberti drew out a Manila envelope from an over-size pocket inside his jacket. "With our thanks."

Mathison opened it eagerly, looked at the prints with interest. "I didn't know they could be blown up to this size. Not so clearly, at least. You did a good job." He riffled through them. Yes, as promised, there were two sets: one for himself, one for Anna Bryant's pilfered files.

"They've been useful," Lamberti conceded. He glanced at his watch again. "How long do you need, Chuck?" he called to the other end of the room.

"Ten minutes possibly." Nield was on his feet.

"We'll make it fifteen to allow you time for a few bright remarks. I'll check the house aerial on the roof." Lamberti turned to Mathison. "You have one up there?"

"There are television aerials—"

"Good. I'll see where I can attach something to help out your radio reception." He left, picking up the large coil of lead-in transmission line in professional style.

Charles Nield shook his head. "I shouldn't be surprised if he is a fully paid-up member in some television or radio repairmen's union, and you'll find yourself with a perfectly legal aerial." He chose another comfortable chair. "Shall we sit down?" He nodded in the direction of the phonograph. "We'll let that play. Background sound is a comfort. Inspires talk." He smiled, and for that moment the quiet impassive face warmed into life. Then he glanced at his watch, casually, yet his eyes promised he could be just as businesslike as Lamberti. "As John said, today is rather exceptional. This is the only way I could meet you without losing any time. That's the real purpose of this visit: identification for future use, if necessary."

"You're vouched for," Mathison said with a grin. "If I meet you in Switzerland, do I know you?"

"I think not—at present. But these things change so quickly. If we have to meet, let me handle it. And it may not be in Switzerland. Austria is what interests us."

"Finstersee?"

Nield shot a quick look at him, then nodded briefly. "I've

141

read your report, of course. What do you really know about that little lake?"

"Just what I wrote."

"That's all? Nothing to add?" Nield hid his disappointment well.

"Only a question of my own. What's so important near Finstersee that would make Yates risk his main operation by starting something on the side?"

"Main operation?" Nield's eyebrows raised slightly.

And now we are getting away from the subject of Finstersee, thought Mathison with amusement. I'll have to earn any direct answers, obviously. "Well," he said, branching off obligingly, "for the last thirty-six hours I've been trying to find a shape to the whole problem around Yates. There just isn't any—if you treat it as one problem. Cut it into two, and you begin to find some sense."

Nield nodded, lit a cigarette.

"You know all this. Or you wouldn't be here."

"Even so, I'd like to hear you out." The voice was friendly, encouraging.

"Let's put it this way. One of Yates's arms stretched toward the United States. In that operation—his main one; it's been going on for two years, hasn't it?—he used the cover of Emil Burch and his business in manuscripts and old maps. But his other arm was free to pick up anything interesting, anything he thought extremely useful. Somehow, through Richard Bryant, he had a chance to make a grab at Finstersee. And he did. So, we've discovered two operations, quite separate in scope and purpose. Yates was their starting point. That's their one link." He watched Nield carefully, but there was only the same noncommittal nod. "And that brings me back to my original question: what's so important near Finstersee that Yates would risk so much?"

"Risk?" Nield asked with interest, avoiding the real question. "Yes, it does seem that way at first. It was the Burch check to Bryant that betrayed him. Yet, how else was he to pay Bryant the customary advance on a contract?"

Cash would be too unusual, Mathison thought quickly, and so would any personal check signed by Yates. Bryant would certainly have asked questions. And no one would ever have seen that check if Bryant had not photographed it for his files. No one would even have known about the contract if Bryant hadn't written Newhart. "We owe a lot to Bryant, don't we? Who was he working for—the British? Then they must know about Finstersee."

"No more than we do. There are always periodic rumors, rather self-effacing ones with very little substance attached, about all that Styrian lake district in the Salzkammergut region. I suppose it's because the Nazi Foreign Office took over Salzburg; Ribbentrop established himself there very comfortably toward the end of the war. So did some Intelligence units of their SS."

"You think they may have left some records behind them?"

"It's one of the guessing games we all play," Nield said with a disarming shrug of the shoulders. "But we don't have to guess any longer about Bryant and for whom he was working. We heard from London this morning. Neither he nor Yates was working for them. They don't believe Bryant was working for anyone. He has been out of Intelligence completely, as far as they know, since he resigned in 1946. That resignation was very quickly accepted, by the way."

"Oh?"

"Nothing serious. A matter of personal opinions. He had a good war record, but in Vienna he didn't measure up. The British made a cryptic comment about that: 'He was the type who liked to choose his wars.' He couldn't believe that a former ally was no longer friendly. The Cold War was beginning to raise its ugly head, and he wouldn't recognize it. Blamed his own side when things turned nasty, and in Vienna they were properly nasty. Anyway, he quit British Intelligence in '46 with some harsh things said all around. Their last report on him, made in 1956, said he had seemingly 'mellowed over the years' and was now less apt to blame the West. At least, he hadn't drifted into the Russian camp, and that was all that worried the British."

"So he has been out of touch with them?"

"Completely."

"And Yates?"

"He bowed out from British Intelligence in 1947. He had been given nothing important to do for almost a year, which means that the British couldn't have been too sure about him. It was all done very quietly, of course."

"Too quietly, it seems now."

Nield looked as if he agreed with that, but resisted any comments and went on with his facts. "He went back to teaching science in school. Then he left for a job in Tokyo, as science editor of an English-language magazine, and branched into running a scientific digest quarterly that was published in Geneva. He came to visit America just over six years ago, in time to impress your Mr. Newhart, who was looking for an international-minded representative in Zürich. His qualifications seemed good, I admit. But as far as being an agent for the British—well, their answer to that question was 'Not on your life!' Which," added Nield with a shake of his head, "is a piece of advice that poor Bryant should have heard." He stubbed out his cigarette in the heavy smoked-glass ashtray that lay on the coffee table. He seemed to be studying its shape. He spun it around slowly. "You will see Mrs. Bryant, won't you?"

"Possibly."

"She might have the answers to a lot of questions."

"She might. But I don't intend to ask them."

"Why?"

"Do you want her killed, too?"

"She may be killed if she doesn't get proper protection. Her husband needn't have died, you know. Not if he had been in touch with us or the British. You just don't go out alone to find—" Nield cut off abruptly. "Not nowadays," he went on. "You need people with you, and behind you; you need a lot of help when you are up against a well-organized machine. The Nazis may be scattered and they may be few—at present, anyway. But one thing they have always been, and that's organized."

"So you believe the Nazis killed Bryant?"

"It's likely." Nield gave the ashtray one last gentle spin. He looked up at Mathison. "You had better know one certainty before you visit Bryant's house again. It will be watched. And anyone who seems to be closely connected with Mrs. Bryant is going to be watched."

"I've already been watched," Mathison reminded him curtly.

"Possibly the Austrians were checking on you. That's understandable in the circumstances. They are neutrals, you know. But what you could face now is not just surveillance by a neutral country protecting its interests. It could very well be Nazis, and that is another matter entirely. If they've been guarding certain lakes in Austria and Czechoslovakia for more than twenty years, they aren't going to let their

144

secrets be discovered now—at least, not without exacting their own price. It may be no more than five years before they judge the time to be ripe for them to come out into the open. And when that happens, they don't intend to come ill-prepared. What they have saved from the past, they'll keep. If they can."

"Bluntly, you're saying that if the Nazis did kill Bryant, because he was edging too close to one of their secrets, then they'll eliminate anyone else who might just share his knowledge."

"Exactly. I hope for Mrs. Bryant's sake—if she does know anything—that she's playing absolutely dumb."

Mathison said with a touch of sarcasm, "Until, of course, you can start protecting her." And what guarantee could there be, anyway? . . . Dear Mrs. Bryant, we assure you that you'll be safe for a month. Or would you prefer six months? There is nothing to fear, believe us. . . . "And how the hell do you manage that?" he asked angrily. Damned if I go near Salzburg, he thought. I'll write her a business letter, enclose the photographed documents for her files. Period. I'm not going to push her into further danger.

"First, we have to learn whatever she knows. Then we can work out a plan to find whatever Bryant was searching for. We'll take the action. And she'll be protected, because we won't let her seem to be connected with us in any way. Don't worry about that."

"What if she doesn't want to tell you anything?"

"Then we'll have to act on our own. And so will three or four other interested countries. It could be a nasty mess. The Nazis might be the only winners." Nield reflected for a long moment. "My own fear is that Anna Bryant or her brother— Johann Kronsteiner—will try to go it alone, and they'll fail. Just as Bryant failed. That would be the real disaster for her."

"Go it alone?"

"Sell to the highest bidder," Nield said shortly.

"She didn't strike me as that kind of—"

"What about her brother? He could persuade her. She sounds the dependent type—the kind of woman who leans on someone else. With Bryant gone, who is she going to lean on?"

"She may have more strength than you think," Mathison

said. He was remembering her flight from the Dietrichs' house, her insistence on staying in her own home.

"Let's hope the Nazis don't hear you say that," Nield said grimly. "Her best chance at present is to look completely helpless. And totally ignorant."

Mathison rose, paced the narrow length of his living room for a couple of turns. His anger was cooling and, with it, his resolve to change his plans, not go anywhere near Salzburg, not ask Anna Bryant any questions. He would have to go. He had no intention of probing into her private business, but someone had to warn her to keep quiet. Someone had to tell her she shouldn't trust people as quickly as she had trusted him. "I'll try to see her and persuade her to play innocent. That won't be difficult for her. She is an innocent." He turned back to face Nield. "You may not like it, but I'm going to advise her to forget all about anything her husband told her—for her own safety."

"That's a start at least," Nield said amicably. The important thing was to reach Anna Bryant. She would decide for herself. He rose, looking pointedly at his watch. "Don't tell me our aerial artist is going to be late." But Lamberti was already ringing the doorbell. Mathison broke off staring at Nield, went to answer it. Either Nield is a good loser, he was thinking, or I've just agreed to what he wanted done in the first place.

Lamberti was regretful. "The super followed me up onto the roof, wanted to see what I was about. He says he won't have any more yards of spaghetti dangling down the side of his building. So no aerial. Too bad." He picked up his box of tools and handed the looped length of line to Nield. "Ready? I bet you can't wait to get out of that fancy dress." To Mathison, he said with a wide grin, "Chuck is really the diplomat type. You may find it difficult to recognize him next time you meet. Well, good luck with your journey. You won't forget what I told you?"

"Phone number, no. Keller, yes."

"That's it. Good-bye."

"Auf Wiedersehen," Nield said.

Mathison turned off his record player, closed the windows, and then stood looking out into the street for a few minutes. Put together the various small pieces of information that

Nield had discreetly dropped here and there, and the total result was an indirect answer to Mathison's first question about Finstersee and its importance. All in all, it had been a fair briefing, Mathison reflected. Incomplete, of course; it had to be. But sufficient to keep him from obvious blunders or way-out guesses that would add to the possible dangers. Danger ... Was there really as much at stake as Nield thought?

The solid block of buildings stared back at him from across the street. His eyes swept over the sameness of its windows, over the small strips of balcony rising in exact tiers like shallow drawers half opened in a giant's dressing chest. Each had its planters of green shrubs, pots of frost-wilted geraniums or newly added chrysanthemums, reminders—like the white chairs and tables—of the city dweller's perpetual schizophrenia: the longing to be in the country, with an open door and garden, while living in the middle of a metropolis.

On impulse, he opened the window wide and looked down on Sixty-ninth Street, eight floors below him. All was late-afternoon confusion: cars parked, cars moving, cruising taxis, an ambulance wailing its way through the crosscurrents of traffic. From the avenues at either end of this block came the steady roar of a busy city, a constant surge of sound. Anyone who wanted to enjoy his miniature terrace must not only keep his eyelids closed, but develop a system of ear flaps too. Then Mathison saw Lamberti and Nield emerge from the service entry and cross the street to a panel truck parked between a battered Chevrolet and a polished Jaguar. New York, New York ... They looked completely authentic, even to the way they walked. And the expert method by which Lamberti eased the light truck out of a tight squeeze into the stream of westbound traffic seemed part of his daily stint. ACME RADIO QUICK SERVICE was the legend that now was putting on a spurt of speed to make the light at the corner.

Certainly quick, Mathison thought, as he closed the window again. The sky was pale blue grayed over with a fine film of smog, clear of clouds, no storm blowing in from the Atlantic, no cutthroat wind sweeping from Canada. Good flying weather, at least. He headed for the bathroom for a shave and shower, pulling off his sweater and open-necked shirt as he crossed the hall. He was back to thinking about the Acme Quick Service boys. But, he reflected as he dried himself vigorously, was all that setup actually necessary? A

147

purely civilian remark, they'd possibly think if they could hear him. They weren't the type to waste time and energy, not even in answering that kind of question.

He weighed himself on the scales. One hundred and sixty-eight pounds, just holding the line. His muscles were firm, thank heaven, and his hair still thick, his color healthy. That was the trouble with being a lawyer: there was a tendency to become desk-bound. He'd make a point of getting some exercise in Zürich, some fresh air free of smog. Would there be any time off at all for some mild mountain climbing? Usually there was never much time off for anything—office work was a slave driver. But after he was dressed in tweed jacket and flannels, he repacked his bag, adding a heavy sweater and socks, thick walking shoes, and a windbreaker. With his two business suits and good shirts waiting for him in Zürich, he was all set for anything.

One last look around the apartment ... He picked a couple of books for company (one was *The Rise and Fall of the Third Reich*, the other *The Last Battle*.). Then he wrote a check and a quick note of directions for Mrs. Pyokari. ("Keep some food in the refrigerator," he added as a postscript, remembering the emptiness that had welcomed him home on Tuesday night.) And that was everything. Except for the unanswered correspondence that had piled upon his desk in the last week. Two invitations to weddings of people he scarcely knew, a suggestion for a weekend at Aspen this winter from a girl he had never liked in the first place, several cocktail notes from acquaintances who did their entertaining in all-at-once style, the usual summonses to black-tie dinners from hostesses eager to find the unattached man to balance the extra woman at their tables. But there were also the first-of-the-month bills, two letters from friends, and a list of engagements he had already made. These he slipped into an envelope addressed to his secretary down at Strong, Muller, Nicolson and Hodge, along with a quickly scribbled note. She could deal with them. And as for the rest— The bachelor syndrome, he thought gloomily. Well, there was one way to get rid of that before you were properly hooked. He swept the pile of cards off his desk into the trash basket.

11

THE LIGHT BREEZE WHIPPED THE BLUE LAKE INTO A DANCE OF broken ripples that sparkled in the early-morning sun. A few die-hard yachtsmen had sneaked down to the little boat anchorages strung along Zürich's left shore, and were spending their breakfast hour in a quick sail. Bill Mathison unpacked, watching them from his hotel room, which overlooked Uto Quai's wide promenade with its constant succession of small harbors and swimming pools, and quite frankly envied them. They were expert in the way they'd sense the change in wind, tacking or veering neatly as they kept close to this side of the lake. Few careened dangerously, even as the breeze quickened, or came to an ignominious jobble with sails flapping helplessly. Fine fun, he thought, just ten minutes away from your office.

And that reminded him to call the Zürich branch of Newhart and Morris as soon as he finished breakfast. Perhaps he'd even wait until nine o'clock and give Miss Freytag the chance to be fully established at her well-run desk before he let her know that he had returned from New York. Come to think of it, his New York visit was all she did know about his recent movements; when he had left Zürich for Salzburg last Sunday, there hadn't been time between his quick decision and his flight out from the Kloten airfield to leave any message with anyone. Not that he had wanted to leave any message; not that he needed to, either. Remembering the cool restraint of Miss Freytag's welcome last week, he had felt he would never be missed if he didn't show up on Monday morning. Possibly Yates had been to blame for the polite-freeze treatment, although Yates had been genial enough to Mathison's face. "Why, Bill, good to see you! Too bad I'm just rushing off." Hearty handshake, hefty pat on the shoulder, a broad honest beam on a big handsome face. That was Yates, good old warmhearted, quick-witted Yates. Where was that son of a bitch?

But by half past eight, Mathison had shaved and showered and changed his clothes and finished the pot of coffee; and the sailboats had already come back to shore. Perhaps the clouds now swelling over the hills around the lake had a special message for yachtsmen. Or offices were open and bustling. It might be time to telephone Miss Freytag.

She was there. She was so upset that she could hardly speak. Yes, she said in the first of a series of monosyllables in reply to his questions: Had Mr. Newhart called yesterday from New York to let her know he was returning? Was Mrs. Conway arriving later today? Had she found a comfortable hotel for Mrs. Conway? Had she any news of Mr. Yates?

"Yes." The dam broke. She was weeping. "Dreadful news," she said in between her tears. "He is dead. He was—he was—"

Dead? Yates dead? "I'll be right around."

"I have to go and identify the body. Oh, Mr. Mathison, I just can't—"

"I'll come at once. Wait there!"

The Newhart and Morris office was only a normal walk of eight minutes from his hotel. Today, Mathison made it in five, cutting away from the lake shore for a couple of blocks until he hit the busy street that ran almost parallel to Uto Quai. There was a short stretch of heavy traffic to be negotiated, and an abrupt rise of wild wind that blew off hats, rattled shutters, tore at awnings, and even broke a window a few steps behind him when a sign swung off its hinges and dashed against the glass. By the time he had reached the small square surrounded by handsome shops and offices, less than two hundred yards from where the window had crashed, the squall had subsided. He chose the staircase to reach the office on the floor above the restrained apothecary shop, whose polished counters had never seen ice-cream soda, hair curlers, or paperbacks in their eighty years of life. Stairs were quicker than elevators for a short haul, just as walking had been quicker than telephoning for a taxi and waiting for it to arrive.

The office was actually a suite of five rooms, spreading in depths to the far-off rear of the building, linked by a narrow corridor. Heads popped discreetly out of opened doors as his running footsteps were heard on the staircase, and then quickly withdrew like a batch of polite turtles. Miss Freytag was in her small office adjoining Yates's room—the large front one with its bow window on a level with the copper-brown treetops in the square. Through the open connecting door, he heard the sound of movement and low voices. He

150

glanced inside. Two men had started to examine Yates's files. Keller's men, possibly.

"They are from Urania Street," Miss Freytag said. She didn't look at him. She was sitting on the edge of a chair, wearing her coat and hat, purse and gloves clutched ready to leave. A grave-faced man, equally ready to leave, stood behind her. He was obviously an official of some kind, judging by the impersonal glance and bow in Mathison's direction. Ordinary plain-clothes detective, or one of Gustav Keller's special security detail? Mathison wondered as he nodded back and then turned to Miss Freytag. She was calm now. Perhaps numb with shock.

"Miss Freytag," he said gently, "you don't have to go anywhere. I'll attend to this matter. But what happened?"

"Thank you, Mr. Mathison," she said in her most precise manner. Her small-boned white face looked up at him briefly. "I must go." The faded blue eyes flickered away from his.

"All right. I'll come with you."

"There is no need. This gentleman will—"

"He can guide both of us. Now let's call a taxi."

"A bus will take us right past the door."

"We'll have a taxi today," Mathison said, keeping his voice gentle. She rose obediently to telephone for one. He noted with amazement that she ordered a small cab, not the medium or large type that cost progressively more. When Freytag got a grip on herself, it was a good one. "What happened?" he asked again.

The grave-faced man answered in German.

Mathison repeated the flat statement in English just to make sure he had got it right. "Yates's body was found in the lake early this morning, about ten miles south of Zürich?"

Miss Freytag ignored the question. The man nodded. He understood English, all right, but perhaps he didn't want to risk his dignity in trying to speak it, for he used German again. "His sailboat was overturned. It had drifted near the shore."

"But when did it happen?"

"Last night. Otherwise, someone would have seen the overturned boat yesterday."

That could be true, Mathison thought, remembering the long stretch of Zürich's suburbs into small towns and villages on either side of the lake. No one would call this area of

151

gentle hills under-populated. There must always be some eyes watching the water. "Was he—" Mathison began, and then stopped, conscious of Miss Freytag. "We had better get downstairs and wait for the taxi," he said. His question was possibly an unnecessary one anyway; Yates must have been trapped in the overturned boat, if they had both drifted in together. He didn't argue, either, that she should stay here and let him have the grim task of identifying Yates's body. She was walking quite determinedly toward the elevator, a tall spare woman in a brown tweed coat with everything—shoes, gloves, purse, felt hat—to match.

It was the man who had been Yates, now lying inside a refrigerated drawer. Miss Freytag barely flinched, but her white face became almost gray. Mathison nodded to the watchful men who were gathered in the room. "That is Eric Yates," he said, and took a firm grip on Miss Freytag's elbow to get her out of there. She was steady enough; it was simply that her feet seemed anchored to the tiled floor, just as her eyes were fixed on Yates's torn lips.

Outside, Mathison decided that a walk would be good for both of them. She didn't speak at all until they had come down through the narrow, twisting streets to the swift-flowing Limmat River that divided the older part of the city in two before it poured itself into the lake. She sighed heavily, looked at Mathison as if she had just become aware of him. "I must get back to the office. Mrs. Conway will soon be there. I must show her every—"

"First, we'll have a cup of coffee." He led her toward a café on the Limmat Quai. "We both need it," he told her. "Just ten minutes to pull ourselves together."

"I don't need—"

"I do," he said firmly. "In fact, I think the doctor prescribes Scotch for both of us."

"But I never—"

"All right. Coffee then. Now come on. This way." He edged her inside the doorway, found a table in that section of the room. The lower half had its usual quota of journalists and professorial-looking types from the University up on the hill. They were talking quietly, reading papers, playing chess. That partly reassured her.

"You see, there *are* women here," he told her, noticing two others at a corner table.

152

The word "women" seemed to distress her slightly. "Yes, ladies do seem to come here," she said, looking at their tweeds and felt hats with approval. She fell silent, but her eyes were beginning to be interested in her strange surroundings. Mathison watched her quietly. She was more than ever a puzzle. She had obviously suffered when the news of Yates's death had reached her, but now there was a dignified restraint, almost an impersonal calm. Was she behaving as she felt she should for the lawyer from New York?

"Do you live in Zürich or in one of the suburbs?" he tried. And that released a small torrent of information. She was delighted to talk about her mother, now eighty-five but really so young at heart, with whom she lived in an apartment near the University. Her father had been a librarian there; he played chess, too; he had passed away ten years ago. So now she looked after her mother, and they lived in the city because it was so much quicker to reach home from the office; her mother was confined to their apartment anyway, so a garden would have been useless. All in all, it was a practical arrangement, much less worrying than traveling any distance into a suburb in case—in case she was ever needed very quickly. She enjoyed her work at the Newhart and Morris office. She had a lot of responsiblility, which she had tried to face as well as possible.

"I had a feeling you almost ran the show," Mathison said.

That pleased her. But, "Oh, no!" she said, "Mr. Yates worked so hard. He was a wonderful man. Kind, generous . . ."

So there she had reached the topic of Yates, bringing it into the placid context of her simple life, his bruised and smashed face receding into pleasanter memories. Mathison relaxed. "He was very good to you and your mother?"

"Most thoughtful. He always sent her flowers at Christmas."

Did it take so little as that to win her loyalty? "I know you must be worried about the possible changes at the office, but I—"

"Mrs. Conway?" she asked quickly. Yes, that worried her.

"Mrs. Conway is here only for a short time, simply to report back to Mr. Newhart and keep him informed."

"I could have done that. I have always done my best for Newhart and Morris," she reminded him virtuously.

"Of course you have. But you seemed so upset on Thurs-

153

day when you telephoned Mr. Newhart that Yates was missing. He thought a stranger might be able to handle a difficult situation more easily."

"I was very upset today, too, when you telephoned me." Her voice was low but calm. "And yet, you see now how controlled I am. Mr. Newhart could trust me."

"But he does. So do I. We all trust you. You are highly capable, and completely honest."

She flinched slightly. "I try to be. But—" Her eyes, which had constantly dropped to his chest level or to his shoulder as she talked with him, looked at him frankly. For a brief instant. Then they were staring at something invisible at another table. "This last week has been terrible. I think I knew that something awful was going to happen to poor Mr. Yates."

"Why?" he asked sympathetically.

Her eyes flickered back to his. She seemed to decide something. She sighed and opened her solid leather purse. "I knew that something was wrong when he did not come to collect these. He had said he would pick them up on Monday morning at my house, very early, on his way to the airport." She pulled out a small black folder and handed it to him. It contained traveler's checks. Not many; two hundred dollars' worth in Eric Yates's name; enough for a quick business trip. "Oh, I'm glad to get rid of these," she said thankfully. "But what will we do with them, Mr. Mathison? We can't put them back in Mr. Yates's drawer. The police started their search of the office with his desk, and I didn't tell them I had the traveler's checks. I mean—how could I? You see, I hadn't told the other policeman—the one who came on Monday morning asking questions about Mr. Yates and his friends in Salzburg. So how could I start telling the police today that I had had these checks all the time? Mr. Yates had asked me to say nothing about his visit to Salzburg to anyone. He was hoping to clear up the mystery of that terrible man Bryant who had worried the New York office with his letter. And Mr. Yates was going to tell you all about it when he returned with a signed confession from Bryant. Mr. Yates said it was the only way to handle this business and smooth everything over without any trouble for anyone. He was thinking of the good name of Newhart and Morris. He always did." She looked at Mathison anxiously, and then

154

at the traveler's checks in his hand. "What *do* we do now?" she asked pathetically.

"I'll deal with this," he promised her. With an effort, he kept his voice casual. "But first, you might tell me just what happened this last week. I thought Yates was in Germany visiting some authors. He left soon after I arrived, didn't he?" He waited for the answer; its truth or untruth would let him know how much or little Greta Freytag was to be believed.

"He didn't go. He learned that one of the authors was in the hospital, another on vacation. So he decided to postpone the trip. He had a lot of work to do at home—studying our readers' reports on recent books and articles, you know. So he didn't come into the office. That's quite normal—he often works at home."

"When did you hear all this?"

"On Sunday, just as we were having one o'clock dinner after I had been to church. Mr. Yates telephoned and explained everything then. He needed some extra money for his trip next day to Salzburg, and because he was so busy he asked me to get it from his desk in the office when I was out for my Sunday walk along the promenade if it wasn't too much trouble. He was always so thoughtful."

"Yes, he thought of everything," Mathison said wryly. "Did he ask about me?"

"But of course. He was sorry he was so busy that he couldn't see you until he got back from Salzburg. He thought perhaps you were working too hard over nothing."

"I suppose he saw the lights burning late in his office on Saturday night. I was a bit of a nuisance, wasn't I?"

"I'm sure he never felt that. He just felt that the only way to solve the problem of Bryant was to see him personally. There is nothing in our files at all about that man."

As I can now well believe, thought Mathison. "And if you had seen me working in the office on Sunday, you weren't to tell me anything?"

She flushed slightly. "Only to assure you that Mr. Yates had the solution to the problem. You could easily go back to New York, and he would telephone you there on Tuesday. He really was upset about all the unnecessary bother you were having. He felt it was a reflection on the integrity of our office."

"And he worried a great deal about that."

"But of course."

"That policeman who visited the office on Monday morning—was he in uniform?"

"No—just in plain clothes like the two who are there now. But he had an identification, and he didn't ask to see any files or anything important. He just wanted to know what friends Mr. Yates had in Salzburg. I thought he might be after that Bryant, too."

But not as a policeman, Mathison thought. On Monday morning, Swiss Security hadn't known about any Richard Bryant in Salzburg; they hadn't even known about any connection between Burch and Yates. None of us knew. Not on Monday morning. "Did the two policemen who arrived at the office today ask you any questions about Salzburg?"

"No. They were interested in a man called Emil Burch."

Then they are authentic, Mathison thought with relief. Burch-Yates was the target for both the FBI and Swiss Security. Gustav Keller had moved in quickly as soon as he had got the excellent excuse of Yates's death. And that changed everything. I won't need to search through these files, Mathison realized; Keller's boys will have done the job. I won't have to meet Keller either; so forget those neat small feet. Strange how things keep twisting in this investigation, just like Yates himself. Every time I learn something new about Yates, I have to change the plans that I thought were definitely settled and straightforward. I didn't really need to come back to Zürich, after all. . . . How often does this kind of thing happen to Frank O'Donnell, or to Charles Nield? How much trouble and effort spent on a project that abruptly ends with the death of a man? Or plunges forward in another direction? Shifts emphasis, changes shape? If I ever meet either of them again, I'll congratulate them on their fast footwork as well as their patience. No one would get very far in counterespionage work if he didn't possess both these items. "More coffee?" he asked quickly, noticing her returning dejection. And keep talking, he told himself. She's too used to being neglected. "Yes, let's have another pot. And have a chocolate éclair. Come on. It looks inviting on that tray."

"I really couldn't."

"Of course you can. It seems to be raining outside. We can't leave yet." He signaled to the waitress and set things in motion. "And what did you tell the policemen about Emil Burch?"

"He is a dealer in very fine maps. Mr. Yates bought two from him. Mr. Yates used to visit the old bookshops in town. He collected ancient maps. That was one of his hobbies."

Yes, Yates had thought of everything, even to an excellent excuse for entering Burch's place of business. Almost everything, that was. But somewhere there had been a slip, worse than signing a faked Burch signature to a check. It had cost Yates his life. "Sailing was another hobby?"

She nodded. "He hadn't so much time for it recently. Last year—well, he used to spend every Saturday afternoon on the lake when the weather allowed." She opened her purse again and found a wallet. "This is the way I am going to remember him," she said sadly. She drew out a snapshot. "I took this, one Saturday afternoon, when I was walking on Uto Quai." The white cheeks flushed slightly as she handed the color photograph over to him. It was Yates, quite unaware of the camera's distant eye, a tall handsome man of fifty with a cheerful face. His hair was wind-blown, his cheeks tanned. He wore Bermuda shorts and a heavy cricketing sweater, its V neck rimmed with his college colors. He had one foot on the wooden dock, the other stretched out to his light sailboat. He had an arm out, too, holding it to someone who was standing on the pier, gripping her hand to help her into the boat. The shape of a slender wrist was all that could be seen. Miss Freytag had cut her out very neatly.

"Who was his friend?"

"No one important. Just a girl who was living in Zürich last year. She left, this spring." Miss Freytag took back her precious photograph. She shook her head as she looked at it. "Why must the good always be taken from us? Such a handsome man."

"And so kind." He was getting pretty tired of Yates's imposed image.

She looked at him quickly.

"So kind," he said, trying to recover his mistake, "in taking a lonely girl for a Saturday afternoon of sailing. What was her name, do you know?" Of course Miss Freytag would know; she would make it her business to find out who was the pretty menace to her daydreams.

"Eva Langenheim. She came to the office to inquire about secretarial work. She didn't get it. But that is how they met. A forward girl. I could hear her laughing during the interview as if she was quite sure of obtaining the position."

"She was in Yates's office?"

"She just walked in. I thought she was a friend until Mr. Yates told me afterward that she was a stranger to him. She was a very forward girl."

"Have you any other photographs? Perhaps one that shows Miss Langenheim?"

Miss Freytag almost choked on her last forkful of éclair. She stared at him. "Now why should you want to see them?" she asked coldly.

"I think the police might like to learn about any of Yates's friends."

"But why would they—"

"They are investigating his death."

"I couldn't—no, I really don't want to talk to them."

"I think you should. Just tell them everything you have told me. They'd be grateful."

"I couldn't," she repeated, panic-stricken. "The scandal—"

"No scandal. Everything will be handled discreetly." He watched her gathering her gloves and purse, buttoning her coat, ready for flight. "Just think of it as your duty," he tried.

That stopped her.

"But don't talk to just anyone who says he is a policeman and flashes a badge at you. Especially if he is trying to question you about Yates's friends in Salzburg."

Miss Freytag was no fool. "Are you trying to tell me that the man who visited the office on Monday morning was *not* from the police?"

The only man who could have known on Monday morning about Yates's connection with Salzburg was either one of his own agents—and he wouldn't have come asking questions— or one of the opposition, who had stopped Yates from making that trip he had been planning to see Richard Bryant. Abduction was a grim word, but it might be the key to Yates's death. Mathison said, "I think that man sounds a bit of a phony. You can find out that very easily, though. Just ask the two detectives who are now working through Yates's files."

"But if he wasn't a policeman, how could he have me followed?"

"What?"

"Followed. After he left, I saw him speak briefly to a man

down in the square. And that man walked behind me all the way home that evening. He was outside the office again on Tuesday. And on Wednesday. And yesterday, too. But today— I could see no one."

"Good God," he said quietly, and saw her flinch. "No wonder you were in a state of nerves when you telephoned New York." That softened her face again. Sympathy was what she needed. Sympathy and praise for a self-sacrificing life, for duty faced and work well done. Yates must have laid them all on with a trowel. And suddenly Mathison felt deeply sorry for the faded blue eyes that rarely dared look at a man directly, for the thin pale lips and the neat lank hair cut in a no-nonsense bob. "Miss Freytag," he said very gently, "you go home now, and I'll take care of Mrs. Conway or anyone else who turns up at the office."

"But this is Friday, and there is so much to do before the weekend." She shook her head pityingly at his lack of knowledge about the running of an office.

"How much work will get done today?"

"But—"

"Just go home like a good girl."

She was half converted. "I really should be there to welcome Mrs. Conway. We are expecting her this afternoon."

He shook his head. "Do as I say." Then he added in a tone as severe as her father had probably used, "I insist."

That did it. She waited patiently as he paid the bill, refused the suggestion that he would call a taxi, made her ladylike good-bye on the Limmat Quai. Unexpectedly, she relaxed. "And thank you so much, so very much," she said with a rush of emotion. "You've been so kind, so thoughtful, so—"

"Good-bye, Miss Freytag. I'll tell the office you'll be in on Monday." He turned away to walk briskly toward the busy square with its rattle of trolleys as they came over the bridge at the head of the lake. And the sooner I get out of Zürich the better, he thought, as he remembered that look of gratitude.

"Mr. Mathison!"

He looked around in disbelief to see Miss Freytag almost running behind him.

"Mr. Mathison," she said, dropping her voice, trying to catch her breath, "that man who followed me on Monday and Tuesday—he was waiting outside the café. I saw him start to follow you. So I thought I had better warn you." She had the good sense to keep looking at Mathison as if they were discussing some afterthought that concerned only them.

"Where is he?"

"He is at the edge of the quay. He is watching the swans. He is wearing a very wet raincoat, dark gray in color. And his hat is gray. It *is* the same man, I assure you," she ended earnestly. "He is quite young, about your age."

"Thank you for that."

"He has fair hair, good features. He looks so nice. It is incredible he should do this, isn't it?"

"Follow people around? Yes, there are more graceful ways of making a living." Mathison's thoughts were racing as he talked. "Miss Freytag, would you mind very much if you changed your plans slightly? Before you go home, will you telephone our office and speak to one of the detectives there? Tell him quickly about this man. Tell him that I am going to try to lead the man right into his arms. Ask him to have a reception committee waiting for us just inside the front door. Will you?"

She nodded, almost smiling. "You have such an odd turn of phrase, Mr. Mathison. A reception committee—yes, I'll try to arrange that." Then her voice changed to a solemn church whisper. "Is that man connected with Mr. Yates's death, do you think?"

"You may be right."

"Then we must see he is caught."

He's worth questioning anyway, Mathison thought. "And thank you, Miss Freytag."

"Yes, we must see to that," she said determinedly as she turned and walked sedately away. She did not glance in the direction of the loitering man. Neither did Mathison. He strolled on, looking neither to right nor to left.

Behind him, the man stopped admiring the slow-cruising swans and followed.

12

BILL MATHISON REACHED THE BRIDGE AT THE JUNCTION OF river and lake, and had to wait for the traffic lights to change. Only then, surrounded by people, did he glance around casually. And there was a fair-haired man in a dark-gray raincoat, now increasing his pace to join the crowd waiting for the signal to go. As the green light flicked on, they surged across in a tightly packed phalanx before the spate of traffic, dammed safely for a brief minute, would again sweep down like a flash flood. Mathison was willing to bet that the Zürich pedestrian was quicker in his footwork than even an old New Yorker.

He headed for the quiet of the broad promenade of Uto Quai, and strolled along the lake. It was comparatively peaceful except for the sparrows; one group clustered on the ground just ahead of him with fiendish chirps. And then he saw that they were intent on pecking one of them to death— the bird had stopped fighting back, was lying in the center of the scrum, cowering and resigned. Mathison pulled out two francs from his change pocket, threw them hard at the circle of sparrows, and sent them protesting into the branches of the trees. "Go on, stupid!" he told their victim, and waited until it had regained enough gumption to fly into the deep cover of a tangled bush. Then he picked up the coins, taking the opportunity as he bent and straightened to look briefly back along the Quai. Miss Freytag had been right. The man was following him.

Mathison's progress slowed to a saunter; he must give Miss Freytag time enough to get that call through. So he studied the hills across the lake as if he hadn't anything else to do. There was scarcely any breeze now, and the clouds had vanished, leaving only sodden leaves underfoot to prove there had been a heavy shower while Miss Freytag and he had been at the café. He stopped twice: once at a boat anchorage, another time at a complex of swimming pool and dressing rooms. But he didn't look back for the rest of his journey. Let's keep the man happy, he thought. No good discouraging him only to have another, and unknown, face following me doggedly around. I learned that little lesson in Salzburg.

But, he wondered now, is there any connection between those men who tailed me in Salzburg and this one? No ... Almost certainly no. Gray Raincoat is simply interested in anyone who may be closely connected with Yates. He must have been hanging around the mortuary on University Street this morning, waiting to see who came to identify the body.

161

He knows who Freytag is, but he becomes curious about me. So he follows us to the café at a time when neither of us is in a mood to notice anything very much. We talk and talk, and he becomes even more curious. I'm the question mark. I may even be a new lead. Is that it? Quite possibly. But in Salzburg last Monday, it was something else again. That American agent, Nield, suggested the Austrians might well investigate any stranger who came asking about Bryant on that particular morning, and in his quiet offhand way Nield could be right. But what Austrian knew of my visit to Bryant's shop except Anna Bryant's brother? (Yet he seemed hardly the type to initiate any surveillance.) And that friend of his, of course: Zauner. Felix Zauner?

As Mathison crossed the bustling street that edged the lower side of the square on which the Newhart and Morris office lay, he stopped thinking of Zauner. The business on hand was right here, now, in Zürich. And if the man who followed him was working for neither the Swiss nor the Austrians, the only way to find out where he belonged was to catch him. Concentrate on that, Mathison warned himself. He reached the square and stopped dead in his tracks. It was almost empty. Across its central garden, there were a few people and some parked cars, but on the sidewalk ahead of him there was nothing but a clear view right to the Newhart and Morris building. And Gray Raincoat knew this square, knew the office entrance. He would not have to follow Mathison. He could stand at this corner, feeling reasonably unnoticed, and mark the doorway Mathison entered; there was nothing to block his sight or confuse his judgment. Damn it, thought Mathison, as he lit a cigarette to cover his indecision, who would have guessed the square would be so empty at this hour? You've made things too easy for him; you'll never get him near that doorway. Or will you?

He began walking, but slowly, to give the man time to get into position at the corner. No doubt Gray Raincoat was already guessing that Newhart and Morris might possibly be Mathison's destination. I bet, thought Mathison, he imagines he can stop worrying. Well, we'll see about that. He threw his unfinished cigarette into the gutter, looked around him quietly, carefully, to add some proper color to his behavior, and stepped quickly into the apothecary's shop that lay one door ahead of Newhart and Morris.

It had dark wood paneling, large jars filled with colored

liquid, a handsome display of mortars and pestles, and a delicate scent of lime. A middle-aged man in a starched white coat was wrapping a box of pills in stiff white paper. Mathison watched, fascinated with the precision of the miniature mitered corners. Red wax, heated over a thin candle flame, was deftly applied and sealed. "Now," said the chemist as he laid the package at one side of the dark polished counter, "what does the gentleman wish?" Polite eyes peered at Mathison over rimless glasses.

"Some cough medicine."

"For yourself?"

"For my sister."

"How old is she?"

"Adult."

"I see. May I recommend one of the usual brands? They are—"

"I'd prefer something you would make up."

"You have a prescription?"

"Unfortunately, no, but I am sure you must have an excellent prescription of your own."

"It will take a few minutes."

"That is perfectly all right." Indeed it was. The longer, the better. Let's make Gray Raincoat a little less sure of me, Mathison thought. How long would it take to make him uncertain enough to investigate?

"Would the gentleman have a seat?" The chemist gestured to the leather armchairs before he vanished behind a screen of shelves, each with its neat arrangement of tightly packed apothecary jars.

And that might be a good idea, thought Mathison, choosing the chair that was cornered near the half-curtained window. Sitting down, he was hidden from any curious eyes on the sidewalk. The man who was following him might even be forced to enter and make sure that Mathison wasn't meeting someone inside this quiet, dimly lighted room. A man in his profession must always suffer from inflamed suspicion and a ruptured faith in the innocence of other men. Would he rise to the bait? Why not? Mathison in those last crucial moments on the sidewalk had tried to look as devious a character as ever dodged inside a doorway. Within five minutes, thought Mathison, I'll know whether I've flubbed the whole deal. Why the hell did I have to be so god-damned clever and tell Miss Freytag to get the detectives to stay just inside the

163

hallway next door? Yet, if they had been out on the sidewalk or even standing down at the corner, the man would have noticed them and taken flight.

So Mathison waited, sitting quite motionless, his eyes on the closed door. All he needed was a man hesitating on the threshold.

The door opened. Mathison was halfway to his feet, but it was only a little old lady in a black sealskin coat who walked to the counter and collected the small white package. The chemist was already out of his hiding place, bowing and smiling and making pleasant talk about the concert last night. For madame's taste, the violins had been too heavily muted. And then, Mathison became aware that someone was standing outside the open door. The man, trying to look into the shop without actually stepping inside? Or another customer? The curtain at Mathison's elbow was opaque linen and blocked any view of the square. If it was the man in the gray raincoat out there, Mathison thought, he is as much on edge as I am. More so, perhaps; he isn't even sure now that I am still here. If only the old girl doesn't nod to me graciously on her way out. . . .

But she didn't. And the chemist, with one last bow over his clasped hands, was retreating behind his screen. Mathison heard her voice saying acidly, "Excuse me." There was a slight shuffle of feet as the man stepped aside. Mathison moved.

He was at the door, his left arm thrown in a strong grip around the man's shoulder, his right hand tightly on a wrist he forced back. "Why, Bobby old buddy, good to see you!" he said clearly, genially, as he applied quick pressure on the wrist and twisted it behind Gray Raincoat. Surprise had given Mathison a moment's advantage; speed did the rest. He jerked the man inside the next doorway, saying, "This way, buddy boy," and swung him into the dark hallway. It was empty.

She didn't telephone, Mathison had just time to think before he had a real scrap on his hands trying to keep the struggling man's hand out of the raincoat's pocket. He was shorter than Mathison, but agile. He twisted around, used his knee. Mathison dodged back so that the savage thrust only grazed him, but even that doubled him up and loosened his grip. The man slipped free. A small automatic came out of his pocket.

164

"That's enough!" a voice called, and a janitor came running down the hallway from some service stairs at its rear.

Thank God, thought Mathison, and then stared at the running man. He was fixing a silencer to the revolver he carried in one hand. Mathison straightened up, and his unspoken question was answered as the janitor said crisply, "Get him moving, Hans! Take him out the back door. Let's leave no mess in the hall."

Hans prodded Mathison's spine with his automatic. From somewhere overhead, perhaps on the landing above, there was a soft movement of light heels.

The janitor looked quickly up at the staircase beside the elevator and then back to Mathison. "Move, you!"

I'm damned if I move, thought Mathison. What I do is shout and drop flat on the floor and hope, all at the same time. He took a deep breath, ready to yell. And at that moment the long menacing silencer stopped pointing. The janitor turned and ran.

Hans whirled around to see what had scared off his friend and hadn't even the chance to use his automatic. Three men had moved quietly in from the square outside and were already within gripping distance.

Two handcuffed him while the third came over to Mathison. He had gray hair cut short, a dark mustache, high color, worried gray eyes. And his shoes were not only brightly polished, but small and neat. Gustav Keller, thought Mathison, and sat down on the stairs, feeling like a marionette whose strings had been cut. He eased his legs, rubbed the inside of his thigh. "I'm all right," he assured Keller's raised eyebrows. "And where did you spring from?"

"We were in a car across the square. I am sorry there was a little delay, but I had to alert my men at the back of this building."

"Lucky you were there." The feeling of complete futility returned briefly as he remembered forcing Hans into a hall without a policeman in sight. He took a long deep breath. "Miss Freytag said she'd call the men upstairs," he explained, shaking his head over women in general.

"She did better than that. She telephoned headquarters and asked to speak with the man investigating Eric Yates's death."

Mathison stared incredulously, and then began to laugh. "That would get action."

Keller's normal smile came back to his round, genial face. "We had a front seat for the performance, you might say. You puzzled us for a bit. That apothecary's shop—" His smile broadened. "Pity you could not see this fellow being gradually drawn toward it." He looked over at Hans, his amusement fading. "He will talk, that one," he predicted. "And now we have two of them. A nice bonus."

I hope, thought Mathison worriedly. The other man was a tougher specimen than the disconsolate Hans.

Keller's relaxed mood ended abruptly as a shot sounded from somewhere outside at the back of the building. Lightly, he ran toward the rear door. Mathison's worry deepened even if that shot had not been fired with a silencer. The man must have made an effort to escape, if shooting had been necessary. Had he managed it? Mathison glanced over at Hans, who may have had the same thought; he had brightened visibly. And then his face grew tense, even frightened. Keller was returning, quite unperturbed.

"Tried to escape," Keller said. "He was shot in the leg. Painful but efficacious." He nodded to his men. "Get that one out of here. His friend has already been taken away." He looked grimly at Hans. "You won't be alone when you stand trial for Yates's murder."

Hans stared at him, his white face turning to look over his shoulder as he was firmly led toward the back of the hall. Then he shouted, "I had nothing to do with it. Nothing. I never—" He was pulled out of sight, protesting.

"I'd put my money on the other man," Mathison said, remembering Hans's relief when he thought his friend might have escaped. "Murder? Was that bluff or—"

Keller's hand went out for silence. He looked up the staircase in annoyance. A small crowd had been gathering on the landing overhead, and now the more inquisitive were pushing the others ahead of them down the steps. "No cause for alarm," he called up to them crisply. "Get back there, all of you! Go on with your work!"

"Wasn't that a shot we heard?" someone asked.

"Backfire. No one is in any danger."

"I told you it was only a motor bicycle," another voice announced, and the group of people receded to their own hall.

"Where are your two men?" Mathison asked. They hadn't appeared on the stairs.

"They had orders to guard Yates's room, no matter what disturbance was created. We've been expecting something. But not exactly this." Keller took a seat on the stairs, too. "Now, would you tell me why that man was tailing you?"

"I suppose he was interested in anyone who seemed to have a close enough connection with Yates. I identified his body."

"Miss Freytag was with you?"

"Yes. She recognized the man. He had followed her earlier this week. So he was definitely interested in Yates. But there was something else I wanted to tell you." Mathison frowned, trying to remember. "Oh, yes—photographs. Miss Freytag sneaked a few snapshots of Yates when he went sailing last year with a young woman. She was apparently a pretty good friend of Yates. But you'll have to ask Miss Freytag very delicately about all that." He tried a small joke. "She's quite a girl, Miss Freytag. Duty, stern daughter of the voice of God . . . That's your best approach."

Keller studied Bill Mathison with something that might have been sympathetic tolerance. "Indeed."

"Was Yates murdered? Can you make that charge stick?"

"I think so, once that frightened little man starts talking. Yates was dead, you know, before he was jammed into an overturned boat. We learned that only half an hour ago. But in any case, we are arresting these men on a weapons charge. And that other fellow—he faces more than that. We shall have to find out what he has done with the janitor, the real janitor, who is German, now a naturalized Swiss citizen. Did he use force or threats to remove the man so that he could take his place? And for what reason?" Life, at this moment, seemed extremely interesting to Inspector Gustav Keller. His eyes actually sparkled with the problems confronting him. "We could have charged them, of course, with your attempted murder. They did threaten you, didn't they?"

"Slightly."

"But it would be much safer for you if we kept your name out of this whole affair. I don't think," Keller added slowly, "that any other member of this group was watching the square. They seem to be slightly understaffed. As far as we have been able to find out, they are only a handful of people."

Mathison looked at him quickly. "Nazis?"

"Possibly. We have had our suspicions for some time, but

they have been careful to avoid all trouble—until this week. I wonder what goaded them into action?"

Finstersee? Mathison stayed silent.

"At least, we now have something to—" Keller stopped short, once more glared up the staircase. "Does no one use the elevator any more?" he demanded angrily, rising quickly to his feet.

Mathison's head turned. He rose, too, looking with surprise and a good deal of pleasure at the girl who stood half a flight above him. She was slender and long-legged, auburn-haired and blue-eyed. Even from this distance, the bright color of her eyes was quite definite and most remarkable. Now, thought Mathison, that's the kind of secretary to have. She must work with the interior decorator on the floor above Newhart and Morris; she certainly didn't belong in the firm, or else he would have seen her last week and his few days in Zürich might have been less work and more fun. "Excuse me, please," he said in German. "I am in your way."

"Not at all. I always step around people on staircases." Her German was extremely correct. "It's a pity to disturb them. A stone step is such a warm and comfortable place. But I am so sorry I scared off your friend."

Mathison, dusting off the seat of his coat, looked around for Keller. He had slipped away.

"I did want to tell him that the elevator is not working. Someone has probably left the door open." She passed him, head high—she obviously did not like to think of herself as an unwelcome intruder—as she walked to the elevator to investigate. Behind her trailed a vague cloud of delicate rose and jasmine.

"Let me," Mathison said, coming to life, following quickly. The door had indeed been left ajar. He closed it. He tried to think of something to say in German, but at the moment all fine phrases had left him. "Do you speak English?"

"With an American accent." She was smiling at last, and her voice was friendly.

"Suits me," he said with relief.

Her blue eyes widened. "You aren't a Swiss policeman?"

"Whatever gave you that idea?" She seemed to be leaving, so he walked along the hall with her.

"They seemed to be everywhere. You know, that was the *third* time I tried to get down those stairs. On the first try, I heard a German voice saying 'Let's leave no mess in the hall,' which rather intrigued me, I must say."

"For my part," Mathison said with a grin, "I didn't know whether to feel relieved or insulted."

"It couldn't have been much fun for you at the time," she agreed. They had reached the doorway, and she was studying him curiously. Then she saw he was watching her with just as much interest, so she looked quickly away at the placid trees and neat flower beds. She plunged on quickly, "I glanced over the banister and saw a man with a gun. Sorry, pistol, isn't it? I always get these things wrong. Anyway, he was aiming it at your back. So I got ready to scream."

"I'm glad you decided you were on my side."

"It was purely instinctive."

"Still nicer."

She laughed and said, "I played coward. I saw three more men slip into the hall just at that moment, and they all had guns—pistols."

"I never thought the difference mattered very much: they have the same effect."

"So instead of screaming—my throat seemed to get stuck— I turned and ran and tried to get two policemen upstairs to go down and investigate. But they wouldn't leave their post. You know, they looked at me as if I might be some kind of accomplice. It was all crazy. Completely crazy. Then the shot was fired—and it *was* a shot; I know motorcycles—and I tried to get downstairs again. But by that time your friend was very much in command. He is a policeman, isn't he?"

"Something like that. But why do you want to know?"

"I'm trying to piece everything together, I suppose. It was a rather bewildering morning, you must admit. I never thought Zürich could be like this," she added lightly. And I've never talked so much to a stranger either, she thought in rising embarrassment. "All that long explanation was really an apology. I feel I almost let you get shot."

"I don't see what else you could have done. Unless you wanted to have two bodies mess up the hall."

"Most untidy. The Swiss would never approve." Then she looked at him quickly. "We *are* joking, aren't we?"

"I hope so," he said and managed to look reassuring.

"Just what did happen here in this hall?"

"A long story."

"Oh." End of that topic, she thought. "Well, I'll say good-bye." She glanced uncertainly down the quiet square. "If I cross that busy street and keep on going, do I reach the lake? It's my guiding point. You see, I've just arrived in Zürich. Dropped my suitcases at the hotel, didn't even have time to get my bearings."

He stared at her unbelievingly. Could this be Mrs. Conway? As young as this? With humor and warmth, totally feminine? Smartly dressed, with quiet elegance—excellent gray wool suit over a blue cashmere sweater, a deep-blue fleece coat over her shoulders, shining black pumps and pretty stockings? She looked as if she had risen late and spent at least an hour on preparing herself for the outside world.

"I was just trying to guess your name. Could it be Conway?"

"Yes," she said, surprised. "Lynn Conway." And now it was she who was staring. "You aren't William Mathison?"

"Bill Mathison." He shook her hand with mock solemnity. "How do you do, Mrs. Conway? Welcome to Zürich, city of Zwingli and numbered bank accounts."

She recovered. "You aren't at all what I expected."

"My sentiments completely."

"But I mean—you really don't behave like a lawyer, not the ones I've met. I thought they kept all their fighting for court."

He said quickly, dodging that subject, "Shall I show you where the lake is? We seem to have taken root on this sidewalk." He fell into step at her side, or almost. It was one of his to one and a half of hers. They had passed the apothecary's shop and he hadn't even noticed it.

"I thought you hadn't arrived yet. I'm really so glad you *are* here," she was saying most seriously. "Tell me—what is going on? Two plain-clothes men in Yates's office, the whole place disorganized, and no one could find Miss Freytag for me. Oh, I know Yates is dead, and I'm not being heartless. But frankly, there is a lot more involved than just a missing contract, isn't there? There must be. . . ."

"A lot more. I'll put you in the picture as much as I can over lunch." And then, as he noted hesitation in her blue eyes—the bluest blue he had ever seen, putting her coat to shame—he added quickly, "You *are* free, aren't you?"

"I ought to telephone Jimmy Newhart," she said slowly. "And there are other calls, too. Miss Freytag, for instance."

"Protocol is always easier to handle after a good lunch.

170

Besides, there is no use calling New York until at least three o'clock."

"Of course. How stupid of me." She was remembering the time lag. "I feel so—so disoriented. It was really a bewildering arrival."

"Where are you staying?"

"The Eden au Lac."

"That's handy. I'm almost next door. Let's walk to your hotel, and you can unpack. I'll call for you there at one-fifteen. Frankly, you don't even need a dab of powder, but I'd better wash and brush up." He was acutely aware that his coat was dust-streaked and his shirt collar had lost a button. Suddenly, he halted abruptly. "Good God, I may be arrested any moment. Would you wait? Please? Won't be a minute!" He was already running back to the apothecary's shop.

She hesitated, and then she waited. She remembered his parting grin. Bill Mathison was a man of surprises, and she didn't meet too many of them nowadays. He kept his word, too. He returned in less than a minute, with a small white package in his hand.

"All ready and wrapped. Not an eyebrow lifted," he reported delightedly. "Not one explanation necessary, just the hard cash."

"A very Swiss package," she said, admiring the neat red seals on the mitered corners.

"Cough medicine. Special brew. We'll feed it to the swans after lunch." He was quite decided they were going to have lunch together. And dinner, too. "Zürich can be a very pleasant place," he assured her as they set off at a brisk pace toward the lake. He liked this new fashion of low heels for women; it let them walk instead of teeter-totter.

"Yes, even thugs don't want to clutter up a hall with any mess. Who were they?"

"Nasty types. The one who pointed his automatic at my spine had been following me around this morning."

"Here? In Zürich?"

"Yates lived in Zürich, remember? But let's leave all that until later and not spoil our appetites."

"I have a thousand questions," she warned him, and glanced at the package in his hand. Cough medicine? She shook her head, trying not to laugh.

"After lunch," he insisted, and had his way.

171

SEDATE SUITS, IMMACULATE CHESTERFIELDS, GRAY HOMBURGS, thin attaché cases grouped in small clusters near the doorway of Bill Mathison's hotel. The bankers were waiting for the cars to take them to luncheon or a conference, perhaps both. The junior men crowded the sidewalk, while the older ones stayed inside the shelter of the lobby, hats in their hands, their heads, with their closely brushed hair, an array of shining gray helmets.

"It will soon be over," the porter told Mathison as he collected his key at the desk. "They start leaving tonight."

"Think of the fun I've missed by not being here this week."

"Please?"

"A very impressive sight."

"Indeed, yes. A very great honor."

"Any messages?" A rhetorical question, as much a matter of habit as of hope. My friends in Zürich, thought Mathison, are not the type to leave messages at a hotel desk. Possibly, too, their business with me is over. Gustav Keller's nimble disengagement this morning is a fairly good indication of that. I'm the fellow who may ask too many questions. Where is quiet Frank O'Donnell, for instance? Any chance of meeting him here, or is he already on his way back to New York to pick up the threads of his investigation of the Burch angle of Yates's peculiar life? And Charles Nield—is he already in Salzburg, concentrating on Bryant and Finstersee? Plagued by his own questions, which kept bobbing up no matter how he tried to push them firmly to the back of his mind, Mathison could imagine the barrage he would have to face over a lunch table today. Lynn Conway was too intelligent not to be curious, and if she was responsible for the Zürich office for the next few weeks, she certainly had to know some basic answers. Just what can I tell her? he wondered.

"No messages," the porter said. He had searched thoroughly through pigeonholes and undercounter shelves.

"Thank you." Mathison turned to face the lobby, straightened his tie, hoped the popped button didn't show, and made his way around tall green plants in huge majolica pots to the quiet corridor where the elevators were hidden.

"Bill!" It was a woman's voice. "Bill, how wonderful!"

Elissa? Good God, he thought, and I didn't telephone her; I forgot all about it. He turned slowly. And it was Elissa Lang, dark hair loose to her shoulders, gray eyes teasing. She was dressed in the same smart fuzzy tweed coat, the same flat-heeled buckled shoes.

"You never telephoned," she said laughingly as they shook hands.

"I just got back to Zürich this morning."

"Where on earth have you been?"

"New York."

"How cryptic!"

"Oh, I had to go there for some consultation."

"Was the contract so involved as that?"

She has a good memory, he thought. Now what did I tell her about Bryant's contract? Nothing very much, surely. Just an off-hand mention when she asked about my business in Salzburg. "No. It was a matter of letting the publisher know the details so he could make up his mind what to do. And how are you?"

"Let's talk about us over a drink in the bar."

"Sorry, Elissa. I have a lunch date for one-fifteen. And after that I have to be at the office. Business. But what about a drink this evening? Or lunch tomorrow." He frowned. "No, tomorrow may be filled with business, too." Or that trip back to Salzburg, he thought. "Let me phone you this evening; I'll be more definite then."

"Come and have a drink now," she pleaded. "Just half an hour. I'm leaving Zürich."

"So soon?"

"I'll tell you all about it in the bar." She turned and led. He could do nothing but follow, glancing worriedly at his watch. Half an hour would bring them to one-fifteen. He would have to keep this chat to twenty minutes. It was always the way, he thought wryly: last week in Zürich, he hadn't talked with one pretty girl; today he had two beauties on his hands. He did remember to pull off his coat, hand it with a tip to an aged retainer in the lobby with instructions to have it sponged and pressed and in Room 307 within half an hour. His jacket had been protected by his coat and looked all right. He adjusted his tie again, and concealed the gape of his shirt at its neck. One of his shoes had been badly scuffed, right over the toe. His favorite shoes, too, dammit. They'll never be the same, he thought with annoyance as he chose a table near the door.

"Nothing intimate?" Elissa asked with that enchanting smile, which she was turning on today in full force. She glanced at one cosy corner where the subdued light scarcely carried, but sat down without any further comment and let him help her with her coat.

"Too many bankers around." There were a few, here, who seemed to be cutting classes. Or perhaps they had business of their own to attend to. The huddled heads looked serious. "Now what's this about leaving Zürich?" he asked, determined to keep the conversation on Elissa. That was the surest way of avoiding his own complicated affairs. "The Martinis are good, by the way. Will you risk one?" He ordered two with neither olive nor pearl onion.

"Purist," she told him. "Remember that funny little café near the foot of the castle hill?"

"Yes. Too much vermouth, you warned me."

"You *do* remember," she said delightedly. "That was a perfect evening, wasn't it?" She was studying the other tables quietly. The room was fairly spacious—it had probably been a small reception hall before bars had become a necessity—with softly shaded wall lights set into its dark wooded panels, and there was no feeling of crowding. Everyone sat at white-clothed tables, small islands unto themselves; there was no bar to stand at, no open array of bottles in front of mirrors, no high stools, not even a visible barman.

"Slightly on the short side," he replied. "How was Schloss Fuschl?"

"Too sentimental for words," she said, "but I suppose that's the right tone for farewell parties."

He said nothing at all. He wished he had never asked. Then he could have enjoyed an excellent Martini without wondering why she had lied to him in Salzburg. But he deserved this feeling of awkwardness that had unexpectedly attacked him; after all, he had set that little trap, and that annoyed him too. Except, he had to know. Her answer had been important to him. He had got it, and it wasn't the answer he had wanted. He looked at her face and thought sadly, You are much too beautiful to tell lies. And why such an unnecessary one?

"You are depressed," she said.

"I was just thinking we seem fated to have an interrupted drink together." If the waiter didn't arrive soon, he wouldn't have time to do anything but gulp it down.

"Couldn't you phone and tell your friends that you'll be a little late for luncheon?"

"No."

"Then it's another woman," she said, laughing. "Why don't you postpone her until tomorrow? And your business appointment, too? Then we could have the rest of the day to ourselves. I'll be leaving soon, and then you'll have all the free time in the world."

"You're always leaving, aren't you?" The drinks had come, and he welcomed the interruption; he didn't need to think what he would say next as he signed his name and room number on the check.

"My grandmother's ill. She has two nurses, and the house is like a morgue. Oh, she'll live to ninety. It's just a matter of—well, senility. She's slipping away gradually as far as memory goes. She doesn't even recognize me. Sad, isn't it? She was such an energetic kind of old lady."

"That's grim." But was it the truth? The trouble with one silly lie was that it kept casting its shadow around. Then he chided himself once more; he was becoming too damned suspicious. Why should Elissa lie about her grandmother? "So you are staying with your friend?"

Elissa shook her head. She said dejectedly, "No, all my plans collapsed around me. My friend gave up her apartment last week and moved to Geneva." Her mood changed to one of amusement. "It would have been pretty useless if you had called that number I gave you. You didn't, did you?"

"I only arrived this morning," he reminded her.

"Oh yes . . . Have you still got it?"

"Right here." He fished out his address book and found the page.

"Let me see," she said lightly, her arm extended over the table, her hand open. "You know, I've had the most awful feeling that I didn't remember that number correctly when I gave it to you."

It was the only entry on the page. This was the first time he had actually looked at it since he had written it down in Salzburg. Then, it had only been a string of five figures, quickly scribbled. Now, they seemed familiar. I've seen that

175

number somewhere else, he thought. He took out his pencil and scored it through. "Where are you staying?" he asked, ready to write her new number.

"Here."

"At this hotel?"

"They managed to find a room for me. I'm sure it is one the bankers rejected. It's a dull little place with no view at all." Her arm had remained lying across the table. Unexpectedly, she picked the little book out of his hand and looked at the opened page. "I knew it," she said in dismay. "Oh, Bill, I'm so sorry. You could have called this number until doomsday and never found me. It was just a matter of the last two numerals: they should have been fifty-three, not thirty-five." She gave him back the address book, opened at the page. "There isn't much use in keeping that. Is there?" She shook her head over her idiotic mistake. Her dark-brown hair swung softly, fell over her brow. She brushed it back carelessly. She seemed completely at ease, and yet Mathison had a strange feeling that she was waiting.

He didn't take the subtle cue; he made not one move to tear the page out of the book and hand it to her with an appropriate joke. Instead, he laughed the whole incident off while he looked hard at a number that had become definitely interesting. "No use at all," he agreed. "Unless I frame it as a memento of our first meeting."

"And always keep remembering me as that nitwit Elissa? Really, Bill, you are a cruel and horrible man."

"That's me," he said cheerfully, and slipped the address book into his pocket. He glanced at his watch, frowned.

"You have to leave," she said slowly. "But must you?"

"I'll have to telephone right now that I'll be fifteen minutes late. I'm sorry, Elissa." He reached for her coat, pulled it around her shoulders.

She didn't move. She looked at him, her dark-gray eyes wide, softly appealing. "Telephone and say you can't come. Please, Bill ... Let's have this afternoon together." She reached across the table, touched his hand with hers. Her fingers caressed his gently.

He drew a quick breath. He raised her hand to his lips, then laid it beside her glass. "I've got to go," he said, as if he hadn't noticed the invitation.

"Then go!" she told him angrily. She looked away, took

176

out a cigarette and lit it before he could reach for his matches.

"I'll call you later," he said awkwardly, and rose.

She ignored him completely. So he left.

But as he again waited for an elevator to make its slow return to the ground floor, she came running into the corridor. "Oh, Bill," she said, and threw her arms around him. "Please forgive me. That was no way to end a drink together. It's just that I don't know when I'll see you again." She reached up and kissed him. "This is how to say good-bye."

"You make it sound much too final." His voice was coldly polite.

"I'm leaving tonight."

Behind them, the elevator opened its door automatically. He glanced at it, easing himself out of her embrace.

"I've just had—" she began, and then took his hand and stepped with him into the elevator. "I promise I won't keep you late," she assured him. "Any later than I have," she emended, and laughed.

"What floor?" He was waiting to press the right button.

"Three."

That was his floor, too. So he pressed and they were on their way.

"I've just had the offer of a job," she said. "It's in Salzburg."

That surprised him. "I thought you were on your way home. Father's orders."

"Oh, I phoned him last night and I think I persuaded him to see things my way. After all, a job is a job; it is not just wasting time trying to learn how to paint. That was what really worried him. He thought I was drifting. But with a steady job, I could earn enough to finish my art classes too."

"That depends on the job, doesn't it?"

"It's interesting, but I'll have free time. You see, there's a man in Salzburg who has quite a big interest in skiing—he deals in sports equipment and arranges competitions and all that kind of thing. He needs someone who can ski, talk several languages, and be a sort of counselor and friend to groups of foreigners who will be coming to the mountains around Salzburg this winter."

"Are you sure you'll have any free time?" he asked, his sense of humor returning. They had reached the third floor. They began walking along the corridor.

"What I wanted to ask you," she was saying as they reached his door, "was this: suppose you were one of my friends in Salzburg and had given me farewell parties and all that, what would you think if I were to return within a week?"

He looked in amazement at the pretty upturned face. It was completely serious. Women will always astonish me, he thought: who else would worry about something that mattered so little? He opened his door. "It would give me a chance for another farewell party," he said lightly.

"Now, Bill—" she remonstrated, and stepped into his room even as he turned to say good-bye.

"I have to telephone." He wasted no time either, but walked straight over to the table beside his bed and picked up the receiver. "Please get me the Eden au Lac Hotel's number," he said crisply. "Call me back when you reach Mrs. Lynn Conway there. No, I don't know her room number." He replaced the receiver, noted that his coat had been returned warm from pressing, and took off his jacket. He hung it over the back of a chair.

Elissa had closed the door behind her and stood with her shoulder against it. "What would you think, Bill?" she insisted. "Would I look ridiculous?"

"Crazy, perhaps; but not ridiculous."

"Then that's all right," she said, smiling. "I don't mind being thought crazy."

"Done your way, it has a definite charm." He was keeping his voice brisk and businesslike. So were his movements. He took off his tie, found a new shirt. "I'm going to change," he said, heading for the bathroom.

"Will you be going to Salzburg?"

"Possibly. There's a day's business to clear up."

"Will you be staying—"

The telephone rang. He picked the receiver up and turned his back on Elissa. "Lynn? I'm sorry. I'm five minutes late as it is, and I'll need another ten. I got all jammed up at this end."

"Don't worry," Lynn said, and she sounded as if she meant it. "I haven't even unpacked. I've had a visitor. Miss Freytag. She came to welcome me and see if I was comfortable and brought me flowers. Wasn't that a nice thought? And we've been having such an interesting talk."

He dropped his voice. "Is Freytag with you now?"

178

"Yes."

"And I told her to take the day off." My God, he thought, surely we aren't going to have her hanging around for lunch. Or are we?

"Well, in a sense it is," Lynn said cryptically, taking care not to hurt Miss Freytag's feelings. "By the way, we had a phone call from your more-or-less policeman. He seemed much less annoyed than he was in the hall."

"Oh?" He heard a sound of movement near the door and turned his head. Elissa was about to leave. She blew a kiss as she held up one glove.

Lynn was saying, "I'll brief you about it when we meet."

"Ten minutes from now? I won't keep you waiting this time."

"That would be fine. I'll be down in the lobby."

"Tell Miss Freytag that her plan worked beautifully. It was much better than mine would have been."

"I'll give her your thanks. Bye, now."

He replaced the receiver and turned around. The room was empty. He hadn't even heard the soft closing of the door. But no harsh feelings, he thought with relief, remembering Elissa's gestured kiss. It was odd though that she had the unexpected good sense to slip away, particularly when she had been left dangling in the middle of a question. But, he supposed, if she wanted to see him again, she'd soon discover where he was staying in Salzburg. She had found out this hotel by remembering his remark about a bankers' conference, hadn't she?

He changed in four minutes, including a fresh tie and shoes and suit. As he quickly emptied the pockets of his jacket on the back of the chair, he found his address book was missing. It should have been in the side pocket where he had slipped it when he was in the bar. Had he dropped it there? He would take a hundred-dollar bet that he hadn't. It had been in his pocket. He was sure of that. Tight-lipped, angry, he locked his door and didn't even wait for the elevator but ran down the three flights of stairs.

At the bar's entrance, he hesitated. He might as well check. The place was almost empty now, and his table was unoccupied. That was good luck, at least; much less embarrassing than scrabbling around strangers' ankles. His luck held. Under the edge of the tablecloth, almost by the leg of his chair, he found the small address book where his foot had kicked it. But how the hell he could have been so bloody careless as to drop it instead of putting it into his pocket—that made him even more annoyed with himself. Well, he had lost a hundred-dollar bet. And, he thought, as he pocketed the book safely but quickly and made for the exit, he owed Elissa a very big apology. Damn it all, that girl unsettled him. She was crazy, certainly, in the way he liked craziness; but there was something else that disturbed him, a sort of elusiveness, a kind of question mark that kept raising its unpleasant eyebrow. Perhaps if he hadn't been caught up in all the troubles that stemmed from Eric Yates, he might not be so ready with his suspicions. Too ready. They were becoming a habit, and not one that he wanted.

Just ahead of him, about to leave the bar where they had been having a leisurely drink, were two immaculately dressed men. Bankers obviously, from smooth hair to dark suits, striped ties, highly polished black shoes. English variety, perhaps. They were collecting their bowlers and navy-blue Chesterfields from a wooden rack near the door. One of them, pulling on his yellow gloves, stepped back as Mathison passed him at high speed, almost blocked his path. "Sorry." That was all he said, scarcely glancing over his shoulder. Mathison stared briefly and with a "that's all right" went on his way. Charles Nield. Charles Nield unmistakably, and a far change from the zippered jacket and flannel shirt of Acme Radio's repair service.

So I know he is in Zürich, at least, thought Mathison as he came out on the broad flight of steps that would take him down to the sidewalk. But how long was he in the bar? Sitting there all the time I was with Elissa?

And there she was too, across the street, waiting on the broad esplanade. She had pretended to be watching the lunchtime sailors who were once more snatching an hour at the boat anchorage, but she must have been keeping at least one of her beautiful dark-gray eyes on the hotel's entrance, for she waved at just the right moment to catch his attention. She came running toward him, disregarding the light traffic, not even noticing the discreetly interested looks from the men she passed. He went to meet her. Elissa was the kind of girl you couldn't ignore; and besides, he was telling himself, you owe her an apology even if it will have to be unspoken. What would she say if she thought he had blamed her for his own carelessness? "Hello again. I thought you'd be halfway to Salzburg by this time."

"I was waiting for you," she said with disarming frankness. "I wanted to tell you why I had to run off so quickly. I discovered I had lost one of my gloves. They were new, too." She held out her hands to display the taupe suède gloves that matched her handbag. "I found it, looking so lonely and forlorn in the corridor downstairs just outside the elevator."

"And I almost lost my address book." In spite of himself, he was watching her carefully. "It was lying under the table where we were sitting."

"I guess we were both a little upset, there. If we meet in Salzburg, perhaps we can begin all over again, forget today, pretend it never existed."

"*If* we meet? We are bound to meet."

"I may be out of town when you arrive. Traveling to the villages will be the first part of my job—just to get to know the local conditions before the snow comes and brings the skiers. When do you expect to be there?"

"Quite soon, I hope. But that depends—"

"On what?"

"The office here. It's passing through a crisis. The man who was in charge of it—well, he has been killed."

"Killed?" Her eyes widened; her lips parted in astonishment.

"Yes. His body is at the mortuary right now. That's how I spent most of this morning. I went with his secretary to identify him—nasty business."

"How was he killed?"

"In a boating accident."

She said nothing. She looked out at the lake with its scattering of sails. "It looks safe enough, doesn't it?" She asked at last. Then as her eyes came back to him, they saw something behind him, farther along the sidewalk. For a moment, they hardened. She said, "But I'm keeping you late again. Good-bye, Bill." She reached up, kissed him full on the lips. With a last gentle touch on his arm, she turned and ran up the steps into the hotel.

That was a quick retreat, he thought with some relief. And Nield and his banking buddy had seen it, too, even if they were engrossed in saying good-bye on the top step. Mathison turned and started walking toward the Eden au Lac. Lynn

181

Conway and Miss Freytag were standing together on the sidewalk, both looking in his direction. They must have had a front-row view of Elissa's farewell, he thought as he glanced at his watch. He was several minutes late, after all. And what's more, he was thinking now, we'll be three for lunch; I know it, I know it, that's my kind of luck today. But he was wrong about that. Miss Freytag was shaking hands with Lynn, ignoring him completely. Before he reached polite hailing distance, she had left for the nearest corner.

"I really am sorry," he told Lynn Conway. If there was anything he hated it was to keep putting himself into a position where he had to apologize. He was usually punctual—and with women that meant being a few minutes early—but today seemed to be one of complete disintegration. What was his calm and cool Mrs. Conway going to think of him? And it was important somehow that she didn't think of him as a philandering dawdler who hadn't enough politeness to keep an eye on his watch. "Everything got very complicated," he admitted lamely. "I haven't even telephoned for a taxi to get us into town. I thought of lunch at the Veltliner Keller." And hang the expense. This would be one way of giving that anemic word "sorry" some real vitality.

"I'd love that another time. But now, wouldn't it be easier to eat right here? There's a pleasant dining room, and the food is good. So Miss Freytag tells you."

"If that's all right with you." It was certainly the simplest solution. The fact that you had always to phone for a cab was a slight tax on patience, although that kind of arrangement did hold down traffic on the streets. "I thought we were going to have Miss Freytag right on top of us for the next couple of hours."

"To tell you the truth, I had a feeling that was going to happen, too. We were waiting in the lobby, and she started talking about the dining room. Somehow I could just see the three of us drifting in there. So I decided I wanted to look at the lake."

"She certainly took the hint." He was remembering Miss Freytag's straight back and high head, not even glancing around to give him a friendly wave as she turned the corner and disappeared from sight.

"It was really so odd," Lynn said reflectively. They had climbed the hotel steps and were now in a small almost

182

private lobby. They could have drinks, he noted, in one of a series of pleasant sitting rooms.

"Here?" he asked, looking at the nearest room. "Or are we so late that we'd better have drinks at the table?" Again he felt that unpleasant feeling of inadequacy; his fault entirely that there wasn't enough time for the usual ritual.

She looked at him, wondered what he really preferred. "Let's find a quiet table."

He insisted on one in a small bright room near a window, where they could look out over the esplanade at the lake. And he began to feel more at ease. Lynn Conway might not be quite so warm and friendly as when he had left her this morning, but she wasn't harboring any resentment about being kept waiting on the sidewalk. "What was so odd about Miss Freytag?" he asked, once the drinks were ordered.

She frowned at the sailboats on the lake. They were few in number now; most were returning to the small anchorage across the street. "Eric Yates used to keep his boat over there, did you know?"

Mathison shook his head.

"That's what Miss Freytag was talking about as we came out of the lobby. She was perfectly all right. A little sad as she spoke of Yates, but perfectly all right. And then—well, she saw the girl across the street. Miss Freytag almost froze. Her eyes actually bulged."

"But why? Did she say?"

"She was about to speak. But the girl was running to meet someone seemingly, and as we came down the steps onto the sidewalk we saw it was you. This time, Miss Freytag froze completely. She kept staring. She forgot everything else. It was really rather embarrassing."

"But why—" began Mathison, and stopped. The whole thing was ludicrous.

"I wished I were right back inside the lobby again," Lynn said, trying to laugh. "Poor old Miss Freytag. Has she some complex about kissable girls?" She looked down at her Martini. One complex I won't develop, she told herself sharply. But it was sad; every time she met a man whom she liked right from the start, she'd always find out that he was either married or about to be married or someone else's property. Not for me, she thought angrily. I'm damned if I do unto other women what they did to me; two years married to Todd Conway and the pretty little secretaries and eager-eyed

183

career girls were already considering him fair game. It would have taken more will power than Todd ever had to steer clear of them. Even his death had proved that: a car smashed up and that bright new starlet with her body ruined for life, all to show how well Todd could handle his shining new Jaguar at ninety miles an hour.

"Freytag had a thing about Yates. Quite innocent, I'm sure. She's just one of those far-worshippers. But she is no fool in other matters. Didn't she say anything at all?" She must have, he thought. What could it have been that brought that strange look to Lynn's face? The light had gone out of it.

"Is it important?" She picked up the menu and brought her thoughts back to the present.

"She is full of surprises."

"Miss Freytag? I thought she was dismally predictable. Except for those few odd seconds. But I'm sure they made good sense to her." And I wish I hadn't been so simple-minded as to mention them in the first place. Freytag's words embarrassed me then, and they are embarrassing me now. It's no business of mine who kisses whom or where or how or why. Lynn Conway concentrated on the menu. "Too much choice. It defeats me," she said. "I'll have lamb chops, and a salad, and coffee afterward."

"I'll join you in that." Mathison's appetite had got lost somewhere among his worries. Miss Freytag as a subject of conversation was obviously dead. Yet, when someone who kept her emotions under such tight control as she did suddenly let loose, it was worthwhile listening to her. He had found that out this morning. "Let's add smoked salmon as a starter, and some wine. Got to keep up your strength for those thousand questions you are going to ask." He had won a natural smile, at least.

"I'll fall asleep," she warned him.

"And miss my answers? Not you," he predicted. And that was a real laugh from her, too. He looked at the spill of dark-auburn hair, gleaming in the rays of sun that struck obliquely through the window. It matched the soft copper of the leaves on the trees outside. He almost blurted out the compliment; a mistake, though, at this moment. So he ordered the food and wine, kept everything businesslike and friendly, let her relax into the natural kind of talk they had enjoyed that morning. And he was relaxing, too. The hard

184

edge of worry was softened; problems seemed less threatening, more soluble. She was easy to be with, this girl. She matched his moods without suiting herself to them. She could surprise without bewildering him; she didn't jangle his nerves, set his teeth on edge. She said nothing stupid and didn't try to seem clever. All that and beauty, too, he thought. Mathison, you're sunk. If ever you'd risk marriage again—no, no, be careful. This one is real danger. Others come and others go, but this is the kind of girl that stays with you in memory. So keep everything businesslike and friendly, no more than that. Because either you marry this girl or you spend the rest of your life regretting you didn't. Marriage? No, you've had it; you certainly have. You're inoculated for good.

Or aren't you?

He listened to her soft voice and watched her expressive eyes. *"What?"* he had to ask, jolted out of his wandering thoughts. "The office is going to be closed down?"

"Until Tuesday. That was what your friend the policeman suggested when he telephoned."

"Inspector Keller?"

"Yes. He seemed quite determined about it. A matter of security. He is putting on a guard, day and night. And he wants to close off the stairway, block the elevator door for our floor, and let his men get their job finished with Yates's files as soon as possible."

"That sounds reasonable." After all, the man who had impersonated the janitor must have had some purpose behind his masquerade. Such as slipping into Yates's office after dark, once all the nice unsuspecting people had put their trust in locks and gone off to supper and bed?

She looked astonished. "Frankly, I thought it was highly unreasonable. But don't worry—I listened calmly and agreed politely. I had the feeling that argument would get me nowhere." She watched his face, added quietly, "I'm rather glad I did. He knows the facts and I don't. You know them, too, don't you, Bill?"

"A few of them," he admitted. And here come the questions, he thought, and braced himself. He began to understand the vague manner of Frank O'Donnell as he avoided talk about highly enriched uranium in Newhart's office, or the offhand style of Charles Nield facing him across a coffee table in his apartment; and he now could sympathize with their predicaments. He glanced around the little dining room with its constant hover of waiters, and wished that he needn't answer any questions at all. Not here, at least. "What about a stroll down the lakeside?" he tried.

"I'm really awfully tired. I scarcely slept last night, and I keep feeling I've lost five hours of my life. Do you remember the story of the mob in London when the calendar had to be reformed? The government passed a law making September third become September fourteenth. So of course there was a vast crowd screaming 'Give us back our eleven days.' The only time that story didn't seem so amusing was this morning. Give me back my five hours, and I'd feel happier right now. You know what? I think I'd like another pot of black, black coffee. There's that telephone call to Jimmy Newhart we have to make. I suppose we'd better take it in my room upstairs? Two waifs, thrown on the street, locked out of their office."

"Sad," he agreed, smiling too. "What did Miss Freytag think of the shutdown?"

"She thought it was very correct—a mark of respect for such a wonderful man as Mr. Yates." She watched the smile disappear from his face. "You don't like him, do you?"

"Less and less."

"But why?" Could he be as jealous of Yates as all this? From what Miss Freytag had blurted out, it could be possible. And yet, she thought, studying Bill Mathison's face, he doesn't seem the type to be jealous of a dead man.

He gave it to her straight. "It's a matter of espionage," he said quietly.

She was motionless. She didn't exclaim, didn't look startled after that one moment of complete shock. "Perhaps we ought to have that pot of coffee in my room," she said. She noticed the obvious relief on his face. "Why didn't you suggest it? Did you think I'd start getting the wrong ideas about you?" So he wasn't as self-confident about women as she had thought, and that discovery pleased her somehow.

"I thought you might already have them."

Did that really matter to him? And why had it mattered to her? She said nothing at all but let the usual interruptions of check-paying and table-leaving act as an excuse for her silence.

She let him do the placing of the call to New York. And it was only as they went up to her room in the empty self-service elevator that she asked, "So Yates was an agent?"

186

Mathison nodded.

"For or against us?"

"Against."

"And Miss Freytag didn't know all this?"

He shook his head.

"Then why should anything she said about Yates be of any importance?"

"It could help fill in the outlines. God knows we started with practically a blank page."

She fell silent again as they left the elevator and walked the short distance to her room. "I've changed my mind about asking questions," she told him as she dropped her coat on the bed and walked to the window. "I'll leave it to you, Bill. Tell me whatever you think I need to know. Fair enough?"

"More than fair."

"And as for Miss Freytag this morning—she hurried away because she couldn't face you. She was absolutely aghast that she had been so rude about your friend; she would never have said those things against the girl if she had only known."

"Known what?" Mathison asked sharply.

"She wasn't explicit. I suppose she meant she hadn't known you were on kissing terms."

"That's only Elissa's way," Mathison said angrily. "I bet she made straight for the first man she saw on the day she came out of her cradle."

"Elissa?" Lynn Conway relaxed.

"Elissa Lang."

"Then Miss Freytag got it all wrong. She mistook your friend for Yates's girl."

"Eva Langenheim?" he asked, incredulous. Miss Freytag wouldn't mistake Yates's girl for anyone else, any place, any time.

"That was the name she blurted out." Lynn looked at him with surprise. His lips had tightened; his eyes had narrowed.

He pulled out his address book, leafed through it quickly. Yes, the page with Elissa's number had been neatly removed. So, he thought angrily, I was right with my first hunch; she did filch the book out of my pocket when my jacket hung over the chair. And she made an excuse for leaving the room, and cut out the page, and—hell, what did it matter how she managed to drop the book under the table where we had been sitting in the bar? What mattered now was the accuracy of his memory. That number must be of some importance if she'd risk so much to destroy it.

He found his pen, sat down at a small desk, started jotting down the figures, making sure they ended with thirty-five, as they had done originally. Or was it thirty-five? Not fifty-three? She had done a good job of muddling there. Clever, clever little Elissa: try one thing and then another and leave them guessing. He studied the number as he completed it. Yes, that was how he remembered it. . . . And then, from the back of his memory, there came a small warning signal. He had seen that number somewhere else. Where?

Across the room, Lynn watched him with more than surprise now. What on earth did I start? she wondered in dismay. He had written down something, was looking at it with a deepening frown, his mind far, far away from this room. She welcomed the knock on the door that brought the coffee tray. She poured quickly, keeping her silence. (He took two lumps of sugar, no cream, she recalled.) Quietly, she placed the cup within his reach. He nodded his thanks. He was taking out his wallet, searching in its small stamp pocket. She fought down her curiosity and went back to the coffee tray for her own cup.

"This may be it," he said, almost to himself. He was unfolding a scrap of paper that had been hidden between the stamps. On it was the telephone number that Anna Bryant had given him: Yates's very private number which Bryant had been supposed to call early last Monday morning. He compared it with Elissa's number that he had jotted down from memory. They were identical. "They match!" he exclaimed, "by God, they match!" and looked up to find Lynn staring at him. He began to smile, and then to laugh.

She found she was smiling, too, although heaven only knew what there was to be amused about. "So we won?" she tried tactfully.

"I wouldn't say that. But we did retrieve something from the disaster." He had spoken lightly, still feeling his success. And then he thought of what might have been, and he sobered up. He looked at her for a long moment. "I think the explanations begin here and now." He rose, stood hesitating. There must be no mention of Yates and his Burch apparatus in America, not one word about the FBI and their problem with highly enriched uranium. No mention either of Charles Nield's interest in Finstersee; in fact, no actual naming of the dark lake. He'd stick to Bryant and his contract, Yates and his confidence tricks, and try to keep everything circulating around Salzburg. That would be enough to shock her anyway.

"Are they so difficult?" she asked sympathetically. She sat down on the edge of the bed and reached for her cigarettes and an ashtray.

"I'm just getting them arranged in sequence," he said, playing for time. No lies. That was the one good rule. "Okay. Here they are. You know why I went to Salzburg originally?" He lit her cigarette, and one for himself.

She nodded.

"Well, this is what happened. . . ." He began pacing back and forth in the small space of unoccupied carpet, and then—as his story really began to flow—he dropped into the armchair. Half an hour later, he had ended.

She was shocked, all right. "So Yates was really the head of a spy ring? And Elissa Eva Langenheim Lang was possibly more than his mistress? Who were they working for? The Russians?"

"I asked about that, but didn't get any definite answers. Professionals are always so damn cagey when they are dealing with amateurs. My own guess is that they were working for Peking."

"Are you *serious?* I mean, Peking is having so many troubles of its own. Have the Chinese any time left to bother with Europe?"

"They won't give up any foothold they have. And they've got strong ones, not only in Europe, but in America, too. Have you ever known a Communist who doesn't plan for ten years ahead?"

"Or who doesn't keep trying?" She shook her head sadly. "Like the Nazis," she added. "You really think the Nazis may have killed Bryant? Because he had some piece of information about them that they wanted to keep secret?"

"That is what his wife thinks."

"And you believe her."

"She was right to fear Yates, wasn't she?"

"Yes. But you can be right about one thing and wrong about others. Is she really to be trusted?"

"You'd have to meet her to know that. You'd have no doubts then." He looked at her frankly, his dark eyes holding a glint of humor. "And if you are wondering now whether I

189

once had any doubts about Elissa, the answer is slightly yes and mostly no. I can be fooled by a woman, I admit it. But Anna Bryant isn't like any woman I've known."

"I'd like to meet her." The remark had been involuntary. She looked at him quickly, startled by the idea that had just entered her mind. "When are you going to Salzburg?"

"Well, since the office is closed for a long weekend, I might take the chance to visit Salzburg tomorrow. The sooner the better."

"Need any help?" After all, she thought, I *am* in the firm of Newhart and Morris; I'm its meanwhile-representative in Europe, aren't I? If I were a man, I'd just say I was going. But as a woman, I can't even seem to be pushing. Won't it dawn on him that I should be there? It concerns the Zürich office, doesn't it? But it hadn't dawned.

He was saying, "No! You keep out of this, my girl." He relaxed a little. "At any other time, yes. But now—no, no, you stay in Zürich."

"And spend my weekend dodging Miss Freytag?" She laughed to conceal her disappointment. "I just thought I might be useful. When you talk with Mrs. Bryant, that is. It is bound to be difficult. She must be in some kind of delayed shock. They seem to have been a really happy couple."

"They were." He looked over at the telephone. "What's holding back New York?"

"If they had been unhappy, I suppose it would have been a kind of release, a bad way out but yet a solution. . . ."

He glanced at her curiously. What kind of married life had she had? She hadn't even mentioned her husband once, all through their conversation at lunch. And that, he reflected, was odd. Women who had been happily married kept dropping their husbands' names; that was one of the little crosses the next husband had to bear. Yet, there had been no touch of bitterness, either, when the conversation had touched on men. "You know," he began, but the telephone rang and cut his compliment short.

"New York," said Lynn, and reached for the receiver. "You'd better break the news about Yates."

"You can handle it," he assured her. "I'll wait until he gets around to Salzburg." And once that's all settled, he thought, I'd better call Keller and get rid of my latest piece of news. It wasn't the most comfortable feeling to realize that he might be the only person in Zürich who knew Elissa Lang's double identity. Not the only person, he thought with a stab of worry as he looked over at Lynn. She was talking intently, her face grave, keeping to the simple facts. Discreet, Jimmy Newhart had called her. Yes, she would be discreet about the information he had given her. But was discretion enough of a safeguard against someone like Elissa Lang? A cold cloud of worry descended on him.

"Your turn, Bill," Lynn called to him. "Jimmy wants to speak to his legal adviser." She covered the mouth of the receiver. "He is terribly depressed. He thinks we are going to be caught up in a whopping scandal. Cheer him up a bit."

And who's going to cheer me up? wondered Mathison as his worry increased. I told her too much, dumb blundering ox. He mustered a reassuring grin for her puzzled eyes, took the receiver, and adopted his very best bedside manner. "Hello, Jimmy! Now you can relax. It's all out of our hands, isn't it?"

Across the room, Lynn gave him her warmest smile, and even with Newhart's strong voice blasting his eardrum, he felt his heart melt.

14

MATHISON RETURNED TO HIS HOTEL, PICKED UP HIS ROOM key at the desk. He was in a gloomy mood. His attempt to reach Keller by phone had been useless.

"A message for you!" the porter called after him. It had been quickly written by the telephone operator and read: *Miss Freytag would like to see you tonight at seven. Bergstrasse, 19. Most important.*

"Where is Bergstrasse?" he asked the porter.

"You go up Rämistrasse and then—"

"It's near the University then?" That was the district where Greta Freytag lived, he remembered.

"Not far. You turn to your right before—"

"I'll let the taxi driver get me there." Mathison went on his way to his room. He would have to call Lynn and ask her to postpone dinner until eight, even eight-thirty. Either that or call Freytag and tell her he couldn't make the appointment. Yet he hesitated to turn her down. *Most important,* for one thing. For another, her feelings bruised easily. She must be thinking that he had been laughing at her all the time she was talking to him about Eva Langenheim. Besides, he owed Miss Freytag considerable thanks. Even a three minutes' delay in the arrival of Inspector Keller and his men would have had unpleasant results for William Mathison this morning.

His call to Lynn pulled her breathless to the phone. He could hear a heavy gush of water in the background, so she was probably running her bath before she took that sleep she had promised herself. "How's the unpacking?" he asked.

"Practically finished."

"I've just had a message from Miss Freytag. She wants to see me at seven."

"Oh . . . Then we'd better postpone dinner. Bill, why don't we cancel it altogether?"

"Cancel it? You have to eat, don't you?"

"I've been thinking of a tray in my room, and then some more sleep. That's how I feel. Honestly. It wasn't just the flight here. So much has been happening, so many things to think about, that I am almost numb with exhaustion. I wouldn't be very good company tonight."

And was she also thinking about Newhart's call from New York? Jimmy had come up with one of his own bright suggestions the minute he had heard the office would be closed until Tuesday: why not go to Salzburg, both of them? Lynn would be a restraining influence on Bill, funny joke ha ha; keep him from overgenerous impulses on the settlement he'd draw up for Mrs. Bryant. (Yes, Jimmy, you get funnier by the minute. One more crack like that and I'll start calling you Scrooge and we'll both wish we had never opened our big mouths.) He didn't argue now. "I'll call you tomorrow," he said quietly, "before I leave for Salzburg. And Lynn, I wish I could take you with me on the trip, but I don't think it would—"

"Be wise," she cut in. "I know. I understand. I really do." Her polite voice told him she didn't understand one bit.

"I'll explain later," he tried.

"See you when you get back," she said. Her voice rose in alarm. "I must dash—the water—" The receiver banged down.

Damn Freytag, damn everything, he thought as he jerked his tie loose, pulled off his jacket, and settled down with his homework on the Nazis that he had begun on the plane. He

was almost through his rereading of *The Last Battle*, searching for the sections that dealt with the breakdown of the
Nazi machine, with the last scrabble for safety and self-
preservation by its top organizers. Some were dead, some had
been tried, some vanished. Names and places, that was what
he wanted to know. Who had been stationed in Salzburg,
worked near there? ...

The telephone rang. Keller, at last, Mathison thought and
plunged for the receiver. But it was Charles Nield's voice,
abrupt and cool in spite of the easy phrases. "What about
having supper with Maria and me and the kids?"

"I have an appointment at seven. Otherwise, I'd be delighted."

"Then I'll pick you up earlier and we can eat at six."

"That's right; mustn't keep the kids up too late."

"We'll save time if you start walking toward the Limmat.
I'm just leaving the office." And that was all.

Mathison closed his book, switched off the reading lamp. It
was now almost half past five. *Start walking toward the
Limmat* ... He had better stick to the sidewalk that edged
the street and not cross over to the darker promenade. He
dressed quickly, and hoped he was getting the message correctly. Nield had sounded in no mood for mistakes.

He picked up the note from Miss Freytag with her address
on it, locked his door, and set out for his walk along Uto
Quai.

It was a cool, crisp evening, and dark. Lights from the hotels
and large houses that overlooked Uto Quai were sparkling
brightly, and across the lake's black waters the low hills were
roped with a glitter of shining beads. There were other
people walking, mostly away from town, with coats buttoned
up and briefcases bulging. Traffic was fairly heavy on the
street, a swift moving stream of taxis and small cars. Mathison kept to the outer edge of the sidewalk, resisting the
temptation to look around or seem anything other than a
man stepping smartly into town. Nield, he reflected, would
have his work cut out for him.

He had barely covered the distance of about two hundred
yards when a small dark car, almost like one of the less-

expensive taxis, pulled up just ahead of him. The front door was open by the time he reached it. Nield's voice said, "Hop in!" He obeyed, and the car was moving forward even as he pulled the door shut.

"Pretty smooth," Mathison said.

Nield said nothing. He was watching his rear-view mirror as much as the traffic ahead of him. He had got rid of his banker's suit; he wore a heavy tweed jacket and flannels and a turtle-neck sweater, and might have been an instructor at the University or one of those self-prolonged students at the C. G. Jung Institute. As he maneuvered the car through the mixture of gardens and trolley-car rails that nested at the head of the lake, he relaxed. "If we were spotted," he said, "they didn't have much time to do anything about it. Thought we would do some sight-seeing while we have a little talk." He swung the wheel to his right and started climbing the busy street that circled around the University's hill. He turned left before they were halfway up Rämistrasse, and now they were driving slowly through the district of narrow little streets with close-packed and venerable houses, occasionally spaced by small squares, that stretched thickly from the University's heights right down to the old guildhalls on the River Limmat. The spread of the modern city, with its bright lights and feeling of space, had given way to the tight dark clutch of the Middle Ages.

"I'd say this was sinister except that it's in Zürich," Mathison tried. The silence in the car bothered him. Nield was not one to lack conversational gambits.

"It's safe enough, even without Keller's men keeping an eye on this street."

Mathison looked quickly out the window. The street was so narrow that even the lights from the few small shops and the three stories of flats above them seemed dimmed. The car was traveling leisurely. He noticed one shop was an antiquary's, another was for secondhand books, and farther on there was another bookshop.

"Thought you'd be interested in this one," Nield said. The sign over its door read EMIL BURCH—DEALER IN FINE BOOKS, MAPS, MANUSCRIPTS. "Too bad we can't risk browsing around inside. It's a cosy setup." He slowed the car still more, bringing it to a smooth stop before the narrow street turned into a small cobbled square.

"Can we risk browsing out here?" Mathison asked sharply.

194

"Keller's men have probably got their eye on us right now."

Nield lit a cigarette. "The ground floor was legitimate business, if you can call any cover that. Above was storage, again perfectly legitimate. The two top floors were Burch's supposed living quarters—when Yates got around to visiting there. A good place to talk with various people who came into the shop as possible customers and then walked quietly upstairs for a meeting, or instructions, or delivery of information. Keller's men have already intercepted two of them."

"And aren't the Nazis keeping an eye on the place?"

"Strangely enough, they never did learn about Emil Burch. They were watching another of Yates's hide-outs, which a Soviet agent was kind enough to point out to them several weeks ago. So Keller learned today from one of the men he arrested—the one who tailed you, as I heard it."

"That other hide-out is the one with the telephone number I was to forget completely?" Mathison was on edge. Nield's quiet watchfulness was disconcerting. "Lucky I didn't." He could be cryptic, too.

"Why?"

"It matched."

"What?" Nield was irritated.

"Elissa Lang's number. She's the girl who was having a drink with me today."

"Elissa Lang . . . Didn't I see that name in your Salzburg report?"

"As an added note in Frank O'Donnell's handwriting, no doubt. I really was damned stupid about all that." If he had just stopped mumbling to himself about invasion of privacy, he might have speeded up this whole investigation by a couple of days. But the truth was he had not believed that either Elissa or her phone number in Zürich was of any importance to anyone except himself. Mathison ended his unpleasant stocktaking as he became aware that Nield was now watching him intensely. "I was just examining my damaged ego," he said with an attempt at lightness. The atmosphere in the car was oppressive; the first thunderbolt should strike any minute. What the hell's wrong, he wondered, apart from my own blunder?

"So your Elissa Lang uses Yates's telephone number?"

"Yes, and we'd better get that word to Keller right away. The trouble with you fellows is that you don't tell people where you can be reached in an emergency. I tried one call from an outside pay telephone, this afternoon, to police headquarters. Keller couldn't be found. All I could do was leave my name and hope he'd figure out my address when he got around to calling me back. Of course, by this time he must have seen Miss Freytag and studied her photographs of Langenheim and Yates. And he must also have heard from Freytag that Eva Langenheim is back in Zürich. But what he doesn't know is that Elissa Eva Langenheim Lang is returning to Salzburg tonight—if she's telling the truth for once."

Suddenly, the mounting tension in the car ended. "How long have you known that Lang and Langenheim are the same girl?" Nield asked slowly.

"Since around half past two this afternoon."

"Oh, well," said Nield, and laughed with relief. He started the engine, and the car moved gently away from the narrow street where Keller's men were within call. "You've answered the question that has been worrying me for the last five hours."

"And what was that?"

"What was Eva Langenheim to you?"

Mathison thought back to the scene in the bar. "That must have puzzled you."

"It scared me stiff. I kept wondering if I had made the biggest blooper of my career when I told you too much in your apartment. Much too much, if you were Langenheim's friend."

"If I had been, what would you have done? Signaled one of Keller's men to put me under arrest?" And I wouldn't be surprised at all, Mathison thought with a mixture of amusement and annoyance, if the signal had been prearranged too. "You were to blink your lights twice in quick succession," he said with a grin, but there was a tightening in the pit of his stomach. That quiet face, with its quiet voice and quiet good manners, which was now intent on finding the quickest way out of the labyrinth of alleys and short twisting streets, masked a lot of unexpected depths. Nield could be a very tough customer indeed.

"Here we are," Nield was saying as he eased the car into a large and long street. There were trolley-car rails, automobiles, people hurrying home or walking out to supper. The shops were lighted and open for their last customers. "We'll pull over near that café and I'll call Keller."

"Tell him I may have been caught napping but I'm not a sleeper."

Nield laughed softly. He liked that. "I'll warn him to have the airport, railway station, and main roads watched. You stay in the car, Bill."

The first name was at least a gesture. "Well in," Mathison agreed. "And don't be long. That appointment I have for seven is with Miss Freytag."

"Where?"

"At her home. It's on Bergstrasse, wherever that is. Somewhere near the University."

Nield paused with one foot out of the car. "Did you arrange this meeting?"

"No. She telephoned me when I was out, and the hotel took the message." Something in Nield's casual voice had caught Mathison's attention. He pulled out the slip of paper with the written message and handed it over. Nield pulled his leg back into the car, closed the door, struck a match, and read the small scrawl of writing.

"Okay," he said, handing it back and getting out of the car. "I'll only be a couple of minutes." He reached for his raincoat in the back seat, drew it on as he stepped onto the sidewalk, and found a tweed cap in its pocket to hide his fair hair. He had given himself a short walk past several shops to reach the café. He didn't seem to be in any particular hurry.

Mathison studied the people strolling past; no one seemed interested in the car, no one was following Nield. Then he studied the broad street, the other parked cars, the occasional trolley, the little shops. It was all neat and respectable, comfortably middle-class, just like Miss Freytag herself. He replaced her note in his pocket, lit a cigarette, and wondered why Nield had been interested at all in her message. Or perhaps Nield had to be interested in everything.

"We've plenty of time before seven," Nield said as he got back into the car. "So we'll continue the sight-seeing. Distances are short around here." The car swung gently into the stream of traffic, and headed along the street, which had started to slope steadily downhill. Then Nield made a left turn into a modern but less brilliantly lighted street. No shops here, little traffic; a residential area of small houses and gardens. "We are on our way to Yates's second place of business. Thought you'd like to see the house with that invaluable telephone number—the one that matched. Too bad we can't go in and putter around on the second floor. I hear he had the very latest in sending and receiving equipment, together with a small developing laboratory, stores of objects all hollowed out to contain microfilm messages for his couriers to carry safely through customs. Ever seen those gadgets? Talcum-powder cans with hidden spaces inside their caps, the same kind of tricks in pocket flasks, hollowed-out lipsticks that look perfectly normal and can still function for les girls, cuff links for the men, specially doctored shaving brushes to conceal film in their handles, hairbrushes that slide apart. Of course, nothing was left lying about; even the heavier equipment was dismantled and stowed away in hollow beams or under floor boards. The small stuff was found inside book ends, and also in the bottom roll of a large Chinese scroll hanging on one wall. It must have taken Yates several hours to get everything ready when he arrived there—two overnight stays a week, regularly—and longer to clear everything out of sight before he left. Only the small darkroom was left intact, supplied with absolutely innocent films and photographs."

"And he risked telephoning from there?" So much care and evasion and trouble, and Yates had given his number to Anna Bryant? And Elissa, too, had handed it over to him? Mathison didn't believe it.

"Not from his place. From the ground-floor section of that house, seemingly quite separate from Yates upstairs. A middle-aged woman lived there, never left it unattended. She seemed to have no connection at all with Yates. But she was the watchdog for the whole house, and in an emergency could put up any special visitor for the night. Yes, it was a very neat arrangement. Yates in the upstairs apartment as a Herr Hase, whose job as a traveling salesman only allowed him a couple of nights at home each week. Downstairs, a widow called Dorothea Langenheim, whose pretty niece Eva visits her occasionally. A fine mess of lies, isn't it?" Nield had been keeping the car's speed down to a leisurely crawl so that now, as he pointed to a modest two-story house with some trees and bushes cosying it away from the other neat little houses along this part of the dark street, he did not have to slow up in order to let Mathison have an adequate glimpse.

He could see no aerial; but there was an outside staircase climbing up the side of the house to Herr Hase's apartment.

"I bet he didn't use that staircase when he slipped down to phone or interview," Mathison said.

"It was kept for his open arrival and departure. When he had business downstairs, he used a hole in the floor and a ladder. The hole was rather expert; it was fitted over with a strong sliding panel covered by a heavy rug. From the downstairs view, it looked like part of the coffered ceiling in Frau Langenheim's living room—an elaborate ceiling for such a modest house. Once the Swiss found a long ladder, library steps actually, which could run along her high bookcases on that side of the room, they became wary of the recessed panels in the ceiling just above it. That, and Frau Langenheim's total ignorance of her upstairs neighbor, led them to visit Yates's place. They found his sliding panel in the floor. Frau Langenheim broke down for one minute, and then clammed up for the duration. However, as the Swiss discover more and more, she may reconsider." They had left the dark quiet street with its pleasant little houses and were entering another that seemed almost a duplicate: some lights in shaded windows, small gardens, some trees and bushes, everything neat and shipshape and Bristol fashion. "This is Bergstrasse," Nield announced. "And there's number nineteen." But he didn't stop; they cruised on at the same even pace.

Mathison glanced at his watch. Its illuminated dial told him he had twenty minutes on his hands before he kept his appointment, and with Miss Freytag one had better be right on the minute, neither early nor late. He looked quickly back at the house, at all the other houses in their measured row. "This isn't Bergstrasse," he said.

"Sure is."

"But she hadn't any garden. That's what she told me when we were talking this morning. At least—" He searched his memory. She and her mother lived in an apartment. A garden apartment like the one Yates had rented as Herr Hase? No, not that. *A garden would have been useless,* he remembered definitely. "That isn't where she lives," he said.

"Could this be it?" Nield pointed to the beginning of small apartment houses, three stories high, that ended the street before it joined the busy main thoroughfare of Rämistrasse.

"More like it, except for the number."

"It's her place all right." Nield drove on, at last pulled up behind a row of parked cars.

"Then the operator at the hotel took down the wrong number?"

"No. We don't think the operator at the hotel took down any number, or any message either. Inspector Keller hasn't been able to reach Miss Freytag all afternoon. Her mother said she had been given a holiday from the office and was going to walk along the lake shore. Just before I called him, he had made one more try to reach Miss Freytag. She wasn't there. Her mother is in hysterics; she has a policewoman with her right now."

"Freytag is missing?"

"It looks as if she might be."

Mathison didn't move, didn't speak.

"Outside your hotel today, was that Miss Freytag standing with Mrs. Conway in front of the Eden au Lac?"

Mathison nodded.

"So Elissa Eva Langenheim Lang saw them both? I wondered what prompted that quick good-bye of hers."

"You believe Elissa—" The thought was so monstrous that Mathison didn't finish it aloud.

"She could have arranged for Freytag's disappearance if she thought Freytag would identify her. She has a mission in Salzburg as Elissa Lang; an important one, now that Yates is dead and she can finish what he began. And as for the fake message to you—perhaps she feared Miss Freytag had told you about Eva Langenheim, perhaps she wants to know whether or not that suspicion is true."

There was one sure way of finding out just what the fake message really meant. "Turn the car and drive back to Bergstrasse nineteen," Mathison said grimly. "Drop me just before we get there, and I'll approach that house on foot."

"I thought I'd do that little job for you," Nield backed and turned the car carefully.

"You aren't my coloring."

"I'll keep my cap on."

"You know damned well that if Elissa has half the brains you credit her with, she has given a precise description of me, or perhaps even a photograph she managed to take with one of her fancy gadgets."

"We'll have to chance that. Because I'm armed, and you aren't." Then Nield tried to play that angle down. "It shouldn't be too risky. Keller will be placing his men around the house right now."

"In that case, you've just argued yourself out of the job. We'll avoid all chances; I go it alone," Mathison insisted. "Up to a point," he added with a grin. "You stick fairly near, will you? I'm no hero."

Nield drew the car gently into one of the deeper patches of shadows, about forty yards or so from the entrance to the house, and switched off the engine. "You can use this, can't you?" He handed over an automatic.

"I once could." Mathison felt the weight of the pistol, liked its balance and grip. "I can always whack someone over the head with it, and leave the marksmanship to you." He slipped the automatic behind his belt. "And just what are you expecting inside that house?"

"I don't know. Neither does Keller. He would like an excuse to get in, though. He didn't have time to explain, but he certainly recognized the address when I gave it to him over the phone. And not favorably."

"So I'm the excuse," Mathison said slowly. No wonder Keller was rallying around so quickly. That might be reassuring in one way, but in another it increased his worry. What was inside that house?

"I'll stick near you. Very near," Nield said as if he sensed Mathison's thoughts. "No, no," he added quietly, as he reached out and stopped Mathison from opening the car door. "No hurry. Mustn't be early."

Mathison tried to relax, looked along the dark street at the quiet house. He was back to thinking about Elissa. Nield was overestimating her, surely. "How could one girl manage all this?" he asked unbelievingly.

"You don't imagine that Yates and Elissa were working alone with only the help of a caretaker, do you? He had a big organization built up, and she must know something of it. Or how else could she have sent you this invitation to Bergstrasse nineteen? She has more power than you think. Or I thought. Or Andrew, for that matter. He's the English friend you saw me with today."

"The budding financial expert?"

"That's right. He is attending the bankers' get-together in your hotel. A very knowledgeable type. I stopped off on my way to Salzburg especially to meet him. We thought an exchange of information on Yates might be useful to both of us."

"And I thought you were torpedoing the gold standard." Mathison glanced at his watch. Three minutes to go.

"Glad I looked authentic. I had a hard time keeping Andrew from setting off after the beautiful Eva, or shall we say Elissa? It doesn't really matter what we call her; all her names are as bogus as hell. But as I kept telling him, you just can't tail people, dressed in your bowler hat and striped pants. He had to settle for a quick phone call after she had gone up to your room with you—that's where she went, wasn't it?—and pray that one of his Zürich contacts could reach the hotel before she got downstairs."

"But she's staying in the hotel."

Nield shook his head. "She was waiting in ambush for you in the lobby. That's when Andrew first noticed her, just as she rushed after you with arms outstretched and head tilted for that kiss. Touching scene."

"Time—" Mathison said, looking at his watch.

"Not quite," Nield said reassuringly. "Give the Swiss a chance to get close to the back door. Now, where were we? Ah, yes—Andrew. He almost popped his bowler when he saw Langenheim. British Intelligence have been looking for her since she vanished from London about three years ago. She was a blonde, then, with a different name, a Canadian passport, and some useful connections—she had haunted the UN in New York for a couple of years before she arrived in England. Well, with a few introductions in the right direction, that face and figure did the rest. She aimed straight for a couple of men who held fairly influential jobs but who liked to fancy themselves as part of the swinging scene. Honest to God, I don't know sometimes which are the more lethal to have around: the ones who want to prove they are virile or the ones who want to be considered intellectual." Nield shook his head, perhaps remembering other men, other places.

"Vanity, vanity, all is vanity?" Mathison suggested. He shook his head, too, thinking of himself. "Elissa must have had a field day."

"She did a lot of damage. And left, just one step ahead of a major scandal. It was partly hushed up, but the British kept looking for her. They traced her to East Germany. Then nothing. Until last spring, when they heard—through a defector, naturally—that she had been sent to Switzerland and had

202

adopted the name and papers of a Swiss girl called Langenheim. But that piece of information came three weeks too late to do them any good. She had already left Zürich."

"And headed for Salzburg."

"New name, new nationality, new papers and passport, new legend." Nield shook his head again. "Poor old Felix Zauner . . . Oh well, it happens to the best of us."

"He employs her?" Mathison remembered the quiet Austrian he had met in Richard Bryant's shop. It was difficult to believe that Zauner could have been another dupe. The man was too intelligent, too cautious.

"In a minor role. So I hear from one of my friends in Salzburg. He thinks she is a decorative piece who is clever enough to keep an eye on any stranger in Salzburg who catches Zauner's attention."

Like me, thought Mathison. He felt stifled. "I'll be late," he said, reaching for the door of the car. The dark street with its far-placed lights had become grim and cold. The neat houses with their drawn curtains no longer seemed safe cosy oases for hot suppers and television.

"Only five minutes late," Nield said quickly, glancing at his watch, stretching his arm across to close the door. "No use messing up Keller's timetable. We may need him." He stopped Mathison from lowering the window. "Better suffocate than be overheard," he suggested. "I have some things to say. About your Elissa."

"Don't worry, I'll keep clear of her."

"The choice won't be yours."

"She may never reach Salzburg."

"That would be nice," Nield said dryly, "but I wouldn't count on it."

"You think she got away?"

"She had several hours to play around with before the Swiss even learned she was heading back to Salzburg."

"That was my—"

"It wasn't anyone's mistake. Drop the hair shirt. And if anyone is cussing himself, it's friend Andrew. There he was, taking time off from high finance to find out what I knew about Yates that he didn't already know, and right across the lobby was Elissa. She may have dyed her hair, but her face and legs are the same. And Andrew is rather a specialist on Miss Langenheim Lang. She was responsible for the suicide of one of his oldest friends."

203

Okay, okay, thought Mathison impatiently, you've got me listening. I believe you about Elissa. What's the warning behind all this? Mathison stared through the darkness at the hunched figure beside him. He couldn't read Nield's face any more than his mind. Was Nield still unsure of him? "All right. You think she got away. But your English friend— wasn't he keeping an eye on her until reinforcements arrived?"

Nield nodded gloomily. "She ditched them neatly. All they did was to give her notice that it was time to get out of Zürich. At least, that's my guess: She is much too clever to ignore any danger signal. And too important an operator to allow anyone to threaten her mission." He looked at Mathison and paused for emphasis. "Anyone."

So that was the warning, that was what Nield's attack of talk had been leading up to. "I get you. I'm the guy who can have her traced to Salzburg." Mathison tried to keep a note of humor in his voice, but he had really started worrying. Not just for himself. For Lynn Conway. She knew about Langenheim Lang, she knew about Salzburg. "Surely Elissa wouldn't act just on a hunch, on some vague suspicion?"

"Depends on how strongly her instincts are working, and how scared she is. How else has she managed to survive? She is one of the best agents the Soviets have turned out in years."

"The Russians?" Mathison's eyebrows went up. "I had it all figured out that Yates was an agent for Peking," he added wryly. Now he began to see why Nield, and Frank O'Donnell back in Jimmy Newhart's office, wouldn't make up their minds too quickly about Yates's employers.

"And you were right. Yates was working for Peking. Since 1958, that is. Before then, he was Moscow's man, a Stalin admirer."

"Don't tell me a tough-minded man like Yates could be taken by a flutter of eyelashes from Miss Langenheim Lang," Mathison said with a touch of bitterness. Not Yates, he was thinking; Yates wasn't the type to let himself be deluded by sweet talk or wide-eyed sincerity.

"Eight years ago, she was in Tokyo. So was Yates, making up his mind to slide over to the Peking side. They met, worked together as Soviet agents. She must have been around twenty then, straight from the KGB finishing school, and a real dazzler. As she is even now, no doubt about that. So when the Russians decided to infiltrate Yates's organization in Zürich, she was the obvious choice."

"She pretended to be converted to the true faith, too?"

"That is how it looks from here. The Russians must have supplied her with a pretty good legend to convince Yates she had come over to his side. He would check pretty carefully before he accepted her and sent her to Salzburg as his ears and eyes."

"But why Salzburg?" Elissa had come to Salzburg before Richard Bryant had even talked with Yates.

"Rumors," Nield said tersely. "These damned lakes were full of them." He glanced at his watch, took out a cigarette.

"She knows about Finstersee," Mathison said slowly.

"How did you reach that idea?" Nield forgot about his cigarette.

"She prepared me nicely." Like an old chest of drawers being sandpapered down for a first coat of paint. "I wasn't to be surprised if I didn't see her around Salzburg; she has a new job that may take her into the mountain villages to arrange for skiing parties this winter. There's a mountain village near Finstersee, isn't there?"

"Unterwald," Nield said very softly.

The moment could be right. Mathison tried, anyway. "What's so important about Finstersee?" It was the same question he had asked back in New York.

"You never give up, do you?" Nield asked with a laugh. He stuffed the cigarette back in his breast pocket. "Better not show a light. Nice dark road, isn't it?"

But Mathison wasn't to be sidetracked again. "I just like to know what's at stake."

"And if you don't think Finstersee is important, you'll pull out?" Nield was making a joke of it, but he was watching and listening carefully.

"I'm already up to my chin. Besides, as you said, the choice won't be mine." Elissa and her friends would see to that. "There are Nazi documents hidden in Finstersee. That much, I can guess. What are they?"

"Names on file."

"Names?"

"Names of men who worked secretly for the Nazis. Men who were anti-Nazi, who belonged to various European and American countries that were fighting the Nazis."

"And yet worked for them?" asked Mathison incredulously.

"Most obediently. Against their will, of course. But they did it."

"Blackmailed?"

"Either blackmailed because of some possible sex scandal, or intimidated because of families living in Nazi-occupied territory, or bribed with the promise of keeping their fortunes, of saving relatives from concentration camps. Totalitarians have many ways of twisting a man's arm without laying a hand on him."

"And the names of these men were never known?"

"Except to a few top Nazis. It's one of the secrets they want to keep until they try to grab power again. Then they'll apply the screws once more, and they'll have a supply of ready-made traitors." He looked at Mathison. "You think I'm too hard on these men? But that is what it was—treason. And if they gave in once, they can give in again. Who would want it known that he had worked for the Nazis? The blackmailing will be very simple next time."

Mathison said nothing at all. Nazis were a long way from recapturing power, even if there had been recent stirrings in Germany of revived nationalism, but that list of names could be used in the fight toward power. And it wasn't only the ex-Nazis or neo-Nazis that Nield had to worry about. The pressure on those poor devils whose names were secretly on file could be applied with the same ruthlessness that the Nazis would use if the list fell into Communist hands. Totalitarians, Nield had said, have many ways of twisting a man's arm. Or of breaking his back.

Nield was reaching into the rear seat for his nondescript raincoat. "Some of them are dead, no doubt," he said in his quiet way, "but enough of them must have stayed alive. And one thing is certain: they were not men who held ordinary jobs. They were a carefully selected bunch. They had talent and ambition and careers that gave enough promise to make them doubly dangerous today. Because they are bound to have been promoted, achieved some importance in these last twenty-odd years. Those who grew too old, have been retired, could still be used as agents of influence. But the younger ones among them—well, they could be used for more than purposes of propaganda."

If any of them had really sensitive jobs, Mathison thought,

then security itself could easily be breached in vital areas. "Have you any idea who these men are? Or how many of them are living in America?"

"No." Nield was pulling on his coat, the angry movement of his hands as he wrenched it around him showing something of his well-concealed emotions.

"But you do know such a file exists?"

"Yes."

"And that it is hidden in Finstersee?"

"That is what we hope Anna Bryant will tell us."

"You mean it was Richard Bryant's death—"

"Partly that, partly your report on what happened in Salzburg on the day he was killed." Nield pulled the belt of his coat tightly into its buckle, checked his pockets again, shook out his shapeless cap. His eyes were on the street ahead. "Come on, boys, come on!" he said tensely, revealing his own impatience.

They waited in silence for a full minute. Then Mathison saw a gleam from a far patch of dark shadow, as if someone had just lit a cigarette.

"Now!" Nield had his door half open. "Got everything?"

Mathison felt the unaccustomed weight of the automatic at his belt. "Everything," he said, trying to fight down a feeling of foolishness. Damn you, he told himself, you heard Nield's warnings and you listened to them and yet you can't quite believe all this is necessary. "Don't worry. I'm not backing out." He opened his door.

"Didn't think you would once you heard what's at stake." Nield stepped onto the sidewalk. Mathison got out, too. The nearer he came to this house, the more he wondered what had prompted him to volunteer so damned readily for a job he knew little about. He was glad he was not alone, even if Nield's company was ominous. He had said he didn't know what to expect, but he was certainly prepared for trouble. Mathison buttoned the lapels of his coat tight to the neck against the sharp bite of cold night air.

They met in front of the car and started walking at a normal pace.

15

THE STREET WAS ASLEEP EVEN AT THIS EARLY HOUR, AND blotted with shadows. A few cars, small, widely scattered under the stretch of trees, hunched close to the curb. There was a faint hint of roast veal from one darkened house, a snatch of a muted Mahler symphony from another, and always the protective curtains or shutters drawn against the night, with only a few cracks of light to show that people did live here. Underfoot, fallen leaves, matted into a carpet by today's heavy rain, dulled the sound of heels on the well-paved sidewalk. A quiet street, a decorous street, a place of neat lives and good order and careful privacy. Greta Freytag and her invalid mother, thought Mathison, might well have stayed here. If Nield had not checked with Keller, or if he himself had not remembered her comment about gardens, he would be walking toward this gate right now without any suspicions. And unaccompanied. He glanced at the silent Nield, who showed no signs of leaving him. Was he going all the way?

Nield seemed to sense his perplexity. He dropped his voice to a murmur Mathison could barely hear. "Sure, I'm breaking every rule, but it may be worth it."

"We're over ten minutes late." And their car parked back there—what excuse for that if it had been noticed? I'm worrying too much, thought Mathison. He envied the cool Nield.

"We misjudged the street number. I'm your old Zürich pal who volunteered to get you here on time. Like most volunteered help, mine was overoptimistic."

"And you're hanging around so we can have dinner together after I see Freytag?" Mathison tried.

"Not bad, not bad at all," Nield said with some amusement. His eyes searched the street for the last time. "There are two men over by that big tree opposite, and that car near the house with the big hedge wasn't there when we drove past, but they are Keller's people, I hope. Otherwise, it seems okay. Damned careless of your hosts. They ought to have had pointmen out. They underestimated you. Or they are under-strength." One last search with his eyes along the street and he halted at the gate. "Or I may be totally wrong. Freytag may be using a friend's house to see you privately." Then his voice became normal again as he began speaking in German. "Here's the house, Bill. This is the number, I think. Yes. At last!" He swung the gate open—it had a fine warning screech—and led the way along the short brick path, his head turned from any watchful window as he looked back at Mathison. He kept talking.

Mathison's confidence began to return. He was even smiling at Nield's ripe Zürich accent (Hier isht das Haus ...) as he pressed the bell and waited for the door to open. Nield had stepped slightly to the side and was standing where no light from the hall would fall directly on him. He was holding a cigarette, shielding his face from the brief flare of his lighter. The men waiting across the road would see the small signal quite clearly. What the hell do they all expect? Mathison wondered.

The door opened. A little old lady, leaning heavily on a walking stick, a thick dark shawl wound around her shoulders, looked at Mathison blankly. Her face was pale and thin, her hair white and frizzed into a fringe across her brow while the rest of it tried to escape from a flattened bun on top of her head. The invalid mother, thought Mathison, and resisted the impulse to glance at Nield. "I'm William Mathison," he said. "Is your daughter at home, Mrs. Freytag? She wanted to see me."

"Oh, yes," she said, and looked out at Nield. She frowned uncertainly.

"I'll wait here," Nield said. He moved casually behind Mathison, glanced into the hall.

"I won't be long," Mathison assured him, taking his cue.

Her frown deepened. "Greta!" she called. That was a normal enough cry, except that there was something in the tone of her voice that sounded more of a warning than of a call to her daughter. That, and the puzzled frown, the uncertain look in her eyes, the lack of invitation to enter, switched Mathison from almost-acceptance into definite doubt. It deepened as a man appeared immediately in the narrow hall and took charge. He was small and thin, a lightweight physically but with quick and highly intelligent eyes. With a glance at Nield and a friendly nod for Mathison, he said, "Come in!

209

Miss Freytag is upstairs. She will be down in a few minutes." He gestured to both of them.

The woman stepped aside, pulled the door wide open to let them enter. Her frown persisted, as if she didn't quite like this development but had no other ideas of how to handle the unexpected appearance of Nield. "Come in, come in," she said, dropping the frown and picking up a more amiable look of welcome. "Please wait in there." Her stick pointed to the room from which the man had appeared so quickly. "I will let Greta know you are here." It was an unnecessary remark: Greta Freytag would have had to be inflicted with instant deafness not to have heard her name called up the narrow staircase and through the thin walls of this house.

Mathison stepped inside the hall. Nield threw his cigarette away and followed, hands deep in pockets, cap pulled down to his eyebrows, looking like some embarrassed lout who was totally disinterested and impatient to leave. "How long will this take?" he was muttering. He seemed to be paying no attention to the hall—unheated and as cold as the air on the steps outside, unfurnished except for one wooden chair—or to a rustle of movement, a creak of floor board, that came from the room Mathison was about to enter.

But the thin-faced man stopped him, with a sharp glance at the woman, who had obviously made more than one unnecessary remark. "Wait here," he countermanded. "I shall go and tell Greta. She may want to see you upstairs." He transferred his sharp glance to Nield.

"We have a dinner engagement," Mathison said, as he managed partly to block the man's view of Nield by stepping between them. He didn't add to the explanation; those quick eyes were clever enough to put the story together for themselves. The man's interest faded. He nodded and ran up the staircase. Mathison moved slowly to the bottom step as the man disappeared from view. From here, he could see something of the room. It was silent in there now, as if the man inside—or two men, perhaps, for the rustle and creak had seemed to come from separate sides of the room—was holding his breath. Mathison turned to look back at Nield, standing beside the lady with the stick, and an uncertain and perplexed old lady she was. "Don't worry," he told Nield, "I won't make us late. I'm glad you came along, though. Never would have found this address by myself. Have you seen anything of Gerri lately? Heard he was opening a new garage. Business must be good." What he had seen of the room was a stretch of bare floor, a wooden table and four chairs pushed back as if people had risen hastily. There were three beer bottles on the table; no glasses, cigarettes stubbed into the lid of a can, a poor overhead light from an elaborate brass chandelier which had been left only one bulb. An empty house, thought Mathison, and now a very silent house. Had the men left by some other door, slipped out by a back entrance?

There was silence from upstairs, too. Nield was listening. He exchanged glances with Mathison but no words, as if he was too busy with his own guesses. He could be thinking that if he had been playing it by ear tonight, these characters in this empty house had thrown away the score and were improvising desperately. The deep silence ended. There were footsteps overhead, and the thin man returned to sight. He was looking perplexed but friendly. He ran lightly downstairs. "I am sorry," he was saying. "Greta must have gone out. We didn't know. But if you would telephone later tonight, you can talk to her then. Or I could have her telephone you when she returns. Where are you having dinner?"

Mathison looked at Nield. "At the Schwarzer Adler, isn't it?" Now I'm stuck, he thought. You handle this, Charlie my boy. And what the hell is going on?

Nield handled it. "What's that?" he was asking sharply, looking up the stairs. He listened quite openly. "I heard something—"

"Nothing," the man said quickly, and signaled for the woman to open the door. She seemed to move very spryly without much help from the walking stick. "The Schwarzer Adler," he agreed with a nod of his head. "I'll give her the message."

"There it is again!" Nield said. "Someone is in pain—perhaps has had an accident, needs help? Didn't you hear it, Bill?"

"No!" said the woman, her voice rising. "There's nothing!"

"Nothing," echoed the man in a more natural tone. "Gute Nacht, Herr Mathison. Auf Wiedersehen." He flashed a glance at the woman, telling her to keep quiet.

"I think I hear something, too," Mathison told him, watching Nield, who had managed to get between the man and the staircase.

211

"Willi!" shouted the woman, closing the door again.

Willi wheeled away from Mathison and saw Nield, his hands deep in his pockets, beginning to climb the stairs, slowly, innocently, looking upward at the floor above. "Come back here, you! I'll get the police!"

"Do that." Nield went on climbing.

The man lunged after him and made his first open mistake. From under the heavy sweater that covered his belt, he drew a revolver while his other hand pulled out a silencer from his pocket. He was fitting them expertly together as Nield swung around to face him.

Mathison heard the shot from the staircase as he turned at the warning rush of heels on the wooden floor behind him. He caught the woman's upraised arm with the stick ready to crash down on the back of his head. Her other hand came at him, two fingers pointed straight for his eyes, but he caught that wrist, too. For a moment she was all strength, and then just as unexpectedly all weakness. Mathison removed the stick from her loosened grip. "For God's sake!" he said in disgust, and dropped her onto the wooden chair as Nield picked up Willi's revolver with a handkerchief. She was crying bitterly. At the foot of the stairs, the thin man had been knocked back a good three feet. He lay there unconscious, his right shoulder smashed by Nield's bullet.

"Look out!" came Nield's voice, and Mathison turned sharply to see the woman dart past him, her white wig askew from the force of a quick rush that dodged Mathison and carried her through the deserted living room. A rear door smashed shut. "Let her go," Nield called, and brought Mathison back to the hall. "Keller's men will take care of her—like the other two." He noticed Mathison's slight surprise. "There were two of them? As well as the woman and this clown?" He nodded at Willi, who was moaning slightly in a strangled whisper, like a man screaming in a deep nightmare.

"That was my count," Mathison agreed. "You have good ears." Nield had been some distance from the living-room door. Mathison glanced at the stairs. "Did you really hear something up there?"

"No. But they didn't want us to explore, did they?" Nield had emptied Willi's revolver, holding it carefully with his handkerchief, and now placed it out of reach of the man's inert arm. "Lesson one: never leave a loaded weapon beside

212

even an unconscious man," he told Mathison. "And if this worries you, we are simply leaving evidence of lethal attempt." Briefly, he examined the singed hole in the pocket of his raincoat. "How do I explain this, dammit? I borrowed the coat."

"You've taken up pipe smoking," Mathison suggested with a small laugh. His sense of relief was growing by the minute. Some kind of trap had been set here for him, but he hadn't been caught. No damage done except to Willi.

"What's so funny?" Nield asked curtly.

You and your legal niceties, the woman's wig, all this business of disguise and subterfuge; and myself, too. "The joke's on me. I really thought she was an old woman. Well, it's lucky we had Keller outside."

"*You* were lucky she didn't carry a gun. And where was yours? Lesson two: never underestimate." He glanced down at Willi. "I need to remember that myself. He was faster than he looked." Distant footsteps caught Nield's ear. Men were in the kitchen, about to enter the living room. "We can leave him now. He'll soon be in good firm hands." Nield was already climbing the stairs, three at a time.

Mathison followed at the same pace. From below he could hear footsteps and voices now coming into the living room. Nield was paying them no attention whatsoever. He was at the top of the stairs, gesturing for speed, pointing to the central corridor that led from this barely lighted landing along the upper floor to the other side of the house. Six closed doors, noted Mathison; three on each side. Nield said quietly, "You take these rooms. I'll try the others." He had drawn his revolver as he moved toward them. Okay, thought Mathison, and pulled out his automatic. Trouble to be expected? He reached his first door, braced himself.

It was unlocked, and the room felt empty. He risked switching on the light. Anticlimax, he told himself as he looked briefly at a nondescript bathroom.

The second door was locked, but it was flimsy enough to be forced open at the first try. He groped for the light switch and flicked it on. The dark shapes in the room became recognizable: a well-furnished bedroom, complete with armchair and a small television set. But the wardrobe door, gaping open, showed nothing but empty hooks and hangers. The bureau drawers were empty, too, and its top quite bare except for a crumpled lace mat, as if someone had been packing in haste. There were two suitcases beside the door, heavy to lift, locked and strapped. "What do you make of this?" Mathison called softly to Nield.

Nield didn't seem to hear. He was standing at the door of his third room, his hand on its light switch. Then slowly he turned away and came over to Mathison. He slipped the revolver back into his pocket. His light-blue eyes had become cold and hard. Briefly they took in the bedroom and the suitcases. His normally pleasant face was as taut as his voice. "Ready for evacuation, I see. Once they got you here alone, knocked you over the head, left you unconscious, they were ready to move out—no doubt calling the police as they left. They had it well staged."

"They'd call the police?"

Nield nodded to the room across the passage. "Over here," he said, leading the way. Mathison stopped abruptly at its threshold. He pocketed his automatic. Slowly he entered.

The room was small, barely furnished. On its strip of thin rug were scattered a brown tweed coat, brown pocketbook, a felt hat, gloves, umbrella. And on the narrow bed against one flowered wall, her face set in a death mask of fear and pain, lay the rigid body of a woman. She was almost unrecognizable in the disarray of hair and clothing. Mathison's breath strangled in his lungs. His eyes shifted unbelievingly toward the coat, the matching gloves and pocketbook, the sensible hat; then back to the silk scarf tightly twisted around the woman's neck.

Nield said quickly, "Touch nothing. Leave this all to Keller's experts." He put out a hand to keep Mathison from lifting the coat to cover the contorted face.

"Very wise," said Keller's voice behind them. He was alone. He stopped at the threshold, his lips tightening. "Greta Freytag?" he asked Mathison.

"Yes."

Keller crossed over to the last unopened door. He kicked it wide, but found nothing inside that narrow room except a cot and blankets. He returned slowly. He looked only at Mathison, kept talking only to him. "So that is what it was: a safe house. They could shelter several people here if necessary, keep them apart from each other while new passports and identities were being faked." He went on to the well-furnished bedroom and glowered down at the waiting suitcases. "The caretaker lived here—the woman who came

214

running out into the night. I see she was ready for flight anyway. A neatly planned operation. Up to a point." He glanced at Nield for the first time, gave a brief nod of congratulations, and ignored him once more. "Have you the revolver with which you wounded the man downstairs?"

"But I didn't—" began Mathison. And then he caught on. Nield, quite silent, was holding the revolver out to him. Mathison took it. Nield didn't seem too happy about parting with it, but he could scarcely object; he was the man who had never been here. "How's this?" Mathison said, passing the revolver over to Keller. And that, he thought, keeps your report in good order. No difficult questions about Nield's presence to be answered. A neat and satisfactory solution for all.

"Thank you," Keller said most seriously. "The police like to check weapons and match them with bullets."

Mathison had rising doubts about that satisfactory solution. "Awkward for me," he suggested.

"But why? You fired in obvious self-defense. The police will find the other bullet somewhere in the staircase wall— the one that came from the wounded man's pistol."

The other bullet? Mathison glanced sharply at Nield. But of course—there had been a silencer on that pistol, and it had deceived him. All he had noticed was a faint plopping echo to the shot that Nield had fired. Christ, thought Mathison, no wonder he lost his sense of humor down in that hall. Willi's bullet must have whistled close.

"The man did fire at you?" Keller was making sure of that.

Nield nodded. Mathison replied for him. "He fired."

"His pistol was empty when I picked it up."

"Oh yes," Mathison said quickly, taking the small handful of bullets from Nield to give to Keller. "It seemed a good idea to make sure he wouldn't sneak another shot. Lesson one, I believe."

Keller wrapped the bullets carefully in his handkerchief. "Can't be too careful," he agreed. "Well, now that we have everything straight, it's time to leave. I would suggest that back-bedroom window. The roof of the kitchen and scullery jut out right underneath it, an easy drop for anyone in training. Except it might be wiser if you, Mr. Mathison, were seen to be leaving by the front door. There are some neighbors gathering down on the street, and it's possible that a friend of this house is pretending to be one of them. So you and I shall leave quite naturally, even if the back way is safe for anyone going out that window for the next five minutes. But just one moment," he finished in the same grave voice, "I have to give orders to get Homicide along here." He looked at the doorway of the room where Greta Freytag lay. He shook his head angrily, slowly. "I did not expect that," he said. Then he was walking to the head of the stairs and began giving instructions to the man who waited for him halfway down.

Nield signaled his good-bye, switched off the light in the bedroom that Keller had pointed out, made for its window. He eased it up gently, looked down at the drop, then around the small patch of back yard. A hedge, some bushes, no lights, an opened gate, cold blackness of enclosing night. He nodded, swung over the sill, and lowered himself out of sight. Mathison, listening intently as he watched Nield disappear, heard a faint thud. Then silence. He crossed over to the window, restraining an impulse to look out and see Nield's second drop into the yard, closed it carefully. He was back at the door and had switched on the light before Keller returned.

Two men followed Keller. They had been assigned their jobs. One went into Greta Freytag's room, the other started a careful check on all the others. "I'll have more help for you in half an hour. Tell Homicide we need both these suitcases intact. Intact! That goes for anything else we find hidden in the attic—there is no need for them to crawl up there, and they know it. So keep them down here where they belong." To Mathison, he said, "Better leave. Soon this house will be too crowded for comfort." He gave one last look at Greta Freytag. "Perhaps," he said softly, "she knew more than she told you. Or whoever instigated this murder thought she knew more than she actually did."

Whoever instigated ... Elissa? Impossible, Mathison kept telling himself. A foreign agent, yes; but someone who could command abduction and murder? Surely not Elissa ... He said, "Who did arrange this?" He wanted more than some of Nield's clever deductions. He needed something factual, something conclusive.

But Keller wasn't going to help him argue out his bitter thought. Keller wanted some facts himself, and he knew where to start. He looked at the handsome troubled face of the young man who stared at him almost angrily. Keller said very quietly, "You may have the answer to that question, Mr. Mathison. Come! We can talk as I drive you to your hotel. I'd stay close to my room for the next few days if I were you. We'll send someone to keep an eye on you. Much safer." He took Mathison's arm and led him toward the staircase.

A friendly gesture? Mathison decided it was only that, and relaxed. "I'm leaving for Salzburg tomorrow. Unless, of course, someone thinks I'm a murder suspect."

"No one will. Miss Freytag was obviously killed several hours ago. Two policemen can swear to the time you entered this house."

"They didn't see me enter it alone." And it would be impossible to mention Nield, far less produce him as a witness.

"You entered along with a young man I had specially detailed to accompany you who is now on another assignment," Keller said calmly. "And are you going to Salzburg on business?"

"Yes. For Newhart and Morris. I'll have to deal with a bogus contract issued in their name."

"How long will that take you?"

"A couple of days."

"You might stretch them a little. Salzburg is a safer place for you than Zürich."

"Is it?"

Keller's quick eyes studied him briefly. "Unless the person who wanted to delay you in reaching Salzburg has as many resources there as here."

She has less of a ready-made organization to help her in Salzburg, thought Mathison—and there he was, putting the guilt right on Elissa Lang's shoulders again. Yet, as Eva Langenheim, she had Yates's group to help her in Zürich. But would they have obeyed her? How could she have asserted authority over them? "Do you think the Nazis were behind all this?"

They had reached the hall. It was empty now. Inside the abject living room, Willi was being guarded by a couple of men. Keller took Mathison's arm once again in a surprisingly firm grip, lowered his voice even more. "This looks better, just in case our casualty is feigning unconsciousness. Those fellows have lawyers, you know, who don't mind carrying

217

messages out of prison. At least we know who he is. One of my men identified him as a Chicom sympathizer who has been organizing antiwar meetings at the University. We thought him harmless." He halted at the front door. "That answers your question, doesn't it?"

"Then he is one of Yates's group?"

Keller nodded. "We have also learned why he was here tonight. He seemed to think he was dying—he's a type that always dramatizes itself—and he made a brief impassioned speech denouncing the poor woman who is lying upstairs. She betrayed Yates to the Nazis. Yes, he really believes that. And *you* were the CIA agent who paid her to play traitor." Keller opened the door. "Now brace yourself, Mr. Mathison. Let's get quickly to the car."

Its driver had the engine running, the door already opened. "Good!" Keller said as they climbed into the back seat and shut out the curious eyes. Far along the street was a sweep of lights. Ambulance, thought Keller; Homicide, too. "And reporters," he said aloud. "I think we've both had a lucky escape tonight, Mr. Mathison."

16

BUT IT WASN'T UNTIL BILL MATHISON WAS ACTUALLY WALKING through the lobby of his hotel that he could really believe he was a free man. He could still feel Keller's tight grip on his arm, a reminder of what might have been. And here was the warm lobby, bright with lights, busy with people (some arriving for dinner, some leaving to eat elsewhere, the perpetual motion of the let's-try-somewhere-else tourists), looking so blandly normal, so far removed from the strange world he had just left with its doubts and dark visions and danger, that it shook him. Keller and Nield, he thought, must have nerves of Toledo steel.

And then, as he waited for his key at the porter's desk, he was startled to catch a glimpse of himself in one of the mirrored walls; he looked absolutely normal, too. The last ninety minutes of his life, for it was almost half past eight, might only have been a particularly hideous nightmare, except that, in undreamlike fashion, its quick succession of events had been logically developed and connected, and the memories it had left were sharp-edged. Tonight he had been administered a grim lesson in realities. He would no longer be able to talk blithely of the end of the Cold War, of the completely different set of problems that the sixties had brought into the political world; the Cold War in its old evident terms might have eased, but the Hidden War was there. Even a peaceful nation like Switzerland could vouch for that, or it wouldn't have men like Keller in its service.

"No messages tonight," the porter told him, unasked. "You did find the Bergstrasse, Herr Mathison?"

"I found it. Oh, by the way, I'll be spending the weekend out of Zürich. I'll be back on Monday." I hope, he thought, and made for an elevator. He found he was more conscious of the people who stepped inside with him, but after one quick glance he paid little attention to the old lady who bickered all the way to the second floor with her companion except to note wryly that she had white hair pinned into a recalcitrant bun and leaned heavily on a stick. He got off the elevator with two ponderous men discussing soft loans, and did not even look to see what door they entered. There was a limit to suspicion. There had to be, or else he would find it a useless instinct when he most needed it in good working order. And that was the strange thing about suspicion: too much of it, and you had bricked yourself into a ten-foot-thick wall; too little, and you were buying the Eiffel Tower. It had been sold twice, he remembered hearing—and by the same crook. He was smiling as he opened his door.

Suddenly, he was alert. There was someone here, someone possibly inside the bathroom. He switched on the overhead light to help strengthen the lamp he had left on near the armchair, closed the door, picked up a heavy ashtray as he moved quickly, silently, along the wall toward the bathroom.

Its door swung fully open. Nield's voice asked lightly, "Friend or foe?" He stepped into the room, looked at the ashtray approvingly and said, "You're learning." He went back to the armchair where he had been sitting. "How did you know?"

"The chair cushion sags just after someone has been sitting in it."

"What, not pure down? Let's complain to the management. Was that all you noticed?"

"I didn't leave the bathroom door half-shut. And I had the

219

window open a couple of inches." Mathison wasn't amused.

"You *are* learning."

Mathison replaced the ashtray. "You teach a hard lesson." And was it necessary? he wondered.

"I was simply safeguarding myself. It would be hard to explain to a valet with a pressed pair of pants just what I was doing here. Without a passkey too. The hotel wouldn't like that." He paused, asked blankly, "What happened to the automatic I gave you? Don't tell me Keller frisked you and took it."

Mathison drew the pistol out of his pocket. "The hotel doesn't like loud noises either." He shook his head over his stupidity. And you thought you were so damned smart, he told himself. "I forgot about it," he added frankly. Or perhaps I just trust my pitching arm more, he thought.

"Keep it. And just remember to remember," Nield said easily. He seemed completely relaxed. He had got rid of his bulky raincoat and unprepossessing cap. His hair, well-brushed, now looked faintly Byronic, and he had found time to change from rough tweeds back into banker's gray. Was he actually staying at this hotel? Mathison wondered as he slipped off his coat. "Give me a few minutes and then I'll be off and you can ring for that drink," Nield told him as he eyed the telephone. "I'm on my way to Austria. I just wanted to make sure that Keller did deliver you to the hotel door."

"Had you doubts?"

"Not really."

"I had. It was lucky we were dealing with Keller."

Nield's voice became crisp. "I assure you that if I had been organizing any clandestine operations in Zürich, like Yates, I wouldn't be here now. Or you either. The Swiss *are* neutral. It doesn't do to forget that. But there is another characteristic about the Swiss: they pay their debts. Tonight we helped them. Considerably."

"Yes. If you hadn't put Willi out of action, the first of Keller's men to enter that house would have caught it. Willi's revolver was lethal."

"Not a kindly type," Nield agreed. "Too much shock value."

"Keller didn't take it so lightly. He told me—"

"The point is," Nield said, turning away any compliments, "what did you tell Keller?" The question was routine, a matter of simple checking; he could stop worrying about

220

Mathison, the amateur who had stepped into a jungle. Mathison had had a shock, possibly a nasty scare, but he was in control—no rush of overexcited words, no dramatics, no braggadocio. And his reflexes were quicker than ever. He would be able to take care of himself, something Nield had not quite believed when he had made this special trip to Zürich. Amateurs were tricky to handle. Too often they fell into extremes after a touch of action: all zeal and zest, or all quibble and qualms.

"The story of My Day," Mathison answered as he lit a cigarette and walked over to the bathroom, stepped just inside and pulled the door half shut. He looked through the crack at the hinge, and could see the entrance to his bedroom. So that was how Nield had known it was safe to come out. "That saved me asking a silly question," he said as he returned and pulled over a chair to face Nield. "I also told Keller I was going to Salzburg. He had no objections. It saves him having to detail a couple of men to look after me, I suppose. He will need all of them in the big roundup. He may also hope that I'll run across Elissa in Salzburg—he calls her Eva Langenheim, of course. At least, if I see her, he wants me to let him know."

"That's one way of dealing with her." Nield's voice hinted that he could think of other ways, too. "But first we have to find her. And I don't think it will be in Salzburg. In any case, that's my job. You keep clear of her."

"Delighted."

"She has to move quickly. She must. She will stop off in Salzburg only long enough to make contact with the KGB colonel who is in control there. I don't think Elissa will turn in a report on her activities today in Zürich. Not yet. Not until the mistakes she made today don't matter."

"Mistakes?" Well that's encouraging, thought Mathison—if true.

"Mistake one: she hadn't time to get advice from her control in Salzburg, who, in turn, would have got in touch with Moscow. And the Center doesn't want bright ideas put into action until they've been studied from every angle. There were some angles she did miss, and that was her second mistake and a very grave one. So she won't say much—at present—about Zürich, but concentrate on Finstersee and ask the KGB man for support in dealing with that problem."

"But he is bound to question her about the four days she spent in Zürich. She wasn't here on holiday."

"She achieved her original purpose in coming here. She had one whole clear day last Tuesday to visit Yates's secret hide-out, where he sent and decoded messages. She could pick up a lot of information there from his special files and notes. If she has done a good job on that, her KGB control will be satisfied. The urgency of Finstersee will catch all his attention."

"You mean she now knows as much about Finstersee as Yates did?"

"She had the time to search for it. The Swiss didn't even hear of Yates until early on Wednesday."

"She'd manage it, all right," Mathison said. Clever, clever little Elissa. "But what angles did she miss tonight?" Not Elissa. Elissa didn't miss anything. "She didn't do so badly. She did eliminate Greta Freytag. She did use some of Yates's people for the job. She did have me detained by the Swiss— or, rather, that was her intention, and if she gets word about the police raid on the house she will think she was successful in that, too. So why wouldn't she make a report on all that?"

"Because four of Yates's Progressive Action party were picked up tonight. That was the first angle she missed."

"You mean she had expected them to get away before the police arrived?"

"And be arrested later, perhaps even weeks later, once the Swiss collected clues and followed trails."

"But now someone may talk." Not Willi; but possibly one or both of the two men who bolted from the house to save their skins. Then Mathison shook his head. "That's little help to us. They won't know her as Langenheim, or as Lang. They can only identify her by a code name. Isn't that the way these boys work it?"

Nield nodded, briefly amused. "They could identify a photograph though. A snapshot of a pretty girl with Yates? Swiss Security must have been searching through Freytag's letters, diaries, photographs for this last hour. And that was another angle Elissa missed: Freytag had photography for a hobby."

Mathison was a hard man to convince. "Would it be likely that Elissa, even protected by using only a code name, had ever met any of those four? Face to face?"

"Normally, no. But today was definitely abnormal. How did she manage to arrange everything so quickly? By coded

222

messages dropped under bridges, or attached to a park seat?"

"I get you. Too little time. And she couldn't risk talking over a telephone. She had to meet them to enlist their help, give them urgent reasons for such action." He was remembering Keller's words.

"And that was the third angle she missed." Nield looked almost cheerful for a moment. "She is bound to check back with Zürich to find out how the action went. She will hear of the arrests at Bergstrasse. She has too much sense to mention that miscalculation in any report to her boss until she can make sure of complete success with Finstersee. She needs a triumph to justify, or excuse, the risks she took today. If she can deliver the Nazis' secret file into the right hands, then—" Nield shrugged his shoulders.

"All will be forgiven?"

"If she doesn't make any more mistakes."

"I thought you said she was good at her job."

"She is. But she seems to have been underestimating us, which sometimes means she could be overestimating herself. And that is unforgivable on her side of the fence." Nield waited for any more objections. But Mathison was silent. "She intends to get that Finstersee box. From now on, that's all she is thinking about. We had better not underestimate her."

Mathison nodded. He was convinced.

Okay, okay, thought Nield, glancing at his watch. He was running later than he had intended, but that last ten minutes was not time wasted. Mathison had to have some reassurance that, if he was being sent to Salzburg after tonight's crisis, he wasn't being sent blindly. He'd know that Nield had been trying to think out all the angles, at least. And he must feel now, as Nield did, that there was some margin of safety. "I think we'll have a couple of days to make our own moves without interference from Elissa and her friends. It takes a little time to get people into position, supply them with some cover, credible justification for being there. Their chief worry will not be us, but the Nazis. And that's our big worry, too. The Nazis have been guarding that file too long to let it slip out of their hands now." He hesitated, added carefully, "You have no questions about Moscow's use of that file?" There was a current fashion, he thought wearily, of equating the Soviet Union and the United States; just two big monsters, no choice between their methods or purposes, too powerful for anyone else's good. A comforting philosophy that rid one of any feeling of moral obligation or of commitment, or even of the need for a study in depth of recent history.

"They'll make use of the names, all right," Mathison said grimly.

Nield could relax. No daydreams on cloud nine here. "And what about us? How would we use them?"

"We'll lock them away in a nice safe place and then—surprise, big surprise—some amiable filing clerk with security standing will try to filch them in a couple of years, and we'll be drunk-lucky if they don't end up in Moscow anyway. Or in Peking, where there will be a new set of Communists with the same old ideas about world power."

Nield's eyebrows went up all the way. "Oh, sometimes we do keep the secrets we learn," he suggested, his words mild enough but his voice sharpening. "What would *you* do with them?"

"Burn them."

"Yes," Nield said quietly, "that's a good solution as long as there is no duplicate list around."

"Duplicate? For God's sake, Chuck—why don't you start worrying about triplicates, quadruplicates—"

"Because I'm not talking about triplicates, quadruplicates, or any other iflicates. The more copies of any document, the less security. Obviously. But even the most supersecret document has a duplicate for insurance. This file of names was moved along with other classified material to the outskirts of Salzburg during the last year of the war. Part of the German Foreign Office went there to escape the Allied bombings of Berlin, and so did SS Intelligence, who controlled this file. Now I ask you, Bill, would they have only one copy of it?"

"No," agreed Mathison, if slowly. He was annoyed with his own stupidity. One bomb landing on a truck that carried important unduplicated documents could leave a pretty big gap in Intelligence. "Then you had better find the Finstersee file. That's the only way you'd be able to keep a watchful eye on its names, warn them that they could be blackmailed into betraying their countries all over again, advise them to let you know if they are approached—" He broke off. "I suppose that's the kind of use you'll have for the file—if you find it?"

Nield nodded. "We'd run a lot of interference, try to block any of the opposition's possible plays."

Mathison watched Nield curiously. What's he trying to make up his mind to tell me? wondered Mathison. I'm beginning to know that look in his eyes. "It will be a headache for you. And a nightmare for those names on the list."

Nield had decided. Very quietly, he said, "The nightmare may have begun."

"A duplicate list has been discovered?"

"It *may* have been discovered," Nield said carefully.

"How do you reach that idea? Is it just a hunch? Or do you actually know?"

"It's a hunch, and all my own, and a hell of a thing to carry around."

Mathison said nothing. If Nield's instincts were flashing a warning signal, there could be some basis in fact for them.

Nield frowned thoughtfully at the middle distance. "The Nazis hid important documents in Czechoslovakian lakes, too. And the Czechs searched diligently, backed by Moscow experts. They found two deposits last year. One of those they publicized quite freely—great triumph for Communist Intelligence, that sort of angle. And indeed it was. But they were pretty cagey about their second find. They were too clever to say nothing at all about it—after all, you can't hide diving or dredging operations done on a big scale—but their description of the contents of the chests they hauled up in the second lake was too simple, too disarming. So the nasty thought keeps coming back: just what was inside one of those chests? Something that was going to be so useful to them that they weren't telling what? The duplicate list of unsuspected Nazi agents?"

That could be a warning signal, thought Mathison, but it wasn't quite enough. "Perhaps."

Nield nodded. "It might not be, and again it might. I've been wondering, you see, why the Communists ever betrayed Eric Yates to the Nazis just when he was on to something as big as the Finstersee cache. The timing of that was all wrong."

This was adding some flesh to the bones, thought Mathison. He waited expectantly.

"It would have been so much more likely that the Russians would keep intercepting his radio messages to the Chicom agents in Warsaw, even let him deal with poor old Bryant all the way to the bitter death, and *then* seize the Finstersee chest while they made sure that Yates got his last reward from the Nazis. On the other hand, I have to admit that the Russians might have been plain stupid, or just too damned clever, which often comes to the same thing. They may have tipped off the Nazis before they knew that Eric Yates was working on anything as important as Finstersee. That would be ironical. And it does happen. Sometimes."

"You don't sound too persuaded."

"I'd be more persuaded if the Russians had been showing any interest, these last six weeks, in the Styrian lakes of the Salzkammergut region—they had located Yates's transmitter some time ago and must have been listening to his messages when they tipped off the Nazis—or even if they had shown one-tenth of the interest they took in Lake Toplitz before the first big finds there in 1959. It's strange how cool they've been playing it. They have sent a couple of men now and again to the villages near Finstersee, but they never seemed interested in the lake itself, only in any strangers who were visiting that part of the country. The Soviet agents may have been checking to see that Finstersee slept on undisturbed." Nield laughed softly. "And we can be stupid, too. We didn't take any rumor too seriously, because the Russians didn't. It's so easy to believe that a rumor is only myth pretending to be historical fact, especially when you've checked once and found nothing. Then the rumor becomes an old wives' tale, just so much hysterics." He became grimly serious. "We should have kept checking and double-checking, no matter what the risks. Two years ago, I lost one friend up there, near Finstersee. That seemed too big a price for any rumor. And yet, we'll pay a lot more, and pay and pay, if the Communists have the Nazi file."

"There has to be a limit to any check and double-check," Mathison said sympathetically. "Or else a rumor could become a mania."

"There's that, too," Nield conceded. He stopped brooding. "It's a hell of a life," he added briskly. "In any case, I've just been spilling out some of my own worries in the last few minutes. Perhaps they are ill-founded, perhaps not."

"I wouldn't neglect them."

"Seriously? Go on, Bill, be honest about them. Now's the

time. We can't afford any afterthoughts once you are on your way to Salzburg."

"No afterthoughts. If your guess is anywhere near accurate, then this whole job of ours has become twice as urgent. Elissa is trying to find the Finstersee file in order to suppress it. If Moscow has already got one set of names, it certainly doesn't want any copy to fall into Western hands. Because the value of this file to them—for any blackmail purposes—lies only in the fact that we don't know what names are on it. Without the Finstersee file, we could neither warn the men whose names are listed nor protect ourselves from them."

"And if my guess is wild, if there exists only one copy of that file?"

"Then we had better find it before Elissa tracks it down." He looked at Nield with a smile. "Still not quite sure of me?"

"It wasn't that," Nield said quietly. "I just wanted to make sure you knew how rapidly we'd have to move. And why. That's always important."

"Especially when you're dealing with an amateur," Mathison said, his grin widening as he recalled that afternoon, back in New York, when he had first met Charles Nield. "I know, I know. I sounded off plenty, before." I was going to Salzburg, but on my own terms. I might have had Anna Bryant killed, and myself, too. "So all right. I'm now going to Salzburg to warn Mrs. Bryant that she's in danger and to offer her our help. I'll also ask her quite frankly what her husband knew about Finstersee. Anything else?"

"No. That should start everything moving."

"You mean, that's all you want me—" began Mathison in surprise.

"It will be quite enough. Keep your visit as natural as possible. I don't want you to do anything to create any serious doubts."

"Elissa," Mathison said wryly, "seemed to have had some doubts about me as it was. And I was being as natural as hell."

"If she had had real doubts, you'd have been as dead as Greta Freytag right now. Look, didn't I reassure you there *is* a margin of safety for you in Salzburg?"

"Sure. I believe you. Or you wouldn't be sending me there. I would only foul up your entire operation."

Nield stared at him, recovered, said quietly, "Elissa's first interest in you came through Felix Zauner when he detailed

227

her to follow you. But—and this is important—he has checked thoroughly on you and finds you above suspicion. I got that from a very good source. So you can believe it. Elissa will, too. All that worries her now is the possibility that Greta Freytag identified her as Langenheim to you when—"

"Not to me," Mathison said quickly. "Freytag told Lynn Conway, who told me."

There was a long silence.

"You know who she is?" Mathison asked.

Nield nodded. "Send Conway back to New York."

"But she is here on a job. She takes it seriously. And what do I tell her, anyway, to explain why she'd be better out of Zürich? What's more, I've no authority over her. If she pulled rank, she could start giving the firm's lawyer a few instructions herself."

"Look here, Bill, most of Willi's group in Yates's organization were picked up tonight at Bergstrasse. But there may be a couple, even three, left in that particular cell for Keller to clean out. He needs a little time to get the information on them, to plan and make his moves. And if they questioned Greta Freytag before they killed her, then they have the Conway girl's name. Zürich is no good for her at the moment, no good at all."

"Keller said he would keep an eye on her."

"That means three men watching her around the clock on an eight-hour basis. Simple, if she stays in her hotel. Will she?" Nield suddenly swore. "Complications are something we expect in this job, but if anything really gets me riled up it's the *unnecessary* complication. How the hell did Conway step into all this?"

"How did any of us?"

Nield calmed down. "How much did you have to tell her?"

"That Yates was engaged in espionage—she saw Keller's men at the office, and she also saw the rhubarb in the hall this morning when Keller came charging to the rescue."

Nield wasn't pleased. "And what did you tell her about Langenheim Lang?"

"Only that Langenheim was possibly Yates's mistress, and worked with him. Lynn had already guessed as much from Miss Freytag's reactions."

Nield's frown deepened. "Get her out of Zürich."

"How?"

228

There was a pause. Nield's face cleared. "Salzburg. She would have the same reasons as you have for being safer there."

There's more than Lynn's safety at the back of that quick mind, thought Mathison. "I turned her down on Salzburg," he said abruptly.

"She wanted to go?"

"Jimmy Newhart suggested it when he called us from New York."

"Then it would be a completely normal thing for her to travel to Salzburg to see Anna Bryant?"

"If these were normal times, yes. Look here, Chuck, you can't possibly want her there. She'd—"

"She may solve a small problem for us. No danger," Nield added quickly. "Her actions will be strictly limited. Yours, too, friend. You'll have plenty of time to sight-see around Salzburg after you've spoken with Anna Bryant. You'll have a few days to relax and enjoy yourself with Lynn Conway—a very natural way to behave, I'd think. Auburn hair, good legs. What is the color of her eyes? No, I'm serious! I need the color of her eyes."

"Blue. Very blue."

"And she'll be wearing that blue fleece coat?"

"Possibly."

"Make sure of that. Now, for what you'll wear—" Nield rose, went to the wardrobe and opened it. "Tweed jacket, I suppose?" He seemed to be memorizing its color and double vents. "You could sport that tie you have on now," he said as he turned to face Mathison. "That's just for tomorrow, when you do your job. After that, dress as you like; you're on your own." He glanced at his watch quite openly, announcing time was running short and silencing any further questions most efficiently. "The important thing is to keep everything *outwardly* normal. You have a real excuse for going to see Anna Bryant, and play that angle hard. Make no secret of it. Any Nazi observer will accept that. Remember, the Nazis don't know you at all, and Elissa's friends are probably just as ignorant about you and Lynn Conway. So it's a perfectly natural business visit to Anna Bryant. Got that?"

"Yes. But I don't like dragging Lynn—"

"Two are safer than one."

Meaning? wondered Mathison. That Lynn lends me something of her cloak of innocence? Or that one person was

229

easier to abduct than two? Or that I'll not risk any chances if I have her to worry about? "Damn your eyes," he said very quietly.

"You'll keep a closer watch on her than any of Keller's men could," Nield said cheerfully. "Now here is your timetable. You'll both visit Anna Bryant tomorrow afternoon—as early as possible. When can you make it?"

"Around half past two."

"How long will it take to discuss the contract with her?"

"You just can't go in and say, 'Sign here!' I can't time myself. Exactly. Or Lynn, for that matter. They may start a lot of conversation, those two. Give us about an hour."

"That would be normal time for such a business visit?"

"Look—I can't talk with my eyes on my watch."

"I think you'd better. Keep it brief. First, business; then, Finstersee. But send Lynn Conway away before that subject is brought up."

"Where? And using what excuse?"

"That's your problem. For Christ's sake, Bill—" Nield looked at him sharply, mastered his brief exasperation. "Do you know where Tomaselli's coffeehouse is?"

"Yes, it's on the old market square." Tomaselli's was a pleasant café only a few minutes from the Neugasse, filled with people at the rush hours, never really empty of patrons who read newspapers and made a cup of coffee last the whole afternoon. He would have taken Lynn there as a matter of course; it was the kind of place foreigners visited to feel they were at home in Salzburg.

"Drop in there with Mrs. Conway after you've seen Anna Bryant. Choose a table in the main room downstairs. You'll have a newspaper under one arm, and you'll carry that small red-covered guide to Salzburg." Nield pointed briefly to the dressing table where Baedeker's short edition lay beside travel folders and a map of the Salzburg area. "It will fit neatly into your pocket."

"I'll also be carrying a briefcase," Mathison reminded him. "Actually, a leather envelope, black in color."

Nield's eyes widened. "Thanks for that. And wear exactly the clothes we discussed. Right? They'll identify you quickly."

"How do I recognize the man we'll meet in Tomaselli's?"

"You won't meet him. He could be one of any of the people at the tables in that room."

The main room wasn't too large, Mathison remembered,

but it was big enough. "I'd better choose a table in its emptiest section, so that he can see us clearly. But how do I pass on the news I got from Anna Bryant?"

"You'll have three possible pieces of information to give him. One: Anna Bryant has what we need and is willing to help. In that case, you lay your newspaper aside on a chair and light up cigarettes as you wait for your coffee. Two: Anna Bryant knows nothing and therefore can't help. If so, unfold your newspaper and—with Mrs. Conway—you can study the concert or movie advertisements. Three: Anna Bryant knows something but refuses to tell. If that happens, you'll take out the guidebook and puzzle over it with Mrs. Conway. Got that?"

Mathison went over the three signals quickly. "If all is well, I relax and smoke. If it's a complete dead end, I give up worrying and start looking for some entertainment. If it's a no-help answer, I turn to Baedeker for guidance."

"That's it. One positive signal, two negatives. If you have to give one of the negative signs, then. that's the end of your job. Enjoy your coffee and cakes. Leave. Your mission is over. We'll handle it another way."

I bet you will, thought Mathison, and I bet you've even got your plans all laid for that too. "And if I give the okay-on-all-counts signal?"

"You'll leave Tomaselli's with Lynn Conway. Don't let her do too much window-shopping. Keep your eye quietly on your watch and get back to Bryant's place within twenty minutes. Don't be late. Please! Because a couple of minutes later, I'll be coming in by the back door. Keep Lynn Conway in the front shop. Make a likely excuse and be in the kitchen along with Anna Bryant to meet me. It will only take two seconds to introduce me—you'll have prepared Mrs. Bryant for that in your first visit. Then you take Lynn Conway and get the hell out, *but walking slowly*."

"And after that?"

"Stay out, Bill. Your job is done. And we add our thanks." Then as Nield saw the obvious disappointment in Mathison's face, he added, "You and I will get together some day when it's all over, one way or another. And I'll tell you what I can, if I can. That's about everything, I think. . . ." He was ready to leave, glancing at his watch again. "You've got it all straight? Repeat it briefly, will you? The timing is important."

Mathison got it straight, all right, and as briefly as possible. Nield was relieved, and definitely pleased. He had a small shock at the end, though, when Mathison added, "Didn't you forget something?"

"What?"

"Your name. Or do I introduce you to Anna Bryant as Chuck?"

"There's no need for any name."

"I tell her you are just the man from Washington?"

"I'm the man who knows someone in Washington."

"Pretty cagey, aren't you?"

"We have to be."

"I think you should have a name. Women like names. They are reassuring. She'll feel uncertain enough, as it is."

"You've a point there. What about Cliff? That will give her something to hang on to." Nield began moving toward the door.

"I suppose a bad joke is better than none at all for an exit," Mathison said. Or for a casual farewell? This might indeed be the last time he'd be talking with Charles Nield—apart from those two seconds they'd have in Anna Bryant's kitchen. Too bad he wasn't going all the way. Again he felt that stab of disappointment, as if he had been cheated of learning the full answers. "I know why you were so keen to have Lynn Conway in Salzburg," he said, joking in earnest. "She's the excuse to keep me in line."

Nield tried to look surprised, even slightly hurt, at such an idea. "Now, Bill," he said in his most persuasive style, "we are just keeping everything as simple and natural as possible."

"Sure. You could have made me meet your unseen agent in the cemetery and had us match the torn top of a Jell-O box."

Nield recovered. "Now *why* didn't we think of that?" He held out his hand. "Good luck!"

"You, too." Then as they shook hands Mathison had one last doubt.

"Yes?" asked Nield.

"What if Anna Bryant isn't in Salzburg? Her brother lives—"

"She's there, all right. She is trying to make an inventory of the shop. She is selling all the equipment, giving up her lease."

"You have good sources," Mathison said, but he felt better

232

about that. Someone had been keeping a friendly eye on Anna Bryant. "I'll call her this evening and make the appointment for tomorrow."

"Just be careful what you say over the telephone. It's quite easy to tap it from the outside, you know." And as Mathison stared at him, he added, "So far, we don't think that any bugs have been planted inside her shop. She turned away two businessmen who wanted to inspect her place with the idea of taking it over from her intact. Very tempting offer. But they made the mistake of coming on the morning of the funeral. So she turned them out. We think they were Nazis, not Elissa's KGB friends. Elissa was too busy in Zürich this week." He opened the door slightly, waited, looked out. He stepped into the corridor. Quickly, gently, the door closed.

Three calls to make: Lynn, Anna Bryant, James Newhart. But first Mathison ordered a couple of sandwiches, a double Scotch, and a pot of coffee. It wasn't too late to reach Anna Bryant—Austria was in the same time zone as Switzerland and didn't indulge in daylight saving either. So he'd call Lynn first, work out the change in plans. He downed the Scotch in order to add to his courage. She would begin to think he was the man who was always late both in keeping appointments and in changing his mind, a variable type, hardly dependable. But there was one thing he had determined to do: he wasn't going to start lying to her. He couldn't tell her much more than she already knew, if anything at all. But no lies, not to Lynn Conway. He wasn't quite sure what he would say or how he would say it, and the longer he thought about it the less sure he was. Lynn wasn't the kind of girl for whom you prepared set speeches. He picked up the receiver before he could start imagining a hundred reasons why she might not want to go with him to Salzburg, after all. He cursed silently, remembering just in time the virgin ears down at the switchboard. And then, as he braced himself for his first sentence, the call went through to Lynn's hotel. And stuck there. Mrs. Conway's line was engaged.

Three minutes later it was still engaged.

Two minutes later, engaged.

"This is important," he said. "I must talk with Mrs. Conway. Could you give her my name when she is free?" He spelled it out carefully. That was all he could do.

Almost ten o'clock, and he could not risk delaying his call to Salzburg. He'd content himself with a cable to Jimmy Newhart telling him about Greta Freytag's death; that would save a lot of backing and filling, and, more importantly, time. Everything was becoming so damned urgent, he thought in a fresh attack of anxiety. All of Nield's careful plans could start falling apart because of one small change, one piece of mistiming. No doubt Nield allowed for that; but if anything went not according to plan, Mathison didn't want it to happen at his end.

His luck began to turn. He reached Anna Bryant in Salzburg. Except that he had the uneasy feeling that she was in some new kind of trouble. She was in a strange mood: angry at first, until she realized who was talking to her; then surprised, and pleased; then restrained, almost diffident, about James Newhart's offer of a very fair settlement.

"One of the editors from the New York office just arrived here this morning. Her name is Mrs. Conway. I think she'd like to come through to Salzburg to talk with you about that contract."

"You will come, too?"

"Yes, I'll bring the legal papers. They won't be complicated. We can clear everything up about that contract tomorrow afternoon."

"I may have to leave— All right, tomorrow afternoon."

"About half past two?"

"I'll be here." She must have turned her head; she was speaking to someone at her elbow, her voice muffled and indistinct but annoyed. Someone else was trying to get into the act, someone with a question or two of his own. Brother Johann? wondered Mathison. Whoever it was, she managed to keep him out of it. Her voice quickened, became stronger as she spoke once more into the telephone. "I'll be here. At half past two. Have you seen Mr. Yates? What did he have to say about the contract?"

"No. I didn't see him. And there is a piece of news I ought to tell you. There was a boating accident. Eric Yates is dead."

"A boating accident." The words were calm, fatalistic. "Well, I'll see you tomorrow, Mr. Mathison." There was a slight scuffle at the end of the line. "Stop that!" she told someone angrily. And then to Mathison, as she ended the call abruptly, almost in tears, "Thank you."

234

Tomorrow ... that was one thing he'd better make sure of. Something had gone wrong in Salzburg. He began packing.

It did not take long. He was almost finished, ready to step out early in the morning and make the first flight, when Lynn Conway's return call came through. She was annoyed. Not with him, but with Inspector Keller. "We argued for at least five minutes over the phone," she told Mathison. "D'you know what he wants me to do?"

"What?"

"Stay in my hotel for the next four or five days!"

"That's dreary."

"It's impossible. I ask you—"

"I agree. Did he say why?"

Lynn's voice changed. "He told me Miss Freytag had died. Very suddenly. Bill, did you know about that?"

"Yes. I was calling you to tell you—"

"I can't believe it. She was so full of determination—the kind of woman who lives until ninety. And what about her mother? I think I'll go and see her first thing tomorrow."

"No," he said quickly. "No. Leave that all to Keller."

"But why?"

"Because I've been thinking over that trip to Salzburg, and I hope you'll come along. It would be more cheerful than Zürich at the moment. I don't suppose the office will be functioning anyway for several days at least."

There was a startled pause. "I'd only be in your way in Salzburg."

"I'd like you to be with me."

There was another pause, and then a small laugh. "Why does everyone want to get me out of Zürich? That was Inspector Keller's idea, too. He offered it as an alternative to the four-day siege." Another pause. "What's wrong, Bill? I thought you'd have found that funny."

"If you join me on that first flight out tomorrow, I'll promise to laugh at all your jokes."

"That's terrifying—enough to silence me for the whole trip. When are you planning to leave?"

"I'll pick you up at six o'clock at your hotel."

"In the morning? Now, *you're* joking!"

"It's the best connection," he said vaguely. "We have to

see Anna Bryant in the early afternoon. I've just been talking with her on the phone. I think she has some new troubles. She's selling everything, planning to move away. Pretty miserable, all around."

"Do you really want me to go with you?"

"I'd like you to go," he said, sticking to the exact truth.

"All right," she said, turning businesslike. "If I can be of help, I'll be delighted. I'll see you at six. Oh, Bill, what's the temperature in Salzburg?"

"Cool and crisp. Why?"

"Clothes."

He had to laugh. The switch from executive to feminine was beguiling. And reassuring, too. "It's fleece-coat weather. Take the blue one you had on today, and that dress you wore at lunchtime."

"But I have something else—"

"Never change a winning game. With that blue coat, your eyes can't lose. Oh, and Lynn—I'll cable Jimmy about all this. You get on with your repacking."

"For four days?" she asked, now serious, no doubt thinking of Inspector Keller.

"Why not? We can hire a car and do some exploring once we get the contract properly settled. We might even drive all the way back to Zürich."

"I'd love that. Good night, Bill." She rang off.

He replaced the receiver slowly, still hearing the happy excitement in her voice. What have I done? he wondered. But it was too late for afterthoughts. He would just have to believe that Nield and Keller were right; if these two hard-nosed professionals couldn't give the correct advice, who could? They had come to the same decision independently. That was at least in its favor.

He finished his packing, called the desk to make reservations for the first part of the journey, checked on the connection at Innsbruck, ordered a car for ten minutes to six, sent a night cable to New York, and buried his worries about Lynn Conway in those of Salzburg. Something had gone wrong there, something to upset Anna Bryant. A family matter? A quarrel between Anna and her brother? None of my business, he told himself as he climbed into bed and stretched his spine. But the sooner he was in Salzburg the better.

236

17

"STOP THAT!" ANNA HAD SAID ANGRILY, AND PULLED THE receiver away from Johann's reaching hand. She ended the call from Mathison with a quick sentence of thanks before her brother tried another grab.

He was just as angry as she was. He caught her by the shoulders. "I wanted to speak to him. Why didn't you—"

"What would you have said? That you had something you wanted to sell to the highest bidder?"

"You're damned right. But I wouldn't have been as stupid as to blurt that out over a telephone."

"No?"

"No! I was only going to ask him if he wanted a look at some of our mountains. I'd guide him around for a couple of days. Why not? The weather is good and clear now. He used to climb."

"He isn't an agent. I told you that."

"He's coming back to see you, isn't he? That's proof of something."

"It's proof that Newhart and Morris are honest, that's all. He is coming to clear up the mess about the contract."

"Oh." But Johann didn't quite believe that was all. "Look, Anna, I can't be here tomorrow. When you see him—"

She wrenched herself free and marched, head high, back through the narrow hall toward the kitchen.

His first impulse was to leave, continue his interrupted journey to Unterwald. He hadn't seen Trudi since Monday night, or rather Tuesday dawn, which was almost the same thing. The funeral, Anna's plans and business arrangements had used up these last four days. And all that time he had his own problems. He could trust Trudi—the Finstersee box was as safe in her room as any place—but he couldn't stop worrying. Today he had telephoned, left a message to tell her he was coming. He had to get back to Unterwald, no matter how late his arrival.

Yet he couldn't leave Anna close to tears, he couldn't leave her unpersuaded and thinking bitter thoughts about him. And there were a few points to clear up. So he followed her.

Slowly. He ought to have told Anna about the Finstersee chest before this, but it hadn't been easy to find the right moment; perhaps there was never any right moment for his kind of news. He had even postponed telling her, this evening, until he was just about to leave for Unterwald. They had been quarreling ever since. The phone call from Zürich had interrupted the savage argument, and at first he had been thankful for it, but now it seemed to have made matters only worse. I've got to make Anna see it my way, he decided, and quickened his steps.

She was sitting in the big armchair near the tiled stove. She had fought back her rage of tears, but her lips were set and her hands were tightly folded. A stranger would have said she made a very pretty picture with her head resting against the high back of the chair; sad but appealing. Johann paused, feeling a sense of guilt. He looked at the delicate face so deceptively fragile, at the tragic blue eyes that seemed helpless, at the soft blond hair that fell in childlike wisps over her ears and brow. "A gentle creature," Felix Zauner had called her fondly. By heaven, thought Johann, he ought to have heard her just half an hour ago.

He went over to her, dropped on one knee beside her chair, took her hands in his. "Anna," he said gently, "we've never quarreled before. Let's not go on with this one. I haven't been deceiving you. Would I have told you I found the box under the three boulders if I were trying to deceive you?"

"But why won't you tell me where you have put it?"

"For safety. Your safety. The box's safety. And mine, too. I had to move it; don't you see that?"

"It was well hidden."

"Yes. As long as Dick was alive and no one was suspicious of his visit to Finstersee, the box was well hidden. But as soon as things have quieted down around Unterwald, as soon as the men from the Gendarmerie have stopped measuring skid marks and asking questions of the villagers and gone back to Bad Aussee, the Nazis are bound to go up to the lake and check that ledge. Then they'll find the box is gone, and they'll search every foot of the woods and that meadow. Because Dick had nothing incriminating in his car, and so he must have hidden it. . . . They would have found it."

"Perhaps not."

"They would have found it. They have only to calculate

the area he covered before they met him that morning. It's just a matter of deduction. These men are trained for it, Anna. I did what was best, for all of us."

She lowered her eyes. So, she thought, Johann would not have hidden the box in the woods or the meadow near the lake. Where could he have taken it last Monday night?

"You see, Anna?" he asked hopefully.

She nodded. "Except," she said slowly, "except that I must know where the box is now hidden. Dick would want me to know."

"Why?" He rose abruptly to his feet, dropping her hands. His voice sharpened. "Don't you trust me to deal with it correctly?"

"Dick would want me to have some control," she said determinedly. "And I don't trust your judgment, Johann—not in this. No, please don't start shouting again. Please, Johann, let's not quarrel any more."

"Who's shouting?" he demanded, forcing his voice back to normal. He began to pace around the kitchen, trying to cage his emotions as much as his body in this cramped space. He thrust a dining chair out of his way, shoving it back against the table, where it should have been in any case. "What's so wrong about selling that box? Sure, you've told me Dick didn't find it for money. But Dick is dead. You are alone. You need that money. And I need you to have it. How can I marry Trudi and support you as well?"

"I'll find a job." She tried hard not to start thinking of *that* problem.

He shook his head. "Not enough to pay all your expenses. You'd have to double up with us in my house at Bad Aussee." He might as well be brutally frank; it was the only way to make Anna realize the harsh facts of life. "Trudi may have her own ideas on that."

"So have I. I won't live with you and Trudi. I'll visit you now and again, that's all." She paused. "I'm coming this weekend."

She's so transparent, he thought, and had to smile. She was going to search his house, was she? He turned to face her, his grin widening. "Anna, Anna ... You're wasting your time. You'll find nothing more in my place than a slashed rucksack."

"Dick's rucksack?" She was horrified. "You left it lying around?"

"No, no. It's mixed up with a pile of old climbing equipment."

"Oh, Johann——"

"Stop fretting," he said gently. "It's safe enough." He sat down at the table, found a cigarette and lit it. "What else could I do? I hadn't time to destroy it last Tuesday morning. I was in and out of my house like a hunted fox. I had to get back to Salzburg to be with you. I'll get rid of it soon, take it up a mountain, drop it into a crevasse. Nothing to it." Anna was silent. Encouraged, Johann added, "Just leave everything to me. Trust me, Anna."

She closed her eyes. So the Finstersee chest was not at Johann's house. And it wasn't hidden anywhere near the lake. Where had he taken it? She sighed, partly because she was tired with the vehemence of the emotions that had spilled around her tonight, partly because she couldn't find an answer to that question. She was near the truth, perhaps so close to it that she could almost put a finger on it, and yet she couldn't see it. Her mind, as Johann would say, wasn't trained for such things. But his mind wasn't trained for such deductions either; that was why he had given something away even as he had spoken to her, and she hadn't the brains to see it clearly. As Dick would have.

"You might have trusted me a bit more tonight when Mathison called you. It's just possible——"

"No," she said sharply, guessing what was coming. "You'll only endanger him too." Did Johann not know what danger really meant? He could climb jagged peaks, descend rock faces, edge his way up chimneys and along razorbacks; did he think everything was as easy to master?

"I still think he is an agent."

"He is coming here with papers to be explained before I sign them, and one of the New York publishers is coming with him too—a woman. It's all simple business."

"Oh." Johann was deflated. His guess about Mathison had been wrong then. "So the publishers are sending a woman along? I suppose they thought she could drive a hard bargain."

"What bargain? They don't owe us anything."

"There are some people who could make a load of trouble for them. And they know it. Smart lawyer, Mathison."

"Johann!"

"Except when he goes boating," Johann said with a wide grin. "He took a dunking in that Zürich lake, did he?"

"You've guessed wrong again," she said angrily. "That was Eric Yates who had the accident. And he's dead."

"Yates has been killed?"

She nodded. And now, she thought, I've no way of communicating with the British. The only hope left—and a faint one—was Bill Mathison's friend, the one he had spoken about, the one who might have contacts in Washington. She almost relented and told Johann about that, but first he must tell her where he had hidden the box. "Where did you hide it, Johann?" she asked very quietly.

"Now how did we arrive back there?" he asked, and rose. "I'd better leave. Trudi will begin to worry."

"It will be midnight before you reach Unterwald."

"That's no problem," he told her lightly.

She stared at him. "Then I think it *is* time you married the girl."

"Come on, I'll get you upstairs and see you safely locked in. The way your friend Mathison did last Monday." He was over at the peg on the door, unhooking his loden cape.

"You don't need to have guilt about not being here then," she said in annoyance.

"I was fairly busy that night," he reminded her.

Yes, she thought, finding that box, hiding it so cunningly, spending what was left of the night with Trudi. "Where *did* you hide it?"

"That's not the question."

"Then what is?" she asked sharply.

"The question is—what is in that box? If you know, you'd better tell me."

"But why—" she began and floundered, suddenly on the defensive.

"Just so that we don't sell it for too little."

"I'm not selling!"

"That's right, you'll give it away."

"Only to the right people."

"Right, wrong . . . Anna, who can know what people are right, what people are wrong?"

"Dick said that if the box fell into the wrong hands, it could mean disaster."

"For whom?"

241

"For the world that is free—and that means us, too, Johann!"

"That was only a matter of Dick's opinion."

"It is only a matter of opinion that the Nazis were wrong—"

"No. They won't get the box. So you can stop worrying about that. But apart from them, it's a free market. I've no set opinions, like Dick."

"Johann," she said wearily, "there *is* a right way and there *is* a wrong way in which the contents of that box could be used."

"Is it as important as that?" he asked quietly. "We've really got hold of something, haven't we?" And then, just as Anna was looking at him with new hope, he added, "But who is to judge how anything will be used?"

"If you couldn't judge the strength of a rope or the hold of a piton, where would you be? At the bottom of the Dachstein Glacier."

He opened his mouth to reply, and burst out laughing instead.

She rose, opened the stove to see if its low fire would last gently through the night, began picking up her purse and a book to take upstairs.

"I'm glad you cook better than you argue," he told her.

She said nothing.

"When do I expect you at Bad Aussee? Day after tomorrow? If I'm not around, you'll find Franz working in the shop. And if he isn't there, you'll find the key to the house on the window ledge to the side of the door."

She didn't answer.

"Anna—I've never known you to sulk. Don't start—"

"And I've never known you to behave like this either." She didn't look at him, but moved toward the door, then paused as a knock sounded. Instinctively, she turned to Johann. He was frowning as he glanced at his watch, puzzled and annoyed. He swore under his breath. The knock sounded again. "Who is it?" she called.

"Felix."

Johann's frown deepened. But he unfastened the chain that he had installed last Tuesday morning after he had returned from Unterwald and learned of the burglary here. He opened the door wide. "Come in, come in," he said heartily enough. "It will have to be a short visit, Felix. I was just leaving."

"So I see." Felix Zauner stared briefly at Johann's loden, which was draped over one arm, and then gave his full attention to Anna. "I dropped in to see if you were all right." He pulled off a glove, took her hand and kissed it. "You know how sorry I was that I couldn't be here for the funeral. I had business in Vienna. Just got back an hour ago."

"Your wife told me you were there," Anna said. "Come and sit down. There is some heat in the stove." Felix was pulling off his heavy coat, but in spite of its weight and the warmth of his dark-gray suit, he looked cold. Haggard too, thought Anna. The thin bridge of his nose was prominent, his high cheekbones were clearly marked, his mouth seemed pinched. "I'll make some coffee," said Anna, if only to break the silence in the room, and moved over to the small electric stove beside the sink.

"I was just about to get Anna upstairs and lock her safely in," Johann said as Felix dropped his coat and gloves and green velours hat on a chair.

"I'll do that." Felix smoothed down the long thin strands of reddish hair that, in spite of his hat, had been blown wild by the wind. "It was Anna I came to see."

"She's tired." Johann looked at Anna uncertainly. Would she start telling Felix about the chest at Finstersee? But even as a sweat broke in the palms of his hands, he remembered that Anna had no idea of Felix's real job or his connections. She might, however, treat Felix as a father confessor. She was in a strange mood tonight.

"I'm all right," she called across to him. "I don't usually go to bed as early as this. It will be good to talk to Felix." And what a ridiculous fuss about seeing me safely upstairs. Who's going to see me safely upstairs tomorrow night, or the next, or the next forever? "You'd better leave or you'll never get to Unterwald until dawn."

"I'll be there before midnight." But he couldn't decide whether to leave or stay until Felix had safely gone. And Felix, standing over by the stove, heating his spine, had noticed his hesitation. "Just one thing before I go," he told Felix. "What help did you get in Vienna?"

"Help? Oh, you mean about the financing of my plans for a ski resort at Unterwald?" Felix was taking out his cigar case, preparing to have a pleasant half hour in a comfortable chair. "They were interested but noncommittal."

You know damn well what I meant, thought Johann. So

there would be no investigation of Dick's murder; they were all going to play it down and call it accidental death. "Didn't you give them good reason to take direct action?"

"Your reason?" Felix smiled, but the gray eyes studied Johann carefully. "They have their own ideas about what should be done." The smile faded. "Of course, my visit was very brief. It seemed a waste of time to me."

He's slipping, thought Johann. I know it. And he knows it. And now in Vienna—does State Security know it, too? Was that why they summoned him so damn quick yesterday morning? Felix Zauner had always seemed so infallible to him that all he could do now was stare incredulously.

Felix said airily, "The truth is, Vienna is rather removed from the situation here. It seems a little improbable to them, at the moment."

"But if you had put in a full report—"

"Are you teaching me how to conduct my business?" Felix noticed Anna looking around at them both. He ended with an easy "There's nothing to worry about. You'll see a ski lift at Unterwald yet. And that will make you a lot of money, Johann. You and Trudi might very well run the inn, once August Grell leaves. He's getting old, you know. And it looks as if his son, Anton, won't be back in Unterwald."

"What did I tell you—" Johann began.

"Last reports say that Anton is staying in the South Tyrol. His girl doesn't want to leave Bozen. So they are getting married, going to run her mother's Gasthof."

"You believe that?"

"For the next few weeks," Felix said smoothly, "we must all appear to believe that."

Johann swung his cape across his shoulders and went over to Anna. He put his arms around her and hugged. "Will I see you on Sunday?"

She shook her head. "I'll have enough to keep me busy here." She tried to keep her voice natural. "And you'll be most of the time with Trudi. Tell her I will come up soon to see her. I do have to meet her and her mother, you know." Johann said nothing at all to that. He just stared at her. Now why? she wondered, turning away in a pretense of fussing over the coffeepot. Why had he gone tense? Why doesn't he want me to visit Trudi?

"Later," he was saying. "She knows you have a lot to face right now. I'll try to get back here by the end of next week.

Franz has been looking after the shop, but I'd better pay some attention to it myself."

"And that is a splendid idea," Felix said. "Need I remind you that the first snow is only weeks away? It's about time you started getting your stock of equipment in order."

"I'll be ready," Johann said. He wasn't amused. "Keep safe," he told Anna as he moved to the door.

"And you take care of yourself, too," Felix said. "Don't play detective. Don't go anywhere near the inn. Or Finstersee. Give them both a wide berth." He drew on his cigar, got it glowing to his satisfaction, and looked up to see that he had managed to freeze Johann in his tracks. "When I left Unterwald yesterday morning, August Grell had as many as eight hunters as his guests. In fact, he seems to be expecting quite a good season this autumn; he has reopened the inn for another month at least." He glanced at Anna and then said deliberately, "I have heard that his guests seemed keener on fishing than hunting—to begin with. But they didn't seem to find what they were fishing for. So today, I hear, they have started beating the woods just above the picnic ground. Strange, isn't it?"

So Felix wasn't slipping after all, thought Johann; not altogether. "Strange," he echoed. He refrained from looking at Anna and asking her silently what she thought of him now. If he hadn't moved the chest from under those boulders, Grell would have his big thick-fingered hands on it this minute. "Are you going back to Unterwald, Felix?"

"Of course. I'm determined on that ski lift."

"Johann," called Anna softly as he opened the door, "take care. Please."

"I'll take care." Of that chest, he thought, and of Grell too. He gave Anna and Felix a very cheerful wave to match his grin. Anna's concern had been half an apology at least. He closed the door, confidently leaving her with Felix and his questions; she'd guard Dick's secret even more now.

"Anna," said Felix Zauner thoughtfully, "did you understand anything I was talking about?"

She concentrated on carrying two cups of steaming coffee over to the table. "About Finstersee and the Grells?"

"About Finstersee. I assumed you and Johann have discussed the Grells pretty frankly."

She nodded, searching now for cream and sugar.

"But about Finstersee, Anna? What did Dick tell you about it before he left here?"

"As little as possible."

"Didn't you wonder why he was so secretive?"

"Not secretive. Just—just protective. There is danger in that lake, isn't there?" She sat down, pointed to the chair across the table from her.

"When Dick phoned from Grell's inn, did he tell you he had found what he was looking for?" Felix took the offered chair. He would have a good view of her face at least. Yet that depressed him; it looked as if she felt she had nothing to hide, as if this visit was just another waste of time. And time was running short for him. Very short.

"No."

"Or that he hadn't found it?"

She shook her head. Her lips trembled, and she made an effort to hold them taut.

"I'm sorry, Anna. I know how it must be painful for you to recall that morning." He gave her a few seconds to re-establish control. She's a brave girl, he thought, and I'm handling this too quickly, yet I haven't the time to approach it slowly. "I'm sorry, Anna. But there was a chest or a box of some kind hidden in Finstersee—"

She looked up at him, eyes startled and wide.

"I heard that in Vienna," he tried. He would at least see if Johann had been gossiping about his real job.

But his remark had no special meaning for her. "They are talking about it in Vienna? It's a piece of common gossip?" She was horrified.

"Not exactly." It had been gravely discussed in a quiet room by three men, two of them with considerable authority and calm impartial faces listening to his explanations, his excuse; his defense, actually. Yet they had believed him, or he would have been asked to resign on the spot. Damn those big-mouthed Americans, what did they expect to achieve from passing on to Austrian Security their piece of information about Finstersee? A pooling of knowledge, such as it was, and a sharing of results? Probably. And they could operate more freely here with Vienna's participation. Clever of the Americans, of the British, too. (There seemed to be some linkup between them.) They weren't always so circumspect. But why had they not contacted him here in Salzburg and at least given him warning of their interest? Why had they gone over his head to the top? So he had been summoned to Vienna, totally unprepared. All he could do was listen, agree to tolerate American-British interest. He had made a tactful protest, of course, a suggestion that such co-operation was hardly neutral behavior. He had been told firmly that the first objective was to discover the Finstersee box; the second was to examine its contents; and after that, neutrality would be observed. "Not exactly," he repeated, easing his voice. "I heard some inside information. It's always very intriguing."

"And dangerous," she said, eying him in dismay. "Felix, you shouldn't talk about it. You must be careful—"

"I am," he told her gently. He studied her troubled face. Now was the moment to ask his last question. "Where is that box hidden, Anna?"

Her face went blank. "But I don't know." Her words had come slowly, but they rang true.

"The truth, Anna!"

She stared at him in wonder. For a brief instant she had seen naked fear in his eyes. "It is the truth. I don't know where the box is hidden."

He kept looking at her. He had barely touched his coffee. His cigar was forgotten.

She hesitated. "Why don't you ask Johann? He is always so full of bright ideas and explanations."

Johann? Dick Bryant had never confided fully in Johann. "He has plenty of ideas," Felix Zauner said, covering his disappointment, changing the subject neatly, "but whether they are good ones or not—that's another matter. Did he tell you he confronted August Grell in the inn? That was last Monday night. He practically challenged Grell that his story about young Anton wasn't true."

"Oh, no!"

"I arrived in time fortunately, kept him from calling Grell a damned liar. I think I managed to smooth Grell down over a long dinner."

"You mean to say Johann actually ate dinner with that man?" This seemed to shock her even more than Johann's indiscretion.

"No, no. I had given Johann his exit cue. Luckily, he had just enough sense left to take it. He went off to have supper with his devoted Trudi."

Did he? Anna began to wonder. "I worry about Johann. Perhaps he—"

"You needn't. He has chosen a good girl to marry. She has a lot of practical common sense. Apart from Johann, of course." He rose briskly. "I hope I didn't stay too long. You look tired."

"No." She refrained from looking at the untouched coffee, at the dead cigar in his hand. They had been little social pretenses to cover his main reason for coming here. Was the Finstersee box so important to him? But why? He hadn't spoken of it the way Dick had talked about it, but surely she could trust him. Should she drop another hint about Johann to Felix? They were good friends. Yet, she remembered uneasily, Johann had had the chance tonight to tell Felix. "I'm not really so tired. Just puzzled. What *are* you, Felix?"

He laughed, dropping his cigar into his saucer, picking up his coat and hat. "A very weary businessman who had a disappointing visit to Vienna. We all want quick success, I suppose. I'll get the financial backing I need eventually. Once these wild rumors about Finstersee die down, I'll be able to interest people in Unterwald as a nice quiet ski resort. Does that explain why I asked you the questions about Finstersee? My interest is simply to have that box found, August Grell removed, and then—well, an abnormal situation will be ended. Businessmen like everything very normal."

Why, she thought as he avoided her eyes, he isn't even coming over to say good-bye.

"One more thing," he said as he reached the door. "Did Dick take many photographs of Finstersee?"

"He always took fifty or sixty shots of every subject he photographed."

"Surely he didn't destroy those he discarded!"

"He kept the three best. Then he would decide which of the three was the one he wanted and concentrate on it."

"So he had two other negatives and sets of prints?" he asked casually, trying to disguise his impatience, his growing excitement.

"Yes. But the thief took them all. She knew just what to look for, and where."

"Are you sure it was a woman?" he asked vaguely. The last flame of hope had flickered and died. Now he was left only with anger. So Elisabetha Lang had taken everything; she had exceeded her mission, no mistake about that. He had instructed her simply to borrow the envelope with the Yates-Bryant correspondence, one envelope in the desk drawer, but she had looted everything about Finstersee. He hadn't even guessed she would know the significance of what he had told her to do; just another small job, trickier than most he had given her but easy enough. She knew the layout of this ground floor; she had had a clear field—or she would have had if Anna hadn't returned so unexpectedly, if she herself had not spent that extra time here. And now Lang was in Zürich, with every shred of evidence, not only of Bryant's interest in Finstersee but also of his strange connection with the man Yates. And I, thought Zauner savagely, am left with nothing. But at least I'm rid of her; at least I no longer have her as a threat at my back. Others of her breed will come, but I know now to entrust them with nothing; give them as little help as possible, keep them ignorant, agree to what they want and do the opposite. I may outwit them yet, but I'll have to be sharper than I was about Elisabetha Lang. Strange that in Vienna today they had called her Elissa. Where did they get that name? And was there some significance—or none—in the fact that they did not inquire too deeply into her employment in Salzburg? "Why are you doing that?" he asked Anna, becoming aware that she was back at the stove again, dropping more briquettes into its tiled belly.

"I'm supposed to be taking you safely upstairs."

"I thought you had forgotten. Besides, I'd rather stay down here for a while. It's warmer. The flat upstairs is so—" She didn't finish. Cold and lonely, lonely and cold, lonely, lonely, lonely, . . . Why say it? "Good night, Felix. I'll chain the door after you." She came forward.

"Have you been crying?"

"Oh, I was just thinking about the burglary. It was such a mean and miserable theft. It was a wonderful collection of photographs. It would have made a fine book." She paused. "And it *was* a woman who entered here. I am sure of that. Bill Mathison is sure. And so is Werner."

"Which Werner?"

"*Your* Werner. Werner Dietrich. He had been working late at the office, and he was walking home. He passed the Neugasse."

He certainly would, thought Zauner. Dietrich had been keeping an eye on Mathison since six o'clock that evening.

"And he saw the woman running away."

"When did he tell you this?"

"When he came around to see Frieda. She stayed with me overnight. He told me to leave it to him; he was putting in a report."

"Dietrich isn't usually so talkative," Felix Zauner said dryly.

"Oh, I suppose he had to quiet me down. I was going to the police about Elisabetha Lang. But you know, Felix, the odd thing is—"

"Elisabetha Lang? Is Dietrich sure it was she?"

"Yes. And so am I."

"But you didn't see her. How can you identify her?"

"I can and will. But what worries me, and Werner, too, is the fact that no action was taken against her. So he is sending a report to Vienna this time."

By God, he would. . . . "To whom?" Zauner asked slowly.

"He didn't say. But he is in earnest."

Yes, thought Zauner, Dietrich is next in line for promotion. He would fill my job nicely. He's in earnest, all right. "It really isn't so odd that no action has been taken. Elisabetha Lang is now out of the country. I doubt if Dietrich's second report will fare any better than his first."

"Surely *something* could be done," Anna protested sharply. "It just isn't right—"

"Right, Anna?" He smiled sadly. "The rights and the wrongs have little to do with it. There's a basic injustice in life."

"Only if we do nothing about it. Accept what is wrong, and you are forever accepting."

He looked at her in surprise. "Life is not quite so simple as that. It isn't a matter of black and white, or even one shade of gray."

"You sound like Johann," she said bitterly. "Don't tell me you have a sense of guilt, too."

"Really," he began, and stopped. He drew on his coat.

"I am sorry, Felix. It is just that I am *tired* of being told I look at life too simply. It isn't naïve to believe that good exists, that evil exists. I have known both of them. I've seen them. I've felt them. They aren't just ideas that you can twist into neat phrases. They aren't words to be clever with. They are too vital. We live by them. Or else we make everything meaningless." Her voice lost its intensity; her eyes softened. "Dear Felix," she said, "I am sorry. I just don't know how to

250

put these things very well." She waited, but he said nothing. "And I didn't mean to hurt you. You aren't like Johann. I suppose I should be glad he does have a sense of guilt. That means he has a conscience. If he hadn't, I'd really have something to worry about." She tried to laugh. Felix kept silent. He looked haggard, almost ill; his gray eyes were watching her and yet she didn't feel he was even seeing her. He is exhausted, she thought, with so much traveling, so many business troubles. "Good night," she said gently.

"Good night." He put out one hand and gripped her shoulder. "Good night, Anna." He left quickly.

He had taken his usual route; not through the vaulted hall, out by the front entrance into the street, but around the flight of stone stairs into the shadows behind them. There lay the narrow door that led into the back courtyard onto which her kitchen faced, and as he opened it she could feel the cold draft of night air brush over the hall's flagstones to touch her ankles. And after that, which way would he take tonight? From the interior courtyard there were three exits, through the hallways of other buildings, into other streets. Strangers to Salzburg could spend weeks of exploring and never even notice these short cuts. Felix would be halfway home before she fixed the chain on the door, double-locked it, pulled over the footstool, and settled down in the armchair by the stove. *If* he really was going home, she added as an afterthought. He had his own problems tonight; she understood them as little as she understood Felix himself. Take the way, for example, by which he always entered and left this house when he came here alone. Dick had used to joke about it, said it suited Felix's reticent nature. She herself had thought Felix enjoyed being more of a Salzburger than the people who had been born and brought up here. Johann, who always used the front entrance on the Neugasse because he refused to wander among other people's garbage cans, had simply laughed and said Felix had a passion for the unexpected.

Johann . . . He would be halfway home, too. It was only eighty kilometers to Bad Aussee over a broad highway, almost empty at this hour and at this time of year. She could imagine how he was stretching all the power he could get out of his jeep, bouncing, swaying, as he whipped along the even surface of the road, the night wind whistling around his ears. He had scared her into complete silence, turned her spine rigid, the last time she had driven with him. He never seemed

to feel cold or discomfort any more than he felt fear. Yet he
wasn't altogether foolhardy, even if he took enormous risks.
He lived by risks, after all. He might take them instinctively,
yet there was a strange intuitive calculation behind them.
Only now—and she began worrying again—he wasn't dealing
with weather and roads and mountains and slopes; he wasn't
dealing with cars or snow bridges or fragmenting rocks or
inexperienced climbers. Perhaps he had been right to move
the chest of documents from the three boulders on the shore
of Finstersee—Felix's report on the hunters and their search
had confirmed that. But remembering the look of quiet
triumph in Johann's eyes, she felt a strange uneasiness cou-
pled to her returning anger. I'll call him around midnight, she
thought, just to make sure he is all right, although that is
more than he deserves.

. But how can I? she thought next. He will be with Trudi.
Oh, why couldn't he tell me the full truth? She felt strangled,
caught in a net of deceit. If she could not trust Johann,
whom could she trust? Perhaps nobody.

18

IT HAD BEEN A GOOD AND EASY RUN TO BAD AUSSEE. JOHANN
slowed down as he entered the little spa, most of its houses
already asleep, a few people dribbling out from the late
showing at the movie house, lights burning in the taprooms
of the smaller inns where the last songs were being sung
about high mountains and sun-filled valleys and hearts longing for their homeland. Entertainment was no problem to the
people who lived here: give them a group of friends, some
red wine, a zither, a few true voices that could sing in parts,
and the hours passed. Normally, Johann would have been
there himself at the Schwarzes Rössl, which he was now
passing, and a burst of laughter almost drew him inside to
share in the rough joke. A small flask of wine would be
welcome, too, and so would the warmth at the corner table
near the stove where his friends always sat. But tonight he
would just have to drop that notion and drive on. Trudi
would be watching the road from her window, running back

to bed and pretending to be long asleep as soon as she heard his jeep coming up to Unterwald.

He passed the larger hotels, all decorously shaded, with their guests no doubt dreaming of the miraculous cures that strange-tasting waters and inhalations and pine-needle baths would bring to their asthma, skirted the park and its little bandstand, edged past the shops and neat white and cream houses that lined the sharply twisting streets.

It was only a matter of minutes to drive through the town area of the small spa. Almost at once, the countryside took over: wooden houses and apple trees, at first in gardens, then in fields; the road climbing up through thick woods and over rushing water toward the hillsides that led to the mountains. Soon even the scattered houses thinned out, the overhead lights ended, and he was entering the loneliness of the narrow route to Unterwald. His own house stood on the left side of its first steep slope, with a rough track cut through the meadow that led to his front door, where a stretch of flat ground made a useful parking lot for his clients and pupils. He was less than five minutes by car from the edge of town and he was in another world, not a rooftop or chimney in sight, nothing but a stretch of sky, clear and star-sprinkled, covering the broad valley below him and the dark walls of mountains beyond. No sounds either, except the sighing of the night wind through the trees.

He left the jeep on the road, wheels turned sharply back toward the bank to help the brakes hold securely, while he paid a brief visit to his place. He would drop off his bag with his town clothes, pick up any business messages from Franz, and then be on his way to Unterwald. Briskly, he walked over the hard-packed earth of the rough track. The dark windows of his house eyed him sadly, reminding him of his neglect in these last weeks. The dead flowers ought to have been taken out of the window boxes, the apples should have been gathered from the tree espaliered up the side wall, the grass on the meadow should have been cut, the piles of logs needed replenishing for the winter to come. Well, he thought, I'll soon be back to normal here and I'll keep Franz busy; there will be lights in the windows and the sweet smell of wood smoke. There would be cars parked outside, and people gathered around his huge stove, talk of weather and the newest equipment and the best slopes and the longest runs, friendly voices and warm laughter.

He felt for the key on the window ledge at the side of the door. But Franz had forgotten to put it there, and he hadn't even bothered to lock the front door. So he must be coming back here tonight, after a few hours in town, to sleep in his room over the shop.

Johann pushed open the heavy door with his shoulder, switched on the light and dropped his bag on the nearest chair. Then he stared in surprise. The room had been pulled apart. The window seats had been opened and searched; the deep drawers below a built-in bed had been emptied; the low chests that served as benches along one wall were gaping wide; the heavy couch had been turned on its side as if to find anything that could have been hidden underneath. So were two armchairs. The only things left untouched were the large table and wooden chairs, visibly innocent. "What the—" he began angrily, and moved toward the big stove, where he would find a heavy poker.

"Far enough!" a voice warned him, and a man stepped through the kitchen door into the room.

Johann measured him with his eye. He was of good height, strongly built, bundled against the cold of the house in a heavy coat. He had a smile on his face, a revolver in his hand. If I can get near enough to grapple with him, Johann thought, that coat of his won't help him at all. Or if I could throw something and duck and make for the front door? But it opened behind him even as he took another step nearer the stove and that poker. He turned to see a second man, as capable-looking as the first, dressed and armed like his friend, younger, even more powerful. Hell, thought Johann, he wasn't out there waiting when I came up the path; there wasn't a movement, or a sound except my own footsteps. He must have slipped around from the kitchen when they heard me come in.

"Back to the road!" the newcomer said, and gestured with his revolver. "You have some questions to answer."

"I'll answer them here," Johann said, and headed toward the stove. "We need some heat in this place. It's colder than the night outside."

"One more step and I'll shoot your knee out." The first man's smile had faded; his revolver looked dangerously ready.

"Do as you're told," a third voice said. "Back to the road!" It was an older man, with graying hair and a dark

254

mustache, who came through the doorway that led from the shop and storage room. He looked lean and fit. He carried a hunting rifle in one hand, a slashed rucksack in the other. He lifted it high to let Johann recognize it. "Out!"

There was no arguing with a rifle. Johann turned to leave. His thoughts raced. The moon was favorable, so was the ground outside—he knew every meter of it by heart—so was the shadowed side of the house, so was the short distance to the trees at the back; yes, there was a chance, if he could trip the young man at the door and let him block it for the few moments needed. There was a chance. He said, "*You*'ve some questions to answer. What the hell do you think you're doing? Mucking up my place, all for an old rucksack that's been left for repairs."

"A rucksack with water stains and lake slime dried on it? Come on, move out! We've waited long enough for you this evening." He nodded to the man at the kitchen door, who moved quickly across the room, pocketing his revolver, to stand behind Johann. "Hands at your back!"

The chance was fading, Johann thought as he obeyed slowly. Handcuffs? These strangers had come well prepared. He brought his elbows smartly up against the man's chest before the handcuffs could be fixed, knocked down the raised wrist of the young man blocking the door so that his shot splintered the wooden floor, shouldered him aside. Yes, there was a chance.

But the man behind Johann ended it. He brought down the handcuffs on Johann's head, sending him staggering to his knees. Roughly, quickly, the handcuffs were snapped around Johann's wrists. Half-dazed, he was pulled to his feet.

The man with the rifle was giving the orders. "Take his other arm," he told the one who had used the handcuffs. "We'll get him to the car, and you—" he looked hard at the young bungler who had fired the shot—"follow us in his jeep. You know where to hide it. And no more mistakes." He swung the rucksack over his shoulder and, with help from Johann's other side, began taking him through the door. "Lose no time," he warned the young man as they passed him. "Switch off the lights, put the key back where we found it." Everything had to be spelled out nowadays, he thought bitterly.

"What about this mess?" The young man looked at the room; the kitchen and shop were equally disordered. So was

255

upstairs. A whole night's job of putting things back into reasonable order. Luckily, there wouldn't be any intrusions; Kronsteiner's assistant had fallen for a hunting trip over the weekend and had left cheerfully this morning.

"No time. Get out of here!" Didn't the young fool know how far the sound of a shot could travel by night? And we had arranged it all so carefully, the older man thought with growing anger; with speed, yes, but with the utmost caution. Certainly, the house search had been thorough, and even if it had not turned up the first prize, there was a pretty good consolation one over his shoulder. A piece of real evidence. Before, they had been acting only on the strength of a deduction. As soon as they had found the broken stalks and grasses by the three boulders, the evidence of green slime dragged off a heavy object as it had been pulled out of its hiding place, Johann Kronsteiner had moved up the list of suspects, to take first place over his sister. Now he was no longer a suspect, but a certainty. They'd get the full truth out of him. If not, they'd raid the Bryant house in Salzburg itself. Kronsteiner had spent the last few days there, perhaps had taken the box with him. The woman would talk to save her brother. Or vice versa. Two captives were better than one when it came to questioning.

Johann stumbled as he was pulled through the doorway, but the unexpected shift in his weight didn't loosen their grip. He opened his mouth to yell instinctively, idiotic as it seemed in the emptiness of the night. But a quick hand went over his lips, clamping down painfully. "Gag him!" the older man said, and a scarf was forced between his lips, tightly knotted behind his head. Then the two men were crossing the meadow obliquely, dragging him in a drunken run toward the upper curve of the Unterwald road, where their car had been safely hidden.

"There's the road!" She pointed to the left as their car came up from the outskirts of Bad Aussee. "Johann Kronsteiner's house is about a hundred—" She stopped abruptly, her gray eyes wide as they stared at the driver beside her. "Did you hear that? It was a shot."

The driver, whom she knew only by his code name of Lev, must have agreed, for he finished turning the abrupt corner, edged the car onto the shoulder of the narrow road to

Unterwald, cut the engine, jammed on both brakes, switched off his lights. In silence, they listened. There were no more shots. "We'll get back to Bad Aussee," Lev said, taking command.

"No! We'll wait. I'd like to go farther up this road." There was little view of the house from here.

"Too dangerous."

"I meant on foot," she said sharply. Supercautious, she thought, and an angry frown hardened the pretty features of her face. Bill Mathison would scarcely have recognized his soft-eyed Elissa at this moment; or Eric Yates his trusted and yielding Eva Langenheim; or the people in Salzburg who knew her as the amiable but aimless Elisabetha Lang. "Wait here," she told Lev, re-establishing her authority. She opened the car door, and found they were drawn so close to the edge of the road that no foothold had been left for her. There was a ditch below her outstretched leg. The light from the half-moon wasn't good enough, and her town clothes, unchanged from Zürich, would hamper her. She pulled her foot back into the car. "You get out," she told Lev. "You'll have a clear view of the road and the house once you are on top of that bank. It's safe enough with those bushes and trees to hide you," she couldn't resist adding.

He didn't like the idea much. But he hadn't liked the idea, either, of bringing her to Johann Kronsteiner's place at this time of night. "He only picked up his jeep at the parking place half an hour before we left Salzburg," Lev had warned her. "If you arrive on his tail, he will guess we've been following him." And she had said, "Not Johann. That's why he likes me: I'm the girl who does unpredictable things. He's an incurable romantic. By morning, I'll have him agreeing with me that his sister—for her own safety—had better confide in him, tell him whatever her husband told her. She's the real key, not Johann. But it is through Johann I'll reach her. So this journey is necessary. If you don't get me to Kronsteiner's place as quickly as possible, I'll hold you fully responsible for the failure of this mission." And that had produced results.

But now, as then, Lev was a hard man to persuade. He was getting out of the car slowly, obviously against his better judgment. Sometimes, she thought, watching his deliberate movements as he climbed the bank, it seemed as if Lev was more in the habit of giving commands than of taking them.

She closed her eyes wearily. She had been traveling for almost six hours and they felt like sixty. First, the precipitous flight from Zürich, her suitcases left in her room (that should keep the thrifty Swiss hoping as they waited for her return), her only luggage a large handbag and a bundle of magazines. Then the brief stop at Munich, using an English passport and a voice to match, just enough time for two telephone calls: one to an emergency number in Salzburg, using the innocuous sentence that ensured safe transportation and special attention when she arrived there; the other to Zürich for news on Operation Bergstrasse. (Mission completed, but unpleasant complications. Poor Willi and his obedient group of Peking Progressives! Small matter to her. She had bowed out of Zürich and of Eric Yates's depleting circle of devoted followers.) In Salzburg (out came Elisabetha Lang's passport again), she had stopped only long enough to grab the suitcase of clothes she kept ready for any sudden trip to the mountains, and to fold one magazine neatly so that it would fit safely into her handbag. A valuable little magazine, brought through customs so casually among the bundle she had carried. Its odd pages between numbers twenty and thirty had enough microdots scattered through their punctuation to give a fairly complete copy of Eric Yates's secret files. At least that was one part of her report on Zürich that would be self-explanatory, perhaps even justification for the "unpleasant complications," whatever that meant.

What was keeping Lev? She ought to have gone herself. She slid across the front seat to climb out onto the road, and then paused, the door half-opened, as she heard the sound of a car. It was somewhere up that road, now traveling away from her toward Unterwald. She gave a small sigh of relief and relaxed. For a moment, she had thought it would come downhill and see her. Then once more she went tense as a second engine started up. This one sounded nearer her, but it, too, began to climb toward Unterwald. She struck a match, glanced at her watch. It was almost midnight.

Lev returned at a quick scramble. And there was a change in his manner. "That house might be worth a visit, but I don't know if we can risk it. It seems deserted, but we had better wait and see. Are there any other houses near that could have heard the shot?"

"If they did, they'll think it was a poacher. Is Johann's jeep still out in front?"

"No. It was the second car to leave. A man locked the front door, and then drove it away. Tall, light-colored hair, fairly young. He wore a heavy coat. I couldn't see much else."

"What kind of coat?"

"Just a dark overcoat."

Not Johann, she thought. Johann might wear a hooded jacket or his loden cape, but not an overcoat. "Then he came from some town or city, not from around here. Who drove away in the first car?"

"Possibly two or three men. They were vanishing into the trees as I reached the top of the bank. The car was parked farther up the road, well out of sight."

And who was shot? she wondered. Johann? "Let's get to the house," she said quickly.

"We can't start until they are out of earshot. Listen! If we can hear them, they could hear us. Besides, we can't risk being seen here. Hasn't Kronsteiner an assistant? If he is out, he may be coming back any—"

"I can handle him," she said, climbing out of the car. "You can bring the car up when you think it's safe enough and have it turned around ready to leave. Keep an eye on this, will you?" She dropped her bulky handbag into the back seat beside her suitcase. "Don't worry. I'm armed." She tapped her coat pocket lightly, and left. Her exhaustion was quite forgotten. Johann might not be dead; he might still have a few coherent words left in him. She broke into a run as she left the steep slope of grayish-white road and started through the moon-silvered meadow.

She found the key in the usual place, but she had to fumble for the lock in the shadowed doorway. Again she wondered about Lev. This supercaution, this instinctive preservation of his identity—could he be much more than he seemed? She had only met him twice before, always in matters of great urgency, and in each case he had been able to relay her requests for immediate help in phenomenally quick time. Could he be close to the top? One of the assistants to the director of the Salzburg network? That nameless, faceless man who controlled them all from some hidden address? Or even the director himself? Not so ridiculous as it sounded. She had heard of instances where direc-

259

tors of networks had made anonymous checks on their agents. If that were true of the reticent, cautious Lev, he could be of great use to her tonight. She would need the most immediate help to establish herself at Unterwald. The key caught at last in the lock, turned heavily. She pushed the door open and closed it behind her as she groped for the light switch, noting with relief that the inside shutters had been closed over the windows. Then she looked around her, and gasped.

With haste, she made a tour of inspection through the whole house, shop and workroom included. The disorder spelled only one thing: she had underestimated Johann's importance. He must know more than she had realized. And by the manner of the search, she could guess the men had been looking for something bulky, something that needed space for its hiding place. The Finstersee chest? At least they hadn't found it. If they had, Johann would now make a very handsome corpse stretched out on that rug. He had not even been wounded by the shot; the bullet had splintered the wooden flooring near the door, and there were no bloodstains anywhere. So they had taken him for questioning, she thought. Poor fool, he would try to hold out. He was just that bull-headed type. ... Yet his stubbornness might just give her enough time to find him. And once he was found, he'd talk out of gratitude. He was that type too.

She locked the door after switching off the light, replaced the key on the window ledge. If any of those searchers came back to the house, they'd better find it as they had left it.

Thoughtfully, she walked back across the meadow, hands in pockets, head slightly bent so that her dark hair swung over her cheeks, slender legs striding out from under short skirt, low-heeled shoes hidden in the stiff frozen beard of autumn grass. Cool crisp silence around her, a feeling of sleeping peace as undisturbed as the view that stretched in front of her—a broad, seemingly endless valley walled only in the far distance by jagged moon-struck peaks. She glanced back at the quiet house with its dark background of pointed trees and curving hills, sharp edges of soaring mountains black against a glittering sky. Poor fool, she thought again, we could now have been making love. What gave you away, Johann?

Lev had the car running, its door open and ready. "Well?" he demanded, his eyes watching the road as if Johann's assistant might appear there at any moment. He relaxed visibly as they started downhill. "What did you find?"

She didn't have to report to him, not if he was really what he said he was. His questions might have been asked out of natural curiosity, but even that was overstepping his job. He was simply a trusted courier who conveyed important messages or people. "Nothing. Only evidence of a very thorough search. Get me back to Bad Aussee. I'll have to sleep there. Beyond the town, past the lumberyard on its other side, there's a safe house. You know it? Good." She settled back into her seat, drew her collar more closely around her neck. It had been cold in Johann's house. Or perhaps it was her disappointment that helped to chill her. If things had gone as she had planned, it would have been so easy. ... Well, I'll just have to replan, she thought, and fell silent.

"You are expected back in Salzburg. You have a report to file."

"I have the first part ready to deliver by you," she said impatiently. "The rest of it can wait. Our first problem now is Unterwald."

"You are moving too quickly."

"So are the men who carted off Johann Kronsteiner."

"I was instructed—"

"We'll talk once we are safely through the town. I'll let you do the driving and you let me get my thoughts straight. Trust my judgment more. I was right tonight, wasn't I? It wasn't any whim that brought me up to visit Johann Kronsteiner."

Lev's thin white face was tight, noncommittal. But she got the silence she needed.

"This will do," she said as they passed the lumber mill, its neat stacks of sawed timber rising house-high over its deserted yard, and entered a narrow twisting road of trees and small gardens and sloping roofs where the moonlight was blotted out and all windows were dark. She waited until he had eased the car into the black shadow of a heavy cluster of trees, cut the engine, switched off the lights. "Now," she said, "here is what I need. First, adequate cover and credentials to get me safely established in Unterwald for a few days. I suggest a faked affiliation with some foreign tourist bureau specializing in Austrian winter sports. I shall say I am making a survey for them of possible accommodations in Unterwald and its surrounding area. That will raise no questions; there is already much talk about a plan to turn the place into a ski resort. Second, I shall need a car. Third, a small two-way radio with which I can reach Salzburg in an emergency. Fourth, I need two men stationed in Bad Aussee or some other neighboring town, ready to get up to Unterwald once I have found what we are looking for."

Lev was sitting very still. "You intend to go in by yourself?"

"Yes. We can't risk any complete strangers blundering around. The Austrians would pick them up and deport them. They've been doing that all summer. So this is what I intend to do: use the Austrians. Let them supply the manpower, do the work, face the risks. When they've found what we want, we can take it. That will be easier than it sounds. I have a contact among them—an important one. Everything he learns, I will learn."

"You can handle him?" Lev asked with the slightest touch of irony.

"I can. He will do exactly what he is told to do, simply because he has no choice."

"The decision to use such a man must come from Salzburg."

"It will come. And it had better come quickly, along with my other requests. Johann Kronsteiner won't last a week. We are now counting in days. Yes, we are going out after Kronsteiner. Or rather, we'll get the Austrians to start the search for him."

"May I tell Salzburg the reason why *he* has become the priority?"

She looked at him coldly. "Because a man is easier to find than a box. All a box needs is a hole in the earth, or a covering of stones, or the hollow trunk of a tree. But a man who is being kept alive, and questioned, must be safely enclosed, and that takes silghtly more space, such as a hut or a barn or a cowshed or stable or anything with walls and a roof."

Lev said slowly, "Are you reporting that a certain box has been taken from its hiding place?"

"Yes."

"By whom?"

"Richard Bryant."

"Proof?"

"No, but plenty of evidence. Salzburg will find it in my

report on Yates. But I think the Nazis must have proof that the box is gone. They were searching for it tonight."

"Have you proof that they were Nazis?"

"Who else? Unless, of course, we let some of Yates's Peking Progressives move into Unterwald. Or gave the West an indication that we've been interested in the Styrian lakes." And if we did either, she thought, then our man in Salzburg has been slipping badly. "So you will report that I intend to search for Johann Kronsteiner, using the Austrians, in order to find that box."

"And then?"

"I'll alert the two agents who have been stationed down here. They can get up to Unterwald within twenty minutes."

"And then?"

"They will have their orders from Salzburg to follow, won't they? My job will be over as soon as I contact them and give them the information."

"Then you do put some limitations on your authority?"

"Is that a criticism?"

Very quietly he answered her. "A little more self-criticism during this past week might have been better for security."

Zürich? She tried to keep her voice natural. "I did only what was necessary to preserve my cover and ensure the success of this mission."

"Such as being seen by Werner Dietrich, Zauner's assistant, last Monday evening when you were in flight from the Bryant house? Oh yes, he was in the shadows nearby, keeping watch over that American called Mathison. Had you forgotten that Dietrich would be somewhere near the American?"

Yes, in the fear and panic of the moment, she had forgotten. "It was no fault of mine that Anna Bryant and the American came back unexpectedly to the house. I was doing a most necessary job. I was given permission to do it." And if I hadn't, she thought bitterly, none of them would have known how close Yates and his Peking comrades had come to the secret of Finstersee.

Lev ignored her justification. "Dietrich put in a report on that incident. Fortunately, we were able to have it suppressed. But he is a very earnest young man, and thoughtful. He is likely to put in another report, direct to Vienna this time. We may have to forestall him in that. Even if we contrive a fairly simple accident, there could be dangerous repercussions."

She could only stare at this man through the darkness, wondering who he really was. Would he reveal his authority? Order her back to Salzburg; back to playing art student, winning the confidence of those who had escaped from Eastern Europe, learning about the resistance groups who had helped them? Back to Moscow, even? Yet they need me here, she thought angrily. Before they could get another agent in place, time would be lost and the Finstersee box, too.

But he spoke simply as if he were indeed only a messenger. "I was instructed to give you that serious warning. I was also instructed, if you seemed capable of completing your mission, to give you this final instruction." He handed her a pencil-thin flashlight. "The message inside is coded, but not microfilmed. You'll be able to read it without any special equipment. Now have you got that report on Zürich? How far does it go?"

She groped in her handbag, pulled out the magazine. "The usual pages," she told him.

"How far does the report go?"

"Up to yesterday." She hoped her voice sounded normal.

"Where will you stay?"

She was closing the handbag carefully. "Stay? Oh, you mean at Unterwald? The Gasthof Waldesruh is the obvious place, I suppose. If it's open." She made an effort to stop worrying about Zürich. "It's possibly wiser if you have someone make my reservation there—perhaps it should appear to be done by the tourist bureau that is supposed to employ me? And there is one other thing I need: the names of any people in Unterwald who may be working for the Nazis."

"We haven't found any."

"Are they as well hidden as all that?" She was incredulous. "But they *are* in Unterwald. That's where the car and the jeep went tonight. They might even have their headquarters there. Haven't we found any trace?"

"The Austrians have been concentrating on Unterwald all this week. We couldn't make one move—"

"They kept us out, did they?" Yes, perhaps they knew something. In that case, Felix Zauner would know too. "I'll try our Austrian contact. Good night, comrade. You will tell Salzburg how urgently I need my requests delivered to me here? Tomorrow?"

"That is not for me or you to decide."

She turned her annoyance onto tugging the suitcase free of the car door, where its strap had caught briefly in the hinge. Everything was resisting her tonight, she thought angrily. "Surely," she said petulantly, "there must have been someone in the village who heard the cars drive up." They couldn't all have been so deeply asleep. "Peasants have toothache and sick kids, don't they?"

"Quiet!" he reminded her, although she had kept her voice low.

Officious oaf, she thought as she hoisted the suitcase and started up the silent road toward a house that was hidden behind trees. Here she was, exhausted, carrying a suitcase and heavy handbag, walking, walking almost two hundred meters to keep him safe and his car unnoticed. And he had to scare her with a serious warning, although he was even then carrying extra instructions for her right inside his pocket. Her age, that's all he was. Not much older. And with less experience, too, that was easy to see. All his excessive supercaution came from too much desk work and too little practice. If she were a man, she'd outrank him any day. And he knew it.

Far behind her, she could hear the car start gently. Without lights, of course. And move slowly, quietly away.

19

"YOU KNOW," BILL MATHISON SAID REFLECTIVELY, "IT'S A strange thing about me and Salzburg. I seem to spend mealtimes slaving over a rented typewriter and biting into ham sandwiches." He finished his fifth attempt at a precise but polite letter to Anna Bryant, widow of Richard Bryant, stating the position of Newhart and Morris, publishers, with regard to a supposed contract which had both originated and ended with Eric Yates, since deceased. "Here it is." He gave it a last glance and handed it over to Lynn Conway. "Just remember that legalese plays hell with prose style," he added as she began to read.

"It's clear and friendly. Hardly sounds legal at all."

"It had better be that," he reminded her with a grin, "or

else Jimmy Newhart will be finding himself a new lawyer."

"And who's going to pay for all your traveling then?"

"Funny girl. At this moment, I wish you and I were—" He cut off abruptly.

She looked up from the letter in surprise. His voice had been in earnest, there. She resisted saying "I thought you liked Salzburg." She knew he did. So she cut out the probing and said, "I'll sign now. How many copies did you make? Three? That's good."

"Businesslike, aren't you?" He was back to light voice, light manner.

"It's always a safe retreat," she admitted. She gave the letter a final check. ... *In addition to the anguish to which you are now subjected, we deeply regret the embarrassment and inconvenience which the matter of the agreement with Mr. Bryant has caused you. It was signed without our knowledge or consent by Mr. Eric Yates, in a private and unauthorized capacity. ... The advance made to Mr. Bryant was drawn on Mr. Yates's own funds, and not on our account. In consequence, neither the agreement nor the advance binds us in any way in connection with the publication of Mr. Bryant's work. ...*

As a token of regret for this unfortunate occurrence, we take pleasure in enclosing our check in the amount of U.S. $300.00, payable to your order. Your acceptance of this check, together with your signature and return of the enclosed copy of this letter, will constitute your full and unconditional release of Newhart and Morris from all liability in connection with the aforementioned agreement and advance, in accordance with the terms of this letter. In any event, we would like to make clear that, as publishers of scientific material, we would not have been able to consider Mr. Bryant's work for inclusion on any of our lists. With repeated regrets, we remain, Very truly yours. ... "It's very clear," she said, signing, handing everything back to Bill Mathison.

He inserted the copies into one large envelope, then checked the photographs he carried in another.

"May I?" she asked, looking at that envelope curiously.

He nodded, spread its contents out on the bed to let her study the photographs quickly: Yates's notes to Bryant, Bryant's replies, the check signed by someone called Emil Burch. She shook her head slowly. "What did Yates hope to get out of Bryant?"

He gathered up the envelopes, placed them with a folded newspaper in his thin briefcase. "Ready to leave?" He was looking at his watch. "We'll just make it."

"Two minutes," she promised him, and left for her room. Not much use asking questions, she was thinking, but the trouble was that they kept slipping out. Security at stake, that was what he had been willing to tell her this morning, security not only of the United States but of the other nontotalitarian nations as well. And if he didn't answer her questions, then it was only to save him from lying. Lies were easy answers to the unanswerable. And who are you to grumble against that? she asked her dressing-table mirror as she made sure her hair was right and her lipstick hardly noticeable. You used to think that men told lies as easily as they breathed. And now you've met someone who wants to establish something honest between you and him, and all you do is quibble because he won't start out lying.

He was waiting for her outside the door of her room. "Where's your blue coat?"

"It looked so sunny outside—"

"Best to take it, Lynn."

"But you haven't taken yours—" She stopped, noting his worried eyes, and went back into her room. The first thing I do when I get back to normal old New York is to get my head examined, she reminded herself angrily. What on earth makes me keep listening to Bill Mathison? Or wanting to please him? "There's one answer you don't have to give me," she told him as she joined him at the elevator. It was a self-service affair, and Bill had kept it in position by jamming his finger on the button and keeping his shoulder against the door. "Forceful," she commented. "You're probably giving the poor thing severe schizophrenia. It isn't programed for your methods."

"I said we'd be there around half past two."

"Are we late?"

"No, no. It's just that we'll take longer to get through the Old Town than you expect. This is your first taste of Salzburg, isn't it? You know, you always ought to wear that color of blue."

"That could become tedious."

Not on you, he thought, and studied her face with pleasure. "What answer don't I have to give you?" he asked gently.

"The reason why you insisted I stay at this hotel." And have a room on the same floor, and next door at that, she thought. She was smiling now, although when they had checked in over an hour ago she had been on the verge of definite rebellion. "You wanted me within screaming distance."

He laughed, and then fell serious, watching her face. "Frankly, yes." Then he was busy holding the elevator door, escorting her into the lobby, dropping their room keys at the desk, taking her arm as they stepped out into the busy street.

"He was in the lobby," Lynn said as they walked toward the bridge over the river into the Old Town. "The Englishman who was on the plane." Both planes at that. The man who had kept them within sight all the time they had waited at Innsbruck, the man who seemed to have little luggage, the man who had checked into their Salzburg hotel right on their heels.

"So I saw."

"He doesn't worry you?"

"He certainly doesn't care if we know he is keeping a close eye on us." And perhaps Charles Nield's banker friend was doing just that. It could be, thought Mathison, that the Englishman thinks I'm his very best bet when it comes to tracking down Elissa. Does he imagine that Elissa is in Salzburg?

"And now he does worry you."

"Not old Andrew."

"He's a friend?"

"A friend of a friend." Mathison glanced around as they were about to leave the bridge. Yes, there was Andrew walking jauntily at a circumspect distance behind them. He wasn't a banker any more. He looked much more like a roving reporter, in well-traveled tweeds, with a raincoat slung over his shoulder. Bowler hat had given place to wind-blown hair, pigskin gloves to bare hands, striped tie to heavy turtleneck sweater.

"Let's forget him," Lynn said, her eyes now wide for the Old Town. But she couldn't quite, for by the time they were reaching the Neugasse she was saying, "Andrew has disappeared. Hasn't been in sight for the last two streets. Now what could have been his idea? To let us know he was there? Reassure us that he *was* friendly? But what now? Perhaps he has decided we are not worth bothering about."

Not Andrew, thought Mathison. He's around somewhere, but he is being more discreet and he will probably stay that way until he is sure there is no hope that Elissa is anywhere on the horizon. "You sound almost disappointed," he told Lynn, and wondered how friend Andrew was going to stay concealed in the narrow stretch of the Neugasse. And then the idea didn't amuse him so much. The minute Andrew saw the name of Bryant over a photography-shop door, that MI6 brain of his would start some quick calculations and come up with the prospect of a bonus: not only Elissa but possibly Finstersee, too.

"Well, it's nice to have such a pleasant-looking watchdog."

"He is hardly that." More like a cat on the prowl, thought Mathison, as they reached the shop. CLOSED the card on the door's glass panel read. "That's all right," he assured Lynn. "Mrs. Bryant is just keeping the customers out. We'll try the kitchen door. This way." They walked on to the hallway's entrance.

It was shadowed, even in daylight, but it seemed smaller now. The garbage cans stood in a black corner, the flight of stairs seemed to twist up into darkness. Lynn's head tilted back, her eyes following the carved design that climbed one pillar, built into a wall, to flower against the vaulted ceiling. Beside it, open electric wiring snaked its way up to a one-bulb lamp. A study in contrasts, she thought: medieval imagination and contemporary determination. "No answer?" she called over to Bill, who had knocked on a door at the foot of the staircase for the third time.

"Perhaps she is upstairs in her apartment," he said, and started to climb. He tried not to sound alarmed. "Coming?"

"Yes. It's lonely down here for a stranger. I suppose if you lived in this kind of house, you'd never think anything of it." She pulled her coat more closely around her. "You were right about this," she admitted as she noticed his glance at her gesture. He wasn't in a talkative mood though, and so she fell silent, too. The steps were steep and worn, and brought them to a dark landing. The first door was that of the Bryant apartment. From somewhere upstairs came the sound of a piano, a succession of difficult arpeggios, far off, muted, but comforting. So was the voice of a child from the floor above. But in answer to Bill Mathison's knock came nothing at all. He tried again. And again.

"Well—" he began, and then stopped. Someone was entering the hall by a back entrance that seemed to lie right underneath their feet. Mathison's hand went out and grasped Lynn's arm, drawing her more closely to him. They stood in silence. The door below the flight of stairs scraped shut; light footsteps came into the hall, walked unerringly. Mathison relaxed as quickly as he had gone on guard. "Hello, there!" he called down to the woman who was unlocking the kitchen door. He let go of Lynn's waist, took her hand, led her downstairs. "Hope we didn't startle you," he said to Anna Bryant. "This is Mrs. Conway—from New York and Zürich."

If anyone was startled, it was Lynn Conway. Even now, she could feel the tight grip of Bill's arm, ready to draw her farther upstairs. What on earth had he been expecting? "I've been looking forward to meeting you," she said warmly as she shook hands with Anna Bryant. "I think Bill was worried in case you had forgotten our appointment."

"I am late and I am sorry," Anna Bryant said, "but I had to be with the Dietrich children this morning. Frieda is at the hospital, you see. You remember her, don't you?" she asked as she shook hands with Mathison.

Frieda? Vaguely he remembered the friendly bouncing blonde who had taken charge of Anna last Monday night. "Hope she isn't seriously ill," he said politely. He walked around the staircase to have a look at the unsuspected door. "Where does this lead?"

"It's a short cut," she called after him. "And it isn't Frieda, but her husband who is in the hospital. He's—oh, well." She opened the kitchen door. "Do come in," she told Lynn. "And I really am sorry I worried you. But there is no need. I worry enough for everyone." She tried to laugh. "Mr. Mathison!" she called again.

"What *is* back there? I'm curious, too," Lynn admitted, hesitating, then running to join Bill. "Why it's a courtyard! These can't be Roman pillars, can they?" She stared at the strange mixture of architecture in this miniature cloister: classical, medieval, baroque—with a touch of contemporary life as well, for in the small open space, beside the covered disused well, were neatly stacked packing cases forming a cubist design, two bicycles, a baby carriage. From a window above came the clearer notes of the piano now attempting some appropriate Mozart. The children's voices were breaking into laughter. Bill had walked around the short colonnade to reach the other side of the courtyard and was looking through an opened door into a dark closed way. There were two other doors on the courtyard, but they were shut, and he could be intruding. So he returned. Lynn was tactfully studying the windows overlooking the well. "I'd guess seventeenth century, but whoever put this place together just grabbed what was handy and used it. I suppose it seemed senseless to carve out new pillars when there were some solid ancient ones lying around."

"Too many doors for my taste," Mathison said, and he wasn't thinking of architecture either. "Where the hell do they all lead?" he asked irritably. He asked that question again, expurgated, as he brought Lynn into the kitchen. He is concealing a load of worry, she realized. But what was there to worry about here?

"Oh, one takes you through to the Mozartplatz. The others go through courtyards and other buildings to the Residenzplatz and the Altmarkt. They are quite simple to use, really, once you know them." She looked at the American girl who was standing uncertainly beside Mathison. Why is she here? Anna wondered. She is pretty, of course, and charming; and she must have some intelligence if she is representing the publisher—but is she? "Please take off your coat. Do sit down." Anna began stoking the ceramic stove. Perhaps, she was thinking, I've learned to distrust too much in this last week. Perhaps last night and my quarrel with Johann and the shock he gave me will never let me trust anyone fully again. Johann . . . He would have liked this girl. She was even prettier than Elisabetha Lang; her clothes were the same smart style, her manner just as ingratiating.

"Let me help," Lynn said.

"No, thank you. I can manage."

Well, that's that, thought Lynn Conway, and tried not to look too curious as she glanced around the strange mixture of living room and kitchen. Anna Bryant was not at all what she had expected. Nor was she welcome. Does she resent me? Lynn wondered. But why? She walked over to one wall, where a panel of mounted photographs caught her eye. "It's beautiful country. Is this near Salzburg?" She pointed to a vista of meadows and trees falling toward a green valley with mountains stretching behind them all.

"That's the view from my brother's house. It's at Bad Aussee."

"Oh?"

Anna closed the door of the stove with a sharp clang. "Johann is a ski teacher and mountain guide," she said stiltedly. "That's his profession."

"And is this Johann?" Lynn was looking at the picture of a skier, caught in motion as he came soaring over a ridge of blue-shadowed snow, bluer sky above, sharp peaks in the high background, a spray of sparkling snow rising behind him.

"Yes."

"Very handsome."

"So women think."

Lynn couldn't hide her surprise as she looked sharply at Anna Bryant. "An excellent photograph. Motion like that is always difficult to catch."

"My husband was an excellent photographer."

"So Bill tells me. It really was too bad that so many of his newest photographs were stolen. Of course, we couldn't have publ—" She stopped short. "Perhaps you'd better read the letter Bill has brought with him, first." She glanced over at Bill, who was taking the two large envelopes from his briefcase. Now it's your turn, she told him silently. I did my best, but it wasn't much good at all.

This is going to be more difficult than I imagined, Mathison was thinking. What has happened to Anna? She was going through the motions of politeness, but her natural warmth had gone; she seemed cold and restrained, almost bitter as she had talked about Johann. There was a hint of nervousness, too. Nervousness or concern? He remembered the angry interruptions in his telephone call with Anna. "Is Johann in Salzburg now?"

"No. He left for Bad Aussee last night. For Unterwald, actually." She watched the American girl, but the name seemed to mean nothing to her. "That is near Finstersee," she said carefully.

"Oh?" Lynn Conway was puzzled but polite. "This is my first visit to Austria, Mrs. Bryant, but I hope I'll see something of your mountains and lakes before I go back to Zürich. Bill has promised to rent a car and take me around. Why don't you come with us, and we'll drive you to Bad Aussee and you can see your brother?" She has been spending too much time indoors, thought Lynn as she looked at the white strained face that stared at her so strangely.

"My brother is too busy," Anna said curtly. "He will be

most of the time in Unterwald. That's where the Seidl girl lives—the one he is going to marry. They got engaged last Monday."

"Monday?" Mathison asked, not concealing his surprise. But I met him here on Monday. And then later that night he was in Unterwald, certainly, but I thought he was there to find out why and how his brother-in-law had been killed. Johann chose strange timing to get himself engaged.

"So much happened that night," Anna said briefly. She looked around the kitchen, thinking now of the Lang girl, who had come here in the darkness to steal. One of Johann's girls. Twice she had been here with him, so filled with interest and questions and seemingly so harmless. Dick had thought her charming, charming and pretty. Johann had been proud of her. And I—I showed her around, showed her where I worked.

"Do you remember our talk then?" Mathison asked, trying to ease his way toward presenting the letter. "I did find out something about Eric Yates. You'll find most of it here." He held out the letter.

She took it from him silently, but before she started reading it she glanced down at the table where he had spilled out the contents of the other envelope. Quickly, she spread out the photographs Mathison had made of her husband's file on Yates. "You really did keep your promise," she said slowly, softly. So Johann was wrong about that, too. Why trust a stranger, he had said, what does Mathison owe you? But I did trust a stranger, and I was right. And here is the stranger, not probing like my friends—like Felix Zauner, and Werner Dietrich, and all those others who kept coming to see me this week, always bringing the talk around to Finstersee, never telling me why they were interested in it or who had sent them to question me. "Oh, thank you. Thank you. You'll never know how grateful I am."

"I don't pretend to be much of a photographer, but I'm glad these prints came out clearly," Mathison said awkwardly. Her thanks seemed excessive for such a small gesture. "Particularly that one." He pointed to the photograph of the Burch check. "It's the one that really interested Washington and got them answering some of my questions about Yates."

"You found out about him?" she asked quickly.

"Some people in Washington were able to find out."

"And what was that?"

"He wasn't working for British Intelligence."

She stared at him. "He tricked my husband?"

All the way, thought Mathison. "Why don't you read the letter, first of all?" It explained more easily than he could tell her face to face. "I typed it," he added frankly, "but James Newhart backs up all I said."

"And that's my signature," Lynn told her, "but he will back that up, too. We can call him in New York if you like." What's making her so difficult? Lynn wondered as she rose and came forward to the table. Poor old Bill, all that work put into the letter and she isn't even giving it her full attention. She had only murmured "Your Mr. Newhart is very kind" as she read about his offer, and almost dropped the letter right there on the table. "Read on to the end," Lynn insisted. Five drafts and a wasted lunchtime, she thought angrily. "If you want to know all about *your* Mr. Yates, you'd better finish it."

Anna read on, and then looked up unbelievingly. "There never would have been a book? Newhart and Morris don't publish—" Her voice trailed off. "Did he want the Finstersee box as much as all that?"

Mathison took a deep breath, glanced quickly at Lynn, wondered how to get her out of the room. Or it might be easier to stop Anna, get her to postpone talking. "Is the letter clear? If you have any reservations about it, just tell me."

"Deceit," she said bitterly. "Deceit right from the beginning. He robbed Dick of everything. But the only thing he did not get was the box itself."

"Lynn, would you leave?" But that was as far as Mathison got. Anna Bryant began to laugh, a strange pathetic kind of laugh that twisted into a sob. Lynn moved quickly to put an arm around her shoulder, take the letter gently out of her hand, help her into a chair. The attack of hysteria never developed, unless the flow of words that rushed from Anna's pale lips was a strange substitution. They stopped Mathison short in his search for brandy, words that poured out about Finstersee and the box which Dick had found and hidden before the Nazis killed him, no one knew of it, it would have stayed there where Dick had hidden it if Johann hadn't searched and guessed and taken it, and Johann had put it in a safer place, he said, safe from the Nazis, safe from everyone, and only Johann knew where it was now, he wouldn't tell her, he wouldn't tell her. ... The rush of words ended in tears.

"Do you understand what she is saying?" Lynn asked, looking nervously at Bill.

Everything had gone wrong, he was thinking, everything; and for no purpose except that Lynn has heard enough to put her into the circle of danger that's now drawn around all of us. "Why didn't you leave?" he said angrily. "I told you to leave."

"And I will," she said, equally angry. "But first I'll get Mrs. Bryant up to bed and fix something for her to eat. She probably hasn't had a decent meal in days. Or slept either."

Anna Bryant was paying no attention at all to their argument. She had recovered her composure with a pathetic determination to keep calm, stay lucid. She kept looking at Bill Mathison. She put out a hand and caught his. "Will you help me?"

He nodded.

"Will you tell your friends in Washington about Finstersee?"

"They know." He glanced at Lynn once more.

"All right," Lynn said, "I can take a hint eventually." She was trying to smile, but there was definite hurt in her eyes. What am I anyway, she thought as she walked toward a door into a long narrow hall, a decorative smoke screen? He'll have some explaining to do before I take one more step with him through Salzburg. If she hadn't left her coat in the kitchen, she would have kept on walking right through the shop and out the front door.

Anna was too intent on her own thoughts even to notice that Lynn had left. "Did they send you here?" she was asking quickly, sharply, and she looked almost bitterly over at the documents on the table.

Mathison said carefully, "I came to bring you those papers. And a friend in Washington—*your* friend, too, Anna— asked me to warn you."

"About what?"

"About talking as freely as you have been doing. He feels you are in considerable danger. And if you want his help, he is willing to give it."

"One man?"

"There are also others."

"And in return I was to tell you where the Finstersee box could be found?"

"No. You could have told him directly. He's here in Salzburg. If you had wanted to tell him, that is." Keep that point clear, Mathison thought; that's the one reason that let you agree to being Nield's little errand boy in the first place. "There's nothing you can tell him now about the Finstersee box," he added, "but you may yet be in danger, and I think you should see this man. He will think of some plan to get you out of Salzburg until it's safe for you to return."

She looked at him. The bitterness left her face. Her voice softened. "It is Johann you must see. At once. Tell Johann he must do nothing about the box until he can meet your friend." She thought over that, made a decision. "I'll go with you to Bad Aussee. This time, I'll win the argument. Last night we had such a quarrel, and after he left I kept trying to piece everything together, to guess where he had hidden it. Not in his own house. That's definite. It was hidden sometime last Monday night—that's the only chance he had. Somewhere between the meadow on Finstersee and Trudi's house."

"Trudi?"

"Trudi Seidl. The girl he is marrying. I thought of going to see her, only—" she shook her head slowly—"Johann wouldn't tell her about Finstersee, or the box, or August Grell. Too dangerous for Trudi. That is how Johann would see it."

You've lost me, Mathison thought, but he wouldn't risk interrupting.

"Johann really believes he is doing this to protect me," Anna went on. "He's that kind of man. He thinks women shouldn't know anything that's dangerous. But then Dick was like that, too." She broke off to glance in the direction of the shop. "And so are you. Oh, really, you are all so foolish! You only add to any danger, don't you see? How can we recognize it when we have to face it? That is double danger, Bill. And it's terrifying—the feeling of not being able to judge the truth is terrifying. This week, my friends became strangers." She looked at him, added, "And it seems as if strangers have become my friends. Can I trust this man you know—this man from Washington?"

"Yes." And I thought the way we met, with the FBI vouching for Nield, was something slightly esoteric, a comedy touch like the Acme Quick Service brothers. Instead, it had let him face Anna Bryant with a direct answer and no private hesitations. "Let me send him here. You can tell him what you told me—and anything else you remember."

"There is a lot to remember," she said slowly. "A lot to tell."

I bet there is, he thought. "You just put all the responsibility onto his shoulders. He can take it."

Her confidence grew. "An hour ago, everything seemed hopeless. I didn't get much sleep last night, of course. I was trying to puzzle out where Johann could have hidden the box, but all I could do was guess. And feel more bitter, more helpless."

"You'll have help now." He picked up Lynn's coat along with his briefcase. "I'll get my friend around here at once. Say half an hour?"

"That will give me time to get my thoughts straight, tell him everything as quickly as possible. What is his name?"

"Cliff."

"What does he look like? I have to be sure."

"I'll come back here just long enough to introduce him. Then I'll leave you two alone. Okay?"

"But aren't you going to see Johann along with me?"

The telephone rang.

"Cliff will do that. Better than I can." He hesitated, made a guess about Johann. "Money may be involved now," he added tactfully. "I couldn't handle that at all, frankly."

"It wasn't money Dick wanted." She was moving toward the shop, where the telephone had given its second ring.

"Lynn will answer it. She speaks excellent German. That's why Newhart sent her to take charge in Zürich until he finds a replacement for Yates."

The phone stopped ringing. "She puzzles me," Anna said, speaking low, as if Lynn were within earshot. "Doesn't her husband object to her traveling abroad like this?" She had tried to make her voice light, keep any censure out of it. I'll never understand American women, she was thinking. Will my daughter be as casual as Mrs. Conway?

"Her husband was killed about six years ago—in an accident."

"Oh," Anna said slowly. She turned away, entered the corridor that led into the shop. She paused again, faced him. "Did I tell you about Werner Dietrich?"

277

"He's in the hospital," Mathison said patiently. God, he thought, how long will it take me to reach Charles Nield?

"He is dying. No hope. He had an accident early this morning. Such a stupid, silly accident. His back was broken; concussion, too. Everyone thinks he really did slip and fall on the stairs outside his office. But he was the only person who could identify Elisabetha Lang."

"Lang? Elissa Lang?"

"Elisabetha. Last Monday night he saw her running away from this house. He was at the corner—"

"I remember him. He recognized the girl, all right. What does she look like?"

"Mrs. Bryant!" Lynn was calling.

"Coming!" he called back. "What does she look like?" he insisted.

"About Mrs. Conway's height. The same kind of figure, the same kind of clothes. Dark hair, dark-gray eyes. She is very attractive."

"Didn't Dietrich report he had seen her?"

"Yes, but the police have done nothing."

Then it wasn't the police to whom he sent his report, thought Mathison.

"Felix Zauner said nothing much could be done because she is now out of the country. She's in Zürich. She went to meet Yates and give him the photographs, that's obvious."

He didn't even try to disillusion her that the photographs had ever reached Yates. He had a new problem. "So you discussed Lang with Dietrich, and with Zauner? Who else knows?"

"Only you."

"Not Johann?"

"How could I tell him? He brought her here in the first place." She began hurrying toward the shop. "Elisabetha Lang was one of his girls," she added over her shoulder.

Lynn was saying into the receiver, "Now that's all right, Trudi. Here is Mrs. Bryant to speak with you. She will tell you I'm a friend. ... No, no, I understand. Please don't get upset about that." She handed the receiver to Anna Bryant, covering its mouth-piece as she told her quickly, "Trudi Seidl. She thought I was you, and tried to pour out her troubles. Now she is in a fluster about me and what I'll think." She retreated to Bill Mathison.

"Troubles?" he asked.

"Johann didn't go to see her last night. And he isn't at his place. She's phoning from there."

"Stood her up, did he?"

"Perhaps."

He looked at her sharply, but she was watching Anna Bryant, who was telling Trudi that Mrs. Conway was indeed a friend. Then Anna fell abruptly silent as she listened to a torrent of words made unintelligible by tears that could be heard across the narrow shop.

"I was afraid of that," Lynn said. "I did try to quiet her down."

Anna Bryant looked over at them. "Please go. Get your friend here at once." Her voice was calm, but her face was white and tense.

"Come on," he told Lynn, and held out her coat for her. "We have an errand to do."

"You go. I'll wait here," Lynn said, watching Anna Bryant.

"Lynn, I need you." He pulled her around to face him. "Come with me. Please." He dropped the coat around her shoulders, hurried her over to the front door, unbolted it. He had wanted to try one of the short cuts, but unless Anna could have given him directions, it might have ended being the long way around to Tomaselli's. "Please," he said again, as Lynn hesitated at the door. To Anna, he said, "Cliff will be here within half an hour. Lock the doors, will you?"

Anna nodded. She was saying into the receiver, "Not over the telephone, Trudi! I'll come up and see you. Tonight if possible. If not, tomorrow. I promise. Mr. Mathison and Mrs. Conway will drive me up to Unterwald." Her eyes, troubled and pleading, looked at Bill Mathison.

"Of course we will," Lynn said, and almost ran down the steps into the street with the force of Mathison's tug on her wrist as he closed the door.

"Bill!" She wasn't amused.

"Just come with me. I'll explain."

"I bet."

"I'll explain. Everything. It's time you knew."

"Now there I agree." She looked at his worried face. Her voice softened. "Please help me on with my coat." She noted that they scarcely stopped walking while he did that. She noted, too, the briefcase under his arm. "I thought that was empty."

"There's a newspaper inside."

"Where are we going?"

"For a cup of coffee at Tomaselli's."

"For a cup of— Oh, really, Bill!"

"And by the time we have drunk it, help will be on its way to Anna Bryant."

"This Cliff person?"

"This Cliff person."

"But why do I have to go along? I should have stayed with Mrs. Bryant. That phone call bothers me the more I think of it."

"Because," he answered frankly, "your auburn hair and your blue coat and my jacket and this briefcase—" he opened it as he spoke—"and this folded newspaper now under my arm will get the message across to Cliff, and no doubts about it either."

She stopped in amazement.

"Come on," he said firmly, catching a sure grip on her arm, "and tell me what bothers you about Trudi's phone call."

They had left the Neugasse and passed through another twist of narrow street. Now they were entering the Altmarkt, a small wide square, empty and placid, edged with handsome low buildings, pleasant shops, and well-dressed window-gazers who walked slowly through a quiet Saturday afternoon. He led her obliquely across the smooth pavement of the square toward a café, restrained and handsome, that stood at one upper corner. Lynn said, "I thought at first that Trudi's pride had been hurt. Johann drove past her house last night, didn't stop. He didn't appear this morning either. So she went down to his house. And she found it in a complete mess. She has been waiting and tidying it up all afternoon."

"A party? Johann's quite a lad. Trudi wasn't his only girl."

"I supposed that, too. Only, she added a strange remark. She had been chasing on a hundred words to the minute, no pause, no stop, not even listening to me saying 'Please, would you wait a moment? Let me fetch Mrs. Bryant.' Perhaps my German isn't so good, not for the Unterwald region anyway."

"What strange remark?" he asked quietly. They were now in the center of the Altmarkt. He measured the remaining distance to Tomaselli's with a careful eye, and eased their pace.

"She said, 'Such a mess everywhere, such a terrible mess, but they did not find anything.' And she broke into tears which took a full minute to control. Then I managed to get through to her that I was *not* Mrs. Bryant, and that threw her into a panic."

They didn't find anything. ... Mathison halted, looked down at Lynn. "These were her exact words?"

"Yes. I didn't pay too much attention at the time—not until Mrs. Bryant started listening to Trudi. Did you see her hands as she gripped the receiver? The knuckles were ridged white. She must have understood at once." And it wasn't good news, whatever it was, thought Lynn unhappily.

"She'd get the meaning." They started walking again, but slowly, while Mathison's thoughts raced on. Johann had disappeared and his place had been searched. Everything had gone wrong. In spite of Nield's briefing, planning, arranging, everything was flying wild, and what signal could Mathison send? Anna Bryant was willing to help, wanted to help; Anna Bryant once knew where the box was, but no longer; Anna Bryant could convince her brother to co-operate, and would; Anna Bryant's brother was missing. I'll throw the book at Nield, Mathison thought in desperation, I'll give such a flurry of signals that his agent will report everything has gone haywire. And that's just about as accurate an alert as Nield could get. That should start him heading for the Neugasse.

Or what if Nield's agent didn't get the message? What if he thought Mathison had gone haywire himself?

"Come on, Bright Eyes. Drop the anxiety. That's an order." He managed a confident grin. "But it's going to be a very quick cup of coffee."

She stopped frowning at the street that ran along the top of the Altmarkt and led to other squares, grander, larger, with domes and cupolas to match. A heavenly place, she was thinking, if only ... She suppressed a sigh. "Even the clouds are baroque," she said as they reached the café's sidewalk, which was covered by a pleasant upstairs terrace. "A pity it isn't warm enough to sit outside. I must come here some summer and watch the dirndls stroll by." She glanced around at some passing capes, and almost frowned again. "There's a man who seems to be walking after us, keeping our exact pace. I saw him as we left the Neugasse. He's dressed in heavy tweeds—"

"Gray hair, beak nose, dark mustache?" Mathison's voice

sounded amused. I saw that bastard, he thought worriedly. "A little too old for you, isn't he?"

"I may be suffering from a father fixation."

"Don't look at him," he warned her.

"I wasn't," she said indignantly. "I was just wondering where oh where is friend Andrew?" This time, she could even produce a small smile.

"That's better," he told her as they entered the café. He took a split second to look back at the square. The beak-nosed man had turned away. No more interest, seemingly. "You're right about friend Andrew. He has deserted us." Mathison tucked the folded newspaper firmly under his arm and steered her to the nearest vacant table.

20

FRIEND ANDREW HAD WATCHED THE TWO AMERICANS LEAVE for Tomaselli's, standing discreetly to the side of a dentist's waiting-room window, which lay on the first floor above a shop directly opposite the Bryants' building.

"There they go," he told friend Bruno, who had made himself very much at home in the dentist's office since he had arrived from Vienna this morning. Beside Bruno's chair were binoculars and camera, and he had set up narrow mirrors on either side of the net-curtained window, angled sufficiently to let him see arrivals and departures from both ends of the Neugasse as well as the traffic on the sidewalk below him. On the table beside the neatly stacked magazines that helped calm the nerves of the dentist's prospective patients, Monday to Friday (closed Saturday—the dentist was an ardent fisherman and hunter, like most of Salzburg's vanishing weekend population), Bruno had placed a two-way radio that looked remarkably like a cigar case. This let him keep in touch with friend Chuck, patiently installed in a parked car on the Mozartplatz within easy approach of the entrance to one of the short cuts to the Bryant place. "I don't suppose there is any need to follow Mathison and Conway into the Altmarkt. You have someone there, I expect?"

The Englishman's diffident way of checking tactfully—if Bruno had not arranged for them to be observed all the way to the Café Tomaselli then he'd better start giving orders immediately—amused the Austrian. "They'll be watched." The wide curve of humorous lips in his round pink face, with its snub innocent nose, and his fine fair hair, thinning away from his high forehead into light tendrils, made him look like one of the angelic cherubs hovering over the pulpit of the pilgrimage church at Maria Plain. But there the likeness stopped. The brown eyes were sharp and watchful, and the husky body, heavy in its clothing of thick tweeds and high-necked sweater, was as hard as Mount Dachstein. There were some who said his heart was as cold as the Dachstein Glacier itself, but his wife and seven children and even old antagonists like Andrew and Chuck Nield would have disagreed violently.

To Andrew, quiet and restrained, his thin intelligent face now tightened in speculation as he looked down at the subdued Neugasse, it seemed that Bruno would be better described as a large hot cup of strong Viennese coffee, whipped cream and all. But Andrew was one of those who had crawled beside Bruno through the darkness on the Hungarian border ten years ago, and helped pull the wounded Freedom Fighters across no man's land to safety. Chuck had been there, too. It seemed as if at least half the attachés and agents who circulated around the foreign embassies in Vienna in 1956 had found their way to that grim frontier. "Well, it's good to be co-operating again," Andrew said. And with official blessing, for a change. No reprimands or demotions this time.

"Less worrying for me than having you as a competitor."

Andrew smiled. The Viennese were masters of the delicate compliment, veiling a direct allusion to several less happy occasions. "Chuck definitely pulled a hot coal out of the fire this time. How much has he told you?"

Bruno's eyes never swerved from the street. "Not as much as I hope he will tell me. But, of course, we see his problem, don't we?"

Yes, thought Andrew, we see it. If Chuck told all he knew, there would be no need for him, or Andrew either, to be here. Bruno would handle everything, and Vienna might not consider it necessary to share the knowledge contained in the Finstersee chest. "You have certainly put up the manpower," Andrew said tactfully. "Pity we couldn't have helped you more there." He had at least two agents drifting into

Salzburg today, and Charles Nield had possibly as many already here. But it was unnecessary to mention that and embarrass one's host. Bruno no doubt guessed. He would have done the same himself if he were co-operating in London or New York. No Intelligence agent let any government, however friendly, take charge of his own private arrangements such as communications with his own government.

"Each makes his contribution," Bruno was saying. "We have the men who know this country in detail; you supplied important information about Bryant and Yates and the woman Lang; and Chuck discovered the crisis and gave us warning. Also, he may have developed the best possible lead."

"Mathison?"

"Mathison."

"Were there no other means of reaching Mrs. Bryant?" Andrew took a dim view of involving anyone but a trained professional in matters like this.

"We tried them. Three days ago, we had two agents contact her. Two days ago, Werner Dietrich. Yesterday, Felix Zauner. Four altogether, two of whom she knows well." Bruno shrugged his shoulders. "No results whatsoever. Perhaps they asked too many questions."

"How else does one get information?" Especially in an emergency situation. "Chuck is really moving very quickly." There was more doubt than criticism in the Englishman's quiet voice.

"Perhaps. But, on the other hand, we were almost too slow," Bruno reminded him. A signal came from the cigar case. "Excuse me, please. Would you watch the street?" Bruno turned to the radio, adjusted it, listened to the message, signed off. "They have just entered the Café Tomaselli."

"I wouldn't mind some coffee myself." One couldn't even smoke here. The antiseptic atmosphere of the waiting room must be kept virgin pure. "Most obliging dentist, though. What excuse did you give him? Police business? Hush-hush capture of a drug ring? Or of diamond thieves?"

Bruno looked bland, busied himself with the radio. Speedily, he made contacts with his other agents, who were observing the entrances to the short cuts that led to the courtyard behind the Bryant place. "All quiet," he reported as he joined Andrew at the window again.

But shouldn't Felix Zauner have been here, doing all this? Andrew wondered. He watched the light foot traffic on the Neugasse below, made a few remarks about this being a very dull time on Saturday afternoon. Most of the Salzburgers seemed to have closed business and headed for the country while those who lived in the country and planned coming into town for a pleasant evening had, as yet, not arrived in any numbers. All this led quite naturally to the question that really interested him. He said most casually, "By the way, where is Felix Zauner?"

"He left for Unterwald this morning. He has some men stationed up there, wandering around as woodcutters, keeping an eye on the lake."

"Does he know we are here?"

"He knows we are co-operating. But he hasn't the particulars." Bruno's brown eyes were quite expressionless. "He left Salzburg before I could talk with him."

"The Americans seem a little nervous about Zauner."

"Oh, they are always worried about any penetration, and Zauner's organization here was certainly penetrated by Elisabetha Lang. But not to any depths; he has only used her in the most routine matters of minor surveillance."

"At least, he has now been warned about her?"

"He was told yesterday in Vienna. He was obviously shocked."

"It's always a pretty hard blow to take."

"Especially with his record. It has been excellent. His potential was high—very high. Next year he would have been considered for a top post in Vienna itself. He may still be, if he has any success with the Finstersee problem."

"Well, he has one trump card. Elisabetha Lang, so-called, has no suspicion that any of us know she is an illegal agent." And for the dispensing of that small piece of knowledge, thought Andrew, I take one modest silent bow.

"I imagine he will find some pleasure in—how would Chuck express it?—in stringing her along."

"Is that his plan?"

"So I was told in Vienna. But it may be the only way of tracking down the KGB man in Salzburg who is running her. We'd like to catch that colonel and the rest of his illegals."

"I just hope Zauner knows who is stringing whom," Andrew said, thinking of Elisabetha Eva. But then, he was something of an expert on the girl with the impeccable passports and papers who was also equipped with the most plausible legends to match that the KGB could fabricate, so that she could be launched illegally across some unsuspecting border, there to settle down for a few years as one of the added blessings to its democracy. "But I agree about rooting up the illegals. They are becoming a plague. It might be a bright idea if the Western nations had a discreet meeting and started a joint uncovering job. We have all had them planted on us."

"First," Bruno said, keeping his eyes on each passer-by in the street below, "you would have to get most Western nations to accept the premise that peaceful coexistence also includes illegal agents. How many would believe that? It is quicker if we just pick off the illegals as they— Now what does this mean? Something or nothing?" He was watching a man who had already strolled earlier along the Neugasse and was returning past the Bryant shop, slowing his pace as he reached the building, taking out a cigarette. He seemed to have some trouble lighting it, and stepped just within the shelter of the door. Now he had decided to finish his cigarette while he stood at the threshold of the hall and casually watched the foot traffic on the street. It was increasing slightly, as if the town was coming awake from its after-lunch siesta.

Bruno reached for his camera, handed Andrew the binoculars.

"Never seen him before," Andrew said, as the field glasses brought the man's face right up in front of him and showed even the tightening of a face muscle, a quick shift in the eyes. He was a serious-looking man of about fifty years, dressed in heavy tweeds; tanned and lean, with dark mustache and eyebrows, strong features, and a beaklike nose. The hair that showed under the slight tilt of his green velours hat was graying, cut long, well brushed. "What is he hanging around for?" Andrew asked irritably. In another fifteen minutes or so, they might expect Mathison and the Conway girl to come around that corner; and then, minutes after that, Chuck would be making his way through the Mozartplatz short cut to Mrs. Bryant's back door. If Mathison's signal for Chuck had been the right one, that was. Otherwise, there would be a no-go message from Chuck and their alternate plan would have to be put into motion: they'd all take off in various directions to meet near Unterwald early tomorrow.

As we should have done in the first place, perhaps, thought Andrew, even if it meant the beginning of a blind search and dangerous risks. None of us are in this business for the good of our health. "That blighter is lighting another cigarette," he said in chagrin. "He's there for the duration it looks like."

"A problem," Bruno admitted. He finished taking his last photograph, quickly laid the camera aside, and began making contact with his three agents stationed at the outlets to the short cuts from the Bryant courtyard. He passed on their reports without comment to Andrew as they came in, one by one. The first mentioned a woman and two small boys using the short cut from the Mozartplatz within the last half hour. The second, at the Residenzplatz exit, had noted three young girls and then—twenty minutes ago—a single man, dressed in a heavy coat, about thirty-five or so, unhurried, carrying nothing, accosting no one, behaving normally. The third agent, near the Altmarkt, had only one man to report, young, fair-haired, dressed in a heavy dark coat, unhurried, carrying nothing, accosting no one, behaving normally, and he had taken the short cut twenty minutes ago.

"They ought to have appeared at least fifteen minutes ago," Andrew said worriedly. "Unless, of course, they are visiting friends in one of the apartments inside that maze."

"I don't like the coincidence of their timing," Bruno admitted.

"Like me to take a look down in the Bryant hall?" Andrew was already moving to the door.

"Yes, that's a— Wait!" The radio had given its muted rasp, three short clearings of its husky throat. "That's Chuck," said Bruno, and began listening to the brief message. "He has just received the signal relayed from Mathison," he reported to Andrew. "He is coming in. Right now."

"Before he gives Mathison time to get here first? What kind of signal did Mathison send, for God's sake?"

"He sent all of them."

Andrew stared in disbelief. "Did Mathison lose his head?"

"Either that," said Bruno, "or he kept it exceedingly well."

Andrew was already out the door.

Bruno's frown deepened as he looked somberly down at the street. The waiting man had decided to move. He was walking briskly up the slope of the Neugasse, passing the other pedestrians, his hands in pockets, head slightly bent. Just then, Bruno's surprised eyes caught sight of a blue coat coming from the other end of the Neugasse. Mrs. Conway and Mathison were walking briskly, too, with none of the conversation that had seemed to flow so naturally between them when Bruno had seen them last. They could scarcely have drunk even one cup of coffee, he thought worriedly. So this was an emergency.

Below his window, he saw Andrew emerge and take in the situation with a glance to his right and one to his left. With scarcely a pause, he started after the man, leaving the exploration of the hall to Mathison and Chuck Nield, who would be approaching the rear courtyard of the Bryant building by this time. Andrew, thought Bruno as he picked up his cigar case once more, had kept his head exceedingly well, too.

Quickly, he called back to his three agents. "Possible emergency," he told them one by one. "Watch everyone who leaves your exit. Signal at once. Be prepared to follow."

Now all he had to do was wait. And speculate.

Down in the street, Bill Mathison and Lynn Conway were entering the yawning mouth of the dark hall.

21

"THAT," SAID LYNN CONWAY AS THEY CAME OUT OF THE CAFE Tomaselli, "was indeed a very quick cup of coffee. The quickest I've known outside of my own kitchen at half past eight of a New York morning." She thought regretfully of the pleasant room they had just left behind: a cosy place for a cool afternoon, filled with rough tweeds and soft voices; newspapers and books at practically every table, students and dowagers and solidly built squires, no one revolting, everyone relaxing and paying little attention to others' vagaries in either dress or brief visits; and not a jukebox or a cigarette machine in sight.

"Explanations to follow," Bill Mathison promised her. "And apologies now." She wasn't really annoyed though, even if she had been a little startled by their quick exit. She was looking almost amused. Speculative, too. "Also congratulations," he added. He could have had a girl with him who wouldn't have reacted so obligingly; someone who would have said plaintively, "Couldn't we just have one more cup of coffee?" or "But I haven't really finished my cake," although at any other time she wouldn't have taken more than one tasting mouthful of the five hundred calories of cream and chocolate on her plate. "And thank you."

"Just obeying orders, sir. You told me to look normal and natural and think up an excuse to get us the hell out. Direct quote, if in less hushed tones. You did impress me, Bill. Where did you learn prison-style talk out of the side of your mouth?"

"From desperation." After remembering every signal, every movement, his mind had gone blank and he couldn't even think of how to move out gracefully. "You did beautifully."

"My excuse was true enough. I really did forget to take our copies of your letter, and they have to be picked up sometime." Even if hardly so promptly as this. But if Bill was in a hurry, she could understand. She, too, kept remembering Anna Bryant's face, taut and bloodless, as she urged them to go, go quickly and send Cliff. So we possibly have done what she told us to do, Lynn thought, but I ought to have stayed with her; she is liable to have real hysterics, and that's one time a woman shouldn't be alone. Lynn glanced at Bill, decided not to mention her fears. He was fully as troubled as she was. As they crossed the square in silence, she tried a lighter topic. "We left our newspaper behind." Our quick-study newspaper, giving a tantalizing glimpse of all the concerts and plays we probably won't have time to go to.

"We don't need it." His pace was increasing.

"What about this?" She handed him the red-covered guide-book which they had also consulted.

"Always useful," he said, taking it with a nod of thanks, jamming it into his pocket as they reached the Neugasse. It was busier now. People had started coming out for their Saturday-afternoon stroll. His eyes narrowed as he saw, some distance ahead and across the street, the thin figure of Andrew in his neutral-colored tweed jacket. He had appeared out of nowhere, merged just as quickly with a group of people passing by. He must have seen Lynn's blue coat, for he had glanced in their direction before he started up the street, away from them. Now, as the group reached the end of the Neugasse, Andrew veered around his temporary friends, and vanished. Just what had drawn him so quickly around that corner? Mathison wondered as he increased their speed even more. Here was the Bryants' shop, and now the entrance to their building. He glanced at his watch. Not bad timing at all, he admitted. Less than half an hour, altogether, since they had left Anna Bryant.

The hall was peaceful, and darker now as the afternoon began to draw to a close. In another hour, its gray shadows would thicken into solid black. Dusk came quickly here in autumn. He knocked on the Bryants' door. Knocked again. Looked at Lynn. Knocked. He tried the handle, and as it held firm his eye caught sight of a piece of paper lying half under the door. It was a folded note. He could make out his own name and the signature—Anna Bryant—but the few lines quickly scrawled in pencil needed better light than the hall afforded.

Lynn touched his arm. Someone had opened the door from the back courtyard and was entering the hall. He had closed it again, for the sharp cut of cold air was no longer striking at her ankles. Then as the man appeared, she felt Bill relax. An Austrian, she thought, noting the loden cape thrown back to show a dark-gray suit with green facings, the short-brimmed velours hat whipped off politely as he bowed. He was about Bill's height; he had pleasant features, light hair with a careful wave, and seemingly no tongue. Quite silently, he waited for Bill to knock on the door.

Bill Mathison said very softly, "She's gone. And left this." He held up the note.

The stranger's face changed completely. He brought some keys from his pocket, long, thin, strange-looking keys, and began trying them one by one in the lock. The third attempt succeeded. He opened the door, stepped inside, beckoned them to follow. Quickly and quietly, he closed and locked it. He turned to face them. Now Lynn could see that his eyes were light blue and his hair was definitely fair. He might look very much an Austrian, but his voice was American. "What's the trouble, Bill?"

Mathison had read Anna's message. He was now puzzled as well as worried. "She was here half an hour ago. We left her waiting for you."

So this must be Cliff, Lynn thought.

Nield took the note. "Well," he said as he read it, "she seems to have changed her mind." He handed the piece of paper over to Lynn Conway.

"Her coat and hat and bag are gone," she said unhappily. "They were lying on that chair." So she really ran out on us, she thought, and looked at Bill. He was taking this badly. His face was taut and white. She read the note. *Dear Mr. Mathison, I am sorry I can't wait. I go to my brother, who is ill and alone in his house and needs me. I will sign the papers on Monday when I return. Anna Bryant.* "But she didn't!" Lynn cried out in relief. "She didn't leave of her own free will." And then relief changed to shock. She stared at Bill, who nodded his agreement, and wondered if she looked as numb as that, too.

"Hold the explanations!" Nield said sharply. "I'll put out an alert first." He pulled a watch from his coat pocket, wound it with three sharp twists. "Mrs. Conway—would you please check through the darkroom and shop, see if anything is disarranged? Bill, you try upstairs." He tossed Mathison his keys. "Keep it quiet," he added, and turned away to concentrate on his watch.

Lynn began moving toward the shop, trying to pull her attention away from Anna Bryant, away from Cliff's voice talking over his disguised radio. Everything was exactly as they had left it. Anna Bryant's leaving had been peaceful. Nothing had been rifled or scattered; no sign of any struggle. If it hadn't been for Anna's small insertion in her note about her brother *alone in his house,* they would all have believed she had simply picked up her coat and bag and walked out.

Slowly, giving Cliff time to talk with his unseen friend, Lynn Conway returned to the kitchen. She stopped at the table, looking down tactfully at the copies of the Newhart and Morris letter, at the photographs that Bill had made of Richard Bryant's correspondence. It was with relief that she heard the door open and saw Bill come back into the kitchen.

"Nothing," he told Nield, handing back the keys, walking over to join Lynn.

"She didn't even get time to file these away." Lynn pointed to Anna's precious photographs.

Mathison stood frowning at the table. Upstairs, in his rapid search through the lonely apartment, he hadn't had time to think. Now, the questions were arising. Whoever forced Anna Bryant to go was working very close to the time Lynn and he had left this place. Was it pure luck? He doubted that, somehow. It looked as if they knew he was coming here this afternoon. Why else had Anna been allowed, perhaps told, to write that note? Even the way she had used his name quite openly—surely she would have kept it hidden unless she had heard it discussed? Had this been her way of warning him that his name had been mentioned, of reassuring him, too, that nothing more was known than that he had come here on business about the contract?

Nield was signing off. He walked over to them, trying to conceal his profound gloom. Everything had been almost under control, even if not according to plan, and now the whole situation was wild, perhaps smashed into a hundred pieces. New dangers, new difficulties added. He repressed a sigh, forced his voice to sound calm and brisk. "The alert is in. The search is beginning."

"But where?"

"Right inside this complex of buildings and courtyards. You see, all the entrances to the short cuts have been watched all afternoon. That was for your benefit, Bill, just in case your visit here caused you some trouble. Anna Bryant has not been seen coming out any entrance, either alone or accompanied. So she must be somewhere inside this maze. Austrian Intelligence is calling in the help of the police to have a room-by-room search. Every shop, back room, storage room; every apartment, floor by floor. It will take some time—" His voice sharpened as Mathison started across the kitchen. "Keep away from that window." He looked at Lynn with a smile, as if to shake her free from her sudden alarm. "We aren't supposed to be here, you know," he said gently. "You were meant to find the note, believe it, and walk away. Come on, Bill, let's keep well out of sight from that courtyard, stay around this table. I want to know just why you sent that flurry of signals from Tomaselli's."

Mathison came back slowly to the table.

"Our job isn't out there, searching," Nield told him. "That's police work, thorough, slow, quiet. No advance warning to Mrs. Bryant's captors or they might cut their losses, try to silence her forever before they make their escape. They won't risk being identified."

"Captors? How do you know there's more than one?"

"The Austrians have seen two men who might be suspects," Nield said briefly. He thought of Andrew now tailing a possible third. "Our job is to find out what Anna Bryant knows. Now, quickly. What did she say? We haven't much time." If any.

All right, I'll give it to him straight, thought Mathison. "Johann is in possession of the Finstersee box."

Nield had had two shocks. Perhaps the open mention of Finstersee was the greater. He tightened his lips, looked at Lynn Conway. "Mrs. Conway, would you mind leav—"

"No need," Mathison said. "Mrs. Bryant—when she decided to talk—talked."

Lynn said quickly, "There was no stopping her. So I know bits and pieces. Bill hasn't got over that yet."

"If I had tried to stop her," Mathison said, "she might have shut up completely."

"She talked freely? To you?" Nield's depression and gloom began to shred away. "Start telling."

"Do I leave?" Lynn asked.

"No," Mathison said. "She stays. Lynn has something to tell, too. About Trudi."

"Who the hell is Trudi?"

"Perhaps the key to everything."

"I think you were right," Nield admitted after an intensive ten minutes. "Trudi Seidl ... We have to get in touch with her as soon as possible and have her answer our questions. One question, actually. How did she know that the searchers could not find anything in Johann's house? If she explains that, she may explain a lot." Nield looked at Lynn Conway for a brief moment.

"No," Mathison said decidedly. "Lynn isn't going to do this. I won't—" He caught his breath. And who am I to say I won't allow her? Wide blue eyes studied him gravely. "Lynn, this isn't your business. Don't listen to him."

"None of you will get any quick answers from Trudi. You might not get any answers at all. She does know my voice, she does know that I am Anna's friend. If Anna can't go to her, I should."

Mathison appealed to Nield. "What about Elissa? Don't you expect her to be up in Unterwald? That's danger."

"I know. That's why I didn't ask Mrs. Conway to go."

"Didn't you?" Mathison asked angrily.

"I thought of it; but I didn't."

Lynn interceded. "Let's say I was on your wave length, Mr.— Cliff?"

Nield shook his head. "We'll drop that name. It didn't bring much luck. And now—" He shrugged his shoulders.

Now, it could be dangerous to anyone who used it. How much would Anna Bryant be forced to tell? "Chuck will do."

Mathison looked at him sharply. He had wondered before and now he began to believe his previous guess. Chuck probably wasn't any more a real name than Cliff, or Andrew either.

"The problem," Nield went on, "will be to get you to Unterwald without rousing suspicion in Elissa or anyone else. There *is* danger, Mrs. Conway."

"Well, at least you've warned me." She wasn't budging an inch. "You'll come with me, Bill?"

"You aren't going in there alone, that's for sure."

"Quick in, quick out. Isn't that what you want of us?" she asked Chuck. She turned back to Bill. "We just won't let danger develop. Heroics aren't my line. So let's think of a plan. Come on, Bill. Put that legal brain of yours to work and keep us safe." She picked up a copy of the Newhart and Morris letter. "Couldn't we use this somehow? Perhaps along with Anna's note?"

And just how long had she been thinking up this little idea? he wondered. "We could. There is no mention in her note of where Johann's house is, so we assume it's somewhere near Unterwald and drive up there to get Trudi to direct us. Yes, I think that should work."

"Just a minute—" Nield began. He looked almost puzzled.

"It's quite simple. We must return to Zürich on Monday morning. We cannot wait for Mrs. Bryant to come back to Salzburg. We need her signature on this letter. So we have decided to spend the rest of the weekend in the country, see the beauties of Styria and the Salzkammergut, and finish our business as well."

Nield considered the idea from every angle. "I'd buy that," he admitted.

"We are just keeping it normal and natural," Mathison told him, and received a sharp stare. "Shall we set off this evening? We'll have early dinner, hire a car—"

"Wait, wait. I don't buy that at all."

"Why not?"

"Too quick. Let's keep it normal and—" He checked himself, grinned. "But there's no other word for what I want. *Normally,* what would you do—if you had to see Anna Bryant before you left for Zürich, and she was up at Bad Aussee with her brother?"

294

"Leave tonight, get there by eight-thirty or nine, finish the business, have tomorrow for ourselves."

"And where would you stay?"

"I'd get our hotel porter to phone Bad Aussee and book us a couple of rooms in some place he recommends. What else?"

"You make it sound reasonable."

"Then what's holding you back?"

"You don't know Unterwald. It may be difficult to find Trudi Seidl's house in the dark. I don't want you wandering around up there asking directions."

"Well, get one of your Austrian friends to meet us discreetly before we reach the village. We'll give him a lift, and he can point out the house." He studied Nield's face. "I gathered you were co-operating with the Austrians. Or aren't you?"

Nield nodded. "With the British, too. We'd have to share the results anyway, so why go it alone?"

I bet that was Washington's decision and not Chuck's, thought Mathison. So I can relax about friend Andrew; one query to be scored off my list. "And you would have preferred going it alone?" he asked with a grin.

"Oh, co-operation is fine, but sometimes we all have our little difficulties." Nield was smiling amiably.

Such as now. But what? "Do we leave tonight or don't we?"

"If you do, you'll have to contact Felix Zauner. He's in charge at Unterwald." Until Bruno can get up there, Nield added to himself. And Bruno he could trust, because he had seen Bruno in action.

"That shouldn't be difficult. I've met Zauner. He will recognize me, all right."

Nield pulled out his watch. "Just let me check first on the situation at Unterwald." He waited for Bruno to answer his signal. "Speed is essential," he told Mathison. "You're right about that. But in this case it's safer to hasten slowly." He glanced at Lynn Conway. "There will be some unpleasant intruders in Unterwald," he said frankly for her benefit. "Nazis, for instance, who consider the Finstersee box their own very special property. We've reason to believe that the Communists are interested in it, too. But the Nazis are very much there, and well hidden. They've had years to get themselves safely installed." He signaled again. Bruno was still busy.

"Nazis?" Lynn asked faintly. Mathison heard the quick

intake of her breath. He put an arm around her waist, drew her closer to him as they stood facing Nield. She tried to laugh off her nervousness, turn it to incredulity. "And Communists, too! Aren't we going to add some of Yates's little band of hope, Peking-style?"

"Just give them enough time to catch their wits," Nield said. "They don't know yet what exactly hit them in Zürich. Once they begin to figure that out, we'll see a couple of them being sent into Unterwald from Warsaw or Prague. But the Moscow boys are several jumps ahead of them. And the Nazis are further ahead than any of us. They've had six full days to think entirely about Finstersee. They've had time to learn some of the things that the rest of us are now trying to find out. They've even had time to plot abductions."

Abductions? Mathison said, "Then you are convinced the Nazis seized Johann?" And Anna, too.

"I'm inclined to believe it. They were at the right place at the right time, and in sufficient strength. Obviously. No one else can make these claims, not even Elissa and her friends." Chuck looked across the darkening room at Lynn Conway. She was much too silent, too motionless. "So that's the background to Unterwald," he told her. And when she kept silent, he added, "You can easily change your mind about going there—provided you change it right now. We'll find some other way to reach Trudi Seidl."

"But I'm your quickest way," Lynn said. "And it wasn't the Nazis or Communists that threw such a scare into me. At least, not so much. It was—it was just the quiet way you talk about them."

"How else?" Chuck asked her with a shrug of his shoulders, and then turned his head to speak into his opened watch case. Bruno was coming through now.

"Let's be tactful," Mathison suggested, and led her into the corridor. She kept close to him, as if she needed that arm around her. Nield's voice was a low murmur, indistinguishable.

Lynn said, "We've wandered into a mine field. One covered with soft green grass. And wild flowers. Like any innocent meadow."

"He said you could back out. He meant it."

"I know, I know. But how can I? I'm the one who can do this job just a little more quickly than anyone else. And you would go to Unterwald yourself if I didn't. Wouldn't you?"

"Well, I might just manage to get through to Trudi. Anna did mention my name, too, over the phone."

But she knows my voice, Lynn thought. "I'm not backing out."

He tightened his grip around her waist. He sensed some hesitation, some afterthought. "What's troubling you?"

"Just the way—the way he talks. So matter-of-fact, so—"

"As he said, 'How else?' "

"I thought the Cold War was supposed to be over." Her voice had an edge of criticism. She looked up at him. Her eyes were puzzled, not quite believing her own words yet unwilling not to believe.

"Sure it is. This is peaceful coexistence," he told her with a grin.

"Don't joke about it," she said almost angrily.

"I stopped joking about it in Zürich." All humor left his face as he remembered the last time he had seen Greta Freytag.

It isn't really fair, he was thinking, that she knows only bits and pieces. She will have to know more if we are to get through this without false steps or blunders. Or even sweet thoughts that could trick her into disaster. Ignorance is a perpetual handicap. "How the hell did we get into this?" he asked, and tried to laugh. "I can think of other ways I'd like to spend a Saturday night with you."

Lynn's silence melted. Through the growing darkness, her eyes met his. And were held. "There will be other Saturday nights," she said. She slipped away from his arm. "I think Chuck has stopped talking to his invisible friend."

Nield was coming toward them, meeting them halfway, his watch in his hand. "The police are searching this building right now. Almost finished."

"You mean, all the time we have been here—?" Lynn asked.

"Almost all of it."

"They certainly are moving quietly," Mathison said. "And the other buildings, too?"

"Yes. The search is working from the outside in. Nothing to report as yet."

"When they took Anna out of here, why didn't they keep on going?"

"It was too light to risk taking her through the streets or squares. They probably have a car parked nearby, but even

297

that could be too far in daylight. We think they planned this operation in two stages. First, get her out of the house before you came back. Second, move her out of this maze of buildings when it is dark and quiet."

"They knew we would come back?"

"And find that note. Its credibility would depend on its timing. She would never have set out alone for Bad Aussee late at night. Using what for transportation, for instance? But at this time of day, you could believe she had gone, taking a bus or a train."

And we were supposed to read the note, go away, come back on Monday, and then wonder what had happened to Anna Bryant, thought Mathison. He looked at Lynn, wondering if she had been following the same line of reasoning. But no, Lynn had other questions in her mind.

"But why does she go with them?" Lynn was wanting to know, almost indignantly.

"If they have Johann," Chuck answered, "then all they needed to threaten was his death unless she went without a murmur."

"And that's how they got in here? With that threat?" Lynn could scarcely believe it.

"And possibly with something belonging to Johann to back up the threat—a ring, the tie he was wearing, anything she could recognize."

"But," Lynn insisted, "how can you *know* that these men are holding Johann?" Always that quiet matter-of-fact voice, she thought as she looked challengingly at Chuck. He deals in pretty big "ifs," and I just don't like them.

"Who else, except Johann, could tell them you were coming today? He was here last night when Bill phoned from Zürich," Nield said patiently.

"Or it could have been someone who tapped the Bryants' telephone," Mathison reminded him, although he believed the Johann theory himself. But Lynn looked as if she needed a little defense.

"I know who has been tapping it," Nield said. "We're cooperating with them."

Lynn felt her cheeks color. She had forgotten about the phone call last night, although Bill had begun with that item in his report to Chuck. At the time, she had wondered why he had even included it, and had decided it was simply legal training: get everything in order, begin at the beginning, don't miss one detail. "I'm out of my league," she admitted. And stop underestimating these men, even kindly, in sweet tolerance. But it was so easy to think they were exaggerating when they dealt with something you found hard to believe.

"And thank God for that," Chuck said. "One Elissa is enough to have around."

Lynn, still embarrassed, turned to the table. It's growing dark, she thought, and became practical. She lifted two of the typed sheets along with Anna's note and placed them on top of Bill's briefcase, ready to go.

"Don't you think it's time we started moving out?" Mathison asked impatiently. And where would Elissa be now? In Unterwald?

Nield held up the watch to explain the delay. "Just waiting for the final okay." There was a gleam of humor in his eyes. "Cooperation."

"What's the situation at Unterwald? Did they tell you?"

"All quiet on the surface. But Zauner has just requested eight more men. He is starting a big search. For Johann, I believe."

"That's quick work. When did he learn about Johann's disappearance?"

"Sometime this afternoon."

"Eight men ... How the hell is he going to account for that invasion? It will have to be a cautious search, give no alarm. As you said, the Nazis would be quick to cut their losses in order to keep themselves unidentified. They're liable to cut Johann's throat, too."

"That's our problem. But Zauner may have solved it. He's a bright fellow, you know."

"He's arranging a hunting party?"

"That's been pre-empted. There is a batch of hunters already occupying the inn."

Mathison looked quickly at Nield.

"They may be authentic. If Zauner has learned anything about them, he is keeping it to himself. He has made a couple of mistakes—Elissa, for one; the Finstersee box, for another. He should have been more on his toes about both of them; after all, he was here, right in the middle of it all. So he may be holding onto anything he has discovered about that inn until he can turn over the Nazis to Austrian Intelligence as his own particular triumph. That would set him up again in Vienna, certainly."

"Pretty sharp."

And that, thought Nield, is why I keep feeling uneasy about Zauner. He's clever, all right. Why then was he so fast asleep about Elissa and Finstersee? "His plan for his reinforcements is pretty sharp, too. He is passing out the word that we are searching for a couple of terrorists, two of the South Tyrol nationalists who have been giving the Austrians a lot of trouble recently. Some of them did set a bomb on the Brenner railroad last week, and Italy—who now owns the South Tyrol—is threatening to cut diplomatic relations with Austria unless something is done about those nationalists. There is a search actually taking place for them, farther west than here. Zauner has simply extended the search to Unterwald."

"And no mention of Johann or the Finstersee box? Just a couple of terrorists who've got to be found, I'd call that pretext pretty near brilliant."

"So do I."

"But how do the villagers feel about the South Tyrol? Some of them may be in sympathy with the nationalists." And what price co-operation then?

"Quite a few, I gather. I've never met an Austrian yet who enjoyed the way the Tyrol was split up, and one of its richest sectors handed over to another country. But these acts of terrorism—well, they are storm troopers' tactics. The Austrians had a bellyful of that in the thirties. And what did it bring them? Annexation, war, ruins, and ten years of occupation. There is at least one lesson to be remembered from all that: men who use terrorism, as a means to power, rule by terror once they are in power. I guess we'd all do well to remember it. Every civilized country has its own interior barbarians." He paused, his thoughts straying for a moment. Then briskly he came back to the subject of South Tyrol nationalism. "I've been told the villagers will co-operate willingly in this search. I believe it. It's one thing to sing about 'Das blutende Herz Tyrols'; quite another to have bombing subsidized by outside sources."

"Outside?" picked up Mathison.

Chuck nodded. "That's the latest headache for the Austrians." He didn't explain, perhaps because he didn't want to startle Mrs. Conway any more than he had already. She had been listening, wide-eyed, scarcely moving. So he smiled for her, said gently, "Every country has its own private troubles,

300

hasn't it? Like people, I suppose." He glanced down at the opened watch, told it, "Oh, come on, come on. Give a signal, will you? Time's awasting." He laughed at his own impatience. "I take that back. Nothing's wasted if it means that everything has been checked and double-checked."

Mathison said, "Which reminds me—did you check on that name Anna Bryant gave me? August Grell?"

"Yes. He's the owner of the inn at Unterwald—the Gasthof Waldesruh. He has been there since the war. He was a refugee from the South Tyrol."

Mathison remembered the bitterness with which Anna had spoken Grell's name. "There's more to Grell than that. He was one of the pieces of prime information that Anna Bryant had for you. He ranked with the Finstersee box."

Chuck's eyes narrowed. He said slowly, "And now Grell has eight guests. . . ." And then his voice quickened irritably. "But surely Zauner would have found out—" He didn't finish. The signal came through just then, and he switched over to his watch. "All clear?" he asked Bruno, and listened intently to a flow of words. "Okay, okay," he said at last. "We'll start moving into Unterwald. By the way, would you ask Zauner to give you all the information he has on August Grell? No, no . . . I haven't any more proof than you have, but I've got a feeling that Grell is worth watching. Can't you get up to Unterwald tonight? . . . I see. . . . Did Dietrich manage to say anything before he died? . . . So it was no accident. . . . Yes, he was a good man. Too bad . . . All right, you clear up this end, and we'll expect you in Unterwald when we see you. Keep in touch. Good luck."

He closed the watchcase slowly, deliberately. No accident, he was thinking. Werner Dietrich hadn't slipped on that steep flight of stone steps; he had been half stunned by a blow on his head and then picked up and thrown down, thrown all the way from the landing to the bottom of the staircase. He had hung on to his life, fought his way back to consciousness for the space of three weak, three vital sentences before he died. He had named the man who had called him so early to his office this morning, had been waiting for him on the landing with a smile and a handshake—a Polish art student, supposedly a refugee; a friend of Elisabetha Lang.

In the crowded kitchen, dusk had softened all outlines into gray shadows. There was complete silence, no movement from anyone. "All right," said Nield, breaking into his own

301

angry thoughts. "It's all arranged. Here's what you do."

"No news of Anna?" Lynn interrupted.

"Not yet. The search has ended in this building, so we can leave any time. There will be a guard in the hall. Ignore him. He will ignore you."

"We just go away and leave her?"

"Mrs. Conway, one of the best men in Austrian Intelligence is staying here in Salzburg until Anna Bryant is found. And the men caught." And also a murderer, and perhaps a lot more with him. "Just concentrate on Unterwald. It's fifty miles away, and the sooner we are all up there the better."

"Is this Finstersee box so important?"

"Yes," Mathison said gently. "And Anna Bryant knows that more than anyone." He looked over at Chuck. "Either you tell Lynn about Finstersee or I'll do that when I'm driving her to Unterwald. Yes, I mean it."

There was a brief silence. "You do it and save time," Nield said. "Have you got those letters to back up your story?"

"Damn. It's too dark to see clearly. May I risk a match?" Mathison cursed his forgetfulness.

Lynn said, "They are on top of your briefcase. Here." She picked up the prepared package and handed it over. "I chose two carbon copies. The note's with them."

Mathison checked them by touch and size, got them safely into his thin leather envelope. "Thanks, Lynn."

"Have you got that red guidebook you waved around in Tomaselli's?" Nield was asking him now.

Mathison fished it out from his pocket, handed it over. Nield opened it at random, tore out a page, handed the book back.

"Now here is how we get you out of Salzburg," Nield went on. "Be ready to leave at seven o'clock. Have a quick but solid supper, and take your heaviest clothes—Mrs. Conway will need something much warmer than that suit she's wearing. There will be a car at the hotel door. A '59 red Porsche. Its driver will turn over some maps to you *and* this page from your Baedeker. Then you will have no worries about stepping into the car or offering him a lift back to his garage. He will accept, and that way he will guide you quickly and safely out of town. You will drop him off when he tells you, and a car will draw out just ahead of you. A black Mercedes with an Innsbruck plate. Follow it all the way, and you'll reach Unterwald in record time. There will also be a car, a blue Fiat registered in Switzerland, keeping at a discreet distance behind you. Don't worry. That will be me."

"Sure you can keep up?" Mathison asked with a grin.

"Just watch I don't tailgate you. Okay, okay. . . . Have you got all that? Now, in Unterwald, your easiest approach to Trudi Seidl will be through Felix Zauner, so you'll have to find him quickly but casually. This is how we'll arrange it." Nield's quiet voice, in short sentences, exact and businesslike, gave them the final instructions. At the end, he paused. Then he added, "There was no need to tell anyone in Unterwald about your arrival. Zauner has been kept informed of most other developments, of course. He's the senior man up there, for the time being. He can pull rank on me. Or on Andrew. We all have to depend on him to some extent. But stick to your story, even with Zauner or anyone else. And as for Trudi—Mrs. Conway will have to use her own judgment on how much she will have to tell about Anna Bryant's disappearance. As little as possible, frankly, for Trudi's own safety. Right?"

Lynn nodded. Now, she thought wryly, I'm going to have to learn how Bill must have felt when he was talking with me in Zürich. "I'll take care."

Mathison, briefcase safely gripped under one arm, groped for her coat on the chair near the door. "Got your bag, gloves, everything else?"

"Yes."

"See you in Unterwald," he said to Nield as he began unchaining the door.

"But no sign of recognition," warned Nield.

"Not even in front of Zauner?"

"In front of no one. Good luck."

And to you, thought Mathison. He opened the door. The hall was lit by its one bulb. A man, leaning against the wall opposite the garbage cans, glanced at them briefly, noted the blue coat that was being draped around Lynn's shoulders, looked away. Silently, they left.

22

AS NIELD HAD PREDICTED, THE DRIVE TO UNTERWALD WAS made in record time. The road, apart from a short stretch of work-in-progress and a jolting slowdown, was well paved and lighted, easy to handle in long bursts of steady speed. The Mercedes, elderly, but capable of a comfortable seventy miles an hour, settled for an average of fifty, allowing for the occasional small town they passed through; it paced them accurately, never allowing them to come too near, never letting them drop completely out of sight. The Fiat, with a more powerful engine than its undramatic exterior suggested, kept at a circumspect distance behind them. Mathison did not have to ask Lynn Conway to study the map that was spread out, ready with a pencil flashlight for emergencies, over her knees.

They talked much. He had the first twenty minutes, once they dropped the driver at a garage just outside of town and the Mercedes slid onto the highway ahead of them. He had so often thought of what he would tell her, from Finstersee to Zürich, that it came out clear and sharp. There was no glossing over the unpleasant truth. And he noted that she was no longer putting up small objections, openly or silently; no longer searching for arguments. She was reaching the same stage as he had last night in Zürich. She was listening. At the end of his account of international realities, there was a little silence. Then she drew one long audible breath. Then a quiet, "Well, there go some of my best preconceived ideas." A small sigh of regret (for them? for herself?) and the beginning of questions—the kind that did not set out to criticize even by implication, but honestly asked for more clarification, more elucidation; the kind that were a pleasure to answer. From there, it became a sympathetic interchange of ideas, a trust in each other as they talked about what they felt and believed. Something she had suggested quickened his mind; something he had said seemed to stimulate her intelligence. Good God, he thought in amazement, for the first time in my life I have met a woman who is as exciting to talk with as to watch, as to be able to touch and sense and feel and possess. Here also go some of my own preconceived ideas; here is a woman to live with forever. Good God, he thought again, and almost missed the left turn into the narrow road that climbed toward Unterwald.

They slowed slightly, as the Mercedes had done, as they neared a lonely house, solitary and dark. "What is he trying to tell us?" Mathison asked, watching the car ahead pick up speed again. "Is that Johann's house, d'you think?" It could have been. It looked desolate, abandoned, an empty black box with a steep rippling lid, set down on a silver-gray meadow. Saw-toothed outlines of trees semicircled a background that rose into rough hills. Light shadows took form, lost shape, drifting over the grass as the clouds veiled and unveiled a moon shrinking into its last quarter.

"Will he ever be found?" Lynn asked softly, as her eyes returned to the twisting road with its side slopes of trees and its dark hints of rising hills, of vast stretches of farther mountains.

"If he is under cover of a roof—yes." That would only be a matter of a careful search.

She rolled up the short gap of opened window. The air was bitingly cold now. "Wouldn't that be too easily discovered?" Houses and barns seemed few. This road, after Johann's place, was a dark piece of nothing. Except scenery. "Wouldn't the Nazis choose something safer? Yet it's too cold at this time of year to keep Johann out in the open. It would have to be some place with shelter. A climber's hut? Or a forester's shack deep in the woods?"

"The people around here must know every bit of possible shelter, so the huts and refuges will all be searched. I'd think that any caves were known, too."

"A cave would have to be deep. There is bound to be a guard with Johann."

"At least one," he agreed.

"I don't see the Nazis freezing to death. They'd want a fire."

"And some light," he added to that. Time was short for the Nazis; they might be keeping Johann awake around the clock to help loosen his tongue. "Something with a bright glare. Yes, the cave—if they use a cave—would have to be deep. And with an entrance that could be covered and show no glow from a fire or a lamp." Mathison changed into first gear for the last steep pull. The Mercedes ahead of them was slowing slightly, as if the village was around the next turn. "I expect the Austrians have already started quizzing the small boys in the village. If anyone knows about caves, they do."

"Or old men who once were small boys?" She looked quickly over her shoulder. "We've lost Chuck! No, we haven't. He's driving without lights now."

"Using ours." And using the sound of our engine to cover his.

"We must be near Unterwald," she said, forgetting about caves as she folded the map, began buttoning her coat, pulling on her heavy gloves. She had taken Chuck's advice—what a strange man, she thought, to have noticed the weight of her clothes and worry about pneumonia—and was glad she was wearing a heavy turtle-neck sweater under her thickest tweed suit and white wool stockings with her strongest flat-heeled shoes. "I'm ready."

"Nervous?" That was a slight euphemism, but better not suggest being scared.

"Excited. And some stage fright, too," she admitted. "I'm trying very hard not to forget any of Chuck's instructions." They had been simple and explicit enough. And yet—

"You won't," he said encouragingly.

"He is really a very strange man, isn't he?"

"You mean you think he may be human, after all?" he teased her.

She laughed.

And that was quite a good way to enter Unterwald.

They had passed a few outlying houses, strung along the road, separated by meadows and small clumps of trees. Now they were approaching an intersection where houses thickened into a solid group. Mathison could see two country roads branching out of it. One of them, a continuation of this route from Bad Aussee, narrowed almost to a trail and kept on climbing past a well-lighted inn to disappear into heavy woods further uphill. The other cut off to his right, vanishing along a dark mountainside. But it was to the left that the Mercedes swung suddenly, and vanished. He made the same abrupt turn, and they were in the main street of the village. The only street. And the street was Unterwald. Houses lined it, scattered from it, but everything focused on it. Lights were in most windows; there was the sound of voices, of laughter, of distant music drifting in snatches; and along the unpaved sidewalk people were walking in twos and threes, warmly bundled in their stylized costumes. "Saturday night in the old home town," he said, watching the Mercedes drawing up in front of a house near which a string of parked cars and an empty bus waited. "And that must be the post office." The place looked like any other house, straight out of an Alpine calendar. If the Mercedes hadn't marked it, he would have passed by. He lined up with the other cars and switched off his engine.

Lynn glanced back as she opened her door and said in dismay, "We *have* lost Chuck." The Fiat was nowhere in sight.

"We always have friend Andrew," Mathison said softly, as he saw the tall Englishman, looped with cameras, step out of the Mercedes. Others followed him. They looked like Austrians from this distance, but perhaps they were only appropriately dressed to let them melt into the local background. They proceeded to do that, quietly, unnoticeably, joining a small collection of other men for some talk, then breaking away in new groupings to stroll briefly along the street before they branched off into the narrow lanes that led behind the houses. With pipes in their mouths, hands in pockets, heavy shoes clumping in broken rhythm, the new additions were indistinguishable from the old-timers. Just how many were strangers, how many villagers? Mathison wondered. "Busy little place, isn't it?" He checked his pockets, tried to look unconcerned, hoped that the weight of Chuck's automatic wasn't as noticeable as he felt. "No hurry," he said as they left the car. "Let's give Andrew time to make contact with Zauner."

"The women walk together, the men behind them. Where are they going?"

"Sounds like preparations for a concert." But not all of these men were following their women into a small building, brightly lighted, near the intersection. It was from there that the tuning up came drifting along the street. "That seems to be a meeting hall. Or a school?" There was a yard beside the building, crammed with small cars. "Quite a gathering anyway." He watched several men dropping out of the small processions to stroll at the same even pace into the lanes. The search for Johann might have begun.

"I'll leave it all to you," Lynn told him as he took her arm and walked her toward the post office. "I'll just fill in if necessary. Oh, Bill—I'm scared."

"No need. And so far it has been easy, hasn't it?"

She nodded. All of Chuck's arrangements had fallen neatly into place. So far. If complications develop, he had said, either use your gumption and improvise or back out gracefully, and we'll try some other way. But at this moment, she thought, there is an awful lot depending on us. That was what scared her.

They stepped from the cool, dark street into a bright

room, small, square, businesslike. Opposite the entrance was a grilled counter, filling part of the back wall. At one end of this was a narrow door, slightly opened, showing a glimpse of living quarters, while at the other end of the counter stood a telephone booth. There was a flag—red, white, red, in three broad horizontal bands—a large map, a moon-faced clock, many notices arranged neatly on one side wall, a wooden table with bench and hard chairs. And people. Far too many people.

"Do you think there is room for us?" Lynn asked quietly as they hesitated just inside the threshold. This was more than Bill had bargained for; of that she was sure. She looked at the jumble of faces turning to stare at the two newcomers, their argument about terrorists abruptly ended.

"Grüss Gott," Mathison said, bowed politely to a woman near the table—middle-aged, heavily built, grave-eyed—who was talking implacably with Andrew. So Andrew was finding the going a little rough, too, was he?

"Grüss Gott. The post office is closed," she announced with the voice of authority. She transferred her severe look to Lynn's blue coat and white stockings.

Lynn said shyly, "Grüss Gott," and smiled warmly as Mathison tried to think of an adequate answer to the post-mistress's firm edict.

Frau Kogel, that was her name. And the others in this room? Felix Zauner was seated at the table, a cigar in his hand, his gray eyes fixed incredulously on Mathison. Two policemen, one stationed near the telephone, the other (a sergeant or inspector of some kind, certainly of higher rank) standing beside the large bulky individual who had broken off his argument to stare at the doorway. He seemed a country-squire type, red-faced, genial, with grizzled hair and well-cut clothes—dark-gray jacket with green collar and facings, trousers striped in green down the sides. His heavy shoes were polished and expensive. Close behind him, obviously cast in the role of listener, was an equally well-dressed man, middle-aged and handsome in a lean way, whose interested expression remained constant. His eyes were alert and watchful. Like a Doberman, Mathison thought as his glance swept quickly around the waiting faces. "Closed? But we only need some directions—"

Andrew cut in quickly, saving Mathison from any further explanation at the moment. "I'm sorry," he said crisply, "but

I was here first. Do you mind?" He turned back to Frau Kogel, who now seemed mesmerized by Lynn's beige tweed suit. "I understand quite fully that the post office is closed for telegrams. But may I at least use the telephone?" His German was good.

"It is to be used only for official business tonight," Frau Kogel insisted. She appealed to the policeman on duty over at the phone booth. "Isn't that right, Karl?"

"We must keep the line open," he agreed.

"But," Andrew rushed on, "this is important. I must call Berne and let my office know I have arrived here."

"Why?" asked Zauner quietly from the table. He had stopped looking at Mathison, his initial surprise either hidden or vanishing. The others' interest followed his; they were all concentrating on Andrew now.

"I am a photographer with New International Press Service. I picked up a rumor in Innsbruck this morning. Two terrorists were said to be in Unterwald."

Zauner raised one eyebrow. "Well, we *are* getting into the news these days."

"And that will please you," the red-faced man observed. His face and voice remained genial, but he obviously did not share Zauner's amusement.

"That depends on the kind of publicity we get," Zauner suggested.

"It will be bad for Unterwald."

"Not if the two terrorists are caught."

"It's all nonsense! Why should they come in this direction?"

Andrew said, "So the rumor is fact, is it? Well, if I can't use this telephone, where's the nearest place I can find another one?"

"At the inn," said Frau Kogel.

"Good. I'll need something to eat anyway, and a couple of rooms."

"Expecting more photographers?" Zauner asked. His interest in Andrew deepened.

"I hope not. Just a reporter who is on his way."

"Only one reporter?" Zauner asked in mock disappointment.

The red-faced squire exploded. "Stop joking, Zauner. We'll be knee-deep in reporters before this thing is finished." He turned back to the police sergeant. "Now, Max," he said firmly, "there is no need to go searching through all the houses, is there? You know the people here."

"I do. But Vienna does not. My report will have to——"

"Nonsense! A waste of time and taxpayers' money!"

"I agree," Max said unhappily, "but orders are orders. You know that, Herr Grell." He went on explaining them, all over again, in his polite stolid way.

August Grell . . . Mathison kept his eyes on Zauner. I can't wait too long, he thought; Grell or no Grell, I can't wait. He went toward the table, speaking in German as a matter of politeness. "Herr Zauner? This is a bit of luck. Perhaps you don't remember me, but we were introduced last Monday. In Salzburg. When you were——"

"Why yes, yes, of course. I kept wondering where I had seen you before. You're the American lawyer. Mathewson?"

"Mathison. And this is Mrs. Conway, also from New York. Mrs. Conway is one of the editors at Newhart and Morris. The publishers."

"Yes, yes, I remember now. You were in Salzburg about that Bryant contract. And what brings you here?"

"We are still trying to finish that piece of business. We came in here to ask for directions. You're just the man to help us."

"I am?"

"Yes. You know everyone around here. Could you tell us where is the Johann Kronsteiner house?"

All talk ceased in the small room. The intense silence was broken by Grell, saying amiably to the police sergeant, "Well, Max, if you've got to search the inn, you've got to. Only please don't cause my guests too much inconvenience. This sort of thing is bad for business, you know. Good night, good night." He bowed to everyone in general, heels together, picked up a loden cape from one of the chairs, and started out. His friend, repeating the leave-taking, followed him. But before they reached the door, one of the notices on the wall seemingly caught their eyes. They stopped to read it.

"It isn't in Unterwald. It's nearer Bad Aussee, I believe," Felix Zauner said.

"Then we passed it," Mathison told Lynn Conway. "Do you mind showing it to us on the map?" he asked Zauner, pointing to the one on the wall. "Actually, we are looking for Frau Bryant. She came up to visit her brother this evening."

Zauner was startled. "Are you sure?" Then he shrugged his

shoulders, studied his cigar. "I thought Johann Kronsteiner was on a hunting trip." He raised his voice, addressed Grell's broad back. "Didn't you mention that Franz had been hired to guide two of your guests?"

Grell looked around. "Yes. He left yesterday with them. They ought to be returning tomorrow."

"Who is Franz?" Mathison asked.

Zauner said, "Kronsteiner's assistant. He left word at the Bad Aussee shop for Johann Kronsteiner to join the hunting party." His eyebrows were questioning Grell.

"That's what he said he would do," August Grell answered. He turned away to finish reading the notice.

"So," Zauner told Mathison, "I don't think you'll find anyone at Kronsteiner's house." His eyes were cold and bright, speculating quickly. There was a touch of distrust too.

"But Frau Bryant is there." Mathison drew Anna Bryant's note out of his pocket, looked at it, then handed it over to Zauner. "You see, we can't wait until she returns to Salzburg on Monday. We'll be leaving then. We've got to get her signature to an agreement between her and the publishers."

"When did you get this note?" Zauner asked sharply.

"Around four o'clock this afternoon. It was stuck under the door."

Zauner studied the note carefully, if only to give himself time. Grell's arrival had been an annoyance. Mathison and Mrs. Conway were a nuisance; but they were negligible, obviously ignorant of Anna Bryant's abduction or anything else that really mattered. But this press photographer? He had made no attempt to establish contact, but perhaps Grell's presence had prevented that. It was with relief that Zauner heard August Grell and his friend moving at last toward the door.

Grell was discussing the notice of a meeting in the school-house tomorrow to consider the development of Unterwald as a winter resort. "We are getting ambitious," he said with a laugh. "First, a ski lift. Now, a resort. Soon we—" He noticed the police sergeant had picked up his coat and was ready to leave, too. "Are you going to start searching us now?" he asked jovially. "Well, come along, Max. Come along."

"It might be a good time," Max said, and plunged into an explanatory apology. And it would be a good time, before the concert ended and the Mitternwald Choral Group and the Tauplitsch Alm Zither Players went up to the inn for a glass of wine and more music. "You'll have a lot of guests tonight, Herr Grell."

Grell did not share his enthusiasm. He said to his silent friend as they buttoned up their lodens, "They'll drink and sing until midnight before they start going home where they belong. And what's to prevent your terrorists," he demanded of Max as they clumped over the wooden floor toward the door, "from slipping onto that bus with the crowd?"

"It will be watched." Max was imperturbable.

"You have your work cut out." The genial voice faded as they passed into the street. Grell was clapping Max on his solid back, an amused but friendly demonstration of encouragement and consolation.

A touching scene, thought Mathison, and looked back at Zauner, who seemed to be engrossed by Anna's simple note.

"If I may interrupt," Andrew said to Zauner, "isn't it possible to let me put in one brief call from that phone?" He had taken out a cigarette, fumbled with his lighter. "May I borrow a couple of your matches? This thing never works when needed."

"Why not try filling it?" He handed over his matchbox.

Andrew picked out four matches, one by one, returned the box with a nod of thanks. "That might be an idea," he conceded.

"Karl," said Zauner, "why don't we let this gentleman—" He indicated the phone booth tactfully. "He won't take long, I'm sure."

Karl had no objections. "Got to keep good relations with the press," he said with a grin. Andrew was already inside the wooden box, closing its glass-paneled door, dialing his call to Bruno in Salzburg.

Now it's my turn, thought Mathison as Zauner rose to face him. But Zauner's usual charm was not much evident tonight; he looked gaunt and tired, and just a little impatient. He handed the note back, saying abruptly, "Sorry I can't help you."

Mathison glanced over at Lynn. She had been keeping very quiet indeed, gradually drifting across the room until she stood at the end of the counter, almost in front of the half-opened kitchen door. What interested her there? He looked back at Zauner. "But you could help us. Frau Bryant may have come up to Unterwald when she found Johann's house empty."

"Frau Bryant is most definitely not here." Zauner was grim-faced. "Good night, Herr Mathison." And that was definite, too.

Score zero, thought Mathison, except for friend Andrew, who seemingly had made contact with a couple of matches that turned into four. But August Grell threw me, and that's the truth. I was keeping it all so easy and natural for his benefit that I had no chance of getting to Zauner. Why the hell, anyway, did Chuck Nield not have him briefed on us? Or perhaps it's my fault; I handled the approach badly. Obviously. Or I wouldn't now have to blunder quickly into the subject of Trudi Seidl. "But doesn't Trudi Seidl live in Unterwald? Frau Bryant wanted to meet her, so why wouldn't she come up here when she was in the district anyway?"

Lynn said very clearly, "Frau Bryant would need some place to sleep, wouldn't she? I don't think she would spend the money on a hotel. Especially when she could stay with Trudi. I know they wanted to meet. In fact, when we last saw Frau Bryant, she asked us to drive her up to Unterwald in our car so that she could visit Trudi." She smiled for Frau Kogel, who had been watching her with covert interest ever since she had stepped into this room. The style and color of every visible piece of Lynn's clothing had been noted by that calm stone-carved face, from buckled shoes to blue coat to beige tweed to white cashmere sweater. "I've been admiring your green apron. It looks very handsome with that rose embroidery on your cardigan. And those silver buttons—where could I find them? In Bad Aussee? I'd like to take some back to New York." Which was all true.

"Now really, Mrs. Conway," Zauner said in English, "how could I possibly help you with Trudi Seidl?" She was quite beautiful, he noticed, shaking off some of his worry and exhaustion; and she certainly could charm. Even Kogel was losing her icebound shyness that terrified most strangers and was adjusting her apron with quick proud fingers, but she hadn't liked him breaking into English. She gave him one of her disciplinary looks before she almost-smiled for the American girl. Who was not so stupid either; she was insisting on German, using it again to answer him, clearly and slowly.

"You could direct us to Trudi's house," Lynn said, "or, better still—if you could spare a few minutes, Herr Zauner, although I know you must be wanting to go to the concert—

you could introduce Bill and me to Trudi. Tell her who we are. Tell her you know Bill, and that he is trying to help Mrs. Bryant."

"Is he?" Zauner asked coldly.

Mathison took out the copies of the Newhart and Morris letter. Tight-lipped, he handed them over to Zauner.

Lynn asked bluntly, "Why don't you want us to meet Trudi Seidl?"

Zauner stared at her. "You do talk nonsense," he said as he turned his back on her to read the letter.

Lynn's cheeks flushed. And Frau Kogel's mouth was disapproving. Quietly, quickly, she began walking toward her kitchen, beckoning Lynn to follow her. "In there," she whispered, and pushed Lynn gently inside, closing the door behind her. She turned to face Zauner, who had swung around as he heard the whisper.

"Where—?" he began. He looked at Mathison, who gave him no help at all. Mathison's hand was out, waiting for the return of the letter. "Very fair," was Zauner's comment on it. "And interesting." It was a leading statement, but Mathison was refusing to be led. There was a marked pause. "Where is Mrs. Conway?" Zauner asked.

"She is with Trudi," Frau Kogel said, and drew her cardigan more squarely on her shoulders.

"You mean Trudi has been hanging around—" began Zauner. It was possible that his annoyance was due to the fact that he, a man who noticed so many things, had not even guessed that Trudi was there. "I told her to stay at home tonight," he said sharply. "She shouldn't be wandering around."

"But she isn't. She is waiting for a phone call, Herr Zauner. From Johann? From his sister? Who knows?" Frau Kogel shrugged her shoulders. "She would feel much worse if she had stayed at home. Here, she can at least hope."

Zauner started toward the kitchen.

"You talked with her enough this afternoon," Frau Kogel said, "and little good it did her. Now if you had found out from Herr Grell just where this hunting party is—the one you say Johann joined—then you could have helped her. So let her be. And if you ask me—"

The telephone-booth door creaked open, and Andrew stepped out. "At least," he said briskly, "I've found my missing reporter. He got sidetracked in Salzburg on an interesting story. An abduction." He glanced at his watch. It was twenty minutes to nine. "I'd better get these rooms at the inn. Wonder if the dining room is still open." Bruno had said he might now be here before midnight. There wasn't much left to do in Salzburg, apart from the police questioning of the two men who had been caught on the staircase outside the attic flat where Anna Bryant had been held. They must have been too confident about her. She hadn't even been tied up. Perhaps she had seemed too obedient, too frightened, too weak. Just the kind of target the bullyboys enjoyed most; they never could resist jibing and jeering and a little secret handling to pass the time of night. She had enough strength to jump. And they had panicked, and ran, as she screamed and fell. Into the courtyard. All the way down. Bloody, bloody hell . . . Andrew forced a smile.

Zauner asked tensely, "Have they been caught?" Was Anna all right? he wondered. He kept a tight grip on his anxiety. "Nasty kind of business," he said, easing his voice. "But you reporters seem to thrive on it."

Mathison only kept staring at Andrew. Anna, he was thinking, Anna Bryant. . . .

"A kidnapping?" Frau Kogel asked in amazement. "In *Salzburg*?" She looked at Karl, who shared her disbelief.

"Thrive?" Andrew raised his eyebrows. "That's putting it pretty strongly, isn't it? Someone has to fill the newspapers for you to read. Three men have been arrested, one on suspicion of loitering with intent near the scene." And I, he thought, did help to nail him down. But that was not much satisfaction, not now. "Of course that charge won't stick," he added, "unless your police persuade the other two to talk about him. How good are they at persuading?"

"I don't think they've had much experience in dealing with kidnappers," Zauner said stiffly. What about Anna? If there was no mention of her, then she was dead. "Perhaps Mr. Mathison, who comes from America, could give our police some tips."

"What about the victim?" Mathison asked, trying to keep his voice casual.

"We'll hear the details when my friend gets here, unless the police are trying to hush up everything. That's one headache all reporters face. Keeps them thriving, I suppose." He grinned widely at Zauner. He's got the message, Andrew thought, noting Zauner's eyes. Was he a close friend of Anna

315

Bryant? The news has hit him hard. And as for Mathison—he was guessing, all right, and guessing accurately; he looked as if someone had just kicked him in the groin.

"Tell me—" began Frau Kogel eagerly, anticipating the pleasure of handing out the mail on Monday morning along with Trudi's troubles, American clothes, and, to top all special pieces of news, a real-live kidnapping right in Salzburg, "who was—" She stopped abruptly as everyone's attention focused on her front door. She turned in annoyance. It was a woman who had entered, a woman in a bulky expensive green coat that just covered her hips. Young, and trying to seem younger with her hair hanging loose, thought Frau Kogel. Pretty, of course; why else were the men gawking at her tight black trousers stretched over her thighs? And she was gaping right back at them. Staring, she was. Big eyes wide. It seemed as if she had frozen right there in the doorway as she kept staring at the American. "Post office is closed," Frau Kogel announced. For once, her official voice had no effect. The young woman hadn't even heard.

"Hello, Elissa," said Bill Mathison.

Felix Zauner looked at him sharply, looked back at Elisabetha Lang.

"Why, Bill . . ." She had recovered from her astonishment, and now showed only delight. "But what fun to find you here. What brought you up to this god-forsaken—oh, I'm sorry." The apology was for Andrew, who was on his way out. "I really didn't mean to block your way."

"I rather enjoyed it," Andrew said with an admiring eye. "Can I give anyone a lift? As far as the inn, that is?"

"It's easier to walk," she told him.

"I have some luggage in the car."

"Oh, you are going to stay there?"

"If I can get a room."

"They'll put you up in the attic—that's what they did to me. And that's what I came to see Herr Zauner about." Her eyes glanced to Zauner. "Isn't there some place else in this village where I could stop for a few days?"

"I'm sorry you find the inn uncomfortable," Felix Zauner said. "Fräulein Lang is an expert on resort accommodation," he told the room in general. "We may work for rival firms, but our interest in Unterwald is the same. Fräulein Lang's job is to advise tourists where—"

"If my attic room is any sample of what they'll find here,"

316

she cut in coldly, "I'll cross Unterwald off my list. So I think you ought to help me, Herr Zauner. Haven't you got a list of your own? I might find something warmer there." To Andrew she said, "You'll freeze in that attic."

"What's the food like?" he asked as he edged past her.

"Venison stew."

"I'll try that as a starter. And I hope you reconsider." He gave one last entranced look and left.

She remained standing at the doorway. It was the only mark left of her embarrassment. "Herr Zauner, would you be so kind as to show me your list?"

"It's in my briefcase at the Hitz place."

"Then why don't we get it right now?"

Zauner glanced at the kitchen door, tightly closed, and lifted his cape. He nodded to Mathison. "Have a good journey."

"Aren't you here for the weekend?" Elissa asked in dismay. "I did hope we'd be seeing each other—once I know where to unpack my things."

"It's just a quick visit," Mathison said. "I thought I'd find Anna Bryant here. I'm trying to straighten out that contract with Yates."

"Poor Bill—he really gave you so much trouble."

"That is how lawyers stay in business."

"Auf Wiedersehen," she told him lightly, with one of her old smiles.

I hope not, he thought. He nodded, trying to keep his good-bye pleasant and nonchalant, and turned away to join Frau Kogel and Karl. His eyes were on the kitchen door. It had opened slightly. He put up a hand for caution, and hoped Lynn would see it. Just wait, just wait a minute, he told her silently. "You're missing a good concert," he said to Frau Kogel. The zither music and four-part singing were coming softly down the street now. They blended well, sweet and true and sad.

Frau Kogel said delightedly, "It's my favorite song." She began to sing, in a voice that was light and young, so much in contrast with her grave face, strong-boned, red-cheeked, formidable in repose, that Mathison stared openly. Her eyes softened as she, too, sang about highest mountains, deepest valleys.

Lynn touched his elbow. "Trudi has asked us to have supper with her."

317

"Where is she?"

"She went on ahead to get the table ready. Come on, Bill. I know the way." Lynn's face was flushed, her eyes excited. "Can we leave, do you think?" She glanced at Frau Kogel, who was going into her third verse, true-voiced, word-perfect. "No, I suppose not."

"Just as well to let Elissa get out of sight."

"Elissa?" Lynn's excitement faded.

He nodded. Elissa and Grell: two pieces of the worst possible luck. And the bad news about Anna. How was he going to break that to Lynn? Nothing has gone right, he was thinking.

"You look as if you had had a shock," Lynn said, and then wished she could take that back. Was Elissa attracting him even against his will? She turned abruptly toward Frau Kogel, who now was on the last line.

"A bad one," he admitted, and wondered if this could be the quick approach to telling Lynn about Anna Bryant. But Lynn had become her calm and businesslike other self, and had taken Frau Kogel's hand before she could start on the fourth verse. Warm thanks, good evenings, best wishes, see you again. And even if Frau Kogel seemed wistful as she saw a little gossip about Trudi was not forthcoming, she relaxed into unexpected blushes when Mathison admired her voice. "Strange mixture," he said as they stepped into the quieted street. No sign of Elissa or Felix Zauner. Only some parked cars, the empty bus, a couple of men talking, lighted windows in silent houses, music flowing from the now-opened door of the schoolhouse at the corner.

"Everyone and everything is," said Lynn, glancing around her. Even if terrorists were not hiding here, they had gone underground in some other village or town where people listened to songs about mountains and valleys, the very thing that the terrorists said they were fighting for. "The irony is always bitter. The sweetest songs are the saddest."

"It's getting to you," he said, listening to the music as he opened the Porsche door. "You know, there is something about a zither—"

A quiet voice said from the floor of the back seat, "Don't look now, but Chuck is here. Help the lady in, Bill. That's right." He waited until Mathison was in the car, too. "Don't pay any attention. I shan't feel hurt. And what kept you so long, anyway?"

318

Lynn said, "I saw Trudi, spoke with her. We are now going to her house for supper. She wants to talk some more. When you reach the corner, Bill, take the Bad Aussee road. Trudi's house is the last one in the village, the fifth from the corner as you go downhill. It's on the right-hand side. You can park off the road on the meadow beside the house."

"Okay."

"Talk some more?" Chuck's impatient voice asked. "Does she know anything at all?"

"She has a box. Upstairs in her bedroom. She says it is some of Richard Bryant's valuable equipment. Johann salvaged it from his wrecked car, wanted it kept secret so it could be sold quickly for Anna's benefit."

Equipment. That might mean nothing, or everything. "Will she let us examine the box?"

"She wants it taken out of her bedroom. I think part of her worry is that the box will be found there." Lynn paused, shook her head sadly. No woman would have hidden it where it was. And tongues wagged easily in a small village. Poor Trudi ... "But she is mostly worried about Johann. She's sure he is in real danger, and when I told her about Anna Bryant being missing—sorry, but I couldn't lie to her. She wanted to know, first thing, why Anna had not come here as she had promised." She paused again. "Was I wrong to tell her?"

"No," Bill said. And if I weren't driving on parking lights and trying to count the houses we've passed, I'd make a grab for you and kiss you until the breath was out of your body. He caught hold of her hand, held it in a tight grip.

"It was right for Trudi," Chuck said. Obviously. "But it could be wrong for you. You've destroyed your amateur standing, Mrs. Conway. If Trudi talks about what you know —"

"I thought of that. But perhaps by that time it won't matter."

Let's hope, thought Nield. He felt the car swerve sharply off the road, bump over some rough grass. As it came gently to rest beside the wall of a house, he raised his head to look out across an open meadow. "Nice trees," he said appreciatively. "I'll wait for you over there. If you have good news, Bill, come out to the door and light a cigarette. Then walk over to that central clump." Nield pointed to a dark mass across the meadow. "I may need a hand with a surprise package I've prepared."

"I don't know how long we'll be." Mathison looked at Lynn. "I suppose we do have to stay for supper?" He released her hand, put on the emergency brake.

"Trudi wanted that. Badly. We reassure her, perhaps, that we are friends, that she isn't alone." Lynn half turned her head in Chuck's direction. "And she wants to be certain that if she hands over the box to the Austrian police that the search for Johann won't stop. That's what worries her now."

"Tell her we'll go on searching." Chuck's voice was definite. We owe that to Anna Bryant, he thought grimly.

"Are you the Austrian police?" Lynn's voice was too polite.

Chuck laughed. "No. I suppose Zauner will act for them. But you can be certain," he added frankly, "I'll stick closer to him than a Siamese twin." He straightened his cramped shoulders, rubbed his back reflectively. "But why did Trudi not tell Zauner about the box if she was so eager to get rid of it?"

"I think Mr. Zauner asked too many pointed questions this afternoon. And there was something that worried her about Johann's house. Zauner came to see her after he had been down there and discovered that it was ransacked. That's how he knew Johann was in trouble, he said. Except, Trudi had been there earlier and had left everything 'tidied up.' So Trudi is convinced he is lying—he never went near Johann's house, but heard about it some other way. It doesn't make sense, does it?"

"He was probably covering up his real sources of information," Mathison said, and looked with amusement at Chuck. "That must be a tricky business sometimes." But Chuck let that ride. He slipped out of the car and set off across the meadow. "One thing is clear anyway: Trudi is no idiot."

Except about Johann, thought Lynn Conway. She sighed, opened the door, and swung her feet onto the cold grass. If I were to give Trudi some really valuable advice, she thought, I'd tell her to forget Johann altogether; the more I hear of that charmer, the more he reminds me of Todd. Then she stopped thinking about her husband, dead six years, still alive in the distrust he had taught her. Was this how he controlled her life, even when she thought she was free of him? She looked at Bill Mathison, coming to lead her toward the front of the house. She stumbled on the dark rough ground, felt the strength and quickness of his arm. Relax, she told herself, learn to trust again. And yet she heard herself asking, very casually, of course, "Elissa—I wonder what she is planning now?"

"Plenty. That's certain. But we'll let Zauner take care of it. He has a small account to settle with her." He fell silent. Then, "The hell with her," he said.

He halted just before they reached the door of the Seidl house, pulled Lynn around to face him. Both arms slipped around her, caught her close. It was a long, long kiss.

From the darkness of the trees, Charles Nield looked at the two distant figures in amazement. "Oh no, for God's sake," he said softly, "not at this moment, not now. Break it off, will you, Bill?"

"What's that?" an American voice asked in his ear. "Trouble?"

Chuck spoke into his midget two-way radio. "Just side thoughts. Here is what you do now, Hank. Get my car down to the last house on the way out of the village. Go beyond it, actually; draw off the road, park in cover; walk back and join me. I'm at the edge of the meadow, in the central clump of trees. Bring that surprise package with you. You had better notify Andrew. He's at the inn. Better notify Zauner, too, but make sure you contact Bruno—he's probably on the road to Bad Aussee right now. Tell him he has to get up here in double time. Urgent. Here. At this meadow. Got it?"

"Action?"

"I don't know for sure. Could be." He signed off. Could be. He looked back in the direction of Mathison and Lynn Conway. They were now entering the house. He relaxed, folded back the small aerial, slipped the gadget—a much-used cigarette case—back into his pocket.

He settled deeper into the shadows, pulling the hood of his jacket tightly around his ears, fastening it closely at the throat, adding wool gloves to keep his hands from freezing. Now, Bill, he was thinking, it's all yours. You have got about a twenty-yard start on Elissa, but once she begins adding up the question marks you'll need every inch of it. I know. I saw her face as she walked along the street with Zauner.

23

THE PARTING SMILE FOR BILL MATHISON HAD LEFT ELISSA'S lips the moment she stepped into the street from the post office. Felix Zauner, two paces behind her, had to quicken his stride to catch up and keep with her. "Better wait until we reach my room before we talk," he suggested tactfully. He had never seen her show so much anger. Her whole face had tightened up, become ten years older. "Relax, relax," he told her quietly. The street might be lighted only by far-spaced lamps, but even they were enough, helped by the general glow from unshuttered windows (a police suggestion for this unusual evening), to let some passer-by see Elisabetha's fury. Elisabetha . . . Elissa . . . Yesterday in Vienna, when he had been asked to give his justification for employing Lang, his three questioners had called her Elissa.

"How far?" she asked tersely.

"Two more houses." As soon as they passed this row of cars drawn into the side of the street, they'd be at Frau Hitz's place, where he now had his room on a weekly basis. The last of the cars was a strange red Porsche, old enough to be put out to hire. Salzburg plates. Mathison had rented it, no doubt. Better not draw her attention to it. Better get her safely indoors before she had another outburst. Where was her prized self-control? "Here we are," he said with relief, and ushered her inside.

"Anyone else here?"

"Not at the moment. Frau Hitz is in charge of the dining room up at the inn for this weekend."

"An old woman with white scragged-back hair?"

"Yes." Not so old, actually. My age, thought Zauner.

"What's amusing you?"

"Let's start talking. We can't spend too long here."

"You mean we'll be watched?"

"Everything is being watched tonight. The search for Johann has started."

"I'm glad there's some efficiency being shown by some-one," she said bitterly. But her voice had lost its shrill note; her face was smoothing out. Those fools, those bungling idiots in Zürich, she was thinking. How did they let Mathison get away? And so soon. So soon . . .

"Even if he belongs to the opposition?" he asked with amusement.

Her control had returned. So had her sense of humor. "But you don't really belong to the opposition, Felix. No longer. You are with us now."

He had to swallow that without one shift of expression on his face. "I am not the efficiency expert around here."

"Who is?"

"A man from Vienna."

"From Vienna?" She unbuttoned her coat, threw it aside, decided that the kitchen table could be too clearly seen from the street, sat down on the lowest step of the flight of wooden stairs that hugged one wall up to the floor overhead. She motioned him to follow her into this corner. "And who is responsible for Vienna entering the picture?"

"Washington and London."

"What?" That had really jolted her. "They know about the Finstersee box?"

"They know."

"And why did you not report this?"

"To whom? You were in Zürich."

That was a neat reminder that she was his only contact. He hadn't been given any other names, any other telephone numbers. "But you had a message this afternoon warning you, among other things, that I would arrive at the inn just before dinner this evening. You could easily have told the man who telephoned you that there was quite a lot of international interest developing in Unterwald as a winter resort. You aren't usually so backward with a neat phrase." Her anger had returned, but now it was cold and wary.

"The man who called me did not talk with me. He gave a message. And then he hung up." And I'm volunteering no information to them, he thought. I may have to answer their questions, but I'll volunteer no statements.

That was Lev, she thought, taking no chances, keeping risks to the minimum. That was Lev, who had delayed her arrival here in Unterwald by all the double precautions and extra arrangements he had made. That was Lev, who couldn't accept her urgent suggestions last night, but had to add some variations of his own. Lev, who was too patient when he should be quick; and too quick when—as in the case of that call to Zauner—he ought to have been patient. She took a deep, steadying breath. "When did you learn that the Americans and British knew about Finstersee?"

"When I was summoned to Vienna."

"And when was that?"

"Yesterday morning."

"You were interrogated?"

"Hardly. I was taking part in a conference."

"Discussing what?"

"International co-operation."

She waited. "Go on. Co-operation between whom?"

"Austria, Britain, the United States."

"Have they men here?"

"Yes."

She waited. When he did not elaborate, she said quietly, "Are we playing games, Felix? Have I got to drag every piece of information out of you with a question? Moscow will not like this. This is not in their bargain. And they insist that any bargain must be kept." She paused, smiled gently, looked at him with wide sympathetic eyes. "You have no choice, Felix. So let's make it easy for both of us. Tell me the names of the chief Intelligence agents who are here, what they look like, what is their cover."

"The Englishman is known as Andrew. You saw him in the post office—as a press photographer. The American is known as Chuck. He hasn't arrived yet. At least he hasn't made contact. So I can't say what he looks like. He is a Swiss climber, visiting some friends on the Tauplitsch Alm, and is supposed to have come along with them in case we must search the mountainsides."

"So the CIA agent is not Bill Mathison?"

"No."

"And who is the man from Vienna?"

This was more difficult to answer. His throat tightened; he looked away. But he answered. "His name is Bruno. He hasn't arrived yet—he was delayed in Salzburg. He is coming as a reporter who works along with Andrew. Their legend is that they are with New International Press Service, head office in Berne. They have heard a rumor, which they are following up, about South Tyrolean terrorists."

"And what delayed Bruno in Salzburg?"

"Anna Bryant was kidnapped and held. The men responsible have been caught." His voice dropped as if it were stifled. "Anna is dead."

She gave an audible sigh of relief. For a minute, she had thought that Bruno had been delayed by Werner Dietrich's accident. "We had no connection with Anna Bryant's death. Believe me, Felix."

"That's right," he said bitterly, "you would never have harmed a hair of her head. But Dietrich was another matter, was he?"

"What have you heard about Dietrich?" she asked sharply.

"He took a long time to die. He regained consciousness before then."

She sat quiet silent, staring at him. "Did he name anyone?" she asked at last.

"Yes."

"Whom?"

He said with a touch of real pleasure, "Your fat friend who poses as a refugee painter from Poland."

"They can't identify me through him. Jan made friends of every art student in Salzburg. His parties were a meeting place for all."

"He is facing a definite murder charge. He may be tempted to talk in exchange for—"

"You don't know us, do you?" she asked contemptuously. "You don't really understand what we are. Jan will not identify me."

But you did, he thought. You identified yourself tonight when you answered to "Elissa," with Frau Kogel and Karl there as witnesses. And had she met Mathison in Zürich, too? Could "Elissa" link her with other clandestine activities there? One thing he did know: she hadn't been having a few days in Zürich just to enjoy a holiday.

She misread his silence. "Jan doesn't know one thing about you. So you are safe."

"I don't like his methods," Zauner said grimly.

"Dietrich was no friend of yours. Why do you—"

"He was a decent man. And a good agent."

"And our enemy. A dangerous man to me, to you. He could have finished us both."

"He would never have had you murdered, Elissa." In his anger, the name had slipped out. Perhaps he wanted it to slip out.

"Elissa? Oh, that name I invented for Bill Mathison?" She

325

spoke lightly, as if the idea amused her. But she was watchful. "Where else did you hear it?"

"In Vienna."

Shock spread over her face. She stared at him unbelievingly. Then at last she asked slowly, "Vienna knew that name?"

He nodded, glanced at his watch. "I have to get back to the post office. It is our headquarters, informal but central."

"Then Mathison told them. He *is* an American agent," she burst out.

"Nonsense. He is a lawyer who came to Salzburg to handle some business from a New York client."

"He, and he alone, knew the name of Elissa." Her voice rose.

"Use your head," he told her sharply. "Stop being so emotional about him. Think, think! Put yourself in the place of the American called Chuck. He has been in Zürich, so he must know something about Yates. And he must have learned something about Bryant and Finstersee, too. So what would he do? Just what you would have done if you had discovered Mathison had any Salzburg connection. You would have planned to meet him accidentally, charm him, disarm him, get him talking. He would have answered your questions without even realizing they were being asked. If, that is, you were a highly intelligent agent."

The quiet sneer ended her panic. She looked at him coldly. She said nothing.

"The name of Elissa Lang was bound to crop up in any talk about people he had met on that one day he visited Salzburg." On Monday; five days ago, no more. Five years, they seemed. "Keep away from Mathison. He is bad for you, destroys your judgment. And I will have no fake suicides here in Unterwald, no inexplicable accidents to Mathison or anyone else. I am responsible for you. If you act stupidly, you will not only endanger your mission but also destroy my future usefulness to your government. They will not thank you for that."

"You are responsible for *me?*"

"I am in charge here until Bruno arrives. My special assignment is to watch you and make sure that you are completely neutralized. Once the Finstersee box is discovered, the others will have more time then to deal with you directly. But now, I am responsible for you."

326

So they really trusted him. "Did Vienna challenge you about me?"

"They asked about you."

"And what did you tell them?"

"Nothing. I protested, of course. I was shocked. I was very unhappy. Like all innocent men who have been duped by a pretty KGB agent."

"Do they really believe that I infiltrated your organization without your knowledge?"

His jaw tightened. "Yes," he admitted with an effort, "they think I was fooled. And for that reason, they believe I will not be fooled again."

"What a blow to your pride it must have been," she murmured. "Next week, I shall find it all very amusing. But meanwhile—" She paused, thinking quickly. She had dropped all emotions, buried them with the remnants of her anger. Zauner had been right: she had let herself get out of control after the shock of meeting Mathison. She had become, for the space of ten minutes or so, a highly unintelligent agent. If Lev had seen her, heard her, he would have had her recalled at once. Disciplined severely. Even— No, no, let her concentrate on what she had to do now. Her cover was completely blown. She would have to get out of Austria once she escaped from this village. But if she completed this mission, she would get a new assignment, new identity, new nationality. If she completed this mission, her return home might earn reward, instead of punishment. That Zürich telephone number she had given to Mathison in Salzburg—a small thing, unimportant, she had used it before. Except that this time there had been Yates's disappearance and his own complicated life to bring the police searching, discovering. Had Mathison memorized that number, made her subterfuge for stealing it quite laughable? He must have told someone about it—the American called Chuck, perhaps—and that number had linked her to the Yates-Langenheim flat in Zürich, destroyed Elisabetha Lang. Such a small thing, so unimportant, a foolish impulse to meet a man again, a weak moment of romantic nonsense—and her cover was blown to pieces. Now she would have to start planning her flight. But meanwhile— "Meanwhile," she said, swinging her attention back to Zauner, "there is a mission to be completed."

He studied her face and felt a touch of sympathy. She

would not accept personal defeat any more than he could. "Don't you understand what I've been telling you?"

"Yes. You were hinting that I am now useless here, that I should escape from Unterwald as quickly and quietly as possible." Did he really believe that solution would end his problems? "But I am not leaving Unterwald, or Salzburg, until the Finstersee box is found. We must get to it before the opposition does. That is possible; you are in charge of Operation Search, aren't you? You will see that I am warned the moment the box is found. And I'll be there to—"

"Hand it over to your own agents, who will just happen to be in the right place at the right time?" he asked with biting sarcasm. "You won't even be allowed within lifting distance of that box. Be serious."

"I am serious," she said quietly. "I don't need agents to help me. And if I can't get near the box, then you certainly can. You may have to deal with it."

"I?"

"But I shall watch, just to make sure. And then I leave. Not before."

"Are you saying that I have to help your agents remove that box?" He was both shocked and angry. This was going far beyond the original understanding.

"We need no agents to remove the box. We simply destroy it."

"Destroy?"

"Complete destruction of box and contents. Those were my official orders, received late last night. Today, I was sent this." She reached for her coat, thrust her hand deep into one pocket, pulled out a padlock. It looked worn and old. "We snap this onto the Finstersee box. In ten minutes, it is destroyed."

"Snap it where?"

"Onto one of the staples clamped together by the padlock that is already there."

"But the box may not have staples and a padlock. It may have locks, instead."

"If it's the same type that was found in the Czechoslovakian lake, it will have two locks *and* a padlock. There should also be collapsible handles at each end of the box. But if it hasn't any of these, we'll have to use this strip of magnetic tape to fix our padlock in place." She held out a small loop of gray metal ribbon and then slipped it back into her other pocket.

"But that's only to be used in an emergency. Much better to attach our padlock near the existing one. Then if anyone noticed it, he would think two padlocks were just another example of the Nazi passion for security. Even if he did question it, he couldn't do much about it. Because, once you snap the padlock in place, and give it a sharp twist to the right, you set a time mechanism working."

"Ten minutes?"

She nodded. "In ten minutes, the box will be blown to pieces and its contents destroyed." She held the padlock up so that he could see that its tongue was at present turned away from the slot into which it would fit. "Safety position," she told him calmly. "It won't slip out of that. You have to turn it toward the slot very firmly, and then snap it hard. Then twist the padlock. Simple, isn't it?" She replaced it in her pocket, almost carelessly, as if to prove to him how safe it was at the moment. "Don't look so upset," she added lightly.

"But others are bound to be killed." The men, for example, who might be carrying that box to a car for transportation to Salzburg. Men standing near. Men in the car itself.

"The box *must* be destroyed. That is an order. You may be in charge of Operation Search, but I am in command of you." She softened her words with a smile. "Cheer up, Felix. I shall leave as soon as I attach that padlock to the box—or watch you snap it in place if I can't get near it. And that's the last you'll see of me. Too bad. I enjoyed working in Salzburg."

She will leave, but someone else will come. Next month, next year, it makes no difference. I am condemned to their service, he thought, and every day I hesitated, every day I postponed making a clear and quick confession to Vienna, has only added another link to the chain that binds me. Perhaps the time to break off must be faced now. And yet, there might be some way out; some way in which I could keep what I have—my job, my reputation, my friends; and, above all, the respect of my family—keep all that and yet be free. Free of this woman, free of her people. Free. Yes, there must be some way out.

"When will Bruno be here?" She was rising from her staircase seat, picking up her coat, looking around Frau Hitz's neat kitchen with a critical eye. Peasant taste, she thought as she looked at the finicky mats with bright patterns on table and chests, the framed lithographs, the faded photographs of men in uniform. Clutter on clutter. "When?" she repeated.

"Tomorrow night." Zauner's voice sounded preoccupied.

She looked at him sharply. "Will he send you away when he takes charge?"

He shook his head. "I have duties to keep me here." Duties? The word twisted like a knife in his heart.

"Good. We'll manage it then. Even if we don't find the box for another forty-eight hours." By tomorrow, she would have two agents established in Bad Aussee, two others on their way. What would Zauner say if he knew she was up here completely alone? He wouldn't believe it. And for her own safety, she did not intend to enlighten him. "I'll get back to the inn."

"Have you changed your mind about the attic room?"

"Yes. The people who stay there are so interesting."

He wondered if she knew that August Grell was the Nazi who had watched over Finstersee. He almost warned her. No, he decided, I'll let her and her friends find out for themselves; they are so damned clever at ferreting out a man's past, are they? "Such as Andrew?" he tried.

She nodded. "I might even see him trying to pretend he doesn't know this unobtrusive American called Chuck. Glance into the street, Felix. I don't want to run into Mathison again if I can help it."

Zauner opened the door. "They've gone," he said quietly. "The red Porsche isn't there now."

"They?" she asked quickly as she followed him into the street.

He cursed his slip of tongue. "Mathison and Mrs. Conway—she's from the New York publishing house that Mathison represents. That contract business, you know."

"I know." Her voice was as cold as the wind that whipped their cheeks.

"We'd better say good-bye. You'll find me at the post office if you need me. And if I have anything to report, I'll telephone the inn and leave a message for you to call Weiss, of your Innsbruck office. Right?"

"Right." And will he? she wondered. "But we don't say good-bye. Not quite yet. Be your usual gallant self and walk me as far as the inn." She started crossing the village street. He had to follow her. "I did not see Mrs. Conway with Mathison. Where was she?"

330

"In the other room."

"Why?"

"She was talking with Trudi Seidl."

"Who's she?"

"Johann's girl."

"How much of his girl is she?"

"He is marrying her."

"Johann?" She looked at him, burst out laughing. Then just as suddenly she fell silent. "And when did Johann decide he was getting married?"

Zauner didn't answer.

"You might as well tell the truth. Because I know it must have been some time since I last saw him, and that was only a week ago. He talked of his future plans quite a lot that night; marriage wasn't one of them."

"How should I know when another man decides to get married?" he asked irritably.

"Well, when did you first hear of it? And where?"

"In Unterwald. On Monday night—no, early Tuesday morning."

"From Johann himself?"

"Yes."

"I see." She listened with rising irritation to the yodeling chorus coming from the schoolhouse. "I begin to see a number of things. Why are you protecting Mathison and Conway?"

Protecting? Perhaps he had been, if only because Mathison had been Anna Bryant's friend. A better friend than I was, he thought bitterly, even if I knew her for years and he only met her three times in his life. "Nonsense," he told her, stopping to listen to the music. It carried sweetly on the night air. "They are a couple of innocents."

"I wonder. Oh, let's keep moving; it's too cold to stand here. Where is Trudi Seidl's house?"

"On the road to Bad Aussee."

"I counted four or five as I drove into Unterwald. Which is hers?"

"The first you saw."

"Not too far away." They had come to the intersection where the Bad Aussee road crossed the main street and then ran uphill past the inn. "In fact, about seven or eight minutes from here on foot? Even less?"

"Less." For an instant, he thought she was going to set off

down the Bad Aussee road by herself. But she changed her mind and started up the dark narrow road toward the inn. "If we were to keep on following this trail," he said, trying to change the subject, hoping to get her mind off Trudi Seidl, "we would reach Finstersee. It's beyond the forest."

"How helpful you are," she said very quietly, "in things that no longer matter. Why do you keep the important things hidden from me, Felix? I shall be writing a report, you know, and the Center will read it carefully. You can't fight them. You'll lose. Too bad. I liked you."

"I've told you all you asked for."

"All right. Where are the Nazis holing up in Unterwald?"

He laughed, if only to cover his annoyance with himself. He had imagined he could keep some things back from this girl, and there wasn't one of them that she hadn't already thought of. If she had kept quiet about them, it was only to bring them out, abruptly, unexpectedly, forcing him into an answer. "I shouldn't ask that question near here, if I were you, unless I lowered my voice to a whisper." He glanced at the inn, brightly lit and welcoming.

"There?" she asked, looking at the inn, too. She had lowered her voice.

"You are right in the middle of them."

She took a deep breath. "And you rather enjoy that, don't you?"

"I thought it would appeal to your own sense of humor."

"How long have you known?"

"Just in the last day or so. I'm searching for proof that can let us take action. Of course, if we find Johann alive, he can give us that proof."

"August Grell—is he the leader of this group?"

"He is certainly one of their top men. He has been in charge of Finstersee for twenty years at least."

"He must feel quite desperate," she said, almost to herself. As I am, she thought. I wonder if Lev could get reinforcements up here tonight? I can't rely on Zauner. He has been too late with much of his information, and even then I had to drag it out of him. Does he really want us to have the box? Or doesn't he care any more what happens to him? I had better get in touch with Lev right away. Dare I risk it from my attic room? "How many of Grell's friends have gathered here?"

"There were eight yesterday."

"There were only three with him at dinner. Are five with Johann?"

"Two, possibly. I heard that three men were detained in Salzburg for Anna's—" He stopped. "They may have come from here," he ended.

She touched his arm as they reached the path to the inn's front door. "Let me know if anything develops. And Felix—please don't cheat. Keep nothing back. Or else it will be really bad, not just for you, but also for your wife and your two sons. Keep your promise." Her voice was soft, entreating. Her eyes were sympathetic, her face sad.

He almost believed them. But there was one thing he could believe: the threat. He nodded curtly, turned away, and walked quickly down the rough road toward the village street. The concert was ending. Soon the people would crowd out; some to drive home, some to walk a little, some to come up to the Weinstüberl at the inn for a glass of wine, some songs, much talk. Saturday night . . . He thought of his wife, Ruth, at home in Salzburg, patiently waiting as she always did, never questioning him, knowing as little about Unterwald as she had known about her release from a Nazi concentration camp twenty-two years ago. A miracle, she had called her release. A miracle I paid for, he thought. And am still paying.

I did not really enjoy doing that, she told herself as she entered the inn's small deserted hall; I didn't enjoy threatening him with his wife and sons. Much better if I could have kept them unmentioned. Now he knows that I have learned a great deal more about his past than he ever realized. I sacrificed a trump card which might have been useful at some future moment. Yet, it was the only threat that seemed to have a definite effect on him. And as for trump cards, the moments for playing them against Felix Zauner were nearing their end. Rapidly. So little time left. She glanced carefully into the dining room and saw Andrew at one table, talking with a couple of off-duty policemen, and August Grell with his three friends sitting over cups of coffee at their own special place in front of the tiled stove. They were almost as silent as the rows of deer heads staring down at them from the wall. They are as depressed as I am, she thought with bitter amusement.

333

She slipped quietly to the staircase, climbed cautiously to her attic bedroom. So little time, she kept thinking. British and Americans already here in Unterwald, Vienna cooperating, so many men at their joint command. Who would have thought they could have moved so quickly? Last Monday, they knew nothing, nothing concrete. Tonight, they were in position and far ahead of her. She must risk making contact with Lev. He must send reinforcements immediately. Tonight. Tomorrow would be too late. Unterwald had become no place for one agent working alone. And how it had become that way was something that baffled and angered her.

Her anger grew once she was in her room. It had been entered in her absence. Police looking for hidden terrorists? They would hardly search inside her suitcase; yet the thin, almost invisible, protective thread that she had fixed at the inside hinge had been torn loose as the lid had been opened wide. The clothes inside were in the right order. But someone had discovered the false bottom to the case, for when she drew out the transmitting and receiving set that lay hidden there, she could smell a slight odor of acid clinging to it. The batteries were destroyed.

She opened the machine to check, make sure, hoping against hope that she was wrong. But she had been right. The batteries were useless. Andrew . . .

Quickly, she replaced everything, left the suitcase where it usually stood, went quietly downstairs. A telephone call to Lev? It would have to be made from here—that horrible old woman and her smirking policeman at the post office wouldn't let her use their phone. And she must not give Lev's emergency number to Felix Zauner; that would be the worst mistake for her own future that she could make. Lev had no liking for her at all; she had felt that last night, felt it today with his final injunctions. He had no liking for anyone except himself. A cold, efficient, cautious, self-protective man. Call him from the inn? He would have her career ended for that, perhaps even more than her career. Because a call from a telephone that must be tapped by the Austrians, even a call with seemingly harmless phrases about an apparently innocent business matter, might endanger Lev's own security. And that was what mattered to Lev.

She stood at the desk, looking at the telephone, hesitating. She glanced once more into the dining room. The two policemen were there, but Andrew was gone.

"Ah, Fräulein Lang," said August Grell, leaving his table, coming toward her, "did you want to make a telephone call? I'm sorry to ask you to wait. I have been expecting an important message for the last half hour. It should come soon, any minute. So would you be so kind as to—"

"No," she said, "I didn't want to telephone. I wanted to have a quiet talk with you."

"If it is about your room—"

"No," she said, lowering her voice even more. "It is about the telephone call you are expecting. From three of your friends? Who went to Salzburg today? They won't be coming back." She watched the genial mask slip for one brief instant and then cover August Grell's good-natured face once more. But his eyes were blue ice. "And Frau Bryant is dead." That was a real shock, a premonition of disaster complete. Again Grell's strong control reasserted itself. "And now that you know how much I could tell you, would you care to hear some more? We have a lot in common, tonight." She emphasized the last word delicately. "An interest in the Finstersee box, for example? Neither of us wants the Americans or British to get hold of it, do we? Oh yes, their agents are here. The Austrians, too. I can name them. Better yet, I think I know one way to get Johann to tell you where the box is hidden."

He took a key from his pocket, went forward to his office door. "In here," he said quietly.

24

A SAD-EYED GIRL, PRETTY AT OTHER TIMES, CHEEKS NOW swollen from crying, looked at Mathison intently as he followed Lynn Conway into the comfortable kitchen. Curtains were drawn over the windows, electric light switched on in special welcome. From a room at the back of the Seidl house came the sound of someone gently snoring. The table was covered with a brightly embroidered cloth and set with a small serving platter of cold cuts, a slab of cheese, crusted bread. Trudi had been busy since she had dashed across the fields to get supper ready for her guests. She had even changed her apron, Lynn noted, and she was no longer on the verge of breaking into tears.

"This is Bill—Bill Mathison," Lynn said. "You can trust him."

Trudi gravely shook hands, watching him. "Frau Bryant spoke of him." She went on watching him as he helped Lynn off with her coat, pulled off his windbreaker, laid them both on a chair near the door. "I am glad you came," she said briefly, beckoning them with her hand to sit down at the table.

Couldn't we deal with the box first? Mathison thought. But no, they definitely could not. Trudi had her own way of arranging matters. It wasn't time that was important to her, but trust. She had accepted Lynn, that was obvious, but she wanted to be quite sure of him. She kept glancing at him as she hurried to the back of the room for the coffeepot on top of a clay stove. Then she lit two oil lamps, bringing one of them over to the table, remembered a serving spoon and fork, rough linen napkins, and turned off the electric light before she sat down at last, taking a chair directly opposite Mathison. Satisfied? he wondered. At least, she was more relaxed.

He made a pretense of eating and concentrated on talk. Someone had to start words flowing. Lynn ate little, and listened. Trudi was frankly hungry—"the first food I've been able to swallow today"—and even answered Mathison freely once he got on the topic of Johann. Yes, it was late last night, almost midnight, that she knew something was wrong. She had been waiting for Johann—he had phoned Frau Kogel in the afternoon and left a message at the post office for Trudi saying he would be in Unterwald that evening—and when it became so late, she went upstairs to her room. But she still waited. If Johann said he was coming, he was coming. Near midnight, she heard the sound of a motor driving up the hill from Bad Aussee. She rushed from her bed to the window. But it wasn't Johann's jeep. It was a dark car, large. It didn't stop, didn't slow down at the village crossroads either, but kept traveling uphill. And then she heard the jeep. It rattled past. There was one man in it, but he didn't signal lightly on his horn as Johann would have done; he didn't even flick his lights. He just kept on at high speed and then took the road to the right when he came to the intersection—only a few farms up there, and then rough open country. Johann might take that direction to go climbing in daylight. There was a mountain towering above that road, the Sonnblick it was called; a cliff face, actually, that was good practice for scaling rock. But he would never go there at midnight. The jeep never came back. She waited and waited, but it never came.

"And the other car? You are sure it went up the hill?"

"Yes. I saw its taillights go right up the hill past the inn."

"Toward Finstersee?"

Trudi nodded. "In that direction. There are forests along that road. When the car reached the trees, I could no longer see its lights." She looked at his worried face. Surprised, she said, "I thought you would have been asking me about the box."

"I'll come to that," he promised her. "But is that all you can tell me about Johann?" And there was nothing much he could ask about the box, except her permission to carry it downstairs. And not much carrying could be done when he was expected to be a polite guest. Women were really astounding, he thought as he noticed Trudi's perfect hostess manner. But at least it kept her calm. He had been afraid of too much emotion when he had entered this room. Emotions were fine in the right place, at the right time; but danger and death couldn't be warded off by emotions. And you remember that, he warned himself. What happened to you out there, almost at the door of this house? He looked at Lynn, and his eyes softened. For a moment, they exchanged a hint of warm laughter, of recollection shared; of astonishment, excitement, complete euphoria. Hold on, hold on, he told himself. Later, later. Not now. He looked quickly back at Trudi, regained his thoughts.

"That's all I know," Trudi assured him.

"Well—about the box—" And what the hell do I say? May I take it? Do I march upstairs into your room and get it?

"I'm glad you were thinking of Johann," Trudi went on. "I was afraid that he would be forgotten. Once you got the box, perhaps he never would be found. You would not do that?"

"No."

She rose. "Come. But you must walk quietly. The stairs creak." She lifted the lamp that stood on the table and carried it toward the flight of wooden stairs that ran up one wall. "Please come, too," she told Lynn, dropping her low voice to a whisper as she glanced quickly at the door leading to the back of the house. The snoring had long since stopped; Frau Seidl was deep in sleep.

They climbed the stairs, lightly, carefully, and followed a narrow wooden passage to Trudi's room. She placed the lamp carefully on a small bureau, opened the massive chest that stood at the foot of her bed. She took out layers of linen, placing them in exact order on the plump eiderdown. "Now," she said, and pointed.

Mathison reached into the chest for a box wrapped in white cloth. It was cumbersome to lift out of its hiding place. He had to strain to keep its weight from settling too heavily on the floor as he put it slowly, silently down. He pulled off its winding sheet, and saw that he could grasp it more easily for its journey downstairs by two handles folded at its sides. The box was both locked and padlocked, a solid piece of work. One thing was certain, this was not the kind of container that a photographer would choose for his equipment. We've really got something here, he thought, and looked at Lynn. Perhaps she, too, had been prepared for disappointment, for her eyes were now wide with excitement.

Trudi was staring at the box with a mixture of dislike and distrust. She didn't move, as if she wondered whether she was doing the right thing. "It is very valuable, Johann said. Equipment that belonged to Herr Bryant. You will see that Frau Bryant gets it?"

Mathison looked at the pathetic, anxious, transparently honest face. "If she is alive," he said very quietly.

"*If?*"

Lynn glanced at him quickly.

Trudi said, "Have you heard something about Frau Bryant—something you have not told me?"

"I heard that the three men who took her away have been arrested. But there was no mention of Frau Bryant. That's what troubles me."

"You think she is dead? Is that what you think?"

"I don't know for certain. But there is a friend of mine waiting outside. He may have learned something more."

"But if she's dead," began Trudi, doubt and fear rising anew, "what do I do?"

"Let's get this box downstairs," Mathison said. "You want it out of your room, don't you?" Trudi nodded. She was close to tears again. "How on earth did Johann carry it up here?" he asked, trying to sound conversational, prosaic, undramatic, anything to calm Trudi. He lifted the box. It wasn't an impossible hoist for one man, just difficult to negotiate quietly on that narrow staircase.

"It was in a large rucksack." At least Trudi had stepped out of his way. Her voice, her movements were listless.

"You haven't kept that lying around, have you?" It could be dangerous.

"Johann took it."

And kept it, perhaps. Hence Johann? Well, we all make mistakes, Mathison thought gloomily. He listened to the sound of a car traveling downhill. There had been several in these last ten minutes.

"I'll go ahead and warn you when you come to the last steps," Lynn said. She had picked up the lamp and was already waiting for him in the passageway. "Come on, Trudi," she urged gently.

"Those cars?" he asked Trudi as he started down the staircase.

"The concert ended some time ago."

And what's Chuck thinking, outside there in the cold? Wondering if I've botched everything? Too damned slow about getting this box? And yet, how else? Mathison reached the foot of the staircase without any clatter. He needed a couple of deep breaths, though, after he lowered the box onto the floor. "I'll find my friend and bring him here. You can talk with him, Trudi." He picked up his windbreaker, moved quickly to the door, took out his pack of cigarettes.

"But I don't know this man," Trudi was saying sharply as Mathison left.

Lynn took charge. "Please trust us, Trudi. I heard Frau Bryant say she wanted to meet this man. He is a—a kind of detective. He was actually on his way to see Frau Bryant when she was kidnapped. She thought he could help her. With that box." And an ugly brute of a thing it is, she thought, looking down at it. "I don't know what is in it, but—"

"It's equipment."

"No. Not that."

"But Johann said—"

"Johann was mistaken." And that is being more than kind to Johann. "Trudi, Trudi—photographer's equipment couldn't have caused so many deaths."

"Many?" Trudi stared at the box as if it contained a nest of adders.

"I have heard of three." Richard Bryant, Eric Yates, Greta Freytag . . . "There may be others."

"Johann?" Trudi asked slowly, fearfully.

"Bill's friend outside, and all the men who are with him, will try to help Johann. I know that. Bill promised you."

Trudi kept looking at the box. "I hate it," she said with sudden vehemence. "There's a curse on it. Get them to take it away. Get them—" She broke off, listened, as she heard brakes screech on the road. "That was a car—stopping. Here."

"Two cars."

"Your friends?"

"I don't know." Lynn almost panicked. "Quick, Trudi," she said as she bent down and tugged at the box. "Give me a hand. Quick!"

Mathison had stepped out of the Seidl house, pulled on his windbreaker, and paused as he lit a cigarette and looked around him. The small front garden, enclosed by its neat waist-high wooden fence, was as quiet as the road that skirted it. So was the meadow to its side, and the small grouping of dark trees where Chuck said he would wait. No one around. The moonlight was half-strength and even more muted by the high wind-blown clouds. His eyes became accustomed to the night, and he walked quickly along the short path that led toward the meadow. He reached his car, parked in the shadows at the side of the house. From there, it was only a matter of sixty or seventy yards to the trees. Had Chuck left? Everything was so peaceful.

But Chuck was there, all right. So was friend Andrew. So were two men bundled up like a couple of local climbers. Chuck said quickly, "You saw the box? What's it like?"

"Locked and padlocked. Not equipment, I'd judge. Fairly heavy."

"Something like this one?" For a brief second, Chuck directed the beam of a shaded torch onto a box at his feet.

The surprise package? wondered Mathison. "Yours looks crummier," he said, much amused, "and a little larger." He bent and groped for the handles and hefted it. "Heavier, too. But not bad. What did you put in it? Bricks?"

"Give Chuck some credit for more artistry than that," Andrew said. "Hundreds of typed sheets, sodden through, not a word legible."

"A slow leak through the years?" Mathison laughed softly. Not bad, not bad at all.

"Come on, Bill," Chuck was saying, "you and I carry this back to the house. Fair exchange. Where's the real thing?"

"It's now in the kitchen, just behind the door."

"Good." He turned to talk to one of the climbers. "Hank, you get to our car, back it up to the meadow. Andrew, you and Chris can cover us from the road and keep an eye out for Bruno. He should be arriv—" He cut himself short, swung around to face the man who was approaching quietly, by way of the trees that edged the meadow, from the fields that lay at the back of the Seidl house.

"Felix Zauner," Andrew identified the man quickly. It must be. The figure was coming from the direction of the village, using the back fields as a short cut. "Yes, it's Zauner. And about time, too." I told him over half an hour ago to meet us down here, he thought with annoyance.

"Keep him with you, Andrew," Chuck said. "Come on, Bill. Let's start moving. Is Trudi expecting me?" He bent down to grip one handle of the box.

"Yes. I told her—" Mathison stopped, straightened up, looked in the direction of the road. Two cars were speeding down from the village. Chuck dropped his end of the box, too. They all looked, not even paying attention to Zauner, who slipped into the shadows around them and then stopped abruptly as he recognized Mathison.

The two cars drew up with a scream of brakes, one behind the other, directly in front of the Seidl house. From the first car, two men slid out quickly and ran up the short path through the garden, heading straight for the door. They did not knock. They shoved it open, vanished inside.

Lynn . . . Mathison broke out of cover and raced across the meadow, tugging the automatic free from his jacket pocket.

The box, thought Chuck, and started after him.

Andrew set off, too, only pausing to call over his shoulder to Hank and Chris. "Watch that second car!" Its engine had been kept running.

Zauner stopped brooding about Mathison, took a step after Andrew, struck his foot against something metallic. He grimaced at the quick stab of pain, stared down in amazement. He knelt and touched the object with his hand. "Get down to the road. Keep out of sight of the cars. Block them off if they start for Bad Aussee."

341

"But they'll be out of sight, too," Hank protested. There was a curve in that road, just at the last grouping of trees on the edge of the meadow. He knew. He had found it useful for parking Chuck's car.

"You'll see them all right if they make a dash for it."

"Are you staying here?"

"Someone has to." Zauner glanced down at the box.

"Then keep your eyes open. I recognized one of the men. They are Grell's friends. But how the hell did they learn about Trudi Seidl's house?"

"Get going!" Zauner told them with all his authority. He watched them move off, two quiet shadows merging with the ragged rim of trees, heading for the lower stretch of the Bad Aussee road. His face was like stone, his thoughts a raging torrent. So they did not tell me they had actually discovered the box, taken it, were even now waiting for transportation. No, that wasn't fair; he had only himself to blame, arriving too late to be told. Late because of Elissa, because of trying to find her at the inn to warn her there was some kind of alert down at the Seidl meadow. *Don't cheat*, she had warned him, and all his determination to help as little as possible had faded away. There was no choice left. ... At the inn, he hadn't been able to find Elissa. Or Grell, for that matter. Frau Hitz, busy clearing the dining room, could only say they had been discussing the lady's complaint about her room when she had last seen them in the hall. It couldn't be, he thought as he stared obliquely across the open meadow toward the two cars parked in their dark huddle in front of the Seidls' garden. It couldn't be. And yet, as that American agent had asked, *how the hell did they learn of Trudi Seidl's house?*

He drew a long deep breath. Hank and Chris were out of sight, must be at the road by this time. He checked in the direction of the house, too. (Mathison and Chuck had entered, Andrew was almost there.) His attention was jerked back to the cars; someone had just stepped from the driver's seat of the second one. Someone who must be alone, for the figure stood hesitating, only its head visible, watching Andrew disappear into the house, deciding perhaps to go after him and even the odds against the two Nazis inside. It wasn't Grell, that was certain. It wasn't any of his hunting friends— their height would have brought their shoulders up above the car's low roof. Yes, it could be ...

Zauner stepped out from the trees' shadows onto the meadow. He whistled softly. Then he raised both arms and signaled wide.

Mathison had entered the kitchen silently, automatic ready. Chuck came hard on his heels, revolver in hand, drawing himself instinctively close to the side of the door before he took the final step inside. They stopped abruptly, lowered their weapons, looked with amazement at the placid scene. The two men weren't there. Neither was the box lying behind the door. The two girls were sitting at the table, their heads turned toward the staircase. Trudi's hands were at her lips, her eyes wide. Lynn held a forkful of meat poised halfway between mouth and plate, as if she had been eating supper when the two strangers from the car had come bursting in and gone rushing upstairs. They were there now, moving around from room to room with cautious footsteps.

Trudi said, her voice hushed in disbelief, "They didn't stop, didn't speak. They knew just where to go."

"Ever seen them before?" Chuck asked quietly.

Trudi nodded. "They are from the inn."

Nazis. Mathison glanced at Chuck, then looked around for any sign of the box. Lynn came to life again. She laid the fork down, drew her legs aside as she lifted the short hem of the tablecloth and pointed underneath. She tried to smile, but her face was strained and exhausted.

"Okay, okay," Chuck said softly, and relaxed. He turned to Andrew who had just entered, put a finger to his lips. From overhead, there came a sharp curse, the voice of one telling the other to hold the light higher, here, here! And then the voice, rising in violent rage, "It's gone!" A wooden lid crashed shut. Footsteps were louder now, stumbling heavily in one last angry search. A bed was pulled across the floor, a door was smashed.

"Let's get them out of here," Chuck said. That first; then I dash for the trees, try to draw them to that other box. If they find it, that will shut them up for good. "Get out of range," he told the two girls, pointing to the back wall of the kitchen. "See what's happening on the road," he said to Andrew. He signed to Mathison to keep well to the side of the staircase. He raised his voice into a drillmaster's yell. "Come down here, you! Drop your weapons!"

There was complete silence. Then instant bedlam. From

outside came the roar of a car starting its way downhill. Overhead, a quick retreat from the staircase; the sound of a window being forced, glass breaking; a scramble of feet over a balcony; two heavy thuds at the side of the house. And at the back of the kitchen, a door was thrown open and a pink-cheeked woman in a flannel nightgown, two gray braids over her shoulders, a stick in her hands, was screaming for police.

Chuck signaled with a nod to Mathison. They both stepped outside. Andrew was there, keeping well to one side of the door, watching the scene on the road with cold amusement. The two Nazis, one limping now, were piling into their car, starting off downhill after the other one. It hadn't gone far, only to the end of the meadow edged by trees.

Andrew said, "There is one person in the lead car. A woman. I think it's Elissa."

"Working with the Nazis?" Mathison asked. He was incredulous. Just when could that have happened?

"One of those temporary pacts they go in for," Andrew said, "and I think she is about to break it."

The woman was out of the car, running toward the central clump of trees.

"She knows where to go," Chuck said thoughtfully.

"She ought to. A man signaled to her from that exact spot. He stepped back into the trees as soon as he glimpsed me. He didn't stay long enough to let me recognize him."

"Then let's get him. And make a show of protecting our possessions. Bill—someone has got to stay here, and you're it. Sorry. But Grell may come prowling around. Anything can happen now." Then he was sprinting after Andrew. Their two vague but discernible figures ran into a stretch of darkness and became nothing.

Mathison drew his back against the wall of the house, kept his head turned to the meadow on his right, put his trust in his senses to warn him of any approach from the left. The meadow was the action point. These two damned fools could get themselves killed, he thought. Did they think the Nazis would let them get anywhere near that box? And yet Chuck was right about making a show of protecting it; the Nazis might otherwise wonder why they could take the box so easily. But not too much show, he told Chuck silently. Or perhaps you are too eager to nail that traitor?

His eyes turned to the road down near the trees. The two

Nazis were out of their car, following the woman. She could run and she could dodge, Mathison noted; she was taking full advantage of the broken light with its strange patchwork of blacks and grays. She was already at the hiding place. He still couldn't identify her clearly.

Then quite suddenly the cloud that had drifted obligingly over the face of the moon lifted and thinned. It was as if a mild floodlight had been turned on the meadow. Chuck was there, caught right in the center; Andrew to one side. "Look out!" Mathison yelled as one of the running Nazis wheeled around, crouched, pointed his arm. Chuck dropped, lay still. Andrew veered, then fell on his face. The two quick shots sent tumbling echoes over the mountain slopes.

The door opened behind him. Lynn was running out. "Bill—"

"Stay back, stay back!" He kept his eyes on the meadow. The man who had fired was crouching there, watching Chuck and Andrew for any sign of movement. Beyond him, at the edge of the trees, the woman was pulling the box out of the shadows as if to make sure of what she had found. And then Mathison saw her face.

She had glanced up when she heard the shots. The quick lift of her head swung her long loose hair clear of her face. In the moonlight, there was no doubt: it was Elissa. Briefly, she stared at the house across the meadow. She recognized my voice, thought Mathison. That look is deliberate. So is that light laugh. Then her head bent once more over the box.

Mathison raised his automatic, steadied his arm, as the crouching man straightened his back and limped forward toward Chuck. I won't carry that distance, thought Mathison grimly, but I'll give him something else to think about. That's one job he doesn't finish. The man was taking aim at Chuck as Mathison squeezed his trigger, ran forward to get within better range for a second shot. He never fired it. Nor did the man, turning to face him, fire back.

From the edge of the meadow where Elissa was rising to her feet, there was a sharp explosion, a violent blast, a burst of raging flame. There was nothing left standing, neither Elissa nor the Nazi who had just reached her. The box was in fragments, nothing remaining except a small glowing heap at the bottom of a wide hole.

25

AS THE ECHOES OF THE EXPLOSION RUMBLED OVER THE HILLS, Lynn had run toward him. Mathison put his arm around her shoulders, and they stood together in silence as they looked across the meadow.

The Nazi was the first to move. He made a limping dash for his car, but several men were there now, and other cars from Bad Aussee. He gave up meekly enough, perhaps under shock.

Andrew rose stiffly to his feet and went over to help Chuck. So he had been hit, thought Mathison. Seriously? He watched Chuck being pulled to his feet. At least he could walk with Andrew's support. Then as one of the newcomers down at the road, a heavy-set man with blond hair and quick feet, ran toward Chuck and Andrew, Mathison remembered the Finstersee box. "Come on," he said to Lynn, and he led her back to the house. Trudi and her mother were in the garden, the door as wide open as Frau Seidl's mouth. This time, she wasn't shrieking.

And now, thought Mathison as he sat down at the table with Lynn opposite him and put one foot on the box, we have nothing to do but wait for Chuck and listen to Frau Seidl's stream of consciousness. It was pouring freely.

It started the moment she stepped back through the door, shivering in her nightdress. "God in heaven, did you hear that? Such an explosion. I thought the Nazis were back. Blasting the Sonnblick. We heard it all the way down at Bad Aussee. That's where they sent us, the people of the village, when they took over here. They made some of the men work for them. My husband had to supply the logs. But everything they built was blasted to bits. The Russians were just to the east, you see; and the Americans to the south. So the Nazis destroyed all the fortifications—because they couldn't get the big guns in place, not in time. Just as well they didn't. Or else there would have been fighting all over Unterwald and not a house left standing. My husband used to say—"

"The Sonnblick?" Lynn asked slowly. Where had she heard that word before? Tonight? She looked at Trudi. The mountain that was mostly a cliff face?

"The Sonnblick," Frau Seidl said, nodding vigorously. "They hollowed out its top for the big guns. It was a secret, but my husband knew what they were doing. So did his friends—the ones who had to haul the timber and the cement and the steel and the electric wires. The Nazis were working night and day. And then it was nothing at all, just explosions and explosions, and it was nothing at all."

Mathison was really listening now. "Heavy guns? Then the Nazis must have tunneled into the Sonnblick. It would be interesting to see some of these fortifications. Where do you enter?"

"There's no entrance left. It was all destroyed and then closed up. It is just a mountain again."

Trudi said, "Get dressed, Mutti. There are people on the road. Everyone in the village is coming here."

Frau Seidl became aware of her clothes. One hand went up to her face, and she blushed like a young girl as she turned toward her room, leaning heavily on her walking stick. At its door, she paused with a new thought. "Who were they?—Oh, yes, the terrorists. And their dynamite exploded. Poor souls." She stared blankly at Mathison. "But why did they keep dynamite on my meadow?" she asked, turning indignant. "We could all have been blown to pieces." She closed her door with a bang.

Terrorists and dynamite, Mathison thought: that would be the tale that would keep Unterwald talking for months. Was Frau Seidl's story about the Sonnblick as much of a myth? "Did the Nazis really take over the village?" he asked Trudi.

She nodded. "They put their troops in the houses. The inn was their headquarters." She spoke absent-mindedly, listening to the rising flood of excitement on the road. "They have forgotten about Johann. The search for him has stopped."

"No," Lynn said quickly. She looked at Mathison for support.

He nodded, watching the door. There were two or three men out there, talking quietly. It could be an informal conference between Chuck and Andrew and the Austrian they had been expecting—Bruno, wasn't that the name Chuck had mentioned? He rose, taking out his automatic once more, crossed over to the door and opened it. Hidden voices made him nervous tonight. But outside were Hank and

Chris and a couple of other capable types. "Just making sure," he told them.

"That's what we are doing," Hank said with a grin. "The others will soon be here." He nodded in the direction of three men coming slowly, a tight confidential bunch, along the garden path: Chuck, Andrew, and the man with light hair and broad shoulders. "All right, Bruno," Andrew was saying. "That just about takes care of everything."

Mathison stepped back inside. "We can all relax," he told the two anxious faces. "There are guards posted around the house. And Trudi, three men are just about to come in. Two of them you've already met; the third is their friend. So you can trust them all. They will see that the box reaches the proper hands." He looked at Lynn. "I'll get you down to Bad Aussee right away. You are practically asleep on your feet."

"I'm tired," she admitted, "but this isn't a night for sleeping. Besides, it's early—just half past ten." *And I'm not going to be packed off to bed, miles away, while he comes back here and I am left alone to lie and worry about him. I may not be able to help much, but I'm staying as long as he stays, even if I do fall asleep standing up.*

"I'm taking you down to Bad Aussee, Lynn," he said determinedly as the door opened and Andrew appeared.

"Just try and make it," Andrew said cheerfully. "We are stuck right here, all of us, until the police get the people off the road and meadow. Don't want too much gaping and gawking, do we?" He had a quick look under the table. "That's right, baby," he told the Finstersee box, "you stay there quietly until we can smuggle you out."

Chuck entered slowly. He had insisted on walking by himself, but he was glad to sit down at the table. Blood was spreading through the shoulder of his coat. He managed a grin for Mathison. "Thanks, Bill," he said very quietly. "At least I can now groan without having a bullet pumped into me." He glanced under the table. "Safe and sound?" He gave a long sigh of relief, and with Andrew's help began to slip off his coat. It took a little time.

Bruno came in at last, locked the door behind him, noted that the curtains were already tightly drawn, went straight for the table and looked underneath. The frown line on his brow cleared away. Until this moment perhaps, he had scarcely been able to believe that the Finstersee box was lying peacefully under Frau Seidl's table. A broad smile split his round, pink-cheeked face; his brown eyes shone as he studied them all. "Congratulations to everyone," he said in a soft, almost gentle voice.

"We still have some distance to go," Andrew reminded him as he began pulling off Chuck's heavy sweater.

"Just let anyone try to get that box away from us," Bruno said. He shook Mathison's hand with a hard grip; he spoke to Lynn; then switched into German for Trudi's benefit. All these politenesses over, he stood looking at Chuck. "And just how did you manage to get that?"

"Wasn't keeping my mind on my business."

Andrew said, "He was watching the trees to see where the man went—the one who signaled Elissa."

"He moved toward the road," Chuck said flatly. Of that, he was sure. Then he gave a yelp of pain as the sweater came away from his shoulder. He looked at Lynn, who was watching and suffering with him. "I told you I liked to complain. Would you mind taking over from this heavy-handed monster?"

If only I knew what to do, thought Lynn as she tried to ease off the shoulder of his shirt. She looked at Trudi for help. "I'll get my mother," said Trudi, and ran.

"Does her mother know about the box?" Bruno asked.

Mathison said, "No. And I don't think Trudi wants it mentioned."

"Do they understand English?"

"No."

"Good. Then we can talk in it. Except"—Bruno looked quizzically at Andrew—"when we are being polite." He was exceedingly polite for the next minute to Frau Seidl, whose complaints and astonishment were outmatched by her compassion for the wounded man who had taken refuge in her kitchen.

"Of course I know what to do," she told them impatiently. "Get away from this table. Trudi, you clear it! Heat some water! You stay with me, gnädiges Fräulein," she said to Lynn, and looked at the wound. "This isn't bad. I've seen worse. Oh, these terrorists ... Why do they have to go around shooting people? You would think the Nazis were back."

Andrew said, "I believe I know where to borrow some brandy." He unlocked the door, slipped into the night.

"Where is Zauner?" Chuck asked.

"He should be at the inn by this time, holding Grell and any friends for questioning. We can't move them, of course, until that crowd out there starts going back to bed." Bruno watched Frau Seidl closely. Had she understood any of that? No, he decided, and relaxed; but he had better rely on speed for extra safety. His words came out more quickly than ever. "He took six men with him. So don't look worried. Grell won't escape. He couldn't have had time to destroy anything either. Zauner is hoping for a nice little haul."

"Did he see the explosion?" And from where? Down on the road? Chuck's face was white and gaunt.

"Stop talking so much. I'll try to answer your questions without your having to ask them." He looked around at the door as it opened, but it was only Andrew returning with a flask of brandy and a neat little antiseptic package.

"Compliments of Chris," Andrew said with a grin. "He's the careful type."

Chuck took a swig of brandy. "Go on," he told Bruno.

"We all saw the explosion from the road—I had just arrived as the shooting started. Felix was as shocked as any of us. And bitter, too. He said, 'They did not even give her one minute.' That's all I heard as I went running over to you. I didn't see him again until just after you had entered this house. He had his plans all ready for the inn. They sounded good to me. So he left at once. Sent you his best wishes."

Chuck looked down at Frau Seidl's strong hands. Lynn had lit a cigarette for him. The women at least seemed to know what they were doing.

"They did not even give her one minute," Andrew repeated slowly. "Meaning? That Felix believes she was given a device to destroy the box but that it was timed to get her, too?" He shook his head. "Pretty drastic, even if she was an agent out of control."

"Far out," Chuck said, and winced, and then nodded reassuringly for Frau Seidl. It mattered little now whether the device had been faulty or ruthlessly accurate. Zauner was what interested him. "Did he speak of anything else before he left for the inn?"

"Only to ask briefly about Anna Bryant's death."

Lynn, opening the package of penicillin, looked up quickly. "Please!" said Frau Seidl sharply, and Lynn's attention was whipped back.

Mathison asked the question for her. "How did Anna die?"

"Suicide. Nothing is quite clear about it. We know what happened. But we can't understand why. Felix took the news badly. He said something about Vienna, something that happened long ago to Anna. He didn't have time to explain, and perhaps he will never explain. But there was no doubt that whatever he knew about Anna made her death seem twice as bad. He is in an ugly mood. So you can relax, Chuck. Grell won't get away. Oh, I agree with you. Felix didn't watch Elissa carefully enough. She outwitted him, and he is chagrined about that." So am I, Bruno's tight voice seemed to say. But he wasn't criticizing one of his own in front of foreigners.

"He didn't do so badly with her," Andrew said. "He did keep her occupied for some time before he brought her back to the inn. At least she wasn't in our way for most of the evening."

"Kept her occupied?" Bruno asked sharply.

"Presumably talking. I saw her arrive at the inn. So, by my watch, I don't think she had much more than half an hour to get those Nazis moving."

Mathison looked at Andrew quickly. Half an hour? Half an hour, not much more ... Mathison's thoughts began racing.

"She made good use of it," Chuck said. He looked at Bruno. "How is the man you captured on the meadow? Singing?" He could tell us a lot, save all this discussion.

"Not yet. He knows that if he starts answering one question, he may tell more than he intends. He will keep silent until we find some piece of information that really will scare him into talking."

Mathison said very quietly, "And how did they manage to get Johann to talk about the Finstersee box? They knew exactly where to look for it—upstairs, in this house. Only Johann could tell them that. So what threat did they use? What made him break down so quickly?" Mathison looked across the room at Trudi, who had stared at him the minute he had spoken Johann's name. She understood that, all right, even if she didn't understand English. "Did they threaten to take Trudi prisoner, too?"

"That's only supposition," Andrew said. "But it's a possibility, of course. It's within their pattern."

Mathison said, "I'm not starting to argue a case about how they learned Trudi and Johann were engaged, or who passed them the word, or why. The point I'm trying to make is that they got Johann talking in a hurry. Everything moved too damned fast. They must have been able to reach Johann in a matter of minutes, once they knew what threat to apply. It certainly loosened his tongue. And again within minutes, the men at the inn had the information they wanted. And acted upon it. Immediately." He glanced at Andrew. "Half an hour, you said?"

"Not much more." Andrew was definitely impressed. "What you're saying is that their speed is the clue to where Johann has been hidden. I agree. He cannot be too far away."

"Except," Bruno said, "he is not in any house or building in the village. He is not in any hut or shack in the woods near the village. That has all been searched. So the hiding place cannot be reached in a matter of minutes. Not on foot, certainly. Not by car either—all roads are being checked."

"There couldn't have been any telephone message," Andrew said. "You have the inn's line tapped, haven't you?"

Bruno nodded. "We have also been listening for any radio transmissions—Grell is bound to have some kind of installation hidden there, or else he could never have functioned properly. We have heard nothing." He looked at Mathison sadly. "You see, Mr. Mathison?"

"Yet they did reach Johann. Quickly. And once his guards knew what threat to apply—Trudi seized, and brought to the place where they are working on Johann, to share his—" Mathison glanced at Lynn, who was listening even if she seemed to be concentrating only on Chuck's arm—"share his experiences," he ended lamely, giving up on the syntax of that sentence, too. But his meaning was clear enough. "He talked, almost at once. Why? Because of the feeling it was useless to hold out? Yet that hadn't made him talk before, had it? But what if he knew that the threat was immediate—that it would not take long to be put in action? You don't lose much time debating what you are going to do if you know that the girl is not far away."

"An interesting point. That kind of threat could get him to talk." Bruno's tone was polite but impatient. "The question still remains: where is he?"

Mathison risked it. "In a cave, perhaps. Up on a mountain

overlooking Unterwald, with some kind of direct communication between the cave and the inn."

They were all staring at him. Bruno's impatience was gone, though. "We are starting a search of the mountains around here at dawn, as soon as there is enough light."

"Dawn may be too late for Johann." And there were a hell of a lot of mountains around here. "What about trying the Sonnblick tonight?"

Bruno took a map from his inside pocket, spread it over the free end of the table. "Why the Sonnblick?"

"You know its history."

"Yes. But the Nazi fortifications were destroyed, sealed off." Bruno pointed to a heavily shaded area on the map. "There it is. It forms the south shore of Finstersee—a steep slope, heavily wooded, pitching into the lake. On its other side, there is a complete drop of sheer cliffs. That is where the Germans intended to conceal their big guns. They made an interior gallery, I heard, all through the top of the mountain to overlook the valley south of it."

"And their HQ was at the inn."

"I'm following you," Bruno said with a small smile. There would certainly have been communications between HQ and fortifications. Something underground, possibly. Overhead lines were too vulnerable in any shelling; and radio contact twenty-odd years ago was not always clearly audible in any emergency. The Germans had had sappers working up there on the fortifications. Bruno frowned. "This is still all in the world of speculation. It's a neat guess, but—"

"Why don't you get Trudi to tell you about the car and the jeep?" Mathison looked at Trudi, whose head kept bobbing up every time Johann's name had been mentioned, and nodded to her reassuringly. "Don't worry," he said in German. He watched Frau Seidl clearing the bowl of water and the scraps of linen away from the table. "Why don't you have a little talk with this gentleman? And keep it short, Trudi."

"About what?" She was frightened. She watched her mother moving with her slow hobbled step into her bedroom.

"About the cars, and the direction they took last night."

Chuck leaned back in his chair. It could have been a half-flask of brandy inside him, or the fact that his wound was clean and adequately bandaged, but he exchanged a small glance with Lynn and winked. Andrew joined Bruno and Trudi. Mathison went back to studying the map. Lynn watched him. I know what he is going to do, she thought, and her heart sank. Chuck touched her hand. "If you just help me over to that chair near the fire—" That would take her mind off the map, at least.

"It's a possibility," Bruno said, leaving Trudi. "Speculative, of course. But certainly a possibility."

"It's the only one we've got," Andrew said. "I think I'll get up to the inn." He remembered the Finstersee box. "No I don't."

"We'll let Zauner handle this." Bruno was pulling out his favorite cigar case from his pocket, adjusting a small aerial.

Mathison had picked up his windbreaker. He lifted the map. "Mind if I take this?" He crossed over to Lynn. "It won't be too long—a couple of hours. Zauner is bound to know all the paths on the north side of the Sonnblick. If there is any entrance at all, that's the place where it will be. I don't see the Nazis swinging themselves up the cliff face like a bunch of monks on Mount Athos."

"The north side falls into the lake," Lynn said, eyes filled with fear.

"But I won't." He kissed her, quickly but frankly, and then looked challengingly at Chuck.

"I said nothing." And damn this throbbing arm. I'd like to see how Zauner handles this operation myself, Chuck thought. He turned his attention to Lynn. "Zauner's men include some of the best guides among these mountains. You know, you have the prettiest hair. I kept watching it when old Mother Seidl was poking and probing." The front door shut behind Mathison. His eyes closed. He heard her exclaim, felt her fingers search for his pulse. "You're a quick learner," he said almost inaudibly. Like Mathison, he thought, and drifted off into unconsciousness.

As Mathison stepped into the cool night, zipping his jacket to the neck, the men guarding the door of the Seidl house stopped their quiet talk, glanced at him inquiringly. "I need someone to get me to the inn as fast as possible," he told Hank. "Can you spare anyone?"

"If you speak German—"

"Enough."

"Then take Karl. He's from Bad Aussee. Knows all the country around here."

Mathison's eyes picked out the tall powerful figure of the

policeman whom he had last seen guarding the telephone at the post office. "Come on, Karl. What's the quickest way to the inn?" The crowd clustered thick on the road. There was an ambulance there, too, and some firemen beating through the underbrush on the far side of the meadow. The police had cleared it of people, roped off the burned patch, lit flares to help get the bodies removed.

"Over the fields to the back of the post office. Then across the village street—"

"Okay, okay. Let's move."

Karl disappeared at a steady run around the corner of the house. Mathison caught up, kept pace, letting Karl choose the way over the rough ground, skirting apple trees, manure heaps, log piles, neat fences, and windows now darkened.

26

"YOU WERE QUICK," FELIX ZAUNER SAID, MEETING MATHISON in the hall of the inn. "I've just finished talking with Bruno. Now what's this idea of yours?" He looked at Karl. "No need for you to—"

"He can stay," Mathison said. Karl not only knew the countryside, but he was a friend of Johann's, too, and a climber in his free time. Karl was comforting to have around. What had seemed stolid stupidity down at the post office when he had kept watch over the telephone had been only boredom. And Karl was no longer bored. He smelled action. Mathison spread Bruno's map on the cramped surface of the reception desk. "How much did Bruno tell you?"

"Not too much. He thought it safer if you gave me the information face to face." Zauner seemed more of his old self, brisk and capable. He listened to Mathison's idea with pursed lips. "Not many people try climbing the Sonnblick along that north side facing the lake. It's too tricky for amateurs, and too dull, with all those trees on it, for the professionals. The close timber defeats the hunters, too, and the ground slopes dangerously—there's no even stance for them. So it isn't a popular place. Deserted mostly. At one time, there were three entrances to the Sonnblick, up near its crest but some distance along the lake. The Nazis made use of these. But at the end they dynamited them. You would have to be the size of a hare to squeeze through the rubble they left."

"Could there have been a fourth entrance, nearer the Finstersee road, that was kept secret?"

"With the Nazis, there could always be anything." Zauner frowned down at the map. "But unless we know exactly where we are heading, we had better wait until the first light breaks. Even then it might be difficult, with early-morning mist."

"At least we can be sure of clear weather tonight."

"Eager, aren't you? And Johann wasn't even your friend." Zauner shook his head, studied Mathison's face curiously.

"I just think we owe Anna Bryant her brother's life. That's the least we can do for her."

Felix Zauner did not argue with that. His face tightened. He nodded.

"Where's Grell?" The inn seemed deserted except for one white-haired woman who waited nervously in the empty dining room.

"We are keeping him out of sight in his own room. The explosion drew everyone out of the Weinstüberl, of course. We'll try to keep them from getting back in, but that may take more men than I have."

"How many?"

"Six altogether besides myself. Three are searching the upstairs rooms, two are on guard outside as you saw, and one is keeping a pistol pointed at Grell. We have got him hand-cuffed to a chair. Excessive? But I'd rather he couldn't communicate with any of his friends, not even by lighting a cigarette at his window."

"He was alone?"

"Yes. Frau Hitz"—he nodded toward the dining room—"tells me there was another man with him, but he left after the big blast. No doubt he is down on the road, trying to find out what happened before he reports back here."

So Grell did not yet know what had happened. He couldn't even have guessed. "I suppose as long as he thinks there is a chance that the Finstersee box was taken by his men, he will sit tight and wait?"

"Absolute innocence. Very aggrieved. Threatening to sue everyone in sight."

"And you haven't told him anything?"

Zauner shook his head.

"What's the present charge against him?"

"Aiding terrorists."

"True in its way." To Mathison's surprise, he was getting along with Zauner a hundred times better than he had expected.

"Come and meet our genial host," Zauner said. "Say nothing, though. Let me make the mistakes." He noticed Mathison's expression. "Another idea?"

"Just a suggestion."

"Oh?"

"If Johann is alive—" Mathison hesitated, aware of the friendly yet mocking eyes.

"I think we can assume he is. Final orders for his death would come from Grell. He would be foolish to give them until he makes sure that Johann's information about the box's hiding place was accurate. If it were a false lead, he would need Johann alive to get the final truth. Which doesn't lessen Johann's ordeal either now or in the immediate future. So if you do have a suggestion, be quick with it, Mr. Mathison. But remember one thing: Grell is not the type to talk. Physical pain won't persuade him."

"I was thinking of shock treatment. The kind he used to jolt information out of Johann, who is also not the talking type."

"Shock treatment?"

"Throw the Sonnblick at him."

"Throw—what?"

"Charge him with knowing that two terrorists are holding Johann hostage in the Sonnblick. Tell him if he is connected with them, he can at least dissociate himself from their violence by revealing the quickest path to its entrance." Then as Zauner considered the idea, Mathison added tactfully, "Perhaps you could do better than that—just as long as it is something to force the truth out of him. All he wants is the Finstersee box. He would sacrifice two men for it."

Zauner nodded. His eyes brightened. "It is only an assumption about the Sonnblick, of course. But a bluff might work. I like your idea. And perhaps I could add a little factual realism to it. Before we put him in his room, I searched quickly and found what I was looking for." He gave an unexpected smile in the direction of Frau Hitz, that unlikely ally, who was now hovering nervously in the background, torn between curiosity at what was happening here and speculation about the explosion down in the village. She had never been allowed to touch that desk or see it unlocked, bless her insulted feelings and indignant tongue. "Let no one into Herr Grell's room," he told Karl. "No one. And if anyone insists, knock him out and tie him up. No one enters." Isolation and shock treatment, he thought as he beckoned Mathison to follow—that might just turn the scales.

It was a comfortable room they entered, but untidy, as if it were rarely straightened thoroughly. There was a large eiderdown-covered bed, roughly made; a huge wardrobe, several chairs, knick-knacks on tables, soft lights, a window tightly shuttered; and a big old-fashioned desk, wide and deep and roll-topped. The place, full enough with furniture and mementos, was positively crammed with men added. August Grell, his gray hair ruffled, face choleric, sat in the corner near the desk with his hands secured behind the back of his chair. A youngish man in rough sweater and knicker-bockers dangled gray-stockinged legs and climbing boots over the edge of the high bed, but the revolver he held balanced on his knee did not look negligent at all. Zauner dropped into the chair that stood in front of the desk, pulling it around slightly to face Grell. Mathison decided to lean against the door just in case Karl did not manage to dissuade any intruder from crashing his way in.

Grell looked at them with contempt. "When does this indignity end?" he demanded.

"In two or three minutes, I hope." Zauner's voice was as casual as his manner. But he wasted no time either. "We know that the two terrorists have taken a hostage. They are keeping him prisoner in the Sonnblick. That is where you told them to hide, isn't it? The Sonnblick?"

Grell was speechless for a few moments. "Ridiculous," he burst out. "Why should I help any terrorists?"

"Your sympathy is naturally with them. You come from the South Tyrol, do you not? But sympathy and ideals are one thing, Herr Grell; violence and cruelty are quite another. Surely, you could not ally yourself with such actions?"

"There is nothing inside the Sonnblick. It is sealed up tight."

"How do you know that?"

"Well—I heard—I assumed—"

358

"You assumed we did not know about the remaining entrance. Stop protecting the terrorists. Or are you more deeply allied with them than I thought? Let me see." Zauner took out a bunch of keys, selected one that unlocked the desk. He rolled it open. "Seems very shallow for such depths, doesn't it?" He tapped the array of pigeonholes. "Really, Herr Grell, you are twenty years behind the times. There are simpler ways of keeping one's secrets nowadays."

Mathison saw Grell's face change from bluster to alarm. For a brief second only. He was in control again as he said quickly, "Are you sure these terrorists are holding a man?"

"Quite sure." Zauner turned away from the desk with regret. It would have given him much pleasure to lift that screen of pigeonholes right out and pick up the interesting objects that lay behind it. Later, he thought, that can come later. First, let him talk. "You never realized that, of course."

"Of course not. I gave them help, yes. As you said, we are of one blood. I cannot bear to see men hunted like animals."

"Not even if they are dangerous animals?"

"I did not know they had committed any crime. I told them of—of the room. Up in the Sonnblick. I had stumbled on it one day when I was out shooting. It is really a cave. Someone must have made it habitable in the old days. It is adequate shelter. No more."

"How do we get there? I presume the path isn't too difficult, if they used it in the dark."

"It is just a short stretch up through the woods beyond the picnic ground at the lake. You follow the beeches, then climb to your right through the fir trees. Their tops cover the door of the room. It seems a part of the rock."

"Is the path clear?"

"Through the beech trees, yes. Then every fifth tree after that has had its lowest branch cut off at an oblique angle." He looked at Zauner with puzzled innocence. "I suppose that was to help find the way when the mist came over the mountain?"

"I suppose so." Zauner toyed with the roll-top, easing it up and down. "Why don't you come along with us? Show us the way. Shout to the two terrorists to come out, give themselves up. They would listen to you. That might save their lives."

"Herr Zauner, I'm exhausted. I would only slow you up. I

359

don't feel well. If I may, I would like to rest in my room. I've told you all I know."

Mathison said, "Is there no way you can talk with these men from here? That would be quickest of all." Zauner was looking at him, almost as if he was saying, "Careful, careful! Let me handle this." So Mathison fell silent.

Grell's handsome face, frank and honest, was completely mystified. "But how could I do that? Using what? There are few telephones in Unterwald, and none leading into the mountains."

He's lying, Mathison thought. Either that or I'm too damned set on my own theories. And we've been too slow; the first moments of shock are over. He now thinks he can out-talk anyone.

Zauner turned to the desk, picked off the screen of pigeon-holes, reached deep into the compartment they had hidden. "What about using this, Herr Grell?" He held out a field telephone. "It's twenty years behind the times, just like you. But it is usable. Like you."

Grell's face went white. "But that is not mine. I admit South Tyrol nationalists have established one of their head-quarters at this inn. That is their equipment inside the desk. I know nothing about it."

"You are guilty, however, of hiding illegal activities. How long do you wish to spend in jail, Herr Grell? Ten years, and you won't be much use to anyone." Zauner held out the field telephone. "If you are as innocent as you say, use this. Talk to the men in the Sonnblick. Give them no reasons, no explanations. Tell them three things, and three things only. An emergency meeting has been called at the inn. They must come at once to attend it. They will leave the prisoner alive." Zauner paused. "No more than that. No less. If you say anything else, Fritz will blow out your brains."

Fritz nodded, raised the revolver.

"I need my hands free," said Grell.

"You don't speak with your hands." Zauner unwound the long cord attached to the field telephone and brought the instrument to the corner. He unhooked the receiver, signaled, listened, signaled again, then held it in position at Grell's face. He nodded abruptly. Grell began repeating the instructions. But he spoke, Mathison noted, in sharp clear German. His soft slurred dialect words had vanished.

Zauner was ready. As Grell's last words ended, he clamped

down the receiver, coiled the cord neatly back into place, walked back with the telephone to the desk. He replaced it, replaced the pigeonhole screen too. Later, he thought expectantly, later. That equipment in there will be worth examining, cataloguing, photographing. The report I'll turn in to Vienna will re-establish my position. Thank God, I can do something honest and normal again. Then he frowned as he rolled down the top of the desk and locked it. How long will I be allowed to function without interference, he wondered. Elissa is dead, but who follows Elissa? Perhaps no one? Not for some time at least. Not until they need me, not until I am promoted. They won't draw much attention to me in the next year or so. They must know that Elissa endangered me this week. I was almost exposed. So perhaps I will be given some time, time to think and find a way out, time to defeat them as surely as I have defeated this Nazi. Zauner pocketed his keys and looked over at the man in the corner. "Fritz, keep a very close watch over this customer. Allow him no liberties."

"Do you mean to keep me handcuffed like this?" Grell was outraged.

"Until we know the men have obeyed your instructions. Now where is the key to the door of Johann Kronsteiner's prison?"

"In my pocket. The right-hand one," Grell added quickly.

Zauner emptied both pockets of Grell's excellent dark-gray suit with its handsome green collar and facings, searched through waistcoat and trouser pockets as well, threw their contents on the bed. "We examine that later," he told Fritz. "But now, you watch him. That's all you do; watch." He picked up Grell's keys, asked him curtly, "Which one?"

"The longest."

Zauner turned abruptly on his heel. As Mathison followed him out of the room, Grell's head sank on his chest. He had stopped straining against the chair. His face was ashen, expressionless.

"Yet," said Mathison as they reached the reception desk in the hall, "I have the feeling he hasn't given up. He is still hoping for some way out."

Zauner half smiled. "I removed it, I think." He opened his fist. On his palm lay a small capsule of white powder. He slipped it into his pocket, shouted upstairs, brought his men down at a run. Two of them he posted with the guards already outside, sent the third to keep watch at the Finstersee

361

road and give warning as soon as Grell's friends approached. Then he made quick contact with Bruno, a brief report, a request for more men immediately. And at last he turned to Karl. "We won't wait for them. You and I will go ahead, leave them to follow. But we can't risk the road to Finstersee. Two of Grell's men will be using it—they are on their way to the inn, from the Sonnblick, and they don't know this district as well as we do. Any ideas for the quickest short cut through the woods to let us reach the picnic ground near the lake?"

"There's a foresters' path through the trees. Not bad. Out of sight of the road, too. Dark, but—" Karl produced a hooded flashlight.

"Could you use an extra hand?" Mathison asked.

"What do you know of mountain country?"

"I used to climb. I still ski."

"Come along."

"The old girl has left," Mathison said as he looked at the empty dining room, and then followed Zauner and Karl outside.

"The scene of the explosion has more attractions, I suppose."

"Grim business."

"Yes." And it might have been I who had to fix that padlock, thought Zauner. Ten minutes, they had told Elissa. They hadn't given her even one. . . . He looked at Mathison and Karl. They had been zipping and buttoning up tight against the night air just as he was doing. "Your eyes accustomed now? Good. And keep quiet. Karl—you first."

They slipped around the corner of the inn, started climbing through its back meadow. Quickly, they crossed the Finstersee road, a narrow track, unpaved, and headed into a forest. At first, it was dense. The moonlight vanished, only to filter through occasional breaks in the rows of trees. Mathison kept his eyes on Karl's back, a solid mass of blackness scarcely visible. Whenever it disappeared from sight entirely, he would put a hand out and reach for Karl's shoulder. He stopped worrying about his feet, but just put one down in front of the other. Wherever Karl could step, so could he. But soon this phase was over. The trees thinned out, dark spikes bathed in soft moonlight. Their pace increased to a quick walk.

Suddenly, Zauner's hushed voice said, "Stop!"

They paused. Mathison took some deep breaths, unzipped the top of his jacket. It was warm in the shelter of the forest. Zauner pointed to his left, where the road cut down to Unterwald from the lake. Through the clear air, they heard voices. A man stumbled over a stone and cursed. A laugh, abruptly hushed. Footsteps grew fainter, until they became lost in the silence.

Zauner said, "So they have obeyed orders. Now we can risk some speed." He set off at a steady run.

The thin figure of Frau Hitz, swollen round with her heavy clothes, came hurrying down the road to the Seidl house. The crowd began just below the house, stretched all down the side of the meadow. Oh dear, she thought, what could have happened? And there was I stuck in the inn, not knowing what to do, no one telling me anything. Her sharp eyes saw the man at the edge of the first group of people. Herr Kraus it was, who had been having dinner with Herr Grell that evening, everything so quiet and peaceful until that woman began complaining about her room. Then the others had been called into Herr Grell's office, and after that—well, she couldn't keep count of the comings and goings. Herr Kraus had stayed with Herr Grell, and that was natural; Herr Kraus was coming to help manage the inn, taking Anton Grell's place. Imagine that young Anton leaving his father and such a good business to go back to the South Tyrol for the sake of a girl, did you ever hear such nonsense? Then there had been that explosion, such a noise, she had dropped two glasses and a carafe of wine. And Herr Kraus had gone running out with all the people in the Weinstüberl to see what was wrong.

"What happened, Herr Kraus?" She tugged gently at his sleeve. He startled her by the way he swung around on her. He stared at her. "What happened?" she asked again.

He recognized her at last—the old woman who worked up at the inn. "I don't know." And he didn't know. There was talk around him of terrorists, of a cache of dynamite blown to pieces, four people killed, five wounded. There had been shots, a volley of shots, and they had set off the dynamite. Talk, talk, and his questions had got him nowhere. "The police won't let anyone onto the meadow." He turned to leave, looking for the last time at the Seidl house. It was well guarded. He could not guess what was going on there either.

"My sister's meadow?" Frau Hitz was all alarm.

"Your sister's?" He stopped. He looked again at the Seidl house. "Then she can tell you what happened."

"I'll ask her. But first I want to see for myself—"

"There is nothing to see."

"She'll keep me talking and—"

"Don't let her keep you. I'd like to hear what has happened, too."

"Yes, Herr Kraus," she said, hearing the voice of her future boss. She retraced her steps to the front path, approached the door. A man stepped in front of her, eyed her silently. It was one of those policemen wearing ordinary clothes who had been in and out of the inn several times tonight. "I'm just going to see my sister," she told him.

"Sorry. There is a wounded policeman in there. No one can enter now."

"But—"

"Orders. Sorry. The man is very ill."

"Dying? Oh dear . . ." She turned away, then looked back. "What *did* happen?"

"People are talking about dynamite. You are from the inn, aren't you?"

"I work there," she said nervously, and retreated. At first, she thought Herr Kraus hadn't waited, after all. But as she made her way toward the meadow through the cluster of people, her arm was grasped. "Just a policeman from Bad Aussee," she said incoherently. "He has been wounded. He is dying. So I couldn't get into the house. The policeman on duty said it was dynamite."

Herr Kraus left her so quickly that she gasped again. She couldn't even see where he had gone. Probably standing down there near the ambulance; that's where the best view would be. She hurried on. In my sister's meadow, she thought again; isn't that just like the Seidls' luck? Always the center of attention, that's what they like to be.

Kraus circled around, came back to the road, decided he had better get back to the inn and report possible disaster to Grell. There was no sign of the Lang woman or of the two men who had gone with her. Their cars had been parked near the edge of the meadow when he first arrived down there, but they had driven off to Bad Aussee before he could manage to reach them and find out who actually was inside them. The Lang woman must have betrayed us, he thought bitterly. We never should have believed her or her bargains.

"A fair bargain," she had said. "Our interests coincide. You want the Finstersee box. We don't want the West to have it. I know how you can get its hiding place out of Johann Kronsteiner—quickly, simply. And in exchange for my help, you must agree to let me see that box, identify it for my report to my government. That is all. The box is yours once I've checked it. As long as you keep it out of Western hands, we shall be satisfied."

Satisfied . . . And when I laughed at that, and asked why she did not want the box for her own government, she had her answer for that, too. "My agents are not yet in position here. I have only one man in Unterwald who might help me. So I have no choice but to come to you. Better that than let the West take the Finstersee box. Besides, you know very well that we already have the duplicate file of names. You lost that one from the Czechoslovakian lake. Do you want to lose Finstersee, too?"

And Grell had listened to her. Perhaps because of her frankness. Perhaps because of her warning about enemy agents pouring into the village—she had been factual about them: Andrew, a photographer; Chuck, a climber; Bruno, a journalist, and all their supporting operatives. Perhaps because there had been no time for argument. It had been a take-it-or-leave-it proposal. And we took it, Kraus thought in rising anger, even I took it. A fair bargain.

He had reached the intersection, was passing the schoolhouse at the corner. The inn was in sight. He stared, stopped abruptly, stepped into the deepest patch of shadow. The inn was all lit up. It was empty, and yet every light seemed to have been turned on. That old woman Hitz would never have left the inn if there had been even one customer remaining there to hand out a tip. The place was empty except for Grell, and Grell was a man who turned out unneeded lights.

Quietly, Kraus stepped closer to the schoolhouse wall and made his way around to the side where he could have the clearest view of the inn. There he stood and watched. In the next ten minutes, he had counted four men altogether; two moving unobtrusively around the back of the inn, two patrolling its front with equal care. Guarding it. As he tried to see any sign of Grell at the lighted windows—Grell's own room had been shuttered, he noticed—six more men crossed the village street from the rear of the post office, moving carefully, two at a time, and headed up over the meadow toward the inn. Three of them joined the hidden patrol. Three moved inside. The inn was not just being guarded; it was being occupied.

Or perhaps Grell had escaped.

Or perhaps he had been surprised.

Only one thing was certain: the woman Lang had at least spoken the truth when she had said there was an army of agents pouring into the village, an army of agents moving with dangerous speed.

He recovered his wits. So what to do? Roads out of Unterwald would be blocked, no cars would leave unchecked, no man on foot. The lower slopes of the hills, the valleys, the villages would be watched. The easy way out was impossible—too vulnerable. Then over the mountains to the east? And after that, strike north? With no map, no compass, no rope, no food, only a revolver in his pocket? The difficult way out was impossible, too, for a man alone. No, not alone. There were still two others. They must be warned. They had climbing equipment and food. Three could make it over the mountains.

And Grell?

Kraus turned away. He would have to circle widely, carefully, to reach the forest on the slope of the Sonnblick.

27

THE LAKE WAS A NARROW STRETCH OF GLASSY CALM RIPPLED by powerful currents that snaked down its spine, shining coldly black under the faint moon. Bill Mathison halted to look down at it. The mountains guarded it so closely that their steep slopes and precipices seemed to keep plunging on, far beneath that dark surface. Only the meadow below him was the lake's one touch of kindness, with a lonely picnic table adding its innocence to the silvered grass. But even there the deep waters pressed menacingly close.

"Not far now," Felix Zauner said, urging him on. Up above them—for the climb was now steep—Karl was finding the last of the blazed trees with his flashlight, and moving quickly. The path was better marked than they had hoped.

Zauner was hurrying ahead, nervous, excited, ready to be jubilant.

"How did Bryant manage it?" Mathison asked in wonder. One man alone. "How the hell did he do it?"

"He did it. You saw the proof tonight, when that box blew up," Zauner said over his shoulder.

"Proof?" What is he talking about? Mathison wondered and tried to catch up.

"Keep behind," Zauner told him. "There's only room for one on this path. Careful, now. One slip and you'd be down those crags."

"The trees would stop me, thank God." It would be a cold and deadly plunge into that lake otherwise. "You know, the box that blew up wasn't—" His heel slipped on one of the large stones embedded between the roots of the trees. Better stop talking, he decided, and concentrate on your footwork. Karl was fortunately being generous with his light. He'd flash it back briefly along the path once he stopped at a marked tree. Since they had heard Grell's two men moving obediently down toward the inn, they had more freedom to move. And talk.

Zauner had seemed to be riding on a wave of mounting exultation. He had been cautious enough to keep his voice to a low murmur, but the short sentences, the quickly related memories, kept coming out. Of Grell: "Did you hear his accent change? He is used to command, that one. He's a German Nazi, too. SS. You were too young to know much about that. I fought his kind all through the war. Yes, this is like old times." Of Grell's men: "They'll follow orders, right to the last letter. No problem there." Of Johann: "He joined my resistance group. Made his way out of Vienna, just a kid of fifteen or so. We raided, and ambushed, and ran; and raided again, all the way down to the Italian border. He was a good courier. Never got caught." Of Grell again: "How do I know he belonged to the SS? Remember that large wardrobe in his room? He had an old coat at the back of it. Insignia cut off. But unmistakable cut and color." Of Grell once again: "He reminds me of one of their colonels I caught. Important man. We were given orders to take him south, hand him over to the Americans for questioning. It was late in the war. . . . My one failure," he added softly, almost inaudibly.

"How?" Mathison had asked.

"We were ambushed ourselves. My men killed. I was left for dead. He escaped."

"Well, one failure—"

"A big one," Zauner had said slowly. He fell abruptly silent. Then they had come to the lake, passed around the meadow, started the climb through the forested mountainside to the crest of the Sonnblick.

Zauner stopped, pointed to Karl's brief signal just ahead of them. It seemed to come from the tops of the trees themselves.

"How the hell did he get up there?" Mathison asked. The answer to that came as he reached the trees themselves. They were backed up against a cliff. Karl shaded the beam of his flashlight but kept it aimed steadily down at the few steps, cut out of the rock, that led to the small natural-looking platform on which he stood. His left shoulder was almost touching what seemed a dark crevice. As he directed the light on it, they could see a door, narrow, small, built of rough timbers to blend with the trunks of the trees that screened it.

There was no talk now. They looked at the door, they looked at each other. There was only one question in their minds as Karl's flashlight found the lock and Zauner plunged the long key into it. Karl pushed the door open. It was dark inside, and completely silent. They looked at each other again and entered.

Johann was lying stretched out on the stone floor against one rough-hewn wall. His eyes were closed, his body scarred and half-naked. If he was alive, he had not heard them. He lay unmoving.

"Find the lights; they must have lights," Zauner said in a tight hard voice that sent Karl searching around the small room with blundering haste.

Johann's eyes opened. He stared at Zauner. "I thought they were coming back. I thought it was—"

"Don't talk," Zauner told him, touched his wrist to feel the strength of his pulse. There was a scream of pain. Zauner let the wrist go gently.

The lights came on. Karl said, "They've broken his wrists. And his legs—they've smashed his knees. Why, he will never —" He broke off.

In silence, they stood looking down at Johann. His eyes closed once more. "That's right, Karl," he said. "I'll never climb or ski again."

Ten minutes vanished in hectic activity. Zauner had come prepared for trouble, even if not quite to the extent of Johann's injuries. Karl administered the shot of morphine, then lit two kerosene stoves, while Zauner made contact with the Seidl house where Bruno was waiting for his report. Mathison found a blanket to cover the chilled body, trying not to put any weight on the broken kneecaps by rigging up supports on either side of Johann's legs. He managed this with a couple of large heavy stones he had discovered in a gallery leading out of the room. Stretched over these, the blanket formed a tent across Johann's knees and was tucked under the stones to keep it secure. That ended his ingenuity; all he could think of next was to light a cigarette and hold it to Johann's lips, while Karl went searching for drinkable water and found a bottle of schnapps, too.

Zauner's radio contact was over. He stowed the small transmitter-receiver into one of the deep pockets of his loden cape and came over to look down at Johann.

"Trudi?" Johann asked with an effort.

"They didn't touch her."

"They kept their bargain." He relaxed a little, but tried to fight off sleep. "Anna?"

"In Salzburg."

"They got the box." His voice was slurring.

"No. It was blown to bits. Now stop talking. I've sent for the ambulance and a couple of guides who know how to get you down this hill on a stretcher. They are on their way. They will be here as quickly as possible. Can you hang on?"

"I'll—" Johann nodded as he drifted into a mixture of sleep and unconsciousness.

Mathison dropped the half-finished cigarette, ground it out under his heel. He glanced at Zauner, decided this was not the moment to tell him about the box. Zauner was instructing Karl to get down to the picnic ground and guide the others up here by the short route. Some of them might even be arriving there from the inn any moment now: they had caught the two Nazis, Bruno had reported; Grell's men had walked into the trap, hadn't even time to draw a weapon. Now, along with Grell, they were already on their way to Salzburg under heavy guard. "That leaves only one of them free. Keep your eyes open, Karl. He might wander up here to find shelter for the night, lie up safely for a few days or take enough supplies to head over the mountains with his two friends. Unless he knows they have been caught. Even so, he might head here. He needs food and equipment if he wants to climb his way out of this country. He won't be stupid enough to try the roads. So keep your eyes open and your revolver ready. Now get going! And take care."

Zauner is good, thought Mathison, he's a first-rate man to have in charge. He hasn't put one foot wrong since he went into action at the inn. I've been watching him, and I'm impressed. Speed, decision, and enough explanation to keep Karl on the alert. It is often as important to tell men why you take a certain action as well as the what and the how of it. But how do I tell a high-powered guy like Zauner that he is completely mistaken about the Finstersee box? Let's hope he sees the joke in it; but he's a proud man, and even if it's his own fault—he arrived late at the Seidl meadow, never did get caught up in Chuck's plan—that won't make him feel any better about it. "You know," he began carefully, "that box on the meadow—"

"Forget about it. No use going over our defeats. Perhaps, in terms of human misery, it is just as well there is nothing left of the Finstersee box. Have you any idea of what was in it?"

"Yes." Three hundred names. Perhaps even more than that.

"Then you know the disaster it could have caused for a lot of decent men. They made one mistake. Do they have to go on paying for it?"

Mathison looked at him in surprise. Nice sentiments, but not quite honest. "You're dodging the main question. They could go on making the same mistake, with the Communists blackmailing them this time. And millions of decent men might have to pay for that." Zauner stared at him. "Sure, the Communists must have a duplicate of the Finstersee file. Why else did Elissa try to destroy it?"

"*Try* to destroy it?"

"That was an imitation she blew up. The real thing is safe."

"Safe?"

"Intact."

"Where?"

"Wherever Bruno and Chuck and Andrew are."

There was a long silence. "Then it is on its way out of Unterwald," Zauner said softly. "They were leaving as soon as——" He broke off, walked toward the wall near the door. Roughly, he tore down the tarpaulin that had been pegged over a slit in the rock, a fissure that served as a window. The cold air swept in, smothered him. He stood there, looked down over the sharp points of trees toward Finstersee, regained his breath.

"Good," Mathison said. "That means they have managed to clear the road of people. Everything is getting back to normal." He watched Zauner with some concern. Had he so much pride that he could see his ignorance about the real box only as a calculated snub by Bruno? "You know, we really did not have a free minute to tell you. Something was always happening. Everyone was really playing it by ear. We just kept one jump ahead of disaster most of the time. If it hadn't been for Chuck's speed—everyone's speed—we would have been left sitting in Salzburg." Perhaps even in Zürich, he thought. God, it has been a long, long day. He sat down on a low wooden platform in one corner of the room with fresh fir branches forming a bed. He looked at a neatly folded sleeping bag and wished he were in it. "They must have used this place regularly," he went on, if only to cover Zauner's silence. There were cans of food stacked on shelves, books, playing cards, even a game of chess set out on an upturned barrel. "A refuge in time of trouble? A lookout?"

Zauner replaced the tarpaulin, began walking around the room. He stopped at the gallery, entered it, stared at the large room at its other end. The moonlight came through the cunningly disguised slits in its cliff wall, striping the vast empty black space obliquely. Ruined hopes, he thought as he heard the wind sigh through the openings. Nothing but ruins. To jump from there would be the quickest way out. The easiest way for me. Not for Ruth, not for the boys. They would have my death to remember as well as my life. I would have neither. The easiest way for me. Has that always been my excuse?

He turned, came back into the small room. Mathison was watching him carefully. Zauner said, "I forgot to tell you— Bruno is taking your car. They need extra transportation. It will be returned tomorrow morning. Frau Seidl will put you up for the night. You could leave now. The others will soon be here. It will take some time to fix Johann for his journey to the hospital in Bad Aussee. No need for you to stay."

I don't know about that, thought Mathison as he looked at

371

Zauner's face. He tried to play down his worries. "Oh, I'm quite comfortable resting my feet for another ten minutes. How is Johann? Could we risk some more morphine?"

"We gave him all I brought with me. The others will have more. Poor fool—did you hear him? He only thought he could never climb or ski again. He never even imagined, once the Nazis had finished with him, he would never draw breath again. Why leave a witness alive? Why leave evidence? Or is that too bloody for your imagination?"

"Not after what I've seen tonight."

"They even had the place to get rid of him finally. Walk into the gallery, Mathison."

"I did."

"There are slits, spaces in the cliff face. All they had to do was throw him out. The victim of a climbing accident, bones smashed at the bottom of a precipice. Oh, they'd stage it properly. A snapped climbing rope, a broken piton."

"You do have a bloody imagination."

"Except for my own benefit. Perhaps that is how the human mind works: we can imagine what may happen to someone else—but we shut off our imagination when it comes to ourselves. Unless, of course, the imaginings are pleasant daydreams. But when they deal with the hard accounting of life? Two and two are four, and not just a fraction over or under four? That's the kind of reasoning we resist. Perhaps we are all poor fools. Always hoping." Zauner stopped looking down at Johann, came over to slump on the wooden platform beside Mathison. "Yet," he went on, almost to himself, "there is such an emptiness, a frightening void, when we do stop hoping. As if life has stopped, too, no meaning left. No more choices, no more decisions; they are all out of our hands. We just wait. Hopelessly."

I could make fifty guesses about this man, thought Mathison, and yet not know. Why is he talking like this, to me—a stranger, an almost-stranger? Perhaps that gives a sense of safety: I am someone he will never see again after tonight to remind him of a bad half hour up on the Sonnblick. Shall I shut him up or let him talk himself out? Mathison looked at the haggard face now staring across at Johann, and said nothing.

"I am to blame for so much of this," Zauner said quietly, his eyes fixed on Johann. "You were right, Mathison. I've been dodging the main question. And for twenty years that

was easy; it wasn't even there any more—va~~~~~
with the Nazis. Vanished forever, I hoped. Dead and b~~~
I began to think. Yes, two and two did not have to make
four." He drew a deep breath. "Two months ago, the threat
rose from its grave. It seemed little at first, something nebu-
lous, something I could deal with in my own way. I found
twenty answers, all rational, all clever, and none of them right.
Because I kept dodging the main question. But this week—
the threat was no longer some thin poor ghost from the past."
He rose abruptly; then stood as if he did not know where to
move. "It was a blast of fire, an explosion." He looked directly
at Mathison. "Don't you understand what I have been trying
to tell you?" he cried out angrily.

Mathison kept his voice even. "Your name is on file in the
Finstersee box."

Zauner laughed suddenly, turned toward the slit of a window once more. "You might have left that for me to say. A
traitor confesses. Redeems himself with one sentence."
Roughly he pulled aside the tarpaulin, stared out at the lake.
"I saved my wife from a gas chamber in exchange for
leading my men into an ambush so that an SS colonel could
be freed. What would you have done, Mathison? No, don't
answer that. It was never your question. You'll have others
to face, but not that one." He looked back at Mathison with
a bitter smile. "Or perhaps you may have to face it—if
enough obedient traitors hand the West over to a ruthless
enemy. At least you've helped eliminate more than three
hundred of them. In one night! My congratulations."

Mathison's lips tightened. He rose, went over to Johann,
looked at his watch.

Zauner's voice changed. Quite simply he said, "It was a job
that needed doing. The file had to be found."

Then give the credit to Richard Bryant, thought Mathison.
He was still too angry to trust himself to speak.

But perhaps Zauner had the same thought, for he turned
away again to look out the window. In clear weather it had a
perfect view of one particular patch of the lake shore opposite: a barren slope of mountain strewn with crags, a small
wandering trail picked out whitely by the moon that led
down to the edge of Finstersee, and a clump of bushes, and a
few twisted trees. "How did he do it?" Zauner asked softly.

They came down through the trees at a sure steady pace,

...eading, two men carrying Johann ... ..., Karl and another policeman forming ... ...p in the Sonnblick room, two more men ... ...atch throughout the night. It was an empty ... Apart from the lights and the heating stove, all ... ...nt and food had been taken away by Zauner's order. ...neard his footsteps on the path," Zauner said softly.

Mathison, whose eyes had been watching the steep rise of trees and crags for any moving figure, tightened his grip on his automatic. "When?"

"About twenty minutes ago, when we were waiting with Johann. He heard our voices, and retreated."

"Why didn't he rush us?"

"Two of us? He would have attacked one, I think; but not two. It's just as well. We'll pick him up without too much difficulty when it is daylight. No use risking any more stretcher cases."

"It may not be so easy to pick him up."

"He will surrender, half-frozen, a pathetic sight. He can plead he knew nothing about Johann—no connection with anything, just a guest at the inn who didn't know what was really going on." Zauner's eyes glanced in the direction of the lake shore as they reached the meadow. "Six hours and he will start thinking that out for himself."

Surrender? Mathison wasn't so sure, somehow. But Zauner knew his mountains—and his Nazis. "Looks damned cold along there. I can feel the lake even from here." That was one thing on which he did agree with Zauner.

They quickened their pace across the frozen grass. Two men with rifles were guarding the ambulance and cars. One of them reported, "A man started coming out of the trees over there. He saw us, ran back, keeping close to the shore. Do we start searching?"

Zauner shook his head. "Wait here and watch. Until it's daylight. I'll send everyone available to join you then. We'll make sure of him."

"One thing is sure," the man said with a laugh. "He has no place to go."

Zauner turned to Mathison as the man left for his car, a cup of hot coffee, an extra cape. "Karl will take you down to the Seidl house. So good-bye. And thank you, Mathison. I'm glad you stayed. On several counts." He almost offered his hand, seemed to hesitate about that.

"What about you?" Mathison spoke cast . .
Zauner uncertainly.

"Oh, I'll be at the inn. There is a lot to clear up."

Mathison just kept looking at him.

"Grell's equipment to be examined, a final report to be made, my full statement to be written," Zauner said evenly. "Not that that is necessary, once they open the Finstersee box. What action do you think they'll take? Is that what is worrying you? But the box is supposed to have been destroyed. So, to keep that myth strong for another year or two, I would imagine my punishment may not be publicized and my record kept quiet."

"The Communists may not be so obliging."

"I don't suppose they will be. They feel virtuous about exposing ex-collaborators with the Nazis—when it suits them."

Well, thought Mathison, he knows what he is facing and he seems ready to accept it. I wouldn't have bet on that half an hour ago.

Zauner, watching him closely, seemed to sense something of his thoughts. "Is this what has been bothering you, all along?" Zauner drew out Grell's small white capsule from his pocket. He broke it open with his thumbnail, scattered the powder wide over the grass. "A symbolic refusal," he said with his light, mocking laugh. "Oh, that never was the answer—not in my case, not with my record. You agree?"

"I agree." Mathison put out his hand. Zauner took it, shook it firmly. "Good luck," said Mathison. He walked over to the waiting car and eased himself into the one small space that was left. They jolted off with Karl's heavy touch at the wheel. Ahead of them, the ambulance was moving slowly, its rear lights rising and falling sharply with each bump on the rough hard ground. Mathison watched them, flinched at one particularly heavy drop. The ambulance slowed, went on.

"It's all right," Karl told him, "they've got the stretcher suspended. It will just be swinging around."

"Hey, Karl," called someone from the back seat as the car bounced savagely over that same rut, "you could use some stretchers in here. Just about lost my teeth down the back of my throat." There was brief laughter, some more simple banter, a feeling of general relaxation. Weapons had vanished; pipes were being lit. The woods closed around the narrow road, wrapping a dark blanket of silence over them

375

28

PERHAPS MIDNIGHT HAD BEEN THE NATURAL CURFEW HOUR for Unterwald, even on a Saturday like this one. The inn was the only place lit. The rest of the village slept. The sparse lights along the main street had been shut off. Windows were shuttered; smoke from the chimneys had died to invisible wisps. A dog barked, and that was all. Unterwald was back into its own world.

And so am I, thought Mathison as the car swept down toward the Seidl house. For the first time in two full hours, he let himself think of Lynn again. Had she waited for him? Or had she left with the others? He kept hoping. He kept trying to guard himself against disappointment: the sensible comfortable thing was for her to go to Bad Aussee, have a long hot bath, a long deep sleep in one of those cumulus clouds that the Austrians called beds. Yes, that was the sensible thing. But he kept hoping.

The Seidl house was as deeply asleep as any in Unterwald. He stared at the dark windows, felt expectation and excitement drain out of him. And suddenly he was tired, just damned tired, completely devoid of energy, nothing but a slow-moving collection of tightening muscles and chilled bones. He got stiffly out of the car. He almost asked Karl to drive him as far as Bad Aussee, but the faces giving him a friendly farewell were as exhausted as his. At the inn, they'd have four hours of sleep, little more, before they started bundling themselves up again for their return to the lake with the dawn. "Gute Nacht," he added to his thanks, and started slowly up the short path.

"Gute Nacht, schlafen Sie wohl!" Karl called to him as he angled the short wheel base of the car to turn back uphill.

He gave them a last wave and opened the door.

The room was dark except for a small pool of light on the table where a lamp stood with its wick trimmed low. From the hearth came the faint glow of a dying fire, reflected

weakly on the ceiling of the room. He ███████████
itself, not with the table blocking his view, bu██████
tired to take the extra steps to check it. It must b███
enough, or Trudi wouldn't have left it. Everything else was in
order—table neat and chairs in place. It seemed in this quiet,
warm room as if nothing at all had happened tonight. Nothing at all. He slipped off his heavy jacket as he made for the
staircase. His feet were as heavy as lead. Better take off his
shoes and keep Mother Seidl deep deep in sleep, avoid a
flood of questions. This was one night he did not want to
search for tactful answers.

There was a quick movement from the top of the stairs, a
lamp held high to catch him on the second step, where he
had sat down to draw off his shoes. He glanced around; but it
was only Trudi. She came down to meet him as he climbed
slowly up the next few stairs. She was barefooted, a shawl
over her thick nightgown. "I heard two cars," she whispered.
"One went to Bad Aussee."

"That was the ambulance with Johann," Mathison whispered back.

"He was hurt?"

Mathison nodded.

"How bad?"

"He will recover. Don't worry, Trudi."

She raised the lamp, looked into his face. She tried to say
something, could not.

"He asked for you."

Again she tried to speak. Then she bent down, gave him a
quick embarrassed kiss on his cheek, turned and ran, her
bare feet pattering on the wooden stairs, the need for silence
quite forgotten. He heard her door close. The staircase was
in darkness again. Better get that lamp from the table to
light my way upstairs, he thought wearily. He envied Johann
for a moment, broken bones and all. He turned to retrace his
steps.

"Bill—Bill?"

He looked down across the room. He saw her struggling
free from a blanket in front of the fire's warm embers. He
reached her as she rose to her feet, her arms outstretched.
He caught her in his, crushed her against him, held her, held
her. He looked down into her eyes. Their lips met slowly,
truly. He kissed her with all his heart.

... om the desperate embrace. ... other. He put out one hand ... cheek. "Lynn ..." I frightened ... myself. I love this girl.

... pulled the dressing gown more tightly ... to her knees in front of the hearth and ... mall log. He knelt beside her to help.

... his?" He looked down in amazement at the mattress ... er his legs. "Camping out for the night?"

That made her laugh. She smothered it quickly, looked at the back wall of the kitchen.

"Don't worry about Mother Seidl. Too much excitement. She's out for the count." I hope so, he added to that. I don't give one damn, anyway. But he kept his voice to a low murmur. "You weren't planning to sleep here, were you?"

"I couldn't sleep upstairs."

"Not in one of those beautiful white beds?"

"A beautiful white iceberg." And in a room at the back of the house where I couldn't even see the road.

So it was a matter of warmth, he thought, and felt the chill of disappointment. "I'd like to have seen you wrestling this mattress downstairs."

"It isn't so big. Trudi helped me. I—I thought I would hear you better—when you got back. But I didn't. Funny, isn't it? I couldn't sleep in a bed, and I fell asleep on the floor. Trudi says she often sleeps down here when winter comes. She—"

"Trudi's fine. Let's leave her alone. What about you?" Her face was too drawn, too tense, yet strangely beautiful. The small flickering flames shadowed her cheeks, made her large eyes seem larger.

"A little—shaken. And you?"

He watched her as she looked at him anxiously. "Recovering rapidly." He dropped on one elbow, stretched his legs gratefully.

"You are exhausted." Her concern grew. "You didn't get hurt?"

"I'd be complaining my head off if I were."

Not you, she thought, not you. She said gently, "You're tired and you're cold. Let me get you some soup; it's waiting over on the—"

"No."

378

"Brandy? Chuck left you some in the—"

"No. Just stay where you are, the way you are. Let me watch you looking so worried. Is it for me?"

"Yes."

"Was that really why you waited down here?"

She nodded slowly. "And it didn't go as planned. I didn't hear you come in. You didn't even see me."

"I didn't dare hope," he said very quietly. He reached out a hand to touch her hair. "Yes, you have the prettiest hair. Chuck may have said that first, but I saw it first. In Zürich— you sat at a window, and the sun on the trees outside matched you. Gleam for gleam." His hand dropped away from the silken strands. His elbow lowered; he stretched back on the mattress. The warmth from the fire began to soak through his body. "It feels good. . . ." His eyes closed.

They opened again as she lifted his head gently and slipped the pillow underneath.

"A mattress on the floor. Crazy. You really are a crazy girl. That's why I love you, I guess." He smiled. "One of the reasons."

"Yes, I'm crazy." She was smiling, too. "I must be crazy to fall in love with a man I have only known for two days." She bent over and kissed him, her hair falling softly over his face.

Sunshine across his eyes; the sound of faraway bells; subdued voices near him. Bill Mathison came slowly out of his long deep sleep, sat up with a start. He looked around the bright kitchen incredulously, pulled himself free from a tangle of gray blankets, rose from the mattress. Near the window, Lynn and Trudi stopped talking. He glanced at his watch and shook his head.

Lynn came over to him. She was dressed in her beige tweed suit and white sweater, her long slender legs immaculate in lace-wool stockings, her buckled shoes polished. Her hair was smoothly brushed, her skin as fresh and clear as the sky outside.

"You're a miracle," he told her, tried to forget his crumpled clothes and wild hair, and gave her a good-morning hug.

She laughed, reached up and kissed him.

"No, no," he said quickly, feeling the stubble of his beard

379

catch against her soft cheek. "I need a shave, a—" But he broke off and kissed her right back.

Trudi was saying, "I have to leave, Herr Mathison. I wanted to say good-bye. And thank you. If you hadn't—"

He cut that short with a quick, "Where are you bound for? Bad Aussee?"

She nodded happily. "But first I'll show you where you can wash. Your bag is upstairs, all safe."

"I'll be domestic and get breakfast," Lynn said. In English, she added, "I better warn you it will be a slice of bread, a dab of jam, and a cup of coffee."

"I'll settle for two cups and spare the rest. Can you stretch it to that?"

"I don't know. House rules, seemingly. But I'll try. Oh, and our car has been returned. And Frau Seidl is at church. She ought to be back in half an hour or so, unless her friends keep her talking. I said good-bye for both of us. She is expecting a lot of company here this afternoon, so we'll never be missed."

"Thanks for the tip. I'll be quick." He paused halfway up the stairs. "What about the rooms overnight?" His smile was wide. "How do we settle tactfully?"

"I've already been through that argument. She won't take a penny."

"Better make that one cup of coffee."

"Herr Mathison!" Trudi was calling worriedly from the upper hallway. As he came running up the rest of the stairs, she burst into new apologies for her haste. "Karl will be here very soon," she explained. "He promised to give me a lift to Bad Aussee. In his sidecar."

"Was he here this morning?"

"Yes, he came to see you."

Mathison looked at her sharply. Her voice had been grave. "Anything wrong?"

She shook his hand, repeated her good-byes, wished him everything wonderful in this world. Only as she turned away to run downstairs did she answer his question. "It was all about Herr Zauner," she said unhappily over her shoulder.

So the news was out, thought Mathison as he shaved and washed in the closet that had been turned into a simple imitation of a bathroom, no doubt for the summer trade. Karl, as a policeman, would have been told that Zauner had been taken away from the inn. But what about Karl's own discretion? Trudi should never have been told. Of course, neither Karl nor she would ever know the real reason for Zauner's quiet removal. But still—He frowned, dressed quickly, putting on a fresh shirt and the spare pair of gray flannels. Bruno really moved swiftly, he was thinking as he carried his bag downstairs, just about as swiftly as old friend Chuck.

"Something wrong?" Lynn asked as he drank the cup of coffee.

"Only something that's to be expected. And nothing to do with us," he added quickly. "Did Karl mention anything about Zauner this morning?"

"The big policeman? No, not to me. He came to offer Trudi a lift down to Bad Aussee, then told us that Johann's jeep had been found somewhere along that little road under the cliffs. It was well hidden, not damaged at all, just as if Johann had left it there. Then Karl took one last admiring look at you, agreed with Trudi that you had been wise to keep guard last night and make sure no terrorist came sneaking around—" Lynn broke into laughter. "You know, that story impressed Frau Seidl, too. She was very touched. No, no, don't look at me like that; I didn't invent it. I was completely numb. Trudi brought it up out of nowhere when her mother came into the kitchen this morning."

He was grinning widely at the picture. And the coffee was good. "Old Faithful, that's me."

"Of course, Karl may have mentioned Zauner when Trudi walked with him to the road. Finished?" She took the empty cup and saucer, carried it over to the sink to wash and dry. He lit a cigarette, strolled over to the door, then remembered the mattress on the floor.

"Okay," he said, picking it up, "where does this go?"

"Trudi said we could leave it. Put it under the staircase."

"No. I'm stowing it out of sight." And let's hope that Mother Seidl forgets to talk about it to her visitors, he thought. He followed Lynn, who had lifted the pillow and blankets, upstairs to a small room at the back of the house. "Nice and quiet. Pity we are in such a hurry. Or are we?"

"And what story do *you* fish up out of nowhere when the mob scene begins in the kitchen?"

"Come on," he said, and they clattered downstairs in a rush of laughter.

She stood, as he packed the bags into the car, looking at

the mountains. "Is *that* the Sonnblick?" she asked, aghast. I would have worried even more, she thought, if I could have seen it last night.

"Oh, we didn't go up that sheer cliff. We went around to the other side. It wasn't too bad. Plenty of trees to hang on to. Finstersee is just below them. Come on, Lynn. Let's move. What about Bad Aussee for some lunch? Then you get out the map and we'll—"

"Would it take too long to drive up to Finstersee? Then I could look at the village, too. We haven't really seen it, you know. Everything is so different in daylight." No more gray grass, black bushes, or even shadowy houses that had all looked so withdrawn, even threatening.

"It isn't far. Just a hiccup of a detour." He helped her into the car, edged it off the meadow onto the road, and started uphill. "Yes, it's all different," he agreed as he looked at the houses they passed, the schoolhouse at the crossroads, the inn on its own high meadow overlooking the village main street with its houses encircled by small gardens and neat fences. Simple and innocent. A smiling place. "Now this is where we start uphill. It's rough going, but direct." He put the car into first as they passed the side of the inn. It was deserted. "Everyone has gone." Even the people down on the street had all seemed strangers. Perhaps it was their Sunday clothes, or the solemn church manners that clung to them even as they grouped on the street to talk. Talk. That at least hadn't changed. He braked quickly. Two men were signaling him to stop. "I know them at least. They were in the car that brought me back last night."

They were two serious-faced types, but when they got near enough to recognize Mathison, they loosened up. "Grüss Gott," they said warmly.

"Grüss Gott."

There was strong handshaking all around.

Mathison said, "Is Finstersee still off limits? Haven't you caught that man you were looking for?"

"They are fishing him out of the lake right now."

"Then he didn't surrender?" Zauner had made it all seem so simple, a matter of routine.

"No. He got Zauner, then he slipped and fell."

"What?"

The grave furrowed face nodded. "He slipped and fell.

Slid. Couldn't stop sliding. It was dark, so he couldn't make sure of his footing."

The other said, "If his coat hadn't caught on a dead tree floating on the middle of the lake, the currents would have had him. We'd never have found the body."

"He got Zauner?"

"One shot. A lucky one for that damned—" The man broke off the rest of his description. The furrows on his face deepened. He looked apologetically at Lynn.

"Zauner is dead?" Mathison asked slowly.

"That's right. One shot."

Dark, they had said; it had been dark. "Why didn't Zauner wait until the light had strengthened fully?" he asked angrily.

The men looked at him in surprise. "But he didn't wait for dawn. He went in just after our car left. Said he would flush the bastard out."

"Well," said the other, "we lost a good man."

"That we did. We lost a good man. Went in alone. Saved the rest of us from five remaining bullets. He was a good shot, that one. Good position, too. If he hadn't slipped—"

"Good-bye," Mathison said, shook hands again. "Grüss Gott."

"Grüss Gott."

Mathison turned the car, drove back toward the crossroads, swung the wheel right. "Hell," he said as he saw he was driving along the village street, "I took the wrong way."

"No," said Lynn, "keep on going. The map says here"— she spread it further out on her knees—"that we'll get to Salzburg eventually. Third-class road, plenty of twists and turns. That means scenery. Or did you want to see Bad Aussee especially?"

He shook his head, went into first, began climbing the hill out of Unterwald. Plenty of twists and turns, he remembered as he went back into third. He slowed down, watched the road carefully. At least he would have to stop thinking about Zauner. He had made it all seem a matter of routine: dawn, surrender of a subdued man. All so easy and simple. And he had known it wasn't. He had made his choice; found the only solution perhaps, even found the only answer to his grim question. The life of his wife, his own happiness, hadn't been the answer; how much real happiness had Zauner had in those last twenty-odd years with the dead men of his be-

trayed platoon staring at him with their accusing eyes? They
had wives, too. . . . "Zauner—" he began, and stopped.

"Would you have stayed up there with Zauner if you had
known he was going in?"

"This is quite a road you picked."

Then he would have stayed, she thought. Thank God that
Zauner had somehow managed to send him away. Thank
God. "You are a stubborn man," she said very quietly.

"I like to finish what I start." He smiled suddenly. "And
that goes for you, my girl. When you marry me, you stay
married. We don't give up."

"Or you'll break my little neck?" Her laugh ended in a
gasp. "Oh!—" But his speed was in control, and the corner
sweeping quickly around the sharp shoulder of the hill was
safely taken. She tried to regain her composure. "There's a
church with an onion-shaped spire." She pointed toward the
mountain slope on her right. So small it was, and old, so
lonely, perched up there on its own meadow.

But Mathison was looking at the signs of a violent skid,
just on his left. A tragic skid. Someone had gone right over
the edge there. The despairing wheel marks were rutted deep
into the soft shoulder, now frozen solid.

"I'm glad you are driving. This would paralyze me," she
admitted. "I'm afraid I misjudged this road." She glanced
down at the map. "But it gets better after this, it says here."

And it did. It still ran high along the mountain's steep side,
but the deep gullies that had turned the road into a twisting
roller-coaster were ended. "Well," Mathison said, "there's one
thing you didn't misjudge. There is plenty of scenery. Good
God, Lynn—will you look at that!" For safety, he brought
the car to a stop, switched off the engine, applied the brakes
firmly. Now he could really look. Hillsides fell away into a
broad stretch of green valley, farmland and forest and
flowing waters, mountains with ice-rimmed peaks encircling it
all in a wide embrace.

They sat in silence. He took her hand and kissed it, his
eyes on the distant mountains. "That's something to remember," he said softly. Then his eyes looked into hers. "And so
are these." He kissed them in turn. "And so is this." He
kissed her mouth.

When at last he started the car, he drove at a steady
speed. Within an easy two hours, they could see the steeples
and domes of Salzburg.